# Gold Rush

### The William Stewart Saga

### A Sequel to An Ocean Away

### Peter Clarke

First published in Australia by Aurora House
www.aurorahouse.com.au

This edition published 2021
Copyright © Peter Clarke 2021

Cover design: Donika Mishineva | www.artofdonika.com
Typesetting and e-book design: Amit Dey

The right of Peter Clarke to be identified as Author of the Work has been
asserted in accordance with the Copyright, Designs and Patents Act 1988.

ISBN number: 978-1-922403-83-4 (Paperback)

A catalogue record for this
book is available from the
National Library of Australia

Distributed by: Ingram Content: www.ingramcontent.com
Australia: phone +613 9765 4800 |
email lsiaustralia@ingramcontent.com
Milton Keynes UK: phone +44 (0)845 121 4567 |
email enquiries@ingramcontent.com
La Vergne, TN USA: phone +1 800 509 4156 |
email inquiry@lightningsource.com

# Dedication

For my siblings and children. Thankfully, all still here.

And

my lifelong friends:

Hank and Jimmy. Gone, but never forgotten.

*God gives us friends to remind us how good*
*He can be, and enemies to remind us how*
*good a friend can be.*

# Acknowledgements

I enjoyed writing this, visiting Ballarat and learning about the events there. The work is all fiction, but I have tried to keep the background to the fiction as close to fact as possible. It wasn't always easy, and I sometimes had to guess. I hope I did so with wisdom and common sense.

Once again, I am indebted to many authors for their wonderful works on Australia in general and on the Eureka Stockade in particular.

# Contents

# CHAPTER 1

# Williams Town

When William awoke, he was cold and damp—the sun was up, but wasn't yet warm. Shivering, he looked around and saw he was in a yard with tools and rubbish scattered about. There was nothing familiar about it. He was lying in a patch of grass, near to a fence. Where was he and how did he get here?

After a while, he began to remember and his first thoughts were of the *Lady Grace* and that there had been much excitement when they decided to leave the ship. Was that last night? He wasn't sure. A group of them had gone to the purser to get their money. Despite his discomfort, William smiled to himself as his memory returned.

\*     \*     \*     \*

The purser was a young man with a gentle, studious face. His eyes protruded a little and William wondered if that happened because he worked with money. He protested at first and tried to talk them out of taking anything. Some of the men argued that they had no money at all and would need some to spend while ashore. Finally, the purser gave them part of their wage, but gave

William only the few shillings and pennies that he had originally left with the purser for safekeeping when he had joined the ship.

"Come back day after tomorrow and get the rest," he said. "That goes for all you men. Come back day after tomorrow and get all your money."

"Why don't you give it all to us now?"

"I don't have it all yet. I have to get it from the agents in Melbourne. I'm going to do that tomorrow, so I'll have it then. Like I say, come back later."

The men grumbled and some wanted to see the Captain.

"It's a waste of time," said the purser. "He'll only say the same thing. You've enough there to enjoy yourselves and you won't be losing or wasting the rest."

Some of the men laughed, and enough of them agreed with the purser that they left.

It didn't bother William that he had only a few shillings. There wouldn't be much to spend it on other than a meal and maybe somewhere to sleep.

Eddie was angry when William told him what the purser gave him.

"It's not their money! It's yours!" he thundered. "Come with me."

As they approached the purser, it was clear Eddie intimidated him.

"How much do you owe him?" Eddie growled, pointing at William.

"We owe him five pounds ten shillings, but I can't give him all of it."

"Well, give him what you can, but you have to give him more than you have."

"All right, all right," the purser muttered, reluctantly handing William two more pounds. William couldn't believe he had earned so much money and there was more to come. He'd never seen so much before.

"What do I need it for?" William asked Eddie as they headed back to join the others.

"It doesn't matter. It's not their money."

The group going ashore comprised three of the able seamen and two of the lookouts, along with William and Eddie.

They all piled into a small steamboat that Eddie secured to take them ashore, asking only a few pennies from each of them to pay for it. The owner probably came out believing he would get a new chum to take ashore, providing a handsome profit, but no one wanted to use his services and he faced the prospect of going back empty. He was a rough and surly-looking type, who no doubt wouldn't take too kindly to coming off second best. But he was also highly negotiable due to his desperation and Eddie took advantage of it. Not a single word passed the man's lips during the trip to shore, which took far too long for William in his impatient excitement.

The men chattered eagerly as they neared the docks, greeted by the sound of music and revelry. Little time was wasted pushing them ashore and the boat hardly arrived before it was gone.

Eddie knew where to go and the others stuck to him like glue.

William was surprised by the rubbish that lay about, the assortment of conveyances and the general rudeness of the people around. No one looked pleased to see them and there were no welcomes. He also had to be very careful where he stepped—mud and animal dung abounded. Despite the hour, a few hawkers were about offering passers-by an assortment of goods. Clothes, tools, meals, accommodation, and even prostitutes, were all available for the right price. The people were dressed as he had never seen before. Most wore funny-looking hats that Eddie told him were called cabbage-tree hats, being made from some local plant. They also wore gaily-coloured shirts, cord pants, and long boots reaching above the knee. Others wore broad felt hats, red or blue jumpers, and moleskin pants. Their brawny throats were bare but they wore silk scarfs around their waist, into which they stuffed revolvers and knives.

"This way," said Eddie, and the men hurried forward to join him.

"Is this Melbourne?" asked one of them.

Eddie laughed.

"Well, when we set out from England, Melbourne was where we were going. But, now that we're here, Melbourne's over there," he said and pointed across the bay. "This here is Williams Town and we're just as well to stay here since we have to go back to the ship day after tomorrow. It'll cost us in time and money to get to Melbourne and there's just as much fun for the likes of us to be had here."

They walked in silence for a while, everyone taking care to avoid the dung, ruts and puddles.

"These are nothing like the docks in England," said one of the men after stepping onto what he thought was solid ground only to find himself ankle deep in water.

"Hasn't been here that long," said Eddie. "There's a lot of traffic since the gold rush started, too. Hard for them to keep up with it. Anyway, we're not going to live here, so who cares what it's like?"

It was darker now and harder to see where to tread, but the sounds of music and revelry they heard earlier were getting louder as they approached a building in the near distance.

"Is that where we're going?" came a question from the group.

"It sure is," said Eddie. "I'm glad it's still here. They come and go in this place. It's called *Sailor's Inn*. We'll get something to eat and drink and whatever else takes your fancy. Before we get there, take some of your money and put it in your shoe. Both shoes if you have enough. That'll make sure you've some left for tomorrow. Their job is to take all your money and yours is to keep some of it."

Eddie stopped, took off a shoe, put some money in it and started walking again. The others quickly did the same.

"It's hard to walk. It's uncomfortable," one of them said.

"Then don't do it," said Eddie. "Your money is your money and your comfort is your comfort and if you can't distinguish between the two, it's of no matter to me."

As they came close to the inn, William manoeuvred himself to be as close to Eddie as possible—he'd never been to such a place and hoped Eddie might protect him.

The building wasn't old, but it did look temporary. It was on a corner and there were verandahs on the sides facing the streets. A handful of customers occupied the tables and chairs—some were drinking beer, but most had spirits. Most of the men appeared to be sailors, dressed in the usual odd assortment of clothes that were borrowed, stolen or bought from the ship's purser. The rest carried revolvers jammed in their belts, but sometimes there was a rifle or a musket leaning against a wall nearby. William had never seen so many weapons and wondered at the purpose of them.

All the women were gaudily dressed, wearing many colours that were hard to define in the poor light from the few lamps that hung along the walls. Insects flicked and snapped against the glass of the lamps, creating a background clatter to the customers as they engaged in animated conversation and competed to be heard over each other.

The groups on the verandah were noisy enough, but the greater noise was coming through the doors that led into the building. The doors reminded William of the half-doors on the cottages back home, but these ones went neither to the floor nor the ceiling, providing no protection against the insects or the elements. Before he could ask Eddie the purpose of them, the men mounted the verandah and bounded through the unusual doors.

The scene outside was orderly compared to the chaos inside. A fiddler was playing in a corner, though the sound of his fiddle could hardly be heard and no one was taking much notice of him. Most of the noise was coming from the people gathered along the bar, who were also drinking both beer and spirits, but they were much more animated than the patrons outside. Half a dozen tables were scattered about and the people seated at them were both drinking and playing cards, focusing more on the cards than the drinking. A few bored-looking women were assisting with a drink for the men at the tables, but those at the bar looked anything but bored—most were the object of men's attention.

"Over here," said Eddie, finding a spot at the end of the bar. "I think we'll all fit."

They made a bit of a nuisance of themselves with a group nearby as they shuffled for some space. There was only one woman in the group and she laughed and sparkled enough to attract the attention of any man. The men in her group bristled and murmured, "Watch it, mate!" as though worried that the new men might steal her affections. When they realised that wasn't happening, the extra space was made available and they all settled down.

"How did he know we're sailors?" William asked Eddie. They had to put their heads close to be heard over the din.

"What makes you think he thinks we're sailors?"

"He called us mate."

"You better get used to it. Doesn't mean a sailor. In Australia, it's anybody. It can be your best friend, somebody you don't even know or somebody whose name you have forgotten."

The others were now clamouring for drinks. Everyone knew what they wanted except William. Eddie collected some money from the others to cover their drink and stopped when it came to William.

"Like I said, Bill, I don't want to be the one to teach you how to drink, but if you've a mind to have something, I'd like to buy it for you."

"What are you having?"

"Whisky."

William shrugged.

"Me, too."

"You might be better with beer. Have you ever had a beer?"

"No."

"Got to be a first time for everything."

"Can't it be a first time for whisky?"

"All right, but don't say I didn't warn you."

Eddie headed for the bar and tried to get a barman's attention. There were three of them working and all three looked like they wished everyone would leave.

At last the drinks were acquired and passed around, and the men decided to leave the bar to go outside where it was quieter.

"Hold on," said Sam Burgess. "That's not going to work for me. This drink is not going to last that long. I've been bounced around an ocean for months and I'm as dry as a barrel of biscuits."

He held out his drink in front of him and said, "To the *Lady Grace!*"

All the men held up their glasses and said, "To the *Lady Grace!*"

All of them except William, who was bewildered by the proceedings, emptied their glass in one gulp.

"Come on, Bill, you too," one of the men said and, before Eddie could stop him, William did the same.

The whisky burned his mouth and throat as it went down. He coughed convulsively, gasping for air.

He wanted to ask, "How do you drink this stuff?" but couldn't find his voice.

The men all laughed.

Eddie patted him on the back and said, "The first is the worst. You have a rest now for a while."

"Rubbish!" said Sam Burgess and took up a collection for another round.

"Steady, Sam," said Eddie. "The lad doesn't need any more."

"If he's going to drink with us, he does."

Eddie and Sam started to eye each other, assessing their chances if it came to a fight.

"Come on, Sam," said Dan Mason, another of the able seamen. "There's no need to make more of it. Let Bill decide."

The group looked to William.

"He doesn't look too good," said Dan.

"I'm all right," said William.

By this point, his head was buzzing but the burning was gone. He looked at the group.

*Good men all*, he thought.

"You men are wonderful," he said. "Best group of men. Let's have another. I'll buy you all a drink."

"You haven't got enough money," said Eddie. "It's a shilling a whisky."

"But we only gave you a few pennies for the first drink!" said Dan.

"I know, but the first one was on me. From now on, you're all on your own."

"Let's find somewhere cheaper," said Pat Clark. "This place is too expensive."

"There is nowhere else," said Eddie. "If you want drink, something to eat or a bed, this is it."

"Well, you lot can keep talking, but me, I'm here for a drink. Who else wants one?" said Sam.

Everyone, including William, gave him a shilling and he headed for the bar.

William was unsteady, had trouble focusing and it was growing increasingly difficult to understand the conversation around him. Ignoring the others, he watched Sam.

Sam got the barman's attention and ordered another seven whiskies. While he waited, he caught the eye of the lady in the group beside them. William saw him smile at her and was astonished to see her smile back. William couldn't tell how old she was, but she had shoulder length black hair, sparkling eyes, an infectious laugh and perfect teeth. William wondered how the top of her dress managed to contain her bosoms as they looked like they were trying to escape. One of the men with her noticed her smile at Sam, looked at Sam darkly and started towards him. The woman held his arm and whispered something in his ear. He stayed with her, but continued to scowl and stare at Sam.

Sam passed the drinks off the bar and re-joined his group.

"You be careful," said Eddie. "You won't have to try too hard to find a fight in here."

"He doesn't look too tough."

"That might be right, but they'll pull a knife or a gun in here as soon as use a fist. Like I say, be careful."

"Well, I'm only lookin'."

"Tell that to the undertaker. He'll be the only one interested."

"Anyway, down the hatch," said Sam.

All the men downed their drinks and before Eddie could say anything to William, he did the same.

"Take it easy, Bill," said Eddie. "You're new at this."

"Who made you his nursery maid?" Sam said sourly.

William wanted to tell him that it was all right but he couldn't find the words and laughed instead. He felt really good by this stage and his laughing turned to giggling. He was in great company, enjoying a drink, and in Australia. If only his da could see him now and join them for a whisky.

Soon enough, the room started to spin.

"What's happening?" he mumbled to Eddie. "The room is spinning."

"Outside, quick!" shouted Eddie, grabbing William and propelling him towards the door, pushing patrons out of the way.

"Christ!" William heard someone shout. "Take it easy. Where's the fire?"

The door was coming fast. He tried to put his hands out to protect his face, but they wouldn't obey the thought. Bile was rushing into his mouth. His head banged the door. It should have hurt, but it didn't. He thought it was funny and tried to laugh again, but couldn't focus.

He tried to ask Eddie what was happening and why Eddie was taking him outside but he couldn't speak. The next thing, he was lying on the verandah, head over the side and being sick into the street.

"There you go," said Eddie. "You'll be all right. Stay here and I'll find a bed for you."

\*     \*     \*     \*

The memory of the night ended with William still at the inn. What happened between Eddie suggesting a bed and him now lying on the grass? Was this the bed Eddie found? Where was Eddie? Where were the others?

He tried to sit up, but his body wasn't cooperating and his head was pounding—probably from when he banged it on the door. Rubbing the sore spot, he found a lump. He looked around. Was this the back of the *Sailor's Inn*? He wished he'd taken more notice when they'd arrived.

His hands and arms hurt. There were lots of red marks and they all itched. He wondered if he'd been bitten by ants, but couldn't see any around.

He stared at a pile of rags for a few moments before realising it wasn't rags at all—it was another man, snoring loudly. He tried to get up again, but the pounding in his head continued and his stomach started to heave again.

Crawling on his hands and knees, he made his way over to the man. He didn't recognise him. The man had vomit all over his shirtfront and appeared to have pissed his pants. He had a big black beard that was speckled with spew. A battered hat was lying nearby, his shirt was torn and full of holes and his pants, which were too short in the legs, were held up by a piece of rope. His shoes were well worn and looked ready to fall apart. He snored soundly.

William reached out and touched the man on the arm. Nothing happened. He gripped the man's arm and shook it.

The man opened one eye and said, "Mine's a whisky."

"I don't have any whisky."

"Then, why did you wake me?"

"Where are we?"

"What do you mean?"

"What's this place?"

The man sat up and looked around.

"I'd say we're in a yard."

"Whose yard?"

The man looked around.

"Dunno. Don't recollect seeing it before. Doesn't look too tidy, though. Hope I didn't pay too much to sleep here."

He looked at William.

"Is it you that smells?"

In spite of how badly he felt, William laughed.

"Might be. Might be you, too."

The man looked at himself.

"Jesus. Someone's pissed and spewed on me. Did you see who it was?" William shook his head and the man eyed him suspiciously. "Wasn't you, was it? You don't look too good."

"No, it wasn't me. At least, I don't think it was. I don't remember much."

"I don't remember anything. Can you see a tank?"

"What's a tank?"

"Christ. Where're you from? Holds water. I need a drink. Need to clean myself up a bit, too. Wouldn't hurt you none, either." He looked around. "There's one."

He got up unsteadily and headed towards a large metal object mounted on a wooden platform. He turned on the tap and water flowed out. He stuck his mouth under the flow, drinking for a minute or so before sticking his whole head under it.

"Jesus. Not half cold."

He flushed some of the water down his beard and shirtfront, took off his trousers, rinsed them in the water and put them on again.

"If I could find the bastard that pissed on me, I'd give him a hiding. What a thing to do to a man."

William took a turn to douse his head and wash himself.

Just then, a door opened at the back of the building.

"What do you think you're doing?" called a voice.

"Nothing," said William's companion.

"Clear out," the voice said. "You're trespassin'. I'll get the police onto you."

"All right, all right," said the man. "Keep your shirt on. We're goin'."

They walked down the side of the building and out onto a road, or at least what William thought was a road. It was little more than two rutted tracks between the trees. The day was warmer now and loudly buzzing with insects and hundreds of annoying flies. William looked up and down the road, neither direction offering any obvious prospect to find Eddie and the others.

"Where's the *Sailor's Inn*?" he asked his companion.

"Why?"

"It's the last place I saw my friends. If I can find the inn, perhaps I can find them."

"I'll show you if you buy me a whisky."

William felt in his pockets and realised he had no money there. He thought it wise to not reveal the money in his shoe.

"I don't have any money."

"I don't believe you. Anyway, if you don't have money, you're no damn good to me."

"My friends will have money."

"Will they buy me a whisky?"

"Yes, they will."

The man laughed.

"I was going to the inn anyway. It's where I work."

"What are you doing here?"

"Like I said, dunno. Anyway, it's this way," he said and headed off down the road, William following behind him. He'd taken only a few steps before he realised there was no money in his shoe either.

*Where did that go?*

"Is it far?" he asked the man.

"No, it's just beyond the corner. Watch where you walk—there's snakes about."

"What kind of snakes?"

"What do you care? Doesn't matter what kind bites you. You're just as dead."

"Snakes can kill you?"

"Jesus, boy. Where're you from?"

"Ireland."

The man laughed, but said nothing.

He saw the man had bites too.

"What are these bites? Are they bad?"

"No—mosquitoes. You'll get used to 'em."

After a few minutes' walk, William asked, "Were you a sailor?"

"Yes," said the man. "How did you know?"

"You don't care about your pants being wet."

The man laughed again.

Shortly, they emerged from the trees and there was a building not too far in front of them.

"That's it," said the man.

"What do you do there?"

"Odd jobs. They pay me in whisky and food."

"If my friends are here, where will they be?"

"There's a room at the back. I'll show you."

They walked up one side of the building and went to the back. They went past another tank and the man had some more water.

William did the same. He was surprised how hot the day had become and how thirsty he was after just a few minutes' walk.

A few unmoving bodies were scattered about the yard.

"Are they dead?" asked William.

"No," said the man, "but when they wake, they'll wish they were."

The man opened a door at the back and stepped inside. William followed. The stench of whisky, sweat and vomit was overpowering.

"Hmm," said the man. "I'll bet the bastard that pissed on me is in here."

"Well, he's here now, anyway," said a voice from the room.

"Eddie? Are you in here?" William asked, looking nowhere in particular as he strained his eyes to see.

"Bill? Is that you, Bill? Jesus, where did you get to?"

Eddie got up from the floor. William's eyes became accustomed to the darkness of the room and he could now see sleeping bodies everywhere. Eddie pushed William back through the doorway and the strange man followed.

"This your friend?" he asked.

William nodded.

"You owe me a whisky," the man said to Eddie.

"Why would I owe you a whisky?"

"Your friend said that if I brought him back to the inn, you'd buy me one."

"That true?" Eddie asked William.

William blushed and nodded.

Eddie reached into a pocket and pulled out a shilling. He was about to give it to the man who reached for it eagerly. Eddie held it away as the man grabbed for it.

"Where'd you find him?" said Eddie.

"Up the road a bit," said the man.

"What was he doin' there?"

"Sleepin'."

"All right. Here's your whisky. Thanks for bringin' him back."

The man snatched the shilling, laughed and walked off.

"Christ, Bill. We looked for you everywhere. I went inside to arrange a bed for you and when I came back, you'd gone. No one saw you leave. Where'd you go?"

William blushed again.

"I don't know, Eddie. I woke up and didn't know where I was. That feller was sleeping near me. Anyway, I'm glad he brought me back."

"No matter. You're here now. Nothing broken?"

"No, I'm all right. I don't have any money, though."

"What about the money in your shoe?"

"That's gone, too."

"Lucky the purser didn't give you more. No matter, I'll lend you some until we get back to the ship."

William blushed again.

"That was stupid," he said. "I don't remember anything."

"Whisky'll do that to a man. Come on—I'll get cleaned up and we'll find some breakfast. I'm hungry and I'll bet you are too."

"Where're the others?"

"Still sleepin'. Probably be there for a while. I missed out on a lot of drinks lookin' for you."

William blushed again.

"Sorry, Eddie. It's not much of a start in Australia, is it?"

Eddie laughed.

"It's no matter, Bill. You're all right and I've got some money that I would have wasted on whisky."

"I'm not going to drink it again."

"We all say that."

Eddie rinsed his head at the tank, drank some water and they made their way down the side of the building and back into the bar.

About a dozen people sat at tables eating. The atmosphere was more sombre than the previous evening. Very little conversation could be heard from anyone.

A big woman dressed in shirt and pants approached them. Her hair was a mass of tangled curls, with a scarf tied around her head trying to bring order to chaos.

"You want breakfast?"

"Aye," said Eddie.

"Just two of you?"

"Aye."

"Use that table," she said, pointing.

"What can we have?" Eddie asked as he took a seat.

"What you're given," she said.

"How much?"

"Six pence each." Eddie handed her a shilling and she shouted "Two more!" as she walked off.

A minute or so later, the woman returned with two large cups of tea, some cutlery, jam and huge slabs of bread on a plate.

"Is this it?" asked Eddie.

"Comedian," she said.

"What's that mean?" asked William when she'd gone.

"Dunno, but I expect we'll find out."

She once again returned with two large plates—this time with massive pieces of steak and two eggs on each.

"All the tea you want," she said. "Just ask."

William had never eaten steak before, nor had he used a knife and fork. He watched Eddie who was already tucking into the steak, quickly cutting off slices, mopping them in the eggs, chewing them and clearly enjoying himself. There was a large bowl of sugar on the table and Eddie heaped several spoonfuls of it into his tea. William did the same and really liked it. True to her word, the woman came back several times to refill their cups.

When they were finished, they went outside and sat on a bench on the verandah. Eddie swatted absently at the insects and flies that continued to buzz around them.

"We don't go back to the ship until tomorrow," said Eddie. "What do you want to do?"

Before William could answer, a voice called from the street.

"Ah! There you are."

A young man was standing there, smiling broadly and holding a horse's bridle. He was dressed in a cabbage-tree hat, a brightly coloured shirt, cord pants, and long boots reaching above the knee—just as William had seen many men dressed the night before. The horse looked as though it had been ridden hard—it was covered in sweat and its flanks were flecked with foam.

"There's who?" said Eddie.

"Why, him," said the man pointing at William.

He tied the horse to a rail and stepped onto the verandah.

"I believe this is yours," the man said, handing William some money.

"Mine?" William responded, bewildered.

"Yes, you dropped it last night."

"Where?"

"Why, here. Your friend here went to find you a bed and you tried to get up, fell off the verandah and the money fell from your pocket. When you stood, you said you had a stone in your boot, took it off and poured some more money on the ground. Then, you started walking down the road."

William stared at him.

"You don't remember?"

William shook his head.

"I was going to chase you down the road, but my friends said you'd be back. We waited and when you didn't come back, I thought I'd drop it by this morning. So, here I am and here you are."

The man laughed again then turned to his horse and untied the reins.

"See you," he said and mounted the horse.

"Wait," said Eddie. "You can't do an act of kindness like that and not let us thank you. Why, most men would have kept it."

"I'm not most men," said the man.

"Can I buy you a whisky?"

"Well, it's a bit early, but don't mind if you do."

The man got down from his horse and joined William and Eddie on the bench. Eddie went inside to get the whiskies.

"He's a good friend," said the man.

"The best," said William, "but it's me who should be buying. You returned my money."

"I'm sure you'll get a chance to thank him and buy him a drink later. Where are you two fellers from?"

"We came on the *Lady Grace*. Came ashore last night. I was stupid and had some whisky, which I don't normally drink. I don't remember anything."

Eddie came back with the whiskies.

"You should have told your friend you don't drink whisky," said the man just as Eddie handed one to William.

Eddie gave the man his whisky too, then held out his hand to introduce himself.

"Eddie Ward."

"Scott Mallard."

"And this here is Bill. Bill Smith."

"Pleased to meet you both."

"What are you doing here, Scott? Do you own a farm?" asked Eddie.

"I've got a place outside town. It's not very big—only about 500 acres. We run sheep and cattle. You probably had one of my cattle, or some of it, for breakfast. If you had breakfast, that is. We do a bit of importing, too. Had some cargo coming in on the *Lady Grace*. I heard last night it had arrived and I came in this morning to arrange delivery. Did you come as passengers or crew?"

"Crew," said Eddie.

"Then I suppose I have to thank you fellows for getting it here safely."

William was only sipping his whisky and noticed the other men doing the same. It didn't seem to be affecting him as much as it had the previous night, though he still wasn't sure about the taste.

"Look," said Scott, "I've got to arrange the delivery, so I'll leave you chaps. But how about I come back when I'm done? I'd like to buy you a nobbler for getting my cargo here. Least I can do."

"What's a nobbler?" asked William.

"Why, that's what we call a glass of whisky," said Scott, shrugging. "Back soon," he said and once again got on his horse.

"He seems right enough," Eddie said as they watched Scott canter away.

"Brought my money back. That makes him right."

He gave Eddie a shilling and a sixpence. Eddie took it and smiled.

"I hope this makes me right," said William.

"Not to worry. I'm glad it worked out. Glad you're all right too. The lads'll tell you I was worried last night. I thought we might find you in a ditch this morning."

"I'm sorry, Eddie."

"Don't be sorry. Sam's fault. He shouldn't have pushed the whisky onto you. Be careful with it, Bill. It sneaks up on you, even when you've had as much practice as I have. Anyway, let's find the others while we wait for Scott."

Eddie got up and headed inside.

"Don't we go around the back?"

"No. We can go this way."

They went through a door at the back of the bar. It was dark inside. Eddie pushed some curtains off a window at the back and light streamed into the room. There were about ten men in there, lying on mattresses.

"Jesus, what're you doin'?" shouted someone.

"Sorry," said Eddie. "Lookin' for the *Lady Grace* boys."

"Look somewhere's else then and pull those bloody curtains."

"That you, Eddie?" said a voice from the darkness.

"Yes. Who's that?"

"Sam."

"The others here too?"

"I think so."

"Christ. Can't you let a man sleep? What's all this fuss 'n' nonsense?" another voice said.

"I'll see you all out front then," said Eddie. He and William went and waited at the front of the inn. The others came one by one, all looking the worse for the drink. Everyone's face was covered in mosquito bites.

"Not too sure about this place," said Sam. "Is Melbourne better?"

"What's wrong with this place?" asked Eddie.

"My head hurts, my face hurts, it's hot, there's a million flies and insects screaming so loud I can't hear myself think. That enough wrong?"

"Don't know about your head and your face, but as far as the rest of it's concerned, Melbourne's no better."

"Where'd you get to, Bill? Find a woman?" said Lucas.

"Leave him be," said Eddie. "We've met a local. He's coming back later for a drink. You're welcome to join us."

"When's that?"

"When he gets here."

"You had breakfast?"

"Aye."

"How about the rest of us do the same. Meet you back here?"

"Where else would you meet us?"

"Just askin'."

The others went inside and Eddie and William sat staring at the dust and the trees.

"It's not Ireland," said William. He thought of his family and a brief sadness crossed his thoughts. What of Mary, too? What was she doing?

"They say there's nowhere like it, but I wouldn't know. Are you goin' to re-join the ship?"

William shrugged. "I suppose so. Not much else, is there?" He was silent for a few moments before speaking again. "What about the gold, Eddie? Do you think about the gold?"

"Let's ask Scott about it when he gets back. No harm in talking about it, is there?"

They waited for the others in silence, both lost in their own thoughts.

William was startled by Sam asking, "Where's the head?"

"Up the back," said Eddie. "A little shed, not the big one. Port side. I'm surprised you haven't found it yet."

"Haven't needed it yet."

"I'll bet."

Sam left and the others sat in silence.

Sam came back and said, "Hope your friend gets here soon."

"Why?"

"I'm ready for a drink. I wonder if that dark-haired girl will be here again tonight. I fancy her."

"She's got to fancy you, too. No point if she doesn't."

"I think she does."

"In your dreams."

# CHAPTER 2.

# A Chance Meeting

The men were still sitting out front when Scott returned later in the day.

They'd idled the day away—sometimes playing cards, sometimes chatting, and otherwise sleeping. William didn't know how to play cards but enjoyed watching, sharing Eddie's triumphs and disappointments. He enjoyed doing nothing, too. The voyage had been long and difficult and it was a wonderful treat to sit around and do nothing. Some men came around the middle of the day, drinking beer on the other benches and chatting. No one paid the sailors any attention and that was all right with them. William thought it odd that the three meals in Australia were called breakfast, lunch and dinner and said so to Eddie.

"It's just how it is," said Eddie. "And there's more than that to get used to."

When Scott got down from his horse and tied it to the rail, he swept off his hat with a grand gesture, leant on the rail and said, "So, you've found some friends in the mean time?"

Eddie laughed.

"Not really. Shipmates. We're all from the *Lady Grace*."

"Then I owe you all a drink. Would you like to start with a beer?"

"Aye, that would do well."

"How about you, Bill? Would you like a beer?"

Eddie laughed.

"Give it a go, Bill. You won't like it, but it'll keep you off the whisky for a while."

William shrugged. He hoped they'd forget about his misadventure with the whisky soon. He was embarrassed all over again every time they raised it.

Scott went inside and returned shortly with eight beers on a tray. They were big glasses with handles. The men took one each and dragged up a couple of benches so they could sit in a group.

"To the *Lady Grace*," said Scott.

"Aye, to the *Lady Grace*," said the others.

William took a sip of his beer. It was warm and none too good. Like Eddie had predicted, he didn't like it.

"Best drink it quick," said Eddie, noting William's sour pout. "It will only get warmer."

"So, what are you lads going to do now?" asked Scott.

"We're back to the *Lady Grace* tomorrow," said Eddie.

"Tomorrow?" repeated Scott with some confusion.

"Aye, tomorrow."

"She's gone. Left this afternoon."

"Gone? She can't be gone."

"She can be and she is."

"Where's she gone?"

"Sydney. Needs some repairs, they said. They offloaded all the cargo and left on the afternoon tide. Captain was in a terrible hurry. Kept shouting at everyone to get their cargo off."

"Jesus, Eddie. What'll we do? They've got our money," chorused the sailors.

"Got your money?" asked Scott.

"Yes, they kept our wages. Said they needed to get some money from Melbourne. Said to come back and get it tomorrow."

"Maybe, they've left it with their agent?"

"Who's their agent?"

"He'll be here later. You can ask him—I'll introduce you. He arranged my cargo."

"This is a right pickle," said Lucas. "No money, no ship. Jesus, Eddie. What'll we do?"

"There's plenty of ships," said Scott. "I can get you on another ship."

"What about our money?" asked Pat.

"If it's not with the agent, then I don't know. Let's not worry about it until he gets here. If he hasn't got it, he might know how to get it."

There was silence for a few moments as the men pondered what would happen if they couldn't get their money.

"What's your cargo?" asked William.

Scott smiled at him, obviously relieved to discuss less painful matters.

"Goods for the goldfields—clothing and supplies. My brother has a store there. I get the goods to him and he sells them."

"The beer was a good idea, but I think I'd prefer a whisky. Who'd like a whisky?" said Eddie.

"We haven't got enough money, have we?" asked Pat.

"Of course we have. Like Scott said, let's worry about that when the agent gets here. In the meantime, what else can we do? C'mon lads. Load me up."

He put out his hand and they all put a shilling in it. Scott tried to as well, but Eddie told him not to.

"This one's on me," he said.

"Well," said Scott. "I bought you a beer for getting my cargo here, so if I'm going to drink with you chaps, I'd rather pay my way, if that's all right with you."

"Aye, as you wish," said Eddie, taking the shilling.

He came back with the drinks on a tray and they all took one.

"Best be sipping," said Eddie. "Got to stretch them out."

"That's all right with me," said William and they all laughed.

"Tell me about the goldfields," William said, turning to Scott.

"Sure. What do you want to know?"

"Where are they?"

"It's not one place, but they are all within a hundred or so miles from here."

"How do you get there?"

"Some people walk. Others ride a horse. Some people go in a cart."

"How do you get your goods there?"

"A dray. That is, a cart."

"How long does it take?"

"About four days. It's a hard trip so I don't do it too often. I go when the goods arrive."

"Can I go with you?"

Scott laughed causing William to blush.

"What're you thinkin', Bill?" asked Eddie. "Are you thinkin' of goin'?" The others leaned forward eagerly, keen to hear his response.

"If I can go with Scott, I am."

"You're serious?" said Scott.

William nodded.

"What about us?" asked Lucas.

"Yes, the rest of us," said Pat.

"All of us," said Dan.

"Not all of us," said Sam.

"That's right," said Eddie. "Not all of us."

"What do you all know about the goldfields?" said Scott. "My guess is nothing."

He looked at their faces. They all looked away and remained silent.

"Look, lads. No matter what you hear, not everyone finds gold. Most don't. They spend all their money on supplies and equipment and join hundreds of others getting there. Most walk there in the heat, the dust and the flies. Some never make it at all and just die on the road. Then, when you get there, you pay for a licence to dig. You pay even if you find nothing. You have to find a spot where there might be gold and you have to know what you are doing to find that spot. No one will tell you. If it's a good spot, there's probably someone there already."

William couldn't believe it. Scott was a right type, wasn't he? He had a shop there, so there was no point in making it sound worse than it was. And why did Pat want to come if it made no sense?

Scott looked at him directly and said, "Don't you believe me?"

William struggled to find the words.

"It's not that. It's, well… it's… I met a man in Dublin. He wanted to come. He said he was coming to get some gold and he made it sound easy."

Scott reached out and gripped William's arm.

"It's not easy, Bill. No, it's not easy. People die digging for gold. You dig down hundreds of feet into the ground, often finding nothing and sometimes getting killed by falling rocks."

"If it's that hard, why do people do it?"

"They do it because sometimes they find a fortune. Why, just a few weeks back some men found enough that they'll never have to work again. But for every one that makes it rich, hundreds go away disappointed."

"Does your brother dig for gold?"

"Yes, but not in the ground. He gets gold from those that dig for it. He has the shop and that gets gold enough for us."

William and his mates were silent.

"Why don't you think on it, Bill? Why don't you all think on it? C'mon. Let's have another drink," said Scott.

"My turn," said Lucas and collected a shilling from everyone.

"I've still got some," said William. "I'll miss this one."

Lucas nodded and left.

"C'mon, Bill. Cheer up. It's not the end of the world," said Scott. "You're looking very disappointed."

"I am disappointed," said William. "Hard not to be."

Lucas arrived back with the drinks and the others started to chat among themselves, mostly about their money and how they hoped the agent could help them.

William was still silent and struggled to contain his disappointment.

"How long have you had the shop?" he asked Scott.

"About a year."

"Does your brother stay there all the time?"

"Mostly. I swap with him when things're quiet down here."

"What do you mean by quiet?"

"When we're not mustering or shearing—they're busy times."

They once again sat in silence for a few minutes as the conversation and insects whined and buzzed around them. The owner had lit several lamps along the walls and moths gathered in hundreds around them, darting in to commit suicide with sharp flashes of light when their wings burned.

Eventually, Scott got to his feet.

"Here's the agent now! We'll find out about your money."

A very well dressed man was walking along the road towards the verandah. He was carrying a coat across an arm and had a fancy hat that was round across the top with raised edges. William could see a white shirt and tie. He had a waistcoat that matched his jacket and trousers and when he stood in the light on the verandah, William could see he was wearing very neat shoes, which had probably been shiny before he walked to the pub.

Scott called to him, "Oscar! We're here!"

"Right," said Oscar. "Who's we?"

"Oh. These are some crew from the *Lady Grace*."

"The *Lady Grace*? She's gone."

"That's what I told them. They haven't been paid all their money. I told them you might have it for them."

"Why would I have it?"

"I thought with you being the *Lady Grace's* agent, they might have given it to you to hold for the men that had gone ashore."

"Why would they do that?"

William decided that Oscar was not as helpful as Scott.

"How can we get it?" asked Eddie.

"I don't know. Why would I know?"

Scott was staring at Oscar as though he'd not seen him before.

"You're not helping. These men are owed money by the shipping company that you represent. I do a lot with you, Oscar and I expect you to be more helpful."

"Sorry, Scott. It's been a long day and a hot walk to here. I'll get a drink and we'll talk some more."

When he came back a few minutes later with a whisky, he seemed more amenable.

"All right. Tell me again what's happened."

"You tell him, Eddie."

"Well, we docked yesterday and we went to the purser to get our money. He said he didn't have enough and had to get the rest from Melbourne. Said to come back tomorrow and get it. The first officer said they'd be in port several days getting repairs done. Then Scott told us the ship has already left for Sydney."

"That's right. They couldn't find anyone here that could do the repair, so they had to go to Sydney. Had to get there quickly for some reason, so they hurried the cargo off and left today."

He stopped speaking, although everyone continued to look at him expectantly. There were more people around them now and others were jostling for positions on the benches or away from the lamps. William noticed that Oscar was sweating and guessed that it wasn't just because of the heat.

"How many of you are there? Are you all from the *Lady Grace*?"

"Seven of us and all from the *Lady Grace*," said Eddie.

"I don't know why this is my problem," Oscar said defensively. "I'm like you. They pay me to do work. Maybe, they tried to find you. No one told me anything about this. I'm sure if they wanted me to do something, they would have told me."

He ran his finger around his collar.

"Christ, it's hot," he said.

The all continued to look at him.

"How much are you owed?"

"They gave most of us some of the money. I suppose two or three pounds each."

"That's not a lot."

"It is when you don't have a lot."

"All right, all right. I'll tell you what I'll do. I owe them some money for the cargo they delivered today. How about, you give me your names and I'll give you a pound each and you can get the rest from them. You'll need to give me a receipt to prove that I've given you the money though."

No one said anything.

Oscar turned to Scott, shrugging and spreading his hands. William thought he looked desperate.

"C'mon, Scott. It's not much, but it's the best I can do. Anyway, there's plenty of ships going to Sydney. You can sign on one of those, go to Sydney and get your money yourself. The *Lady Grace*'ll be there for a while, they say."

"Oscar, I think that's very generous. It sits well with me. What do you think, lads? Eddie, you seem to be spokesman. What do you think?"

"That'll work for me. I'm sure it will work for everyone. Well, lads?"

The others nodded their agreement.

"Then let me buy you all a drink and I must be off," said Scott. "I've got a family that will be wondering where I am."

He didn't wait for assent, but disappeared into the bar and came back with a tray and eight whiskies.

"I didn't ask this time, Bill, but I'm sure you're in a mood to celebrate."

"I'll get some paper," said Oscar and disappeared into the bar.

"Thanks for your help, Scott. I know he didn't want to do it," said Eddie.

Scott nodded.

Oscar came back, got their names, wrote them on the paper and said, "I've written 'Paid one pound by Oscar Longhorne of

Longhorne Agents, Williams Town on behalf of the owners of the *Lady Grace*'. I've put the date and the time and I need you to sign beside your name. He opened up his wallet and handed them one pound each.

The men that could read and write signed their name as requested. Lucas, Pat and William all asked which was their name and put an x beside it. Oscar wrote 'His Mark'.

"Thank you for the drink, Scott. I'm glad things have finished well. Good luck, gentlemen."

Oscar took his coat from a hook on the wall and set off into the darkness.

"I must do the same," said Scott.

"What about the goldfields?" said William.

"What about the goldfields?" said Scott with a smile.

"You said we should think on it. I haven't finished thinking on it yet."

"Do you still think you might go?"

"Aye," said William.

"The rest of you?" he said, looking around at the others.

They all shook their heads.

"All right, Bill. I'll see you in the morning. We'll talk some more."

He went to his horse, got on and called, "See you!"

"Let's go inside," said Sam. "I'm sick of the insects."

Once inside, they found the same spot at the bar they had used the night before.

"Ah. Here you are," the barman said to William. "They were all looking for you last night."

"It's all right," said Eddie. "We found him. Seven whiskies, please. Some water, too."

The barman came back with the whiskies and a small jug of water.

"Here's a trick, Bill. If you mix a little water with the whisky, it goes further, lasts longer and doesn't knock you around so much."

Sam wasn't paying attention to any of the men and William noticed he was smiling at the same woman from the previous night.

*At least I remember her*, thought William.

He was very careful after the previous evening and took his time with his whisky. From time to time he added some water as Eddie had instructed and managed to stay with the group.

Sam, on the other hand, was becoming progressively drunk and evermore flirtatious with the dark-headed woman.

Eddie and the others were in an animated conversation about the owners of the *Lady Grace* and whether they'd left without paying the crew deliberately.

William saw a look of apprehension cross Sam's face. He looked towards the other group and saw the woman's companion detach himself from the group and walk over to Sam.

The woman's companion wasn't tall, but he was rangy and looked very tough. He had a full beard, a weather-beaten and brown face, and his lips were set in a straight line. He was dressed in the standard coloured shirt, scarf around the waist, moleskin pants and long boots.

"All right, pretty boy, what're you lookin' at?"

"Who, me?" said Sam, feigning innocence.

"Well, I don't mean Santa Claus," the man retorted. "Mister, you've been askin' for it and now you're going to get it. Outside."

"What have I been askin' for?" said Sam.

The man looked at the barman who simply shrugged.

"This," said the man and drove his right fist into Sam's face. Sam dropped like a bag of potatoes and hit the floor with a loud thump.

The bar fell instantly silent and the man eyed William's group menacingly.

"Anyone else?" asked the man. "No? Wise decision."

He turned and walked back to his companions, and the noise in the bar resumed.

"I suggest you get him out of here," said the man behind the bar. "At least until he sobers up. Take him out the back, if you like. I presume you're all staying another night. You're welcome to be in here, but your friend is not."

"All right," said Eddie. "Here, help me, Dan."

They carried Sam to the room at the back and when they re-emerged, the man behind the bar said, "That'll be threepence each for the night."

Eddie gathered up the money, put in for Sam and passed it over to the barman.

"Have you got something to eat?" asked Eddie.

"Not now. Too late." He turned to the room. "Last drinks!" he called.

"Aye, then we'll have another."

"Is that six?"

"You'd better have one too, Bill. It'll help you sleep."

"Aye," said William, still shocked by what had just occurred.

He stole a glance at the woman's group. They were laughing and chatting as though nothing had happened.

They put their money on the bar and stood, uneasily and warily glancing at the other group.

"Don't worry, boys. He's done. I warned Sam," said Eddie. "Let's take our time with these."

The men nodded apprehensively and sipped their drinks in silence.

"What are you going to do, Eddie?" asked William.

"I'll catch a ship to Sydney, or anywhere else for that matter. Company didn't want to pay us the money. It's as simple as that. Still, we didn't jump ship and thanks to Scott we got some of our money, so it's not all bad."

The others nodded in agreement.

"What are you going to do, Bill?" asked Pat.

"I'm going to the goldfields, if Scott will have me."

"Why?"

"Dunno. I like the sound of it. I might be lucky. Scott said some are. No reason it can't be me. Besides, I might find a rich girl there."

Eddie laughed.

"What was funny about that?" asked Dan.

"Nothing," said Eddie, laughing again.

'What about you, Pat? What are you going to do?" asked William.

"Same as Eddie. The sea is what I know."

"Me too," said Dan.

"I suppose that goes for me," said Paul.

"And for me," said Lucas.

"You'll be on your own," said Eddie. "I suppose that's not new for you. We'll miss you, lad. Good luck to you."

"I haven't gone, yet. Nor has he asked me. It's all just talk at the moment."

"Time for bed, then. Tomorrow's another day." Eddie finished his drink and headed for the back room.

The others followed. There was no one in there apart from Sam and he wasn't moving.

"Piss first," said Eddie and took a few steps outside the back door. William joined him. They both looked up at the sky as they emptied their bladders.

"I like the stars," said Eddie. "I feel sometimes I have only to reach up to touch them."

"I'm the same," said William.

"Bill, will you really go to the goldfields? Scott made it sound difficult and dangerous out there."

"It was difficult and dangerous on the ship."

"Aye, that it was. Well, good luck. I hope you find some gold. Bill, I'm goin' to the docks early in the mornin'. I'll take the other lads, too. We don't have that much money, so we need to get on a ship as soon as we can. If we can get on one, we will and we won't be back. If it doesn't work out with Scott, come lookin' for us, but what I'm sayin' is, we might be gone."

When they finished, they faced each other and shook hands.

"I understand, Eddie. You've been a good friend and I'll always be grateful to you."

They turned back into the room, selected a mattress each, rolled it out and made themselves as comfortable as they could. The mosquitoes whined around them, an annoying periodic silence indicating one had landed to feast.

# CHAPTER 3

# Deciding to Go

William was roused by movement in the room. Someone had opened the curtains and the faint light of dawn penetrated the window. The mutterings from the others made it clear that the mosquitoes had feasted merrily for most of the night.

"We're off, Bill," said Eddie, gripping William's hand in the half-light. "Good luck. If you make it rich, don't forget your mates."

The others all did the same in turn and filed from the room, leaving William on his own.

He tried to sleep, but the ever-whining mosquitoes wouldn't allow it. He couldn't believe that there could possibly be an unfed mosquito left in Williams Town. In frustration, he got up and went to the head. He washed and drank at the tank before heading to the front to await breakfast. The sun was well up by then and as the mosquitoes disappeared, the flies took their place. Swatting absently, William wished the cook would hurry—he was starving and waiting only made it worse.

It was all he could do to not run after Eddie and the others. What had he been thinking? How stupid was it to stay here? Scott said he would be back, but there was no reason for him to come back, was there? Eddie was right. William should have gone with the others. How long ago did they leave? Could he find them?

The big woman stood in the doorway.

"You want breakfast?"

"Aye," said William, relieved not to have to think about his stupidity any longer.

He got up and as he did, he heard the clatter of a horse cantering on the road. Scott was coming and William almost shouted for joy.

"Him too?" the woman asked.

"I expect so," said William.

"What kind of an answer is that?" said the woman. "Yes or no to breakfast for him?"

"Yes, I suppose," William responded.

"That'll be a shilling then," she said.

William gave her the shilling just as Scott arrived.

"Thought you'd still be here," said Scott. "Are you having breakfast?"

"Aye, and I've arranged it for you too. Hope that's all right."

"Aye, I'm starving. I wanted to get here before you changed your mind, so I left home at dawn. I thought I'd have breakfast here anyway, if I had missed you."

"Why did you want to get here before I changed my mind?"

"Well, I've been thinking on it. My brother could do with some help. I know you can't read or write, but I think you've got a good head on your shoulders." He stared at William and smiled. "Though, by the look of it, the mozzies have done their best to chew it off. Let's talk over breakfast and I'll tell you what I have in mind."

William got up and, as he did, Scott gripped his shoulder. "I'm glad you're still here."

They went inside and the woman pointed at a table.

"There," she said.

"Righty-o," said Scott, sitting down and rubbing his hands as though warming to his task.

While the woman busied herself bringing the breakfast, Scott leaned forward with his arms and elbows on the table and spoke.

"I'm taking the goods to Ballarat today. I normally take a couple of my men to help out, but we're busy at the moment and I can ill afford anyone. So, if you come, I only have to take one man. Then, if you want, you can stay with my brother and help out in the shop. They're busy there, too, so I know he could do with some help."

"Aren't there other men there that can help?"

"You'll understand when we get to the goldfields. There's excitement every day with new finds and opportunities. People drop everything and rush off, filled with hope and expectation."

"Why won't I do that?"

Scott looked at William and laughed. William blushed.

"No, no, Bill. Don't be embarrassed. I'm not laughing at you. We'll agree that you won't run off for a month or two. I'm a realist. I know you'll want to dig sooner or later—everyone does. But in the meantime, you'll learn a lot from others' mistakes. They'll be coming in and out of the store. You'll learn what they do right and what they do wrong. You'll learn that what most people do is mostly wrong. You'll learn that gold is only ever where you find it. And mostly, it's someone else that's finding it." He sat back. "What do you think, Bill? Are you up for it?"

"Aye," said William, his face flushed, heart beating hard. He could hardly contain his excitement.

"I'll pay you," said Scott.

"How much?"

"Well, it's like this. I'll take you up there and feed you on the way. I won't pay you on the journey. Way I see it, it's good for both of us. When we get there, I'll pay you a pound a week and give you somewhere to sleep and provide your food. It'll be good food. You'll eat what my brother eats. We'll clothe you from the store and we won't charge you for that. You'll buy your own whisky and beer. Anything I've forgotten?"

"What if I want to come back?"

"You can come back with me next time I come up, or with someone else if you want to come back sooner. Though you'd probably have to pay them."

He looked at William for a few moments.

"I don't think you'll want to come back."

"Why not?"

"Dunno. Hunch."

They busied themselves with their breakfast. Both men were hungry and William enjoyed it every bit as much as he had the day before. He looked at Scott. The man looked honest. All the dealings so far had been good. He'd arranged for his friends to get some of the money they were owed. William tried to see a problem.

"Tell me about your brother."

"What's to tell? He's younger than me. We own everything together. He's a good man. You'll like him. He'll like you."

They sipped their tea.

"Are you in?" said Scott.

"Aye, I'm in."

"Good," said Scott, extending his hand. "Let's shake on it."

The men shook and William liked the feeling of confirming an agreement with a handshake.

"What now?" he asked.

"Why, I'll ride into the docks and collect the dray. It should be ready this morning. I'll come back and get you. Then, we'll be off to Ballarat."

"Why do you need two men?"

"You'll see," said Scott, laughing.

"Can I come with you now?"

"If you wish. I'll have to explain it to the horse—he may not like it."

"How will you do that?"

"Sorry, Bill—poor joke. Get your things. I'll wait."

"I don't have any things."

"All right. Let's go then!"

They walked over to the horse. It raised its head warily, as though surprised to see two men.

Scott climbed into the saddle, but left the left-side stirrup free.

"Which way?" asked William.

"Which way what?"

"Which way will I walk?"

"You won't walk. You'll ride with me. Put your left foot into the stirrup, I'll lift you up and you can ride behind me."

William put his foot into the stirrup; Scott grabbed his arm and lifted him to sit on the horse behind the saddle, his feet dangling.

"Hold the saddle at the back. We won't go fast. You'll get used to it," said Scott. The horse moved off in the direction of the docks.

William was very nervous at first. He thought he might fall at any moment. Fortunately, the horse moved off at a walking pace and William became accustomed to the side-to-side movement, but he was grateful to have the saddle to hold. Scott maintained a chatter about the weather, the road, the bush and commerce. William was content to listen. He tried to avoid touching Scott, but it was very hard to do as the horse's gait caused them to fall forward and back. Scott didn't seem to mind when William fell into his back but for his part, William was very uncomfortable being so close to another human being for such an extended time. He looked forward to reaching the end of their journey—he knew it wasn't far as he and the others had walked from the docks.

# CHAPTER 4

# Trouble in Williams Town

They reached the docks soon enough. There was the usual bustle and noise, but this time overlaid by the sound of a strong onshore wind. The horse threaded its way casually between the traffic on the street. There were other horses and some people on foot, and Scott pointed out drays—some being pulled by horses and others by bullocks. The bullocks were very big beasts in large teams, moving very slowly and deliberately, pulling massive loads. Scott said that they would use horses to pull their goods, as their load was not that big.

"Be faster, too," he said. "Bullocks are good for heavy loads, but too slow."

Scott stopped the horse at a rail outside a large building. He swung his left leg across the pommel, took his right boot from the stirrup, slid on his back to the ground and said, "Wait here. You can get off the horse if you like, but hang onto the reins. I don't want him wandering off. You either, for that matter."

He threw the reins to William and went into the building.

"How long will you be?" said William. "Can I tie the horses to the rail and have a look around?"

"I don't know how long but sure, you can have a look around. Do you need to buy anything? There's a good general store over there. Everything will be cheaper here than Ballarat, even though it's my store." Laughing, he helped William off the horse, tied the reins to the rail and disappeared into the building.

William looked up and down the street, taking in the sights, sounds and smells of Williams Town. To his left was the bay and the building into which Scott had gone, being only one of many. Some were big enough to be warehouses, but they all had a temporary look about them, as though they had been quickly built for a short-term purpose. There was animal dung everywhere, in some places piled up, probably by the traffic. Wind blew dust about and even though it was early in the day, many people were moving about with purpose. William guessed that, like Scott, those with carts were collecting from or delivering to the docks. Not many people took any notice of him but some said, "Mornin'" as they hurried on their way. He decided to have a look in the general store that Scott had pointed out.

Pushing the door open and stepping inside, a bell tinkled to indicate his entry. William's nostrils were pleasantly surprised by many smells, some unfamiliar, but all pleasant. Goods were everywhere, haphazardly piled about. He couldn't see any customers—perhaps it was too early. He saw a girl standing on a ladder, stacking cans into the shelves. She stopped when she heard the bell and looked over to him.

"Can I help you?" she asked.

Everything about her reminded him of Mary. She had a pert, pretty face—freckled and inquisitive. A floral dress with ruffles at the neck and arms framed her prettiness and took his breath away. He tried to speak, but all that happened was that his mouth moved about silently. She laughed and he added to his embarrassment by turning bright red.

"Well," she said. "Was the question too hard then?"

He shook his head.

"No. I'm just looking about."

"Well, sir, you look honest enough, so you may look about. If you see something that you wish to buy, I'll be right here."

"Is this your store?"

"No, it's my father's. Who wants to know?"

"My name is Bill."

"Well, Bill, mine is Jessica and I'd be pleased to give you some help if you need it."

She went back to her packing and William strolled about, looking at the goods and hoping to find an excuse to continue the conversation. He manufactured and discarded excuses at a rapid rate, strolling by the piles of goods and feigning interest. Several times he glanced at her, but she was focused on her task and didn't pay him any attention. He probably needed some more clothes, but he might be better to ask Scott what to get as he had no idea what would be suitable for the goldfields. His meanderings took him to the back of the room where there were stacks of axe and pick heads, and barrels of handles. They all looked new and he supposed such things would be needed in the goldfields. The handles were smooth and the metal was shiny. He ran his hands over them and delighted in the touch.

The doorbell tinkled and two rough-looking fellows stepped into the store, closing the door behind them. One of the men approached Jessica while the other stood keeping his back to the door. It was clear to William that they hadn't seen him.

"Can I help you?" said Jessica, still standing on the ladder.

"Yes," said the man walking towards Jessica. "We'd like all your money, so get down from there and fetch it for us. That's a good girl."

"I'll do no such thing and you'd best be off if you know what's good for you."

"Come, now, lass. There's no need to try my patience. I know your father is not here. I know you're on your own, so be a good girl and fetch the money before my friend here loses his patience. He's not as nice as me and might decide he wants more than your money."

The man by the door made a noise like a growl, as if to emphasise a lack of niceness.

William looked at Jessica who appeared scared but defiant. She remained on the ladder and the man stepped closer.

"C'mon, lass. I'll not ask again. Get down from there and fetch your money."

"You fetch it yourself."

The man laughed.

"I know there's more than in the drawer. I seen your father take it from the drawer when there's too much, so we want it all. I'm done with talkin' now." His face hardened and he placed a hand on the ladder.

William slipped one of the pick handles from the barrel and crept silently towards the man, keeping the piles of goods between them so the man wouldn't see him coming. He hoped the man by the door would be occupied by his partner's dealing with Jessica.

"Now, that's a pretty dress," said the man. "I might take it for my friend over there." He moved his hand from the ladder to Jessica's dress, fingering the cloth.

"You keep your hands to yourself," snapped Jessica, pulling the dress from his grasp.

"Feisty, too, eh? I like 'em feisty!" shouted the man in the doorway.

"You might," said the man at the ladder. "But she's mine first. Come down from there, girl. You first, the money second."

He grabbed Jessica's dress and tried to pull her from the ladder. She reached for one of the cans and threw it at the man's head. It missed and crashed onto the floor, clattering as it rolled along. He laughed, the sound of his laughter and the rolling can hiding the sound of William's final few steps to reach him.

Without hesitation, William swung the handle with all his might, striking the man on his outstretched arm. There was a sharp *crack!* as the man howled with pain and folded his injured arm into his body, sinking on his knees to the floor. Swinging the handle again, William whacked the man across the head and he slumped to the floor.

"Look out!" called Jessica as the man from the door ran towards William with bunched fists.

"I'm ready," said William quietly and he turned towards the man, holding the handle and ready to strike again.

The man hesitated. The piles of goods left little room for him to approach any way other than directly, so he couldn't feint or move about. His face was contorted with rage as he shouted at William.

"I don't know who you are, mate, but you'll pay for what you just done!"

"Really? And who is it that will make me pay?" said William. "You don't look bright enough and your friend surely wasn't."

The man was so focused on William that he failed to see Jessica raise another can. This time she didn't miss and it hit him right on the forehead.

"Christ!" he screamed, both his hands rushing to his face.

William swung the handle again, crushing the man's fingers against the side of his head.

"I've still one hand left," he yelled and charged at William, fist bunched and ready to strike. Blood was pouring from his forehead where the can had struck.

William used Lucky Gordon's tactic and stepped slightly to the side. He didn't use his fist, but jabbed the pick handle into the man's face as hard as he could, like he was clearing a coalbunker. He had the full weight of his body behind the blow and the man stopped when the blow landed. It hit him on the bridge of the nose and there was a mushy sound as the cartilage collapsed. Blood exploded into his eyes and he had no choice but to try to clear them. William swung the handle in an arc over his shoulder and brought it down as hard as he could on the man's head. The man slid to the floor, partly covering the body of the other man, who was still lying motionless.

Jessica was frozen on the ladder, with a hand to her mouth.

"Oh, Bill. Are they dead?"

"Do you mean, is it safe to come down from the ladder? I think it is."

He put out a hand and helped her down.

"No, I mean, are they dead? Have you killed them?"

"I don't think so. It'd probably take more than one blow to do that."

"But you hit them so hard!"

"So did you."

"I didn't mean to. I just thought it might help."

"It surely did. Now, we probably need a policeman. Can you get one?"

"Yes, but will you be all right if I leave you here with them?"

William hefted the pick handle.

"I'll keep this nearby and hit them again if I need to. How long will it take to find a policeman?"

"A few minutes. I won't have to go far."

The door tinkled again.

"Are you in here, Bill?" called Scott.

"Aye," said William.

"We're ready to go. We have to leave now. Bring whatever you have bought and we'll be on our way. Ah! Miss Jessica. And how are you?"

Scott walked over, touching the edge of his hat.

"And what's this?" he said, pointing at the men on the floor. "What produce has your father decided to sell now?"

As he stepped closer, his face took on a more serious look.

"Good Lord! What's been going on? Are you two all right?"

"Yes," said Jessica, "but it's all thanks to Bill. These two men were bent on mischief and he stopped them. I was just going for the police."

"You'd best be quick about it. I'll stay with Bill. The sooner they're in police custody, the better."

Jessica hurried away and the tinkling bell signalled her departure.

William told Scott what had happened and was just finishing the story when Jessica returned with two policemen. The police had brought a handcart. The men were bundled into it and the police left.

"Bill, I've been thinking. Please let me give you something to thank you for your help. Is there anything in the store that you would like?" said Jessica.

William saw Scott smiling and tried not to blush again, failing miserably.

"Oh, I'm sorry," said Jessica. "I didn't mean to embarrass you."

"There's no need to give him anything," said Scott. "I'll sort him out. He's coming to Ballarat to work with me, so we'll fit him out when the time comes."

"Oh. Ballarat," said Jessica, disappointment in her voice.

"Yes and we must away. Will you be all right now, Miss Jessica? Will your father be here soon?"

The question was hardly from his lips when the door tinkled again.

"Jessica? Why is Scott here? Hello, Scott. Checking out the competition?"

Scott laughed.

"No, Andy. As a matter of fact, we're just leaving."

"We? Who's we?" said Jessica's father, looking at William.

"Oh, Daddy. This is Bill. There was some trouble and he was wonderful. I might have been killed!"

William was embarrassed as Jessica took his arm, pressing close, but revelled in her touch. Her hands were so soft and he realised that she smelled like Hannah, who he had met on the ship from Belfast to Liverpool.

"He did, did he? Then you'd best tell me about it."

"Jessica can tell you," said Scott. "Like I say, we must away."

He pulled a reluctant William by the arm, tipped his hat to Jessica, nodded to her father and all but dragged William out the door.

"Oh, Bill!" called Jessica. "Come back soon! Come back anytime! You'll always be welcome. And, thank you! Thank you so much!"

"Over here," said Scott as they emerged from the store. "We're loaded and ready to go. And we have to go. Now. We have to get out to the bush before nightfall."

William looked over and saw a large dray piled high with what he presumed were goods, covered by canvas. The canvas was old and dirty, as though it had seen much use, and it was held in place by ropes criss-crossing it. There were six horses harnessed to the dray, standing silently, still as statues. A driver was seated at the front of the dray, reins in hand, looking bored. Scott's horse was tethered at the back—it too looked bored.

"You climb up with the driver. I'll ride my horse."

William started to climb onto the dray.

"Who the hell is this?" shouted the driver to Scott.

"He's the bloke I told you about," said Scott. "Bill, this is Mike. Try to ignore him—most people do."

William reached the seat, uncertain what to do about the driver. After a few moments, he stuck out his hand.

"Bill."

The driver ignored his hand.

"Mike," was all he said.

"Fair enough", said William and he settled in for the ride. His mind went back to the driver who took him to Belfast.

*I suppose he was quiet at first. Then, the horses are the same as his, so it'll be good to work with them. How long ago was that? A lifetime?*

The driver flicked the reins and the dray moved off. The horses worked together in perfect unison, their hooves thumping on the ground. The dray wheels crunched on the road, insects buzzed, and the wind continued to blow dust about them. There was more traffic than earlier in the day. It was hotter, too, and the traffic more irritable. Pedestrians, riders and sulkies were able to avoid the larger traffic, but the drays needed more room and were all moving slowly.

"Jesus!" shouted a driver with a large wagon and more bullocks than William had fingers. "Watch what you're doing!" he yelled at Mike as Mike tried to overtake.

"You don't own the flamin' road!" Mike shouted back. He encouraged his horses to move faster with the reins, but they ignored him.

"I might not own the 'flamin' road', as you call it, but if you're not more careful, I'll run that puny thing of yours off it! Then let's see what you have to say."

"All right, all right," said Mike, "but can't you move to the left a bit? We don't have all day."

"Well, since you ask so nicely."

The bullock team continued steadily down the road, moving imperceptibly to the left. Mike's team moved past it, also very slowly. All the other traffic was forced to wait, as the wagon and the dray abreast occupied the whole road.

"Thanks!" shouted Mike, waving as they finally moved in front of the bullock team. The bullock team was so long that William couldn't hear the driver's response.

The traffic thinned out quickly as they moved out of town, though there were people walking, riding, and pushing carts like the ones William had used to move produce in Ireland.

"Where are they all going?" William asked Mike.

"Goldfields, like us," Mike responded.

Finally, near to dusk, Mike pulled the dray off the road onto a grassy area. There was one other dray and several people camped there already.

"This'll do us," said Mike. "This is the best place to stop. Scott likes to stop here and I like to please the boss."

"Bill, help Mike with the horses," said Scott, pulling alongside the dray.

"You worked with horses?" Mike asked William.

"No," William replied, not wanting to create expectations.

Mike started at the front, unharnessing each of the horses in turn. Once he removed the harness, he would slip a halter and lead on each horse. The horses didn't seem to mind and set to eating grass, as though biding their time for something else.

"Take each horse to the creek to drink," said Mike. "The others will want to go too, but only take one at a time. Bring it back as soon as it stops drinkin'. Don't let it bluff you into stayin' and eatin' the grass at the creek. It'll try to be boss, but won't try too 'ard if you show it you're in charge."

William took a horse's lead and led it to the creek. It followed obediently. There was a small incline down to the creek. The water bubbled over rocks and there were plenty of pools to choose from. It was cool in the glade and William enjoyed being out of what was left of the sun for the day. The horse walked out into the first pool and drank noisily. It stopped, raised its head and turned to look at William as though to say, "I'm done." William pulled on the lead and started to walk back to the camp.

He'd taken only a few steps when a voice from the shadows in front of him on the creek bank said, "Nice looking horse. I need a horse like that. How much do you want for him?"

William tried to see into the shadows, but couldn't make out any detail of the speaker.

"Well, he's not mine, and I don't think he's for sale."

"Well, if he's not yours, you won't mind if I just take him."

The man stepped out of the shadows. He was holding a revolver.

William hesitated. He'd never confronted a revolver before. The man was in his path, so he couldn't avoid him, nor could he just give him the horse.

"We have a problem," said William.

"What problem is that?" said the man.

"He's not my horse, but that doesn't mean I can let you have him. In fact, it means the opposite. It means I can't let you have him. I'm responsible for him. So, if you want him, you'll need to use that revolver."

"If I have to, I will."

"If you do, it'll be the last thing you ever do," said Scott, coming up behind the man with his own revolver.

The man turned quickly, ready to use his weapon, but hesitated when he saw that Scott was ready to shoot.

"Aw, mister. I was just havin' some fun."

"That so?" said Scott. He continued to walk, keeping his gun pointed at the man. "Let me know when you decide what to do," he said. "We might fire at the same time and we might kill each other. But if you kill me, my friend there will kill you, so you'll be just as dead either way."

"Which friend?" said the man, a broad smile on his face.

"Why, me," said William who had moved up to stand behind him.

"You don't have a revolver," retorted the man, still looking at Scott.

"No, I don't," said William, "but I do have this very large piece of wood."

"All right," said the man. "Like I said, I'm just havin' some fun." He lowered his revolver.

"Good, good," said Scott. "Wise decision. Bill, take his revolver." Turning to the stranger he said, "Let's all have some fun, shall we? Take off your boots and pants and throw them in the creek."

"Not likely."

Scott didn't hesitate. He took the final two steps and belted the stranger over the head with his revolver. The man collapsed.

"Bill, pull off his boots and pants and throw them in the creek."

William did as he was bid and remarked that the man could do with a bath.

Scott laughed.

"He'll get one. When he comes to, he'll go looking for his boots and pants in the creek. He won't find them tonight and by the time he does in the morning, we'll be long gone."

"We still have to water the rest of the horses."

"Hmmm. That's right. I'll stay here, you take the horse and go back to camp. Bring some rope and another horse. We'll tie him up and the mozzies can feast on him overnight."

William did as he was instructed and when he returned the stranger was awake, cursing Scott for taking his pants and boots. Scott ignored him and tied his hands and feet to saplings about a body length apart.

"There. That'll keep you until the morning. We'll come back and let you free then."

"Christ, mister, have a heart! Like I said, I was only havin' fun."

"So are we," said Scott. "Here, Bill, you keep going with the horses and I'll stay with our friend to make sure he gives you no more trouble."

"Christ, mister. I can't give you trouble tied up like this."

On the final journey, William brought a canvas sack to fill with water for them to use in the camp. The stranger was still tied and looking very angry.

"All done," said William when the last horse was watered and the canvas bag was filled.

"Oh, mister. Can't you let me go now? I won't give you any trouble. I promise, mister."

"No, you can lie there and think about your sense of humour," said Scott, making his way up the bank. The stranger continued to yell and curse as they walked away.

"What about wild animals?" William asked Scott. "What if something attacks him?"

"Well, there's only two-legged ones around here, and he's no target for them without pants and boots. No, I'll come down and free him in the morning before we leave. Now, let's have some supper. I'm so hungry I could eat one of our horses. I hope Mike has been busy, but I'll bet not."

They arrived back at camp and Mike was sitting on a log, waiting.

"You two all right? What took so long? Bill said you had trouble, but didn't say what."

"I'll give you trouble," said Scott. "Why didn't you start our supper?"

"I got the fire goin'."

"Did you feed the horses?"

"Yes. Gave 'em some oats."

"Well, I should be grateful for small mercies."

Scott fetched a pan from the dray and pulled a loin of mutton from a sack, cut off some chops, put them in the pan and set the pan over the fire. While he was doing this, Mike grumbled about having to do everything as he put some water from the canvas sack into a billy, placed a long stick over the stone, wedged one under the dray and put the billy on the other end over the fire. Once the water was bubbling, he threw a handful of tea into it. He waited a few moments, stirring it a little with a stick from a gum tree before lifting it off with the same stick. Once it was cool enough to hold by the handle, he poured three mugs of tea for them. He put three large spoonful of sugar in his own and nodded his head at one of the other mugs.

"Pannikin's yours," he said to William.

"Pannikin?" William asked.

"Aye, pannikin," said Mike.

Scott pulled a loaf of bread from another sack, cut off some large slices, placed a chop between two of them and passed it to William.

"It's what we eat out here," said Scott.

"What about me?" said Mike.

"You only looked after the horses. He saved one from being stolen. Means he goes first."

Scott passed Mike some bread with a chop and Mike tore into it with gusto. He ate his food and sipped his tea alternately.

William did the same, but grimaced at the taste of the tea.

"Put some sugar in it," said Mike. "Tastes better."

Mike turned to Scott.

"How'd he save the horse?" he asked between mouthfuls.

"There was a fellow by the creek with a revolver. Thought he'd take the horse. Bill stopped him."

"Wasn't all me. Couldn't have done it without you," said William.

"Might be so, but you weren't giving up without a fight."

Mike looked at William and held out his hand.

"Thanks, Bill. Don't know what I'd do without me horses."

William shook his hand. Did this mean he was accepted?

"Where's the fellow with the revolver now?" asked Mike.

"Well," said Scott. "We left him at the creek, tied up without his boots or pants."

"He'll be gone by mornin'," said Mike.

"How do you know that?" said William. "Scott did a pretty good job of tying him up and he might have trouble finding his boots and pants in the dark."

"There's two of 'em. I've heard about these fellows. They run a pretty good racket, stealin' horses and sellin' 'em. Might have been better if you'd shot 'im."

"Ah, well," said Scott. "You can shoot him in the morning, if you want."

"If he's still there, I might do just that."

They all went back to their eating.

When they were done, Scott said, "It's been a long day. Normally, Bill, we'd smoke a pipe, tell some stories. But me, well, I'm ready for sleep. We'll do without the tent for tonight and in the future, if there's rain or wind, well, you can do it. You or Mike. I don't care who."

Scott walked over to a tree, pissed on it and yawned noisily. When he came back to the dray, he reached in where they had already untied the canvas, pulled six blankets out and dropped four on the ground. He crawled under the dray, wrapped the blankets around himself and could be heard snoring within seconds.

"I'm tired too," said Mike, walking over to piss on the same tree.

When he came back, he reached down, picked up the blankets and threw two to William.

"These are yours," he said. "Scott uses two to keep warm, but, well, I use one for warmth and the other for a pillow. It'll be a squeeze, but we can fit three side by side. Scott's in the middle. That's the best spot, so it's for 'im. No rain or wind tonight, so we'll just sleep under the dray. If there's rain or wind, we'd put some sides on. You'll have to remember that. It'll be your job. Thanks again for me 'orse. The one you saved is the best. 'Night."

Mike rolled one blanket around himself and the other into a bundle and crawled in beside Scott, careful not to disturb him. Like Scott, he was asleep in seconds.

William sat by the dying fire, enjoying being on his own and reflecting on the events of the day. He'd heard that the journey might be dangerous, but in the space of one day, he'd had two serious confrontations. Well, three if you counted both men in the store. He wished he could have spent more time with Jessica. Scott had bundled him away so quickly. Perhaps, if Scott was headed back to Williams Town, he could come too and say hello to Jessica. Was that what people did? Jessica said he could come back whenever he wanted. He wasn't too sure about her da. He might not find the prospect of William's return so attractive. Still, she *was* pretty.

He looked around for a moment. There were several other fires winking in the distance. Mike had said Scott liked it here. Perhaps other people did too. Or, maybe that was as far as they could get in a day. He looked at the blankets in his lap. They looked old and worn and like they needed a wash. He wondered who else had used them. Well, no matter. Fatigue swept over him and the prospect of sleep was most welcome. He went to the well-used tree then wrapped one blanket around himself as Mike had done, rolled the other one for a pillow and crawled in beside the other wheel.

There was very little space under the dray. It would be easy to forget in the night, rise up quickly and give himself a nasty smack on the head. Still, he hadn't done it on the ship, so it was just a matter to think of himself as being on the ship. He thought about the ship then and how he was so glad to no longer be on it. He thought about Hall, too. Perhaps that's why he wasn't frightened of a fight. He didn't think any good could come of that fight, but maybe something did. Then, he thought about Eddie, too. *Where is he now?*

# CHAPTER 5

# Trouble for Scott

William woke stiff, cramped and cold. He'd woken several times during the night, so took no time to realise where he was. He could smell cooking and peeked through the wheel spokes, spotting Scott hunched over the fire. He looked behind him then and saw that Mike was still asleep.

He crawled out from under the dray and saw that his boots had found their way into the open during the night and were now wet with dew. *No matter. Not the first time to pull on wet boots.*

"How goes it?" said Scott. "Sleep well?"

"Well enough," William responded.

Scott nodded at the canvas bag.

"Can you fetch some water? Take care though—our friend might still be there. If he is, don't untie him. He'll ask you, but don't do it. That's a two-man job."

William collected the bag and headed for the creek. There were wisps of smoke coming from other fires and, despite it being summer, the morning was chilly. A heavy dew lay on the ground and in no time at all it mattered not that his boots had already been wet. It wasn't far to the creek and William approached the spot where Scott had tied the thief. Like Mike had said, he was gone. In some ways, that was worse. He could be hiding nearby and ready to exact revenge. William looked around carefully and waited a few moments, listening for any unusual sound. Not that he'd know unusual. He hadn't been there long enough to even know usual.

Birds called to each other and there were lots of other creatures twittering, croaking and nattering. There was a slight mist under the trees that hung in a canopy across the creek. A sweet, cool smell lingered in the air and the creek water rustled and bubbled over rocks and around fallen timber. Very little sun was visible and William suspected that it would be cool there all day. It was a peaceful place and hard to imagine yesterday's confrontation happening there at all. He thought he'd better not stay too long or Scott might worry that another misfortune was underway. Turning, he decided it might be a good idea to wash his hands and face while he was here too. He crouched by the side of the pond, his feet sinking a little into the coarse sand, and filled the bag before swishing his hands in the water. He noticed a slight woody smell as he washed his face and head. It was so good after the heat and dust of the day before. If he had more time he would have liked to take off all his clothes and wash himself fully—it had been a while since his last proper wash. Scott and Mike didn't seem to fuss, so he'd have to make the opportunities for himself.

Standing, he took one more look around before heading back to the camp.

"I was just about to come looking for you," Scott said when he saw him, a look of irritation furrowing his brow. "Our friend still there?"

"No," said William. "Rope was gone, too. Like Mike said, I suppose he had some help. Do you think he's still about?"

"No," Scott shook his head. "He'd be worried that we'd all come looking for him. I gather from Mike that he and his mate aren't too popular in these parts. Anyway, put some water on to boil, let's have our breakfast and be on our way. We've a full day's journey to the next good creek."

"I thought to have a wash in the creek," said William. "Is it safe?"

"Safe enough," said Scott. "You have to do it away from the camps though. People don't like you stirring up the water where they get their drinking supplies. I plan to wash up at the next one, so I'll show you the ropes. There's a better swimming hole there anyway."

Scott noticed Mike pottering with the horses at the dray. They were already in their harness, so it was obvious he was wasting time to avoid being given another task.

"C'mon, Mike! Get a wriggle on. Day's wasting and you aren't helping. Get the tea made and let's hit the road. Won't do you any harm to wash at the next creek, too. People can smell you a mile off."

"What's that?" shouted Mike.

"Nothing," said Scott. "Just get moving, will you? We've wasted enough time already."

When they were done with breakfast, Mike just dumped the billy, the pannikins and the frying pan in a hessian sack and tied it to the back of the dray. Mike and William climbed to the seat, Mike clucked to the horses and muttered, "Let's go."

The dray rolled forward slowly and the day's journey commenced.

"How long will it take us to get there?" William asked.

Mike shrugged by way of response.

William settled into the solitude of the journey. Scott went ahead from time to time to scout out the track. It wasn't a good road and William guessed he was looking for difficulties and dangers that might need to be bypassed. The country changed as they moved through it—sometimes open fields and sometimes wooded areas. Occasionally, they saw another rider or walker. One time, there was a man with a broken handcart who asked them for help.

Scott got down from his horse, looked at the cart and announced it to be broken beyond repair. The man asked if he could ride on the dray and Scott looked at Mike who shook his head.

"Somebody will be along that will appreciate some help, so it's either press forward or back on foot, or wait. Not much else to do," said Scott.

They moved off, leaving the man sitting beside his broken cart, his face crumpled and looking near to tears.

William knew better than to ask Mike why he shook his head.

They crossed a couple of almost-dry creeks where the horses struggled with the dray going down to the creek, although it was only a few feet, and then again, pulling up the other side.

Mike called sounds of encouragement and the horses responded. William marvelled that they knew what he was asking them to do and resolved to spend some time with them when they camped at the end of the day.

One time, William saw some strange animals bounding along.

"What are they?" he said to Mike.

Mike laughed. It was a pleasant sound.

"They're called kangaroos," he said. "The young ones are good to eat."

At last, with the sun casting long shadows, they pulled into a stand of trees. The wind had increased as the day went on and the temperature began to drop. Long, dark clouds scudded across the sky.

"This'll do!" shouted Scott.

Mike manoeuvred the dray into the centre of the clearing. The horses hung their heads, clearly pleased to stop for the day.

The horses were unharnessed and William took them one by one to the nearby creek, just as he had the day before. They seemed to have no energy this time to protest or to assert themselves, and were docile and easily led to and from the creek. On the first visit, William looked around carefully to be sure he was alone, then stood whispering to the horses and patting them as they drank. One horse put its head against his chest when it was done watering, as though to thank him. It made slight snickering sounds as it nuzzled against him. Its hair was harsh to his touch, and thick with dust.

"Do you wash them?" he asked Mike when all the horses were watered.

"Sure," said Mike, responding quickly to the question. "Not often enough though. They love a wash. It's too late today, but we can do it in the mornin', if we are up early enough. We can take them all down. They won't wander off if there's a wash to be had. I'll do it if you help."

"C'mon, you two. You're wasting time. There's work to be done and no time for talking. Bill, you get some water. Mike, you start the fire and get on to the chops. We'll all be up early and have a bath in the morning. Us and the horses."

"All of us?" asked Mike.

"Yes," said Scott. "You two as well. Won't do any of us any harm."

The horses were hobbled and set to grazing.

Scott roped off an area to keep them close.

"The thieves might still be about and they have a score to settle with us. They'll take our horses for sure if we give them a chance."

"Do you still want them hobbled?" asked Mike.

"I think so. Can't hurt and will slow the thieves down some if they try to run them off."

Once supper was done, Mike and Scott lit up pipes while William sat and watched. Smoking was nothing new—most men did it in one form or another.

"You got a pipe?" Mike asked William.

"Leave him be," said Scott. "He's just getting used to whisky."

"Tell me about the horses," said William, looking at Mike.

"What's there to tell? They're a wonderful animal. You treat 'em right, they'll treat you right."

"How long have you had them?"

"Me? They're not mine. They're Scott's. I just look after 'em and drive the dray."

"They listen to you."

"Aye. That they do. They want to please. With enough patience, you can train them to do anythin'. Not as strong as bullocks, but faster and strong enough for what we want. Not as affectionate as a dog, but just as faithful. Dangerous sometimes. If they are frightened, they'll lose all reason—buck and jump and run. Then you have to be careful. I've seen some terrible accidents. The new chums buy 'em in Melbourne and head for the goldfields. Don't know what they're doin'. Lose the load and the horses on the steep sides of a creek. You have to shoot the horse if it's hurt. Better to shoot the people. They're what cause the trouble."

"I'm done," said Scott, knocking his pipe out on a log nearby. "Might be weather tonight. Mike, help Bill put some sides on the dray."

Mike said nothing but rose and took some canvas from the back of the dray, which he and William tied to the wheels on the side.

"That'll stop the wind and the rain if it comes. Make sure your things are under cover tonight—it looks nasty."

When they were done, Scott and Mike went to a tree and William heard Scott ask, "How's the meat going?"

"One more meal is all," Mike responded. "It's not too hot, but I don't think it'll last much longer. Even then, it's a stretch."

"Ah, well. Vegetables until we find someone to sell us some more."

Scott came back, wrapped himself in his blankets and crawled under the dray.

"I'm off too," said Mike, crawling under the dray.

William sat for a little longer by the fire. He could only discern the whereabouts of the horses by the flickers of the firelight and the sounds of their snuffling and chewing as they moved around the roped off area.

Lightning flashed in the distance and the faint sound of thunder came to him on the breeze. It became colder all the time. He shivered and hugged himself against the chill, leaning closer to the fire. Looking forward to the morning, he thought it would be fun to wash the horses and clean himself at the same time. He hoped Mike would still want to do it come morning. Scott was quieter about it, but William guessed that Scott was content to let Mike handle the horses and the responsibility that went with it.

The storm came closer and William was confident it would be a wet night. He couldn't see how the extra canvas would hold rain out.

He fetched his blankets and crawled into his place. Mike and Scott were already snoring loudly. *Nothing remarkable about that.*

William woke in the middle of the night to the sound of heavy rain and wind. Water was pouring everywhere and it was like being on the ship again. He couldn't tell if Scott or Mike was awake, but there was little point in knowing. He guessed this was a night to be endured. Lightning flashed continuously and thunder roared all around. There was a crash and the horses whinnied. He guessed it to be a falling tree.

Crawling out into the weather without thinking, William went to the horses. They were jammed in one corner of the roped area, moving in a tight circle as though trying to find a way out. He didn't doubt they would only have to push against the rope for it to break and set them free, yet they didn't show any resolve to do so. Slipping under the rope, William walked to the horses whispering what he hoped were soothing words to settle them. He told them the storm would not hurt them and that the thunder and lightning would be gone soon and they would be all right. Their agitation disappeared when they saw him, and they walked over slowly, one or two nuzzling him at the front and back. He patted them alternately, smoothing down their necks and backs and chatting about how he'd been through worse storms than this one. Gradually, the rain did ease; the wind abated though the cold became worse. He was now wet and shivering but enjoyed the warmth being generated by the horses. They were content to stay with him and when they were close, they formed a kind of windbreak.

The sky began to lighten with the imminent dawn and William found a peace standing amongst the horses, watching the sky changing its pastel colours. He saw pinks, yellows and greens eventually change to a blue, and the first rays of a dawn sun splashed over the trees. Nearby a large tree had fallen and he was glad they had not been near it. He doubted anyone could survive such a tree falling on them.

Scott and Mike stirred under the dray. Both emerged dripping wet, but appeared to think nothing of it.

"Have you seen Bill?" Scott asked Mike.

William could see Mike shake his head.

"Bill!" called Scott. "You about?"

"Aye. Just seeing to the horses."

"Are they all right?"

"They seem to be, but I'm no judge."

William stood in the midst of the horses, being nudged and nuzzled. There were quiet snorts and a few of the horses that appeared to resent William's attention to the others pushed their way in, creating gaps and spaces as needed.

"I think they're all right, too," said Scott. "You might have lost a job, Mike."

Mike looked crestfallen and cross all at once.

"I'm just fooling around, Mike," said Scott. "Bill'll have his work cut out for him when we get to Ballarat, but the horses seem to have taken a liking to him."

"Well, let's get on with it. There's still a long way to go," Mike muttered in response.

"Are we going to wash the horses?" said William.

"Aye," said Scott, "That was the plan, wasn't it? Sun's hardly up so there's time to do it. What do you think, Mike?"

"Well, not too much need after the rain, but now's a good time. There's no one else here, so no one to complain if we mess up the water. Besides, the horses'll like it well enough."

"And ourselves, too?" said William hopefully.

Mike walked to the dray and fetched a brush from the back while Scott grabbed a large piece of soap.

"Take the lead horse," Mike said to William. "His name's Bertie. He's a good'un. You lead 'im, the rest will follow."

Mike put a halter and lead on Bertie and busied himself taking down the ropes he had put up to contain the horses. He was still doing it when Scott and William were ready to go.

"You take 'em. I'll finish up 'ere. You take this brush. Scott'll show you what to do."

William took hold of the lead and set off for the creek. Bertie came along without hesitation. Scott ambled beside William and the other horses followed after glancing at Mike a few times as though to check that it was all right.

"Mike won't come," said Scott. "He doesn't fancy the idea of washing. I'm surprised you do. Most people don't bother."

They reached the creek.

"There's a good swimming hole a little further up. I'm going to head for that. I'll use the soap and bring it back for you."

"What do I do with the brush?"

"Oh. Splash water on the horse, then rub him down. He'll stand still as can be. I think aside from rolling in mud, it's their favourite thing to do."

Scott headed off and William set to work on the horses. Like Scott said, the horse stood still, snorting softly, sometimes stamping its foot and playing with the water.

When the horses were done, William was surprised that Scott hadn't returned yet. Nonetheless, he took off his own clothes and splashed about in the creek until he thought himself to be clean.

As he was putting his clothes back on, he started to fret that Scott still wasn't back. He worried about the horses, but they didn't seem to want to go anywhere, so he set off looking for Scott. To his surprise, the horses followed.

Trees stood close to the water and the walk was tough-going. There were large boulders and fallen trees aplenty. In a few places, the water gushed down several feet through small waterfalls, and he had to negotiate them by climbing around. He thought it strange that Scott had come so far when had said the better pool was not that far away.

Looking back, he saw the horses gathered around something on the other side to where he had walked. He'd been too busy negotiating the boulders and timber at that point to look around carefully. Even though he didn't want to waste time, he thought he'd better retrace his steps to see what had taken the horses' interest.

The day was already much warmer and he was running freely with sweat—his bathe in the creek was almost a forgotten memory.

It wasn't long before he arrived back at the spot and saw Scott slumped in thick bushes beside the creek.

*Is he dead?*

He leaned close and saw Scott's chest gently rising and falling. Relieved, he tried to sit him up and put his back against a log, but it was an effort. Scott was a big man—at least, too big to be moved easily. He used his hat to fetch some water from the creek, wet his hand and wiped it across Scott's brow.

Were the horse thieves around? Had they done something to Scott?

Scott groaned and shifted. It was only then that William noticed the blood on the back of his head. He tried to see the wound, but it was lost in the matting of Scott's thick hair.

Splashing some more water onto Scott's head, he shook his arm and called softly, "Scott. Scott. Scott, what's wrong?"

Scott stirred and opened his eyes.

"Bill? Is that you, Bill? Where am I? Christ, my head hurts. Have I been drinking?"

"We're somewhere on the road to Ballarat. You went off for a swim. And no, you haven't been drinking, unless you found some drink hidden in the bush somewhere."

"Ah, I think I remember… I started to climb a log and lost my footing. I guess I fell and hit my head."

"I thought the horse thieves might have taken their revenge on you."

William looked behind and all the horses were there, and Bertie with his halter.

"Can you get up on to Bertie?" he asked Scott.

"I'll try," said Scott.

"Here, I'll put him beside this rock. You can climb on from there."

It took all their effort to get Scott up and onto the rock. Bertie, for his part, stood patiently and didn't object when Scott gripped his mane fiercely to assist himself in getting on and to prevent himself from falling.

William led Bertie back down the creek and the others followed dutifully.

Scott moaned and swayed a lot, but was still on Bertie's back when they arrived back at camp.

"Jesus!" shouted Mike. "Where the hell have you two been? It's not as though I could send out a search party! I didn't want to leave the dray."

"Scott's been hurt," said William. "I don't know how badly. Can you have a look? Will you know what you're looking at?"

"Don't worry about me. We have to get going. Mike, harness the horses. Bill, you ride my horse. I'll ride with Mike."

"I've never ridden a horse."

"Now's as good a time to learn as any—just talk to him first. He's a good horse and won't mind another rider. And make sure you get on from the left. Mike, get me up on the dray. I think I'm about to faint."

Mike struggled, so William helped to get Scott onto the dray seat. Scott stretched out, leaving little room for Mike.

"No matter," said Mike. "I'll fit on somehow. I'm worried about him. What'd he do?"

"Said he slipped and fell."

"That's not like him. I wonder if something else is wrong, too. This is no place to be sick. There's a doctor in Ballarat, but that's about four days away. I don't like this, Bill. I don't like this at all. I wonder if we should go back. It's only two days to go back."

"We're not going back," said Scott.

"Well, you're the boss, but I don't think you're right," said Mike. "Here, Bill, help me with the harness."

While they were working on the harness, Mike whispered, "He won't know if we're going back or not. What do you think? Should we go back?"

William looked at Mike. He'd gone from being an outcast, to accepted, to now helping make decisions. Things were moving quickly. But, why ask him? How would he know what to do for the best?

"I think we should do as Scott says. Is there an inn or a homestead on the way?"

"There's a small town at Bacchus Marsh. That's about two days from here and I've heard there's sometimes a doctor there. I suppose it's two days back and two days to Bacchus Marsh, so Scott'll say one's as good as the other. All right, Bill, let's press on, but if somethin' happens to Scott, we both have to remember what was said 'ere."

"You fellers at it again? Standing around talking doesn't get anything done. Let's get on with it."

Mike climbed onto the seat and the horses moved off. William was still trying to get onto Scott's horse, but it wasn't about to be left behind. William couldn't hold it and it kept trying to follow the dray.

"Hold his head towards you with the headstall. If he can't see forward, he'll stop tryin' to follow and you can get on."

"What's the headstall?"

"The part that's on the side of his head."

William pulled the headstall with his left hand and put his right onto the saddle. He slipped his left foot into the stirrup as he had seen Scott do, and swung himself up. The horse waited patiently now, as though resigned to the new development.

"That's the idea," said Mike. "Now, just let him walk. He'll be keen to follow, so you won't have to do anythin'."

William was surprised by how high he was—not like the ship of course, but it was still some way to fall. It wasn't long before things settled down. The dray plodded along and William followed behind steadily.

Mike turned and called.

"You'll have to have a look ahead, like Scott did. We can't go into a wash or gully where we can't get out. This thing can't go backwards."

"But he's only going as fast as the dray. How do I get him to go faster?"

Mike stopped the dray.

"Come up here beside the dray. I'll take the horse. You take the dray. You'll be all right with the horses. They like you well enough."

Feeling uncertain, but trusting that Mike was right, William swapped with Mike and Mike rode off straight away.

William looked down at Scott. His face was deathly pale. His chest was rising and falling, so he was still alive, but clearly hurt.

"C'mon then!" he called to the horses and flicked the reins as he had seen Mike do. To his astonishment, the horses moved off.

Without thinking, William chatted away to the horses. He told them about the journey to Australia and how lucky they were to be on land.

"You wouldn't like it on the ship," he found himself saying. "It moves too much."

He would tell people in later years that he was sure the horses all nodded and agreed with him.

Mike came out of the bushes in front and pulled up beside the dray.

"There's a wash on the other side of those trees. There's still some water in it. It's not too deep, but you'll need to get the horses moving to get them up the other side. So, slowly down and then, at the bottom, get them moving. Do you think you can do it?"

"Won't know unless I try," said William.

"Aye," said Mike. "Good on you, Bill. That's the spirit."

They reached the wash and the horses went straight into it. They steadied themselves as they went down, jamming their hooves into the soft earth to prevent the dray going faster than they wanted.

When they reached the bottom, William called softly to them.

"All right, lads, now's the time. Let's give it our best."

Once again he flicked reins and the horses reacted immediately. They strained against the harness and increased their speed a little, moving through the water quickly. The dray rattled and clattered on the stones in the creek, reaching the other side of the wash and up they went. Dirt was flying, hooves scraping in the soft earth. The wheels started to sink, one side more than the other. The dray started to list to the side.

"C'mon, boys! We can all do better than that!" William called to them, once again flicking the reins.

All the horses strained as one and the dray lurched forward, came out of the soft patch and reached the top. The horses didn't stop, but continued to strain until the dray had fully cleared the wash.

Mike sat astride his horse, a huge grin on his face.

"You'll do, Bill. You'll do all right. I couldn't have done that better myself. I think Scott might be right. You may have been born to be a horseman. Let's keep moving, though. We want to be in Bacchus Marsh by tomorrow night." He looked back at the wash. "Won't be too many more vehicles getting though that without it drying out. Glad we got to it early today."

William was pleased that he had done well. He wasn't sure how he had done it, but knew it was more about the horses than it was about him.

"Are there others about? I haven't seen anyone since the camp on the first night," William said to Mike.

"There's a few ways to go and different goldfields to go to. There'll be others about. Might have got away before us too, so they'll be in front. Track was used today before us back there."

Once again the landscape changed over the course of the day. Sometimes they passed through wooded areas, and other times open meadows. William could see some mountains in the distance, but Mike wasn't around to ask about them. He hoped they'd go around. They were imposing even from a distance.

There were a few more small creeks that were easily forded. The horses sometimes stopped for a drink, but Mike advised to not let them have too much. Scott lay on the seat, periodically groaning. Once he woke and asked where he was, but was unconscious again before William could answer.

Darkness was nearly on them when they finally stopped for the night. They had not seen anyone on the road, but there were several other camps scattered about the meadow.

"I'll leave you with the horses," said Mike. "I'll check out the other camps. We might be lucky and there might be someone who can see to Scott. Here, I'll help you get him down. I'll use some canvas and build a tent for him. I don't think we should share the dray. If he hits his head, it'll go badly for him."

Mike grabbed some canvas from the back of the dray and built a tent using saplings and rope.

"That'll do him, I think. Has he been conscious at all?"

"A few times, but not for long."

"We'll try to get some food and water into him later. He'll rest quietly for the moment. You see to the horses. I'll see to the camps. Fill the bag with water, too, while you're down there. And, Bill, keep sharp. You're on your own if something happens."

William put a halter and lead on Bertie, picked up the bag and headed for the creek. All the horses followed. Mike disappeared into the dusk.

When they reached the creek, William told the horses to wait while he filled the bag. They looked uncertain, but did as they were bid. He found he had only to drop the halter on the ground and Bertie wouldn't move. Once the bag was filled, he took Bertie to the creek and all the horses joined in. It was a bit of a free for all as they jostled with each other for a spot to drink. William decided there was a hierarchy and he was at the top, Bertie was next, and the other spots moved about over time.

Once they were done, he headed back to camp with the lead in one hand and the bag in the other. He hung the bag on the back of the dray, checked on Scott, fished around in the dray for the rope, and made an enclosure like Mike had done the night before. By the time he was done, he could hardly see his hands in front of his face. It was hard work to find wood for the fire, but he did so as he waited for Mike. He was surprised how much he fretted that Mike would be safe. If something happened to Mike, he had no idea where he was going or how to find Bacchus Marsh.

From time to time, he checked on Scott. His breathing was steady but apart from checking that, William had no idea what else to do.

Just as his fret moved from unease to anxiety, Mike arrived out of the darkness.

"Did you find someone?"

"No," Mike said. "But I did get some more meat. One group had too much, said it wouldn't last and we were welcome to part of it." He was a shadow in the night, indistinguishable from all the other shadows. "How's Scott?"

"I don't know. He's resting and seems to be breathing all right, but I have no experience so I'm not sure."

He had some experience, but such things were of doubtful value and better left in the past.

"Well, let's get a fire going, some meat cooking, make a good billy of tea and see if we can feed Scott."

William was amazed at how easily Mike got the fire going in the dark, cut off some of the meat, got it into the frying pan and loaded the billy. He settled down to wait and William thought better than to say anything—no point in praising someone who wasn't interested.

"Horses all right? Can't see in the dark."

"Yes. I roped off an area like you did last night. They seem happy enough."

"Did you have any trouble?"

"No."

"Good. Fetch that bread from the dray. Should still be all right." William passed him the loaf and he inspected it. "Hmm. Not too much longer. Still—doesn't go off like meat. If we don't want it, the horses will take it and be grateful."

"Bread?" exclaimed William.

"Yes. Don't know why, but they love it. See to the tea. Meat's ready."

William did as he was bid.

"How will we feed Scott?"

"See if he's awake. Shake him a little, if you have to, but not too much."

William moved over to Scott's tent. It was a warm and sticky night. Insects buzzed about and there was the incessant whine of mosquitoes. He shook Scott gently.

"What is it?" muttered Scott.

"We've got something to eat. Would you like to eat? We've got some tea, too."

"Yes, I'd like to eat. Help me get up. I don't think I can eat or drink lying down."

"Here," said William and he helped Scott over to the dray and rested him against a wheel.

"Now I need a piss," said Scott. "Help me up again, will you?"

William helped Scott to his feet and they took only a few steps. Scott fumbled with his buttons and William hoped he wouldn't ask for help.

"Jesus. Just made it," Scott said, the emptying of his bladder sounding like rushing water.

Once he was done, William helped him back to the wheel and went and fetched him some bread, meat and tea.

"Oh, that's good," said Scott between mouthfuls, but stopped way short of finishing everything he was given.

"Do you want the rest of it later?" asked William.

"No, thanks. As good as it was, I feel that I might be sick soon."

"Well, hold it down as long as you can," said William and helped Scott back to his tent.

"I'm still worried," he said to Mike, joining him back at the fire.

"Worryin' doesn't help," said Mike. "We'll be there tomorrow night. At least, I hope we will, but worryin' won't get us there faster or make Scott better."

"What if there's no doctor?"

"Then we made the wrong choice."

"Would you care more if it was you?" snapped William.

Mike stared at him by the light of the fire, then shrugged as though deciding not to make more of it.

"We're in the bush, Bill. Out here, even a right decision can cost a life. Of course I care for Scott. I've known him a long time, but we've made a decision and we'll stick to it. It's not whether it's Scott, or me, or you for that matter. It's just that all we can do is hope we made the best decision, but we won't know until we get there. So, let's call it a day and hope for a quick journey, with good weather tomorrow and a doctor at Bacchus Marsh."

William woke early the next morning. It had been a cold night and he hugged his blanket tightly around him. *Perhaps it would be better to use the other blanket too and find something else for a pillow?*

His feet poked out from under the dray and were damp with dew, no doubt contributing to his being cold. At least his boots were still underneath.

A small part of him dreaded checking on Scott. He'd been part of the decision to press on and he could only hope it would prove to be all right. He hadn't known Scott long, but liked him a lot.

"You awake?" asked Mike.

"Yes," said William. "How could you tell?"

"You stopped snorin'."

"How's Scott?"

"I'm about to check. I didn't hear him in the night, but then, I probably couldn't with the noise you made."

William heard him crawl out from under the dray.

"Scott? Scott? You awake?"

He came back to the dray.

"He's still out to it, but at least he's still breathin'. Let's get to it, Bill. The less time is wasted, the sooner we get there. I know I told you not to worry, but if ever there was a cause for worry, it's how Scott looks this mornin'."

William crawled out as well, struggling to get his boots on to his wet feet while hunched under the dray.

"For Christ's sake, Bill. Let yer feet get wet. It'll do 'em no harm and save you a trip to the creek to wash 'em. I'll see to the dray, the horses and Scott. You stir the fire and see to some breakfast."

They both saw to their allotted tasks, muttering irritably to themselves when things didn't go to plan.

"Hell, Bill. Nothing seems to work when you're in a hurry," said Mike when William called that breakfast was ready. "I'm nearly done. See if Scott's awake. You might be able to give him something to eat and drink."

William went to Scott's tent.

*Mike's right. He looks terrible.*

"Scott?"

William shook him gently by the shoulder.

"Uh?" said Scott.

"We're almost ready to move. You want some breakfast?"

"I need a piss more. Why do I want a piss when I'm not drinking anything?"

"No idea, but let me help you."

He got Scott out, and helped him to piss again.

"Put me on the dray," said Scott. "I can eat and drink up there."

In spite of Scott being awake, it was a tough job to get him on the dray and William was glad when it was done. Scott was half lying, half sitting on the seat and Mike gave him some bread and tea.

"I don't want much," said Scott.

"I know," said Mike. "I put lots of sugar in the tea and spread some fat on the bread."

"Good enough," said Scott. "I'm sorry about this, fellers. I'll get better soon, I promise."

Mike gave William a knowing look.

"We won't be long," said Mike. "We'll have ours quickly and be on our way."

When they came back to the dray, Scott was asleep on the seat. He had consumed little of the bread and only a few sips of the tea.

"Bill, same as yesterday—you take the dray, I'll take the horse."

He cast a look skyward.

The sun was already casting warmth through the glade, and long shafts of sunlight were coming through the branches of the trees.

"I figure it will take all day. Push the horses a little, will you? When we're closer, I'll go on ahead and try to find a doctor. So if there's one, he'll be there when you arrive. You won't see much of me during the day, just look for me ahead. I'll work out the best way and come back and signal. Keep an eye on Scott. If he wakes up, just give him some water. There's a road of sorts, but lots of tracks as people move around muddy areas, or parts of the tracks that have been washed away."

He nodded and galloped off.

*Pretends he's on top of it, but he's as worried as I am.*

William glanced at Scott and tried to make him comfortable.

*These seats aren't designed to make sick people comfortable. They aren't designed to make anyone comfortable.*

"C'mon, Bertie. Let's go."

He flicked the reins and the dray moved off to follow Mike.

A long, hard day followed. Several times he worried that Mike had been gone too long and he must have missed the way. Then he would spot Mike on a hill, or amongst the trees ahead. Once he heard a distant shout and was surprised to see Mike about a mile away, waving his hat in the air, and sitting astride the horse and beside a row of trees that would conceal another creek.

The creeks were always welcome. The sides were never high, so it wasn't hard to go down one side and up the other. There had been no more rain, so the water was never high, either. He would stop and allow the horses to have a quick drink. One time, he got down and filled the canvas bag, which he hung on the side of the dray near to where he sat. He could reach it and moisten Scott's head and lips from time to time. It was warm in the sun and he worried that the heat might make Scott worse. He wished he'd used some saplings and canvas to rig a cover for Scott. He missed Mike. It would be better if Mike stopped from time to time to at least confirm that Scott was still all right, but he was simply showing William the path and moving on without talking.

The country they went through was largely unwooded and undulating, and they never went far before crossing a creek. There was no one else on the road. They'd seen people earlier in the journey, but none now. He wondered if Mike was taking a faster route, but didn't have a chance to ask him. He saw more kangaroos and marvelled at their mode of travel—he'd never seen anything before with legs that didn't walk.

The movement of the dray caused Scott to slip about in the seat. It was sometimes hard for William to keep an eye on the track and check on Scott at the same time. He learned to trust Bertie and the team to avoid stumps, logs and holes in the road. The horses seemed to understand that Scott was ill and though William encouraged them to keep moving faster, they were able to avoid trouble on the road. William was aware of a stirring of affection for the horses and understood why Mike was grateful he had prevented Bertie's theft. The horses in kind seemed to understand that William was in charge and concentrated on doing their best for him.

The sun's shadows were longer now, and the air a little chilly. He hadn't seen Mike for a while and couldn't shake the feeling they were lost. A few times there'd been so many tracks he just guessed which were the right ones to follow. He looked at Scott. He was sure Scott was paler than he had been in the morning, and he worried that he hadn't stirred all day.

"This is the bush," Mike had said. Well, it was no place for the faint of heart.

He'd been frightened on the ship, but not like this. He was responsible for Scott, the horses and dray and all the goods on it.

What if he was lost? He hadn't talked with Mike about what he should do. Should he just keep driving? Would Mike find him?

Mike had told him not to worry, but this wasn't just worry—he was frightened.

Just when he thought perhaps he should stop, Mike galloped out of the trees ahead. He reined in beside the dray.

"Were you worried?" Mike asked with a smile.

"More than a little."

"You're good at that worryin'. How's Scott?"

"I don't know. I think he looks worse, but I don't know. Is it far, now?"

Mike laughed.

"Not far and good news, there's a doctor there. He's at an inn in the town. I've seen him and he's waitin' for us, so let's get movin'. It'll be dark, soon."

Mike walked the horse beside the dray.

"Horses are tired," said William.

"I know, but move it along. There won't be a moon, so we can't travel once it's dark."

"C'mon, lads. You heard the man."

William flicked the reins and the horses quickened their pace. It wasn't long before they came to a timber bridge over a river.

"This is the Lederderg," said Mike. "Lot more trouble to cross before they built the bridge. Once you cross, stay to the side of the road. There's been some traffic and the ground is soft and marshy. We'll get bogged if we're not careful."

William did as he was bid and kept the horses moving. The country was flat with scrubby bush and it was hard to even distinguish the road. He was glad Mike was with him. He doubted he could find his way on his own. After a while, he thought he saw some lights in the distance.

"That it?"

"Yes. I'll ride on ahead now and tell the doctor you're here. Pull up outside the inn."

"How will I find the inn?"

"We'll be there on the verandah. You'll see us."

It was too dark to see well, but William could make out the inn. He looked at Scott.

"We'll be there soon. Mike's got a doctor for you."

The ground was boggy and William had to keep well to the side of the road. It wasn't much of a road, filled with ruts, soft spots and potholes, winding its way through trees and scrub. The dray lurched about, more so than at any time in the journey so far. It was all William could do to keep Scott on the seat.

He was well pleased to pull up outside the inn where Mike and a man William supposed to be the doctor were waiting at some steps.

There were several people seated at tables on the verandah on either side of the steps, but no one took any notice of them. William guessed that a man being treated by a doctor was somewhat commonplace in Bacchus Marsh.

The doctor ignored William and moved up quickly to look at Scott.

"Waste of time to look at him out here. We'll have to get him inside. Get him down and follow me."

Mike and William got Scott down as carefully as they could, but it wasn't easy. They didn't know how to carry him properly, so one took his legs and the other took him under the armpits while his head lolled about.

The doctor went through the front door and into a hall. There was the sound of conversation to one side, coming through a doorway. A man came through a doorway on the other side and said, "Bring him in here. You can lay him on that lounge there."

While they lay Scott on the lounge, the man brought a lamp from a table nearby to help the doctor see. There were other lighted lamps mounted around the walls, but the doctor muttered, "Thanks, James. Can you get me some cloth and water, too, please? I'd be most obliged."

The man hurried away. William and Mike stood nearby.

"What happened?" said the doctor.

"Like I said, Doctor, he told us he slipped and fell off a log. We weren't there, so we don't know. Bill here, he found 'im. Tell the doctor, Bill."

"He'd gone on up the creek while I washed the horses. Said he was heading for a better place to swim. He didn't come back and I went looking for him. Found him unconscious beside the creek. I found a wound on the back of his head."

"Yes, I saw that. It looks nasty. But there's more here than a bang on the head. You two see to your horses and dray. Put them in the yard beside the inn. You'll see other animals and things there. It'll be safe enough. James and I will see to your friend."

Before Mike and William could leave, the man came back with some cloth over his arm, a jug and a bowl. He looked at Scott closely.

"I know this man," he said. "He's Scott Mallard. Has a store at Ballarat. He's been through here a few times. What happened?"

The doctor ignored the question and said, "James, I want to strip the man down. Can we have a room?"

"Of course, there's one out back you can use."

"We can pay," said Mike.

"Don't worry about that," said James. "I'm sure he'll get a chance to return the favour."

"No, he'll want to pay," said Mike.

"Then, I'll sort that out with him. Help us move him."

William and Mike picked up Scott, who groaned softly but didn't wake. They carried him down a dimly lit hallway, following James who was carrying a lamp. He opened a door into a small room with a bed and washstand.

"I want to wash him down," said the doctor.

"Then put him on the floor," said James. "It'll be easier to clean up afterwards. I'm sure he's been on worse. We'll put him in the bed when he's clean."

William and Mike started to leave.

"No, stay with us," said the doctor. "You can stand in the hall if you're uncomfortable, but before you do, one of you can fetch the water and cloths from the front room."

"I'll do that," said Mike, before William could even open his mouth. Mike hurried away and when he came back, the doctor had already stripped Scott. Mike tried to hand the things through the door without looking.

"For God's sake," said the doctor. "It's only a naked man."

He sponged Scott down quickly, making a mess on the floor.

"No matter," said James. "It'll clean up," as he pulled down the bed covers. "He won't want the covers anyway. It's still warm for this time of year."

"Let's get him on the bed. You two, make yourselves useful."

Once again, Mike tried to do his allotted task without looking at Scott. The doctor looked on, shaking his head.

When Scott was on the bed, the doctor said that Mike and William could see to the horses and asked James to hold the lamp as he began inspecting Scott. Mike said that he could do the horses on his own and William could stay in case the doctor needed more help.

The doctor started with the wound on Scott's head.

"It's nothing," he said, shaking his head. "Might have stunned him for a few moments, but there'd be no lasting effect. Hold the lamp closer, James."

"What are you looking for?"

"I think he's been bitten."

"There's bites all over his face."

The doctor shook his head, looked at James and smiled.

"No, those are mozzies or sand flies. I think I'm looking for a snake bite."

"How would a snake bite him?" asked William, who had continued to stand in the room, curious.

"I think he's slipped on the log and fallen into the bush. A snake had probably found a nice sunny spot near the bushes and curled up, sunning itself. Then, Scott here landed on or near to it, disturbing its tranquillity. The snake did what snakes do when startled, it bit the antagonist and left before any retaliation took place."

"I thought snakes killed people?"

"Not always. It might have been small, or have recently caught prey. There's lots of types of course, with some more deadly than others, but the fact that your friend is still alive says it might have been a young, black snake."

The doctor continued his search.

"Ah, what do we have here?" he said, inspecting an area near Scott's shoulder. "How did we miss this?"

There was a red, swollen area with lines of red running away from it.

The doctor looked at William.

"See here," he said. "The redness is key, but in the middle of the swollen area, you can see two distinctive puncture marks."

William leaned close, intrigued.

"My guess is that the snake bit your friend through the cloth of his shirt. It meant that he didn't get the full load of venom and that's probably what saved his life."

"Wouldn't he feel the snake bite him?"

"He banged his head on something. I reckon that he banged his head and the snake bit him at the same time. Anyway, now that we've found the problem, we have to work out what to do about it. The venom is in him now and there's nothing we can do about that. He'll need rest, food and plenty of water as his body recovers. The good news is that if he was going to be dead, he'd be dead by now, so in my opinion, he'll live."

"He's welcome to stay here," said James.

"That's good, because he's not going anywhere for a day or so."

"We were on our way to Ballarat," said William.

"Least of all, to Ballarat," said the doctor. "I'm staying here for a few days, attending to other matters. I'll look in on him and make sure that he's all right."

"You and the other fellow can stay, too, if you like," said James. "There are rooms upstairs."

"I'll have to talk to Mike. He'll know what to do."

"Of course," said James. "You can sleep under your dray in the paddock next door, too. Many do. It doesn't cost anything to sleep there, but the rooms do cost. Scott can have this for as long as he needs it, but business is business."

William laughed. The doctor and James joined him.

Scott stirred.

"What's happening?" he whispered. "Where am I?"

"You're in the Woolpack Inn, Bacchus Marsh," said the doctor.

"Who are you?"

"I'm a doctor."

"Good," said Scott. "Well done, Bill and Mike. We got here. What's wrong with me?"

"I believe you've been bitten by a snake, but since you're not dead yet, I doubt you will be. From the snake bite, anyhow."

"How long will I be here?"

"Only a few days. You're young a fit and shouldn't take too long to get over it."

Scott was silent for a while. Then he said, "Bill, Mike, can you hear me?"

"Mike's not here," said William, "but I can hear you."

"Keep going to Ballarat, Bill. If you and Mike can get here, you can get to Ballarat. I'll stay here and Mike can get me on the way back." He was quiet again for a few moments. "How long have we been here?"

"Just arrived tonight."

"Good. You leave in the morning at first light. You can get there in two days. My brother needs all the goods on the dray, so the sooner he gets them the better. He doesn't know about you, but Mike can explain. He'll be pleased to see you and that's for sure."

He stopped to gather his breath.

"Have you met James yet?"

"Who's James? There's a James here," said William.

"The licensee of the Woolpack. I expect you've met him. I wouldn't be in this bed if you hadn't met him, so your James and the licensee might be one and the same."

"Aye, he's met me," said James. "And more than that, I'm here and you're welcome. I'm glad you're going to be all right. I've told the doctor that you can stay as long as you like."

"Thanks, James. We'll sort it all out later. I'll cover any costs for my boys. I'm tired now. Bill, you tell Mike to get going. Leave tomorrow. He'll understand."

Scott's speech slurred, his eyes closed and he fell asleep as they watched.

They left the room and James pulled the door closed quietly behind them.

"It'll get stuffy in there," said the doctor.

"Aye, but which is better? Stuffy or noise and mozzies?"

"He's under your roof. You do what you think best. My job is done and I'll bid you goodnight. I'm going to get some supper and head to bed. I've had enough excitement for one evening."

"As you wish, Doctor. Bill, why don't you find your Mike, help him if you need to, then bring him to the bar and I'll stand you both a drink."

"We should buy you a drink," said William.

"No reason you can't do that too," said James.

William went outside and wandered around in the dark for a while before he found Mike in the yard beside the inn. There were other horses and drays in the yard, but Mike was the only person. William guessed any others were in the inn.

"Mike, the doctor thinks Scott will be all right. Says it might take a few days for him to get well though. Thinks he's been bitten by a snake."

"Christ. How would that happen?"

"Doctor thinks it might have happened when Scott fell off the log. Doesn't matter, anyway. If the doctor thinks Scott will be all right, then that's good enough for me."

"Know all about doctors, do you?"

"What's wrong, Mike?"

"I don't want to be stuck here for weeks."

"You won't be. Scott wants us to keep going. Says we're to leave first thing tomorrow."

"Scott said that?"

"Exactly what he said. Said if you and I can get the dray to here, we can get the dray to Ballarat."

"All right. That's fine by me."

"James said he'll buy us a drink."

"Who's James?"

"Feller that runs the place. You met him. He arranged the room at the back for Scott. He's happy for Scott to stay there until he's better. Said we can have a room too, if we want."

"That'll cost money. I'd rather stay out here."

"Scott said he'll pay."

"Doesn't matter. I'd still rather stay out here. You can stay inside if you want. I won't mind. Anyway, how do you know about doctors?"

"I don't," said William, choosing not to go into his history. "I'll stay outside, too. Let's get that drink. It'll be nice to get away from the mosquitoes for a while."

"Shouldn't we look after the horses and the dray? Someone might pinch 'em."

"James said they'll be all right. We can ask him about them and come back out if we don't like his answer."

"Be a fine way to thank the man—question his honesty."

"Mike, we've got another two days to go, according to Scott. Settle down. You're the boss when Scott's not here, so you tell me what to do and I'll do it. I'm just as happy to not have a drink if that's what you want, but I would like to get some supper."

He couldn't see Mike's face in the dark, but knew he was upset about something, he just didn't know what. It might be a long two days without Scott.

Mike hesitated for a few moments then said, "All right. Let's go get a drink. I suppose it can't do us any harm."

They walked back to the steps, climbed them and walked into the bar.

James was talking to a group standing in the corner.

"Ah, here you are!" he called when he spotted William and Mike. He hurried over to join them. "I thought you had both got lost! Let's introduce ourselves."

He held out his hand.

"I'm James. I know you're Bill and you're Mike. I'm pleased to meet you both. What'll you have? This is on me. Least I can do for you."

"You don't owe us anything," said Mike.

"Yes, I do. Doctor's here for one of my men who lost an arm in a thresher. He'll stay for a few more days with Scott here. Might have gone early otherwise, so I do have to thank you. Anyway, that's how I see it."

"Beer," said William and Mike at the same time.

"Good choice," said James. "Too hot for anything else, anyway."

"It was cool last night," said William.

"Storm always does that, then it heats up again," said James. "Anyway, it'll be cold enough soon enough."

"I could have told you that," said Mike.

William thought James frowned at them. He was lively and animated and looked quite young—probably a good type to manage an inn. Makes people feel comfortable. *Perhaps he's wondering about Mike behaving as if something's wrong.*

They finished their beers quickly and James said, "Let's go out back. There's a dining room there and I could do with some supper. I'm sure you could, too."

They went back out to the hallway and walked towards Scott's room, but turned left into another room before they got to it. When James pushed the door open they were hit by warmth, noise and delicious smells.

The room wasn't big, but it was crowded.

"Edie!" called Mike to a stout, flustered woman. "Can you handle another three?"

"Of course! Might just be slow is all. Full house tonight. Dunno where they've all come from. Border Inn hasn't closed, has it?"

"No such luck. Where do you want us?"

"Over there," she said pointing at an empty table in the corner. "I'll be with you in a few minutes."

William looked around as they headed to the table and was surprised to see that neither he nor Mike was out of place. Most of the guests looked like travellers—dirty and dusty, and dressed in the standard colourful shirt, moleskins and boots. Some were in animated conversation while others just looked tired.

"We've left our horses and drays in the yard beside the inn," said William as soon as they say down. "Will they be all right? Might something be stolen?"

James shook his head.

"It will all be all right. Some of the guests will sleep there. Nothing's ever been taken from there."

"First time for everything," said Mike.

James looked at William quizzically. William shrugged.

Edie arrived.

"What'll you have?"

"Nothing too fancy for me, tonight. Some chops?"

"And your guests?"

"What can I have?" said William.

"Why, soup, chops, steak, ham, brawn, tongue. If it comes off cattle, pigs or sheep, you can have it. We'll give you some vegetables, too, but I'm not sure what's on tonight. Lucky dip, I guess."

"Steak. I'll have steak."

"Me, too," said Mike.

"Coming up," said Edie and moved away.

She was back moments later with plates, knives and forks and a plate piled high with slices of bread.

"We bake our own," said James, pointing at the bread. "Best in Bacchus Marsh. I'll get some butter. Some jam, too. We make our own jam, as well."

Edie came back later with three plates as ordered and a third plate with potatoes and some green vegetables. William wasn't sure what they were. He would try some and ask Mike later.

"Can we have butter, dripping and jam?" said James.

"You're the boss."

"And tea?"

"You're still the boss."

The steak was perfect—easy to eat and delicious. William hadn't realised how hungry he was, nor how good it was to eat something other than chops. The vegetables were good too, although he didn't recognise the taste. He'd mostly only ever eaten potatoes, although his ma had sometimes grown beans, peas and sprouts and they made a nice change. He smiled.

"Can you share the story?" said James.

"Oh, I was just thinking that I'm doing all right for an Irish boy. Steak, bread, butter and vegetables. They'd knock you over the head and steal this from you, back home."

"Where's home?"

"Belfast."

"I was born here, but my parents came from Dublin, so maybe you can call me Irish, too."

"My parents are from Ireland too," said Mike.

"Where in Ireland?" asked James.

"Dunno, never asked. Never thought it mattered."

When they were done, William asked how much and James reassured him that he'd talk it over with Scott.

They went out to the hall.

William wanted to check on Scott, so the others waited while he crept into the room. Scott was sleeping soundly. There was a mug and a plate beside the bed, so William thought that he'd been fed.

*Doctor's done a good job.*

He joined the others outside the room.

"Can I buy you a whisky?" he asked James.

"Aye, that you can," said James.

"Me too?" asked Mike, looking happy for the first time that night.

William decided that he'd find out what was wrong sooner or later, and was better to think nothing of it until then.

They went to the bar. There were fewer people than before, but those there were noisy and lively.

"Three whiskies," called James. William went to the bar to pay. The barman wouldn't take it.

"I hear Scott's good for it," he said. "Orders are to take nothin' from you. Sorry. Orders are orders."

William picked up the whiskies and returned to the others.

"Where did you meet Scott?" James asked William.

"Met him in Williams Town. I'd come in on the *Lady Grace*. It's a steam ship. We'd come ashore the night before and the ship left without us. Scott offered me a job in the goldfields. I took it."

"And you?" James asked Mike.

"Why, I met 'im in Ballarat. Down on my luck, I was and 'e needed a driver. I'd had dealin's with 'im before, so I was pleased to work for 'im. Haven't regretted it. 'E's a good man."

"That's what they say," said James and drained his whisky. "You lads stay as long as you want. I'm off."

He held out his hand.

"Good luck with the rest of your journey. Come inside for breakfast before you go. Edie'll be there and I'll tell her to take care of you. And, don't worry, we'll look after Scott."

He turned, nodded at the barman and left through the door.

"Do you want any more?" William asked Mike.

"No. I'm done. Let's go."

He too drained his whisky. William tried to do the same and it burnt and stung his throat. He wished he'd put some water with it. It burnt all the way down.

They went out the doors, down the steps and walked to the yard. There was a glowing of cigarettes and pipes around the carts, drays and wagons, and the low murmur of men chatting.

William marvelled how easily Mike found his way in the dark. Mike found the dray, pulled blankets from the back, tossed two to William and crawled underneath. William needed a piss, but had no idea where to go. It was too dark to wander around and he doubted it would be well received by his neighbours if he went nearby. He walked over to the closest dray. The men stopped talking when he emerged from the dark.

"Hello," William said.

The men said nothing.

"I need a piss," said William.

"Good for you," one of the men replied.

"Where do I go?"

"Find a fence. Fence's best," said the same voice.

He retraced his steps to where they had come in to the yard and pissed on the fence there. He could hear the men laughing. He knew it was at his expense, but didn't know why.

*Nothing is easy. Nothing is ever easy.*

He wrapped a blanket around himself, used the other as a pillow and made sure his boots were under the dray. He could hear the horses moving about in the darkness and hoped Mike had given them something to drink.

CHAPTER 6

# The Road to Ballarat

It was just light enough to see, but the beauty of a splash of sun on the nearby hills momentarily took William's breath away.

There was a lot of noise around—animals moving, men talking, and harnesses rattling and clinking. There was the smell of wood smoke and animals, both strong and pervasive. William pulled on his boots and crawled out from under the dray. There was no dew this morning. He saw Mike with the horses and harness.

"We need to be gone," said Mike.

"What about breakfast?"

"I've been to the kitchen already. I got us some bread and some cheese. That'll have to do. I got some more meat, too. That should see us through to Ballarat."

"You're the boss," said William, as he walked over and pissed against the fence.

"I've saddled the horse," said Mike when he got back. "Which do you want? The horse or the dray?"

"I'll take whichever you give me to take."

"You take the horse, then."

"I don't know the way."

"It's time you found out. There's plenty of wheel and horse tracks now. There's a number of roads to Bacchus Marsh, but only one road from here to Ballarat and it's well used, so you'll have no trouble followin' it."

"You're the boss."

"Stop sayin' that."

William shrugged, took the horse by the reins and walked over to the gate, which was really no more than a piece of rope stretched between the posts. He unhooked it and stood waiting until Mike drove the dray through, then re-hooked it, mounted the horse and set off to the west, away from the rising sun. There were already tracks of horses and wheels on the road, as Mike had said there would be. William relaxed a little. After a few moments, he realised that the issue wasn't where to go—it was how to ride the horse. He talked to the horse and explained the problem. He asked the horse if it remembered him, then decided it didn't.

*Is this Mike giving me trouble for something I've done?*

He decided it didn't matter. If he was going to survive in Australia, he would have to know how to ride a horse and he supposed this was as good a time as any to learn. He looked back and saw that Mike was some distance behind already, so he could try things out.

William relaxed the reins and the horse went faster. He pulled on the reins, first to the left and the horse went left, then to the right and the horse went right. It wasn't only easy—it was fun.

William was taken aback as he rode through the rest of the town. He'd thought the inn was it, but there were two more inns, some shops and some houses. The country was still flat and scrubby, though he could see some cultivated areas, animals grazing and hills in the distance. The road headed towards the hills. Maybe that's why Mike took the dray—there might be some difficulties on the route ahead.

He noticed a river to his left and wondered if it was the same river they had crossed the night before. He thought they might cross the river, but it swung away from the road again and before too long there was another river to the right. The road ran straight between the two rivers, which had no doubt caused the ground to be soft and boggy.

Eventually, they came to a creek. The creek crossing didn't look easy and he decided to try up and down the creek for a better crossing.

*That's what Scott would do.*

He turned the horse to the right and followed the creek a little way. There was no easy path through the scrub, so he let the horse find the best way. It wasn't long before he'd moved away from the creek and could no longer see if there was a better crossing. He decided to head back and turned the horse's head to retrace his steps. With a shock, he realised he couldn't work out which way was back. Letting the horse find the way was a mistake, because he'd taken no notice of the path or the landscape.

"Mike!" he called as loud as he could. He succeeded only in startling the horse and almost fell from the saddle. Straining his ears, he hoped for Mike to respond, but heard nothing.

All he could hear was the constant hum of the insects around him. One would occasionally buzz louder than the others.

He struggled to keep his panic in check. He didn't want to shout again and risk falling from the horse.

All right. How did they find their way around on the ocean? He knew they used the sun. Where was the sun when they set out this morning? He knew it moved about the sky, but it wasn't that long ago that they'd started. He'd turned right at the crossing. Put the sun to his left and he'd have to find the road.

He had a plan and his panic subsided.

"C'mon horse, let's see if you and I can find Mike."

The horse moved off and William used the reins to move it left and right, always keeping the sun to his left.

It wasn't long before he came to the road. Relief swept over him and he resolved to be more careful in the future.

Then he realised he wasn't out of trouble yet. He still had to find Mike. He hadn't crossed the creek so, keeping the sun behind him, he set off up the road.

He'd seen Scott kick the horse in the sides to get it moving, so he did the same, wanting to get to Mike as soon as possible. The horse started to canter.

"Jesus!" screamed William as his testicles were crushed each time he came back to the saddle. "Stop!" he screamed. "For pity's sake, stop!"

The horse continued to canter.

William pulled on the reins and the horse stopped.

*This riding is not as easy as it looks.*

He started the horse walking again by flicking the reins. Cantering was out of the question until he found out how to do it without terrible pain.

It wasn't long before he came up on Mike, stopped at the crossing.

Mike heard the horse and looked back.

"How'd you do that?"

"Do what?"

"Get behind me."

"Oh, I went to look for a better crossing."

"There's nothing wrong with this one."

"Why'd you stop, then?"

"Saw you ride off into the bush. Thought I'd wait. Thought you might get lost. Did you get lost?"

"For a while. I made a mistake. I let the horse decide where to go."

"Always mark things. Hills, big trees, use the creek. How'd you find your way back?"

"Used the sun."

"Clever boy. Let's get going. You all right on the horse?"

"I have a question. How do you stop your balls bashing on the saddle?"

Mike slapped his thigh and roared laughing.

Even though Mike was laughing at him, William laughed too.

"It's hard to explain," said Mike, trying to control his laughter. "When I saw you cool as can be drive up on the dray to the inn last night, I thought I'd like to get my horses back today. Then I thought if I did that, you'd be on the horse and at some point, you'd lose the cool as can be."

William blushed, stopped laughing and realised why Mike had been out of sorts the day before. He'd obviously resented William's ability with the horses.

"It's how you sit. You can't lean forward at all. So, sit straight up and sit right on the bones of your arse. Go with the horse. Go up when he goes up and down when he goes down. People try to stand in the stirrups, but you can't. Your legs aren't strong enough to do that for long. So, it's all to do with how you sit. Keep working on that and you'll be all right. While you're thinkin' on it, take this."

He handed William some bread and cheese. Then he clicked his tongue, flicked the reins and the dray moved off. The crossing was easy. William followed, walking the horse and practising sitting up straight.

Once they crossed the creek, the ground rose slowly and became less boggy. The sun was now overhead and blazing down, the heat reflecting from the landscape around them. Trees became sparse, the scrub thicker and the road more dusty. William shaded his eyes with his hand. The line of hills was to his right and not becoming closer, so he guessed they were heading northwest. As they climbed, he could see some hills to the left and looking back, he could see that there were two rivers—one staying to his left and the other heading towards the line of hills to his right. He shivered despite the heat. This was no place to get lost.

The open ground continued and the track was easier to follow. At last, they came upon a creek and they let the horses drink. Mike got down and filled the canvas bag with water. He filled a pannikin, which they shared.

"I was tryin' to get to Ballan tonight," said Mike. "We won't make it, even if we hurry. Not enough day left."

He squinted at the sun.

"There's a good creek before there, that'll do fine. We'll leave early tomorrow and we might make Ballarat by nightfall. There's more creeks to cross, so keep checkin' those crossin's. Put the pannikin in back when you're done."

He climbed back on the dray, clicked his tongue and the dray moved off.

William rode ahead to check the crossings. He didn't try to move the horse any faster than a walk. The track was easy to follow and the dray easy to see even from some distance ahead, so there was no point in testing his new posture. He also had no desire to repeat the agony of the morning, but knew he would have to sooner or later.

*Tomorrow. Yes, tomorrow will be soon enough.*

There were no issues with crossing the creeks and William stayed with the dray once the shadows lengthened and the day was nearly done.

Finally, near to dusk, Mike said, "Camping spot up ahead, just through these trees. We should have enough daylight left to settle ourselves in. Been a long day. Stay with me, Bill. Only two of us to handle any problems."

They came out of the trees into a small meadow. Trees encircled it all the way to a creek that William could see not far away.

"It's strange. Haven't seen anyone else all day. I thought there'd be someone here. Still, more room for us."

He stopped the dray just short of the creek and beside the track.

"This'll do. You see to the fire and supper, I'll see to the horses. You do Scott's horse, though. See to 'im first, before the fire."

Mike stood watching.

William tried to get down from the horse, but his legs wouldn't work. He stood in the left stirrup and tried to haul his right leg over, but everything hurt too much.

Mike started laughing, slapped his thigh hard and said, "Well, if that don't beat everythin'. New chum on a horse—more fun than a night at the pub. C'mon Bill, I'll help."

He grabbed William by the left leg and dragged him roughly from the horse. The horse was startled and moved several paces away. Mike grabbed William when it became obvious he couldn't stand.

"Sit for a few minutes. Always happens. Fun to watch, not much fun if it's happenin' to you. Here, on this log. I'll need help, though. Won't be able to do it all on my own before dark. Get movin' as soon as you can."

Mike went to the dray and unharnessed the horses. He put a lead on Bertie and took the horses for a drink. Scott's horse started to follow.

"Let 'im come. You've got your work cut out with the fire."

It took William several minutes to get up and get moving. His legs felt like they belonged to someone else. They wouldn't do anything he wanted and it took an enormous amount of effort to collect wood and get the fire going. It took much longer than usual and Mike was back just as he was putting the meat on to cook.

"What's happened, Mike? Will it always be like that after a ride?"

"No, it gets much easier. You're usin' a lot of different parts of your body. You'll be really stiff in the mornin', but you've got to get back on and keep at it. Then, one day it's fine and you won't hurt at all, unless you stop ridin', then you have to go through it all again. C'mon Bill, let's get supper done, turn in early and be away at dawn. I'll bet you don't feel like doin' much, anyway."

When supper was done, they crawled into their blankets under the dray and the next thing William knew, Mike was shaking him awake.

"We're wastin' daylight, Bill. I'd swear you'd sleep all day if I let you. I've harnessed the horses, and cooked the breakfast. All you have to do is eat it and we'll be on our way."

William struggled out from under the dray. Mike was right. He was much stiffer this morning and walking was almost impossible.

When they finished breakfast Mike said, "Horse or dray?"

"I thought you said I had to get back on the horse."

"I think that's right, but I'm givin' you a choice."

"I'll take the horse."

"Good lad. We'll make a horseman of you yet. I've saddled 'im."

"That was my job."

"Aye, but hard to do when you're sleepin'."

"Sorry, Mike."

"No harm done. It's all right with me. So up you get and let's get on with it."

William struggled to take the few steps to the horse and struggled even more to get on.

"Lead 'im over to that log, stand on it and get on from there. You'll find that easier, I think."

William did as Mike suggested and found it much easier to get on, but when he sat, it was like someone pierced his arse with needles.

"Jesus, Mike. I can't imagine going through this every day."

Mike laughed, flicked the reins and they were off. William followed carefully and decided that today was not the day to practise going faster.

They crossed a few more creeks without problems and before long drove through a town, William riding beside the dray. He hoped Mike would talk about it, but "Ballan" was his only comment as they passed an inn. He could see a river to his right and presumed they would have camped there if they had made the town the previous night. Despite the early hour, there were a few people about, but none showed any interest in the strangers. William decided that strangers were not unusual in Ballan. The road was terrible—rutted, pot-holed and dusty. The dray lurched and swayed as Mike tried to find the best way through. The town was nothing to speak of, being only a few shops and houses and an inn. It wasn't long before they left the town, after which the road improved and there was another creek to be crossed.

The country was so different to Ireland. It had none of the softness or greenness of his home valley. This was all harsh, dry country of rolling hills and scrub. They sometimes saw more kangaroos that either hopped away quickly or stood and stared as though wondering about the strange creatures they saw. There was little water in any of the creeks they crossed. There were so many creeks that William wondered at the purpose of them all, as there wasn't enough water to fill them.

William also wondered about the road and its direction. It meandered like a creek, first going one way and then another, without apparent logic or reason. It wasn't as though it tried to avoid the creeks or the hills. Sometimes it wandered around the side of a hill, and at others went straight over it. For several hours they'd been heading towards a wooded hill that stood out from the landscape, but now they skirted around the side of it. There were others like it on the horizon that gave some feature to an otherwise monotonous view. Occasionally, he saw sheep or cattle and guessed there would be houses and people about, but saw no evidence of them. The people would have to be brave and adventurous, being isolated in such a vast land.

Fluffy, white clouds scudded across the sky, but did nothing to lessen the heat from the sun. The wind wasn't strong, but it blew warm and dry from the northwest.

On and on they plodded. Insects chirped, whistled and buzzed. The dray wheels crunched and crackled on the uneven road, the horses' hooves pattered, and the day rolled on as monotonous as the landscape.

They and the horses had drunk some water when crossing creeks that had some, but it wasn't enough. William was always thirsty and wondered why Mike didn't stop more often, though he knew they were hoping to reach Ballarat in the day.

Mike stopped at a creek and said, "Not far to go now—only a few more miles. We'll rest here for a few minutes, water the horses and then we'll be on our way."

He reached into a sack on the seat.

"Here," he said, pulling out some bread and cheese. "Have this. It's the last of it."

"I'm going to get off the horse."

"I wouldn't if I were you. You'll have trouble getting off, then you'll only have to get on again. So, why don't you wait? We're nearly there."

"My arse is so numb I can't feel it."

"Better that way. If it's not numb, it'll be hurtin', so leave sleepin' dogs lie."

It was cooler near the creek and the pool where they stopped was large enough for all the horses to drink while still harnessed. Mike fetched a pannikin from the dray, walked a little upstream, filled it and gave it to William who drank most of it.

"Thanks. I needed that."

"I can tell. Besides, it's the last good water you'll have."

"What do you mean?"

"Well, water at the diggin's is all used for findin' gold or washin', so there's little that's drinkable. Gotta boil it. Tastes awful, so you'll drink only tea."

William enjoyed the coolness in the glade. The wind wasn't as warm, birds called to each other and frogs croaked.

"Who on earth came all the way out here to find the gold?" said William.

"I've always wondered that too. It's a long way from anywhere. Might have been lost. Anyway, ask Scott's brother. I suppose he'll know."

The mention of Scott's brother brought William back to the purpose of the journey.

"What's his name?"

"What's whose name?"

"Scott's brother."

"Ah. Tom."

Mike looked at the lengthening shadows.

"Time to get movin'. Say goodbye to peace and quiet. Not much of it in the diggin's."

"Why're you calling it diggin's. I thought it was Ballarat."

Mike laughed. "You'll see."

They rode out of the creek and back into the sunshine. The day might be ending, but there was still plenty of heat in the sun. William regretted not having more water.

He rode up beside the dray.

"Tell me about the goldfields," he said.

"Not much to tell. A lot of men working hard, mostly for nothin'."

"Why do they do it?"

"Enough men get rich that everyone lives in hope. Now, Scott and Tom are the smart ones. They make their gold by trade. The others, well, they get the fever and it never lets them go."

"Have you tried it?"

"Aye, but a waste of time it was, pure and simple, a waste of time. It's not far now. You can ask Tom questions. You'll both have all the time you need for that."

They continued on through the landscape, the sun still blazing although the day was nearly done. The sameness persisted all around, but it seemed to William that they were now climbing a hill. Hills began to appear through the trees, sometimes sharp-pointed and mostly thick with trees. He could see tents beside the road in the distance, but they rode by these and paid no attention to them. A buzz of machinery like steam engines came to his ears, along with shouts of men and the noise of animals. There were a few trees on both sides of the road that kept him from seeing much more. His curiosity was such that he forgot the discomfort of the saddle and thought it might be time to ride ahead, and started to move off.

"Let's stay together," said Mike. "This is no time to get lost."

As the trees thinned out, William saw Ballarat Flats spread out before him and knew he would never forget the sight.

## CHAPTER 7

# Ballarat

The sun was in his eyes, but weak enough—as the day was nearly done—for him to clearly see the diggings. There was some order to the tents that were nearby, with a few wooden buildings sprinkled among them. But in the distance, William could see tents scattered across the diggings in total disorder. It reminded him of the hill overlooking Belfast. He thought he was looking at a valley, but would later discover that it was a flat that looked like a valley because it was largely denuded of trees. There were hills to the left and the right, what looked like a lake ahead, and a river with creeks running into it. It wasn't God's work that took his breath away—it was man's. The evidence of work was everywhere. And it was a mess. The road ahead was churned into a sea of mud. Animals and vehicles moved along it, but he could see no order to their movement. There was a lot of yelling and cursing as people fought for the best way through.

The tents were mostly on the flat, but there were a few others on the sides of the hills that he could see. They were on both sides of the river, but the largest concentration was slightly to his right.

"Main town's over there, but you wouldn't know it. Hard to tell in this mess where anythin' is," Mike said, pointing.

William looked and saw that it was true. There were some more buildings, but no more order to the right and in the distance.

He next became aware of the smell and was reminded of the odour in the air as he approached Belfast. "Tanning," the driver had said at the time, but he couldn't see any evidence of tanning here.

"What's the smell?" he said to Mike.

"Bit of everythin'", said Mike. "Shit, people, animal parts. Not much good when you're downwind."

"Animal parts?"

"Yeah. There are lots of butchers here. Diggers mostly eat meat, but not all of the animal gets eaten. Bits that aren't are often left lyin' around or dumped in a hole to rot. See over there where the dogs are fightin'? There's a butcher right there and he must have been cuttin' for supper. Matter of fact, nearby's where we're goin', so you'll get to see it up close. That's Tom's shop down there. C'mon. Be dark soon. We need to get the horses stabled."

They continued down a slope and finally went to a tent with a fenced off yard beside it. There was a small, wiry, dishevelled man sitting outside the tent on a stool, smoking a pipe.

"Mike," he said, as they approached.

"Joe. I'll be needin' your services. Usual price?"

"Aye. Tom good for it?"

"Aye. I'll take the dray to the shop first. This is Bill. He'll leave his horse now. I'll be back soon."

"He'll have to unsaddle 'im. Tell 'im that's not part of the service."

"I think he knows. Do you know that, Bill?"

"Aye, I know."

"Well, then, unsaddle him and put the saddle on the dray. Bridle, too."

William nodded and tried to get off the horse. His body hurt so much, he almost cried out with the pain as he tried to swing his right leg over. He twisted his left foot out of the stirrup and lay on his stomach across the horse's back.

"Your friend looks like he might be new to a horse," said Joe.

William slid to the ground and took a few moments to settle himself before reaching under the horse to undo the cinch strap. He then slid the saddle and blanket off as one and walked painfully and carefully over to the dray. Mike was grinning from ear to ear. William walked back and took the horse by the bridle. He leant his head against his neck and whispered, "Thank you." The horse nodded. He walked it over to Joe who stood and slipped a rail out of place, allowing William to walk the horse into the yard.

As he passed Joe on the way back, Joe said, "Take it easy, Bill. You'll hurt for a bit, but it'll pass. Happens to everyone."

William climbed painfully onto the dray, Mike flicked the reins and said, "I'll be back soon."

"I'm not goin' anywhere," said Joe.

It wasn't far to the shop. When they arrived, Mike stopped and said, "You wait here. I'll get Tom. Don't let anyone touch anythin'."

It wasn't yet dark, but there were two lighted lamps hanging on poles outside. People stood in front of the shop chatting. Mike walked past them and went in. William was cold, tired and hungry, but Mike didn't come back. Several people went into the store, but came back out immediately and waited outside. Other people emerged with goods and walked away. No one said anything to William, nor did they touch the dray. Traffic moved up and down the road, some hurrying as though to get somewhere before dark.

At last, Mike and another man emerged.

"This here's him," said Mike. "Bill, this is Tom."

Tom walked over and shook hands. The handshake was firm and friendly. His eyes sparkled, his dark hair was slightly receding, and his smile was broad and welcoming.

"I'm very pleased to meet you, Bill," said Tom, stepping back and staring, as though doing another appraisal. "Unfortunately, the day's not done yet. You and Mike will have to unload the dray. I've some customers to attend to, but when I'm done, I'll help. Mike will show you what to do. He tells me that you are stiff and sore. Well, some work might help to loosen you up."

He turned and walked back to the store.

"C'mon everyone, store's open again."

The people standing outside the store all followed Tom as he went back in.

Mike looked at William and smiled.

"C'mon, Bill. Let's get to it. One of us has to be outside at all times. Goods'll go missin' if we don't keep an eye on them. We'll stack everythin' just inside the tent, so while one's in there, one's out here."

It was dark when they finished unloading the dray and William was past exhaustion. They hadn't seen Tom at all—the steady stream of customers must have kept him busy.

Tom had been right about the work though—most of the stiffness was gone from his body.

When they were done, Mike took the dray and horses to the stable.

"Go on in," said Mike. "Tell Tom we're done. I'll be back soon."

It was William's first real look inside. The room was quite big with a wooden floor. Aside from where they had stacked the goods from the dray, goods were stacked almost without order. There were boxes, bottles, tins, bags and clothes stacked about, and in some cases, piled on top of each other from the floor to the ceiling. The tent was made from canvas over wooden poles. Tom was just on the right inside the door at a table, serving some customers. Other customers wandered about the store, selecting goods for purchase.

"Pull that door shut," said Tom when he saw William. "I'll be finished shortly. If anyone tries to get in, tell them we're closed for the day."

The door was canvas over a wooden frame. It didn't look strong and William wondered how it stopped anyone getting in. Some people arrived at the door, but made no fuss when William told them the store was closed. They simply turned and walked away.

Mike arrived back from stabling the horses. He went and sat on a chair at the back of the store. William continued with his job of turning people away. He was really tired and wanted Mike to do it, but Mike didn't offer and he didn't ask.

Eventually, the last customers left and Tom was done. He walked over and slid a pole through some holes in the wood attached to his side of the door.

"Won't stop a stampede or an army, but keeps the wind out," he said. "C'mon, Bill, let's see to some supper and get you to bed."

William hadn't seen it before, but the back wall was mud and bark and there was a fireplace near to where Mike was sitting.

"C'mon Mike, you've done it before and can help. Bill, you can have Mike's chair. We'll get some supper in two shakes of a lamb's tail. All the modern conveniences here, Bill. Inside fireplace."

William sat in the chair and drifted to sleep almost immediately.

Tom shook him awake.

"All right, Bill. Supper's ready. Drag your chair over here. You'll be more comfortable."

William saw another table like the one at the store entrance, though this one was smaller and set near to the wall beside the fire. There were three plates with some meat between two slices of bread.

"Bread's store bought," said Tom. "Got it from the local baker. Don't have time to make it myself. Eat up. Sooner that's done, sooner you can get to bed. There's some tea for you, too. That's your pannikin. Help yourself to sugar."

Mike and William ate like they'd been starved. Tom took his time and they watched him as he finished.

"If you need a piss, out the front and down the side. Piss on the nearest tree. If you need a shit, you'll need to go further afield and you'll need to take one of the lamps and a shovel. Take them from in here."

"What's the shovel for?" asked William.

"Bury what you leave behind," said Tom.

"I'll show you," said Mike. "I need to go."

"And do what?" said Tom.

"I'll need to take a lamp," said Mike. William thought he looked embarrassed.

"We'll need to take two lamps," said William.

The men stepped outside with their lamps and shovels. Mosquitoes found them immediately. Away from the store, William looked towards the sky. It was filled with stars. He looked towards the tents and saw many fires. He could hear music and singing.

Mike stopped with him.

"Hasn't started yet. Most are yet to finish their supper, then you'll hear plenty of music and singing. C'mon and look where you walk. It's not only Tom's store that uses the area out back."

Once they reached the back of the tent. Mike said, "You go that way. I'll go this way." He walked off without further comment.

William walked as he was bid, holding the lamp out in front. The shadows flickered and danced as the flame moved. He couldn't really see the ground, but followed what looked like a path. When he thought he was far enough away, he stepped into the bushes, used the shovel to dig a hole, pulled down his pants and did his business. The area smelled like he'd found the right spot. When he finished, he walked back to where he'd left Mike, but Mike was nowhere to be seen. He waited a few moments and then decided that perhaps Mike had been quicker and was already back at the tent, so he headed back.

Stepping through the door, he saw only Tom inside.

"Where's Mike?" said Tom.

"I waited a while, then decided he might be here already."

"Didn't you see his lamp?"

"No, I didn't. It was dark out there."

"I don't like this," said Tom. He reached to the wall behind him and pulled down a revolver.

"Do you know how to use this?" he said.

"No."

"You'll have to learn."

"Why do we need it?"

"There's people here that would rather take our gold than find some themselves. They might have grabbed Mike, hoping we'd come looking for him and while we're out, they'll help themselves."

"How have you managed on your own?"

"Hasn't been easy. I'll tell you later. Right now, I have to find Mike. You stay here. Call out if anyone comes through the door, or cuts a hole in the tent."

Tom left, carrying the revolver.

After a few minutes, there was a scuffling at the door. William looked about for a weapon and decided the shovel would be good enough. He waited so that he'd be hidden behind the door when it opened.

The door opened slowly and a stranger stepped in, his back to William.

"You in here?" called the stranger. "Tom wants some help."

William said nothing.

"Don't know where he is. Might still be outside," said the stranger. "C'mon. Let's get to it."

Footsteps sounded on the floor. Two men came in, their backs to William.

William brought the flat of the shovel down hard on the first man's head. He fell forward onto a pile of bags. The second man swung to look at him.

"Tom!" yelled William, as he drove the handle into the man's stomach. Tom appeared in the doorway moments later, his revolver levelled at the men.

"Ah, I thought so," said Tom. "Well done."

The first man was unconscious, but the second man was gasping, struggling for breath.

"What'll we do with them?" said William.

"This," said Tom, and brought the barrel of the revolver down hard on the second man's head. He stopped struggling and lay still.

"Did you find Mike?"

"Aye, he's outside, curled up in the bushes, his pants around his ankles. You'd think even a thief would be more courteous and wait 'till a man was finished."

"Maybe they waited 'till he was busy pulling up his pants. Shall I get the police?"

"No. They don't have time for me and I don't have time for them. We can deal with this. Take your lamp and find Mike. I left my lamp beside him, so you won't have trouble finding him. Bring him back. I'll look after these two."

William took his lamp and went to find Mike. He saw a lamp flickering in the bushes and headed towards it. There was Mike, lying on his side with his pants around his ankles, as Tom had said. Mike groaned softly. William roused him to wakefulness.

"What happened?" said Mike.

"Thieves belted you on the head, by the looks of it. Might've killed you if you hadn't been wearing your hat."

"Help me up," said Mike, but struggled to get to his feet with his pants around his ankles.

"Jesus," he said. "Look what they've done to a man. On second thoughts, don't look until me pants're up."

Mike stood and William held him by the shoulder, looking away as he set his pants right. He started to move, but William steadied him while he picked up the shovel.

"Here," said William. "This way. No point in stepping into anything."

William took the two lamps in one hand and the shovel under his arm, placing his other arm under Mike's armpit. They stumbled awkwardly back to the tent.

"Ah," said Tom. "I was beginning to think something more had gone wrong. These two are still out. How're you, Mike?"

"I've been better. These're the two?"

"Must be, although I haven't spoken with them. Bill, get Mike to the table and see what damage they might have done to his head."

William got Mike into a chair and checked his head by the light of a lamp.

"Looks all right," said William. "Big lump, but no bleeding."

One of the men on the ground moaned softly.

"Jesus," he said as he came to. "What happened? I came into the store to buy some nails and someone hit me."

"What would you want with nails?" said Tom.

"I'm buildin' a house for my missus."

"This your missus?" Tom asked, nudging the other man with his foot.

The man shook his head.

"No, he's my mate. He's helpin' me."

"Where're you building your house?"

"Oh. Over by Specimen Hill."

"Wake your mate up."

The man shook the other, who moaned a few times.

"What happened?" he said.

The first man started to answer, but Tom stopped him by prodding him with the revolver.

"I'll give you everything this has got if you open your mouth."

The man looked frightened.

"Not much happened," said Tom, to the other man. "What're you doing here?"

"Came in to buy some things," said the man.

"And, who's this?" said Tom, indicating the first man with the barrel of his revolver.

"He's my mate," said the man.

"And what did you want to buy?"

"Some grog," said the man.

"What did your mate want to buy?"

He looked nervously at the other man who was staring fixedly at Tom.

"He came in to get grog too."

"I forgot," said the first man. "That was it. I came to get grog. Not nails. Grog. Do you have any? We can pay."

"Nails?" said the second man. "What would we do with nails?"

"All right, boys. I've had enough of this. I want you to look behind you. The feller you hit is called Mike. I don't think he likes you too much. That right, Mike?"

"That's right, all right," said Mike.

"Are you going to hand us over to the police?" asked the first man.

"No," said Tom. "I'm going to do something much worse. I'm going to hand you over to Mike. Get up."

"We didn't mean to hurt you, mister," said the first man, looking at Mike.

"And I won't mean to hurt you, either," said Mike.

"Don't you move, either of you," said Tom. "Over here, Mike and take the revolver. They're all yours."

Mike walked over and took the revolver.

"Outside, both of you," he said, indicating the still-open door with the revolver.

"Like I said, mister. We didn't mean to hurt you," whined the first man again.

"Like I said, outside."

"You're not going to shoot us, are you?"

"Thinkin' on it," said Mike. "Which one of you hit me?"

"He did," said the men at the same time, each pointing to the other.

"I've heard of this," said Mike. "Honour amongst thieves. Let's go."

Mike ushered them both out the door, the men still whining that they didn't want to be shot.

"Go with him, Bill. He might still need your help."

William went outside. Like the men, he was afraid that Mike might shoot them.

"All right. That'll do," said Mike, stopping them under the lamps at the front of the tent.

He turned to William, still keeping the revolver pointed at the men.

"Are you going to shoot them?" said William.

"No, I'm not goin' to shoot 'em, but they'll wish I had. You're about to see goldfield justice."

"What are you goin' to do?" said one of the men.

"This," said Mike.

He brought the revolver down hard from above onto the ear of one of the men and then the other, before either man had time to realise what was going on and avoid the blow.

"Jesus, mister! You've torn off me bloody ear!" shouted one, while the other just screamed.

"Now, get out of here before I change my mind about shootin' you."

Mike and William stood for a few moments and watched the men run down the road towards the diggings, both still screaming and both still holding their heads.

William was surprised to hear gunshots from the diggings.

"Are there more robberies down there?" he said to Mike.

"Might be. Claim jumpin', robberies, lettin' off steam. More than one reason for a man to fire a gun."

"Were you really thinking of shooting them?"

"Never used a gun in my life and not about to start now. I've got a revolver in the cart, but haven't needed it. Scott and Tom keep one close to hand. Diggin's are dangerous, as is the road to and from. You'll need to get one, or at least learn how to use one if you plan on stayin'."

"What about the police. Can't they help?"

"Out here? Now there's people that know how to rob. C'mon, Bill. Let's get inside. I've had enough excitement for one day. Besides, my head hurts."

They went back in and Tom was busy sorting through the goods they brought from Melbourne.

"Ah. Thought I'd start while I waited. They've gone?"

"Yes," said Mike, "And they won't come back. But you'll recognise them if they do—their heads look different to most."

Tom just laughed.

"Let's turn in. I'll sleep here, you two at the back. Mike, show Bill."

"Aye."

Tom secured the door then rolled out some blankets in the doorway—one underneath and two on top, and a fourth rolled up as a pillow. "'Night," he said as he crawled in between the blankets.

"This way," said Mike, leading William to the back of the store. They went in behind some stacked boxes. The light wasn't as good in the corner, but it didn't worry Mike. He pulled some blankets from a stack, threw three to William and kept three for himself. He put two blankets on the floor and rolled another as a pillow. "'Night," he said and like Tom, got between the blankets.

Both Tom and Mike were snoring before William had even made his bed.

His last thought before sleep claimed him was that he was so tired he could sleep anywhere.

# CHAPTER 8

## Working at the Store

William could hear the murmurings of conversation as he came out of sleep. He couldn't see anyone from behind the boxes, nor could he recognise the voices.

He got out of bed and looked around the corner. Tom was at the long table near the door, serving a customer. There was no sign of Mike.

"Tom. What do you want me to do?"

"Ah, Bill. If you need to go outside, do that. Otherwise, just sit by the table at the back and I'll be with you soon."

He turned back to the customer.

William went out through the door and was blinded by the sunlight. There was some traffic on the road, and not much noise from the diggings. It was already warm and the sun was higher in the sky than he expected. The smell wasn't as bad as the day before. The wind was coming from the east, not blowing from the diggings as it had the previous night. He went out around the back and was surprised how different things looked in the daylight. There was more scrub than he thought, and more trees to choose from. It was also easier to pick his way around the leavings of previous visitors—no wonder the place smelled. He found a tree that partially hid him from view, pissed on it, and went back to the store. Tom was on his own.

"Did you sleep well?" Tom asked him.

"No trouble at all. I think I could have slept anywhere."

"That's how you looked."

"Where's Mike?"

"Gone back to Melbourne—left at daylight. He didn't want to wake you. Told me to thank you for helping him last night. You won't know, but it's Sunday, so not much happens. I'd promised that customer some of what you brought from Melbourne. We don't trade much on a Sunday, so you and I can have a chat. C'mon, let's get you some breakfast and we can get acquainted."

He closed the door and secured it, then busied himself at the fire cooking the standard chops and making some tea.

"I'd like to help," said William.

"Later, you can. Mike told me Scott has organised for you to work here. Said Scott would have told me himself, but he's still at Bacchus Marsh and might be for a few days. Mike's taken his horse and will leave it with him there, so Scott can join us when he's better."

"How did Mike take the horse and the dray? He can't ride both."

Tom laughed.

"Scott's horse wouldn't want to be left behind. It'll just follow the dray. What did Scott hire you to do?"

"Help in the store."

"Help with what?"

"He didn't say."

"You good with numbers?"

"No. I can't read or write, either."

"You sound like you can read and write."

"That's been said before."

"No matter. There's plenty to do that doesn't involve reading, writing or numbers. Store's more than a one-man job. If you're up for the learning, I'm up for the teaching."

"I'm up for it. Scott said if I change my mind after a few months, that'll be all right."

"That's all right with me too. So, let's shake on it and I'll show you what to do."

They spent the next few hours going around the store, Tom showing William how and where to put the new goods from Melbourne, how to stack cans, boxes and bottles, how to refill the lamps, and where the brooms and rags were kept so they could keep the store as clean as possible. Nothing was hard; it was simply a matter of remembering it all.

At last Tom said, "Let's stop for lunch. I'll show you where everything is and we can take turns with meals from now on."

As they ate, William said, "Can I ask some questions?"

"Of course."

"Where do we wash?"

"You wash?"

"Yes."

"Not many do."

"I know, but I do."

"Where'd you learn that?"

"Dublin."

Tom laughed and William blushed.

"Sorry, Bill. Not laughing at you. I thought you might have said your parents. No matter. I wash too. I've got a tub out back. I usually go out in the evenings, when it's harder for people to see me. Mozzies love it, of course. You're welcome to do the same—wash I mean. Not bite me, like the mozzies. Gets a bit cold in winter, but then there's no mozzies. So you've got to take the good with the bad."

"Where do I get the water?"

"There's a barrel on the side. I have to buy water. You can't drink it. You can only make tea, or use it for washing. There's a pannikin on the side you use for either the tub or the billy. Sometimes in the summer you can take a walk away from the diggings and find a creek in the hills and swim there. Some families do that."

"The meat?"

"Hangs in a bag on the other side of the cupboard. Goes off too quickly, so I get more from the butcher every other day."

"What do you do with what's left over?"

"I give it to the dogs."

"I didn't see any dogs."

"Other people's dogs."

"You should have a dog."

"I had one."

"What happened to it?"

"Dunno. Stolen or eaten, I suppose."

"You should get another one."

"I will. Thieves're less likely to be interested if there's a dog about."

"Do we sell meat?"

"We don't sell anything that's perishable. Only stuff in boxes, cans, bags and jars. Clothes, too, of course."

"Where's the tea and sugar for the billy?"

"There's tea and sugar on the shelf there, near the stove. Bread's in a box on the top shelf. Less chance of things getting it there. I get a new loaf from the baker every other day."

"Who uses out back where Mike and I went last night?"

"Mostly people in the tents near us. Sometimes if someone is taking a short cut from Sovereign Hill, they'll go through there. Why?"

"I wondered. I guess not everyone uses a shovel."

Tom sat back, laughed and looked at William.

"You'll get used to it. That it?"

"How do people pay for what you sell?"

"Money or gold. Mostly gold."

"Where do you keep it?"

"Why do you want to know?"

"So I can make sure no one steals from you."

Tom studied him for a few moments.

"In a box, over there, behind the table."

"Do you send it back with Mike when he brings things from Melbourne?"

"No—too dangerous. If people knew we did that, Mike's life would be worth nothing. No, we pay the government to take it to Melbourne. They go mostly once, but sometimes twice, a week. They have an armed escort. Thieves sometimes take them on, but mostly it reaches Melbourne."

There was silence for a few moments.

"That it, now?" said Tom.

"Yes, that's it."

"Good. Let's get back to stacking. I want to be ready for tomorrow. Word'll be out that we've had a delivery and they'll all be here early."

They spent the rest of the day unpacking and stacking. It wasn't hard work, not like on the ship, but the bending and standing took a toll on a body worn out by the rigours of the journey from Melbourne. William was glad when they stopped.

He was surprised to hear singing. Tom saw him listening.

"Sunday church in Ballarat," he said. "You'll hear that. I like it, but I don't go. You can go, if you like."

"Not for me either. I used to hear it coming from the church back home, but I never went in. I like it too though. Do I have time to go out back?"

"Sure you do. I'll get you a shovel."

"Don't need one."

William went outside. The wind was back from the southeast, carrying the smells of the diggings.

*I got used to the ship, I can get used to this.*

The sun had gone and the breeze was cooler now. It was nice to stand in it after a hard day. He went back in.

"I'm going to have a wash. I'll be a few moments."

"Don't need to tell me."

"Well, you might think the thieves have got me, like last night and come looking for me, leaving the store with no one to guard it."

Tom smiled.

"Good answer. We'll get on. Soap's on a piece of wood under the tub."

William went around back, picked up the tub and took it to the barrel. He put several pannikins of water in it, took it back behind the tent and pulled off his clothes. It was cold and he shivered when he slid his boots off. He stepped into the tub and gave himself as good a wash as he could manage. He loved the feeling of being clean. Putting his clothes back on, he thought they could do with a scrub too, but he had nothing spare. Scott had said they'd clothe him from the store, but Tom hadn't said anything about that, or money either.

It didn't matter. Scott would sort all that out when he came. Perhaps, he could find a creek the next Sunday. *Be good to have a look around, too.* He was still curious about the diggings and how it worked.

He put the soap back on the wood and the tub over it, walked up into the bush, pissed against a tree, and returned to the tent.

"Good," said Tom. "My turn. Close the door after me. You'll learn how to talk to the customers as time goes on."

Tom left and returned all scrubbed and fresh after a while.

"Do you have any spare clothes?" he asked William.

"No," said William, blushing.

"We'll sort that out now. I'll bet Scott said he'd do that and you didn't want to ask."

William said nothing, but knew he was red from embarrassment.

"I thought so," said Tom laughing. "Let's get that done and then you can get supper."

It wasn't long before William was fitted out with standard digger's clothes of serge-shirt and moleskin trousers.

"No choice, I'm afraid," said Tom, laughing. "That's all we keep. You can wash the other stuff tomorrow when we have time. So, you do the supper and ask for help if you need it."

William did a creditable job of getting supper. Tom said nothing, just watched.

When they finished eating, William said that the wood was getting low and where would they get more?

"We can either buy it or fetch it. Fetching is getting harder, since everyone's doing the same. If I feel like a walk, I fetch it. Black Hill is good, but it's steep."

"Where's Black Hill?"

"Back up the hill and to the left. Look for it in the daylight. You can't miss it."

"How did you do those things when you were here on your own?"

"If someone I trusted came by as a customer, I'd get them to hang about for a while. Give them something for free. Sugar, honey or tobacco would always work."

They sat in silence for a while.

"If you want to look about outside, you can. We can't go together, of course. Someone has to mind the store. There's not much to see when it's dark, and it can be dangerous. Drunks and thieves are always about late at night. But, there's still enough light outside. Go for a look around. I'll look after things here."

William nodded, got up and went outside.

The sun was slowly disappearing in the west, casting long shadows from the few remaining trees. There was some traffic about, mostly heading into Ballarat. The wooden buildings in the distance had lamps already burning. Many of the tents in the flat had fires burning outside them and people sitting around. William guessed they were still eating their supper. He wished he had someone with him who could explain it all—he didn't want to walk too far and have to find his way back in the dark. Mosquitoes whined and swirled about him. He slapped at them, but knew it was a waste of time. There was little point to the walk as it only emphasised that he knew nothing about digging for gold. Scott had been right. He'd take the chance to learn about it.

He started back to the shop, taking care to walk to the side of the road. It was still churned up and muddy, no doubt still wet from recent rain.

When he walked in the door, Tom looked up from where he'd been working.

"That didn't take long."

"I need someone to explain it to me. Besides, the mosquitoes were feasting off me."

Tom laughed.

"Diggers love to hear about things from home. There's lots of Irish here, so I'll bet someone comes in, meets you, and invites you back for supper. That'll happen soon enough and they'll be pleased to show you over their claim. I'm nearly finished here and then I'm going to turn in. It'll be a busy day tomorrow."

William headed off to his bed at the back, curled up and was asleep in no time.

He woke to Tom calling, "C'mon, Bill! Time you were up. There's work to be done." He'd been dreaming about the ship and was glad to leave those dreams behind.

They finished a hasty breakfast and were hardly finished before the first customers arrived.

The customers were mostly men, although a few women called by, and everyone expressed interest in the new store hand.

There followed a busy day of helping Tom in a dozen different ways. William wondered how Tom had managed on his own. Fetching, folding, carrying and keeping an eye on the store kept William so busy he was relieved when Tom suggested they stop for lunch. While they were seated, a man came in and Tom called to him to join them.

"I've already eaten," said the man. "But I won't say no to a cuppa."

Tom poured him some tea while he introduced William.

"This here is Bill," he said. "He's helping me until he catches the fever."

The man laughed.

"That'll be soon enough. Mine's Jack. Used to own a store myself, then caught the fever. Now look at me."

William thought his clothes were yellow, but realised the man was covered in mud.

"Rain didn't help," said Jack. "Now we're all splashing about in mud. Where're you from, lad?"

"Belfast."

"I'm from Dublin, but aye, I've bin there too. Didn't much like it. Not much work and hungry all the time. Then, took off for California. Gold ran out there and now I'm down 'ere where I met the missus. She and the kids don't like it much workin' in the diggin's. Should've kept the store that I set up 'ere. Tom 'ere, now 'e's smart. Well, at least, Scott is. That right, Tom?"

"Bill's been wondering about the diggin's. You got time to show him?"

"Sure I do, but not now, maybe later. Do you need 'im 'ere, later?"

"I can spare him for a while. Anyway, you'll need him to help you carry what you'll buy."

"Don't plan to buy anything. Just came by for a cuppa."

"C'mon Jack, pull the other one."

Jack laughed.

"We need some rope. What we've got is frayed and gone to hell. We'll need about eighty feet. Can you do that?"

"Aye, we can do that in one and a quarter inch. But you'll need Bill to help and I can spare him now, so finish your cuppa and let's get to it."

Jack and Tom stepped out the rope from a coil.

"How much?" said Jack when they were done and the rope was rolled up on the floor.

"Hmm," said Tom, figuring in a book. "I make that eight pennyweights."

Jack pulled a piece of cloth from his pocket and poured gold from it onto the scales until the gold matched the weights. A few pieces fell to the floor, but he paid them no heed.

"C'mon, Bill. You can help me and Tom can mind the store. It's not much to carry, but the job'll be easier for two."

William looked at Tom who nodded.

Jack split the rope into two roughly equal coils and they each took one, with a piece joining them.

"Thanks for the tea," said Jack as he waved and left, William following close behind, the distance determined by the length of rope between them.

They walked down the road, side by side. The road continued to fall. There were both large and small shops on both sides of the road, but not many customers. He was on the inside and had to walk in all the mud. There wasn't much traffic, but there was enough to splash William with mud. He jumped to avoid some.

"Pay it no mind," said Jack. "It's only mud and will wash off soon enough."

He stopped and looked at William's new clothes.

"I suppose I wouldn't want to get them dirty, neither. But, you'll find out soon enough that the diggin's aren't for stayin' clean. You been to other diggin's?"

"No."

"Thought so. Where'd you say you're from?"

"Belfast."

"How's things there?"

"Better."

"Better than what? 'Ere?"

"No, better than before, with the famine."

"Now, that was a bad business."

"Did the gold really run out?"

"Where?"

"California."

"No. Too many people lookin' for it. Like 'ere."

It seemed to William that they'd been walking for some time when Jack said, "There's my tent. See yonder."

Jack pointed to a group of tents in the distance, on a flat, near a creek.

"Claim's not far above it. Makes it easier to shepherd the claim."

"Have you got sheep there, too? I don't see any."

"No. There's no sheep," said Jack laughing. "We call it shepherding when you have to stay by your claim to stop others jumpin' it. If they start workin' it, they claim it's theirs. I'd shoot any bastard that tried to do that to me. We'll go to the tent first, then the claim and drop the rope off. I'll show you how the claim works."

William had been looking around as they walked. He wanted to be sure to find his way back and was intrigued by the activity around him. Tents were scattered about and there were piles and piles of dirt. The road they followed was more or less flat, but he could see hills around—some near, some far. There was no clear distinction of where people would dig and where they would pitch their tents. Constant noise assaulted his ears—people shouting, dogs barking, machinery creaking and crunching. The ground underfoot was no less muddy. In fact, he decided, the only type of road was a muddy road. Men along the creek were rocking things that looked like baby cradles, but couldn't be because the men were pouring dirt and water into them.

They reached a point where the road forked. They turned left and crossed a creek. The ford was flat, although he decided it would be hard to cross when in flood. The water was muddy, unlike anything he had seen on the journey to the goldfields. Mike had said the water would be undrinkable. Jack stomped through the creek, not looking for anywhere to keep his feet dry and William had no choice but to do the same. Water came into his boots and they started to squish.

William could see Jack's tent more clearly and the creek near to it.

"Canadian Creek," said Jack. "Used to be much better for gold. We're all scratchin' around now, all tryin' to see if it's played out. All goin' deeper. Lot of gold came out of 'ere. Lot of alluvial stuff and shallow holes. Gettin' harder all the time. Too many people if you ask me. Same as California."

"What's alluvial?"

"Gold that's not in the quartz reef any more. You can dig it right out of the ground."

William slipped on the muddy track and dragged Jack down with him.

"Sorry, Jack," said William.

"No harm done, Bill. I shoulda carried the damn thing myself. Just bein' lazy."

They scrambled to their feet and moments later, arrived at the tent.

The tent up close was a miserable affair—canvas held up by poles, patched and sagging. There was no visible chimney, but there was small fire at the front smouldering among some stones. There was a tripod of iron standing over it with a hook for a billy.

"Darlin'? You there, darlin'?" called Jack. "Got someone for you to meet."

A woman emerged from the tent, bending low as she came out. Two girls followed. The girls stood behind their mother, peeking out from behind her skirt. It reminded William of Hannah and her children.

The woman was much younger than Jack. She had a fine, strong face, and sparkling eyes and appeared to be smiling. Her clothes were neat, but muddy like Jack's, and it was obvious that she too had been working. Digging must be a family affair.

"So, who is this, then, that you've no doubt brought home for supper? Tell him supper's not ready yet."

"This is Bill and he can do his own listenin'."

"Bill, is it? Where are you from Bill?"

"I work with Tom, at the store," said William, stuttering and not sure why. He was embarrassed at the woman's frank stare.

"Well," said the woman. "Bill, from Tom's store, you can't be calling me darlin'. You'll be needing to call me Bridie and these are our girls, Missy and Polly. Missy and Polly, this is Mr Bill."

'Hello, Mr Bill," said the girls in unison.

William delighted in the sound. It was just like his own two sisters. There was a sudden ache for his family.

"Now, Bill is from Belfast and don't you be makin' fun of 'im," said Jack. "I've brought 'im to tell us the doin's back home. We're goin' to look at the shaft, then we'll be back. I thought I'd give you a warnin' there'll be another for supper."

"Doesn't look like he eats much, so maybe no warning was needed."

"Needed or not, you've got it. We'll be back soon. C'mon, Bill. I'll show you the diggin's."

Jack turned, and walked back the way they had come.

William was uncertain what to do, torn between saying something to Bridie and following Jack.

"Off you go, Bill. Don't keep Jack waiting. We'll talk later. There'll be time enough."

William followed Jack and caught up with him. They crossed the road and started up a hill.

"Not too far," said Jack. "Still, hill's tough when you do it all day. Stay close to me. Careful where you walk."

The ground had been torn up by digging. There was no order to the holes and not all of them were filled in. Jack was right—William needed to be careful and some of the holes looked deep.

"How deep are they?"

"Some go down to eighty feet."

"Did they get gold?"

"No. Most of 'em were duffers. I thought I'd try higher up."

"Why?"

"A hunch. I figure the gold at the bottom has come from up on the hill. Didn't matter when there was plenty of gold at the bottom. Now, I think most of it has gone."

"Why aren't others looking higher up on the hill?"

"Not everyone is as smart as me."

Jack stopped, looked at William, and laughed.

"They're looking further up the creek, over the other side of the river and even north of Ballarat."

"Are they finding gold?"

"Some are. There's a gully further up the creek where they found some big nuggets just a few months back."

"What's a nugget?"

"Gold comes in all shapes and sizes. Bigger bits are called nuggets. Enough of this. We'll be there soon. Then you can ask all the questions you want. I'm findin' it hard to walk and talk at the same time."

William could hear the sound of machinery.

"Are they steam engines I can hear? I think I heard them when I arrived."

"Yes. They use them in the bigger mines to crush the ore and to pump water. Fellers like us don't use 'em. Can't afford 'em."

They continued to pick their way around the holes and the heaps until Jack stopped beside a freshly dug hole. There was very little left in the way of brush or scrub on the hill, though there was more growing towards the top.

"This is it," said Jack. "What do you think?"

"About what?"

"About my chances."

"How would I know?"

"Two of the fellers that found the big nugget a couple of months back had been here only a few months. Said it was their idea to dig where they did. Said they felt it was a good spot. Thought I should ask you."

"What's the thing across the top?"

"It's a windlass. I use it to pull the buckets of dirt up."

"Why don't you just bring up the gold? Leave the dirt down there?"

"That's the trouble, you see. The gold is mixed with a lot of dirt. I bring up the buckets, take them down to the creek and Bridie and the girls help me to cradle it. Separates the gold from the dirt. It's what I mean about the hill. It's hard work carting the dirt down all day. Still, I'm bettin' this is a good spot."

"How deep is it?"

"I'm down about fifteen feet."

"How do you know when to stop going down? Do you stop when you find gold?"

"Unfortunately, you don't always find gold, so there has to be another reason to stop. Well, down the bottom of the hill, it's when you get to the clay. Up here, I think it'll be when I get to the hard rock. Gold's heavy and falls until it gets caught on somethin' it can't go through, like clay or hard rock. Clay down there, rock up here. I haven't dug up here before, so I'm guessin'."

"Do you know, before I left Ireland I heard you just walked up, picked up the gold and stopped when you had enough."

They both laughed.

"I wish. We all wish," Jack said.

William peered into the hole.

"It looks dark down there."

"It is. I've got some lamps down there to help me see. Sometimes, if I'm not tired, I'll keep workin' after dark."

"What's the rush?"

"Water. If it rains, the hole will fill and collapse. Some people shore them up with wood and bark to stop them collapsin'. Doesn't always work. Have to do it with deep holes, of course— too dangerous if you don't. Fellers gettin' killed all the time takin' risks."

"How do you get down?"

"Hand over hand on a piece of rope. There's toe holes in the sides. Can't do it too often or you'll cause a collapse, then you've got to abandon the hole, or dig the rubbish out."

"Can you make it wider?"

"You stake a claim and get a piece of ground eight feet square. You're only entitled to work one claim at a time. You can get a couple of mates and register claims side by side, then you can go deeper and wider."

"How would they know?"

"You'd be surprised what they know. Costs you three pounds a month to have a licence to be in the diggin's. You pay it whether you find gold or not. They're always checkin' on it, so they know what's goin' on. More's the pity."

*How right Scott was. Jack's a good man and he's telling me things that would take weeks of heartache to discover.*

"C'mon, Bill. Let's go back for supper."

"Won't someone jump your claim?"

"They all think I'm mad comin' up here. If I find somethin', I'll need to be careful, but at the moment, no one's interested."

Twilight was coming on and there was a chill to the air. They weren't that high up on the hill, but they had a better view of the flats below. Fires were starting to wink around the tents and the noise of the cradles had subsided. Dogs barked and people called to each other. The steam machines had stopped working and the valley was almost tranquil. There were a few people moving on the road, mostly towards the town that William could see in the distance.

It took little time to get back to the tent. William followed Jack carefully, but stopped from time to time to view the tent and its surroundings. The tents were not pitched in any order, and none were close to the creek. There were many different sizes. Jack's looked as ragged as any other, but if anything, it was bigger.

Bridie cooked at the fireplace outside the tent. She had the standard steel tripod and billy, an oven sitting in the coals, and something steaming in a pot.

"Ah, here they are, girls," said Bridie as they approached. "Hunters from the hills returning. What, ho, boys? Laden with gold, no doubt?"

"Enough, darlin'," said Jack. "One day I will be and then you'll be feastin' on humble pie."

"I hope so. It's a dish I'm looking forward to. The bigger the helping, the better. Wash up first, then c'mon in. The girls are hungry and ready to eat. No doubt, you are too."

Jack went around the side of the tent. William followed. There was a barrel of water from which Jack ladled some water into a worn, metal pan. He picked up a piece of soap from a stump, washed his face and hands in the pan and dried himself on a piece of cloth hanging from one of the tent's ropes. He threw the water onto the ground and said, "Your turn."

William did the same.

They walked around to the front of the tent and as they did, William could clearly see the shapes of Bridie and the girls moving around inside.

Jack saw him looking and said, "I don't like that. It's like everyone has a window into our lives. I'll be glad when we find some gold and can get out of here. Back to a proper home. It's what Bridie wants. I want it too."

They stepped inside and William could see that the well-lit tent was split into two unequal sections.

"It was my idea," said Bridie, busy at the table, as though reading William's mind. "Everyone asks, so I know what you're thinking. It gives the girls some privacy when, Lord knows, there's little enough."

William blushed.

"Now you've gone and embarrassed our guest," said Jack.

Bridie stopped working and looked at William.

"That I have and who knows why. It might be because I said I know what he's thinking. Don't worry, Bill. I don't know what you're thinking. It's just that everyone asks that question. Here, sit down. Jack has done a good job of making the table and chairs. Right fancy, they are. He's good at those things. Has to be, I suppose."

The girls and Bridie seated themselves at the table. Jack and William did the same.

The table was covered with a cloth. There were spoons, bowls, damper on a large piece of flat wood, and the pot that was on the fire was beside it, also on a piece of flat wood.

"I've made some stew. We get sick of the chops. I managed to get some vegetables. I hope you like it. Here, give me your bowl and I'll serve you some."

William passed Bridie his bowl and she ladled some stew into it. Without asking, she cut off some damper for him.

She then did the same for the others. William waited and was glad he did.

They all lowered their heads.

"Lord," Jack said. "Thank you for the meal we are havin' and for bringin' Bill to us. He'll tell us of your doin's back home. Be good to find some gold, too. Don't be forgettin' us, now. Amen."

They all ate quietly. William was glad he knew how.

No one spoke at the table. Dogs howled and barked in the distance and the evening was punctuated by the occasional gunshot. From time to time, they could hear people talking nearby.

"That was really good, Bridie," William said. "I used to have it on the ship, but it was never as good as this."

"Thank you, Bill. You are most welcome."

Jack pulled out his pipe.

"Do you smoke, Bill?"

William shook his head.

"Time enough to start," said Jack. "Now, tell us about Ireland."

Everyone looked at William. It was as though he'd been asked for the location of the gold. Even the girls looked interested.

"I don't know what to tell you," said William. "I grew up in the country. I came into Belfast when I left. I don't know much. The famine and the disease are gone, if that's what you want to know."

"That's good. Is there work for everyone?"

"I think so. I got some work on the docks. They seemed to need people. It was busy."

"That's good."

Jack was silent for a few moments, then he went on.

"The Irish stick together out here. They call us the Tipperary Boys. We always want news, if we can get it. We don't fight each other so much. I never liked the English so much at home. They took everythin' and gave nothin'. Here, it's the damned police. They check if we have a licence. Ridin' roughshod through the camps. If you don't have a licence, you get fined five pounds and the police get half the fine. It's a terrible system. The diggers look for gold and the police look for diggers. It's that stupid Charles La Trobe. What kind of a name is that, anyway?"

"Who's Charles La Trobe?"

"He's the Lieutenant Governor of Victoria. Has been since 1851. The licences are his idea. It's not fair chargin' a man to look for gold. Oh, that gets us mad, all right. But it's how they police it that we don't like. If you hear people shoutin'', 'Joe! Joe!' you'll know it's the police lookin' to find unlicensed diggers. Sometimes, they do it all day long and there's nary time to dig."

"Who shouts 'Joe'?" asked William. "Is it the police?"

"No, it's the diggers," said Jack.

"There's a funny side," said Bridie.

"Aye, but only if you don't get caught. If you get caught, you get chained to a log or a tree, or stuck in a cell with men who've done a lot worse than avoid a licence fee, and you're left there until the fine is paid."

"C'mon, dear. Don't work yourself up. Tell Bill about Kelly."

"Oh, Kelly. There's a lad. Most of the fellers get away by hidin' in a shaft, or even crossin' a drift to another shaft. Not Kelly."

"Oh, Daddy! Tell us about Kelly!" shouted the girls in unison.

William loved being with this family. The daughters were enchanting, Bridie lively, and Jack the centre of their attention. Would he and Mary have been like this?

"Well. Kelly had vowed he would never pay for a licence. He'd only been on the diggin's a few months and had always found a way to avoid it. The whole thing was a game to him. One day, he was in his tent and heard the police comin'. There were shouts of 'Joe! Joe!', but also the cries of protest from the diggers. He had no chance to get out, so he dons one of his wife's dresses and bonnet and stands in the door way."

The little girls were hugging themselves and looking excited.

"A police sergeant come up to Kelly and says, 'Where's your man?'

"'And what would your business be with him?' says Kelly." Jack impersonated Kelly with a high-pitched voice. As soon as he did, the girls squealed with delight. Bridie laughed out loud at the sound and Jack smiled, clearly pleased with the girls' reaction.

"'We're on a licence hunt and we want to see his licence,' says the sergeant." This time Jack impersonated a deep voice.

"'Well,' says Kelly. 'That would be my brother, but there's only me and my sister here at the moment, so you'll have to wait until he gets home. Will you come in for a cuppa while we wait?'

"'No, miss,' says the trap. 'I don't have time right now, but would your brother mind if I call on you. I didn't know such a comely lass was here at the diggin's.'

"'I'm afraid, sir, that I am already spoken for. May I introduce my sister? She's not spoken for and would appreciate being called upon by a gentleman such as your fine self.'"

The little girls screamed in delight at Jack's high-pitched voice.

"So, Kelly signals for his wife to come to the door. She, of course, is afraid of the trick that Kelly has played and afraid for Kelly should the sergeant discover that he has been played for a fool."

"Tell Mr Bill, Daddy. Tell him what happens!" shouted the girls together.

"Well, Kelly's wife goes to the door. She's so afraid and shakin' and she can't believe that Kelly is so stupid. Why bait the police? Weren't things already bad enough?

"'C'mon, dear sister,' says Kelly. 'There's a very nice man here at the door. He'd like to meet you. Don't be shy, darlin' sister. He won't mind you havin' only one leg.' Kelly looks back into the room. 'Oh, darlin', you're havin' trouble getting out of bed, are you?' Kelly looks back at the trap. 'Oh, Sergeant, poor thing. She's so big, she can't get out of bed. Spends a lot of time in bed, she does. But then, so would you if you were as big as she is.'

"The sergeant says, 'Please tell her not to worry. I'll call on her some other time. Thank you for your time, miss. Please give my regards to your sister.'

"'Oh, Sergeant. She'll be so disappointed. But a busy man like yourself has responsibilities. Goodbye, Sergeant.'

"The sergeant leaves and Kelly turns back into the room to find his wife has fainted."

The little girls' laughter and squealing filled the tent. The sound of it caused the three grownups to laugh heartily as well.

"Did he get away with it? Surely the sergeant found out he was tricked?" said William.

"Nope, never found out and Kelly still doesn't have a licence."

"Off to bed, you two. Mr Bill will be leaving soon."

"Tell Mr Bill another story, Daddy, please. Just one more? Please?"

"Missy and Polly, that would be delightful, but I have to go now," said William, catching Bridie's look. "I've been gone too long already. It's dark outside and I'm afraid of the dark."

"You are not," said Polly.

"Well, perhaps just a little," said William. "But afraid or not, I must go. It's been good to meet you all. I hope I can come again."

"Of course you can," said Bridie. "You will always be welcome."

William stood and headed for the door.

"I'll come with you for a little," said Jack. "It's dark out there and best not to get lost."

He took a lamp from the ceiling post.

"I won't be long," he said to Bridie.

"Goodnight, Mr Bill," said the girls.

"Goodnight, girls. Goodnight, Bridie."

William and Jack walked out into the darkness. The night was moonless and the lamp showed only the ground near their feet. He was glad Jack was with him. It would be a treacherous journey without any experience.

"I don't know how they do that," said Jack.

"Do what?"

"Say everything together like that. It's like their minds are joined," said Jack.

"Are they always like that?"

"They are now, but always? I don't know. They're not mine. Their da was killed in an accident. He and Bridie used to come to my store when I had it. Well, when he was killed, I took to lookin' after Bridie and the girls. Weren't no hardship. She's a fine woman and the girls treat me like I'm their da."

"How was he killed?"

"Bill, it was the silliest thing and leaves you wonderin' if there's a God at all, much less one who cares. His claim was down on the flats below Golden Point, not far from where we are now. Was just him and Bridie workin' it, like we do now. He'd bottomed and was gettin' payable gold. It started to rain and thunder near the end of the day and she took the little ones back to their tent, leavin' him to clean up. An hour later, when he hadn't come back, she went lookin' for him. He was floatin' in the pit. It had half filled with water and he couldn't swim. We all supposed he'd been tryin' to grip something on the side, but with the rain, it was all slippery and he couldn't get a hold. He'd probably been callin' for help, but with the thunder and all, there was no one to hear him. Bridie was inconsolable. She blamed herself. 'If only I'd gone back sooner,' she kept sayin'."

"Wouldn't other diggers have been nearby?"

"No one can understand it. There were other claims all around and people workin' them. We decided that he'd stayed past the time when the others left. He must have worried that the pit would fill with water and he'd lose his find. Men don't always use their head when it comes to gold."

"Wouldn't the others check on him?"

"Mostly they do, but sometimes the diggers think someone else is doin' it."

"That's a terrible end for someone."

"It's not just him, Bill. There are hundreds of stories like that. I think God takes a holiday when men look for gold."

"It's sad for Bridie and the girls, but she's lucky to have you. I'm sure she's a fine wife."

"She's not my wife. Yet. We talk about gettin' married, just haven't found the time. Call each other husband and wife, though. I suppose it's a lie, but it makes things easier. And Bridie, she worries that I'll get killed too. So, Bridie and the girls live in one half of the tent and I live in the other, waitin' for the day when we have enough gold to open a store in Melbourne."

"But the girls call you Daddy."

"Aye and I don't mind. Matter of fact, I like it. Watch the creek here now. If you fall in, you won't be the first, but might be good if you did. It would lighten our mood. Give me somethin' to laugh at."

The path ahead was clearer now, and lights from the shops around them highlighted the direction of the road.

"Not far up the hill for you now, Bill, so I'll leave you and head back. I'll take the lamp. You shouldn't need it, but your boots will be a mess when you get to the store. Thanks for comin' by. We like company and you're good company. The girls like you too. I know Bridie does. Be seein' you, Bill."

William felt rather than saw Jack's hand outstretched. He took it and shook.

"Thank you, Jack. I enjoyed meeting your family."

The men headed off their separate ways and William knew in a few minutes that Jack had been right—he could no longer see where he walked, and his boots squelched with every step. Unfortunately, he had some idea what was underfoot.

# CHAPTER 9

# Reunion with Scott

William stepped into the store and before he had a chance to check his boots, he was startled with a shout.

"Ah! Here he is! Welcome back, stranger!"

He looked up in surprise and there was Scott sitting with his brother, a bottle of whisky between them.

"So, what have you got to say for yourself? Come on in and let's have a look at you."

"I can't—Tom'll kill me. I've got half the road on my boots."

"Well, I'll come to you then."

Scott strode over to William and shook his hand warmly.

"It's good to see you. Tom says you are settling in well. How about you? What do you think?"

"More importantly, Scott, how are you? Fully recovered? You look good."

"I'm as fit as a fiddle."

"Come on, you two. Enough of the talking. There's whisky here. Pull up a chair, Bill. Scott has brought a very nice Islay whisky to celebrate," said Tom.

"What are we celebrating?" William asked.

"The way I see it, my being alive and no small thanks to you. You being here, and no small thanks to me," said Scott. "So, give those boots a bit of a lick and a spit at the door and let's celebrate."

William cleaned his boots as best he could and joined the others at the table. Tom poured him a generous whisky.

Tom and Scott raised and clinked their glasses and waited for William to do the same.

"To us," said Tom and Scott at the same time.

"Aye. To us," said William.

The other two downed their whiskies in a single gulp. Scott noticed William hesitate. He laughed.

"Tom, Bill needs to be careful. He's new at this game. You sip it, Bill. Take your time and that way we can enjoy your company for longer. Tom said you went with Jack to look at his claim."

"Aye, that I did and then he asked me to stay for supper."

"Did you meet Amy?

"Do you mean Bridie?"

"Yes. Her name is Amy, but Jack calls her Bridie. So you met her?"

"Yes. I met her and the girls."

"Did he tell you about Alf?"

"Alf? Who's Alf?"

"Alf was Amy's husband."

"Yes, he did. Said he was killed in an accident. Drowned in a pit."

"That's true, but it's not the whole story."

"What's the whole story?"

"Alf was alive when Amy went back to check on him. He was floating in the pit, hanging on to roots and things in the side. He was nearly exhausted. Amy said she'd run and get help, but he begged her not to. Said he was exhausted and wouldn't last much longer. Said could she lie beside the pit and reach down and hold his hand? The water would keep rising and he'd eventually be able to crawl out. She did what he asked. Lay down in the mud and the water and held his hand. The first diggers found her like that in the morning. The water not only stopped rising—it fell. As it fell, she couldn't hold Alf anymore. He eventually let go of her hand and drowned. She was too exhausted to move. They think Alf died not long before the first diggers arrived."

"Why didn't Jack tell me that?"

"They don't want the girls to find out. Bridie told them to stay in the tent while she went to look for their father. They did what they were told. If they'd ignored the order they might have gone to someone for help, but they didn't. Jack tells it like she stayed with them, but she didn't. She held Alf's hand until they both ran out of strength, then he drowned."

*I know what that's like. Trying to hold someone's hand to stop them drowning.*

The men sat in silence for a while, each lost in his own thoughts.

"Thank God for whisky," said Tom, once again raising his glass.

"Aye," said Scott. "Helps us to cope with life, such as it is."

"I suppose you didn't go back to Melbourne?" William asked Scott.

Scott shook his head.

"Mike brought my horse. I came up here before going back. I wanted to be sure you were settled in. After all, I employed you and left Tom holding the bag. What do you think of the diggin's?"

"It's nothing like I thought it would be. I heard you'd pick up as much gold as you wanted, then go home."

They all laughed.

"You were right to give me the chance to learn for a while," William continued. "The men work really hard and it's dangerous, too. I've heard that many seem to think it's not worth it."

"Most don't get much, but those that find a lot, they think it's worth it. Where're they doing most of the digging now, Tom?"

"There's still gold to be had in the gullies and on the flats, although it's getting harder to stake a claim—too many people. They've found some new areas. Some are having luck around Dead Horse Gully, north of here, Sailors' Gully in the south and at Little Bendigo."

"Where's Little Bendigo?"

"Why, north and east of here. Not far away. Just a few miles. Most interesting thing is that they've found some deep leads. Well, it's not too deep at Little Bendigo and that's how they found one of them."

"What's a lead?" said William.

"More whisky first," said Tom, topping up their glasses.

He continued.

"A lead is an old river bed. See Bill, country around here didn't always look like this. Hills, valleys, rivers and creeks were in different places, flowing different ways. The gold was leached out of the quartz and finished up at the bottom of the creeks and rivers. Then, millions of years ago, the whole lot was covered in lava, pushed sideways, up and down, burying the old rivers and creeks and leaving the gold in them. New hills, rivers and creeks were formed and they are what we see today. There's gold around the new creeks, but there's gold in the old ones too, and that's what they found last year at Little Bendigo and now they call it the Eureka Lead."

"Is a million a long time?"

"A very long time."

"How did they find the lead if it's buried?"

"Ah. It's near to the surface where they found it. They were digging normally for surface gold. Diggers who found it realised what it was. They followed it for a while, but it went down, a long way down, and it became too dangerous to go that deep. They decided that if it was near to the surface at Little Bendigo, maybe it was near to the surface somewhere else, too."

"Jack said there's gold all over the place. Maybe, there's more than one old river bed."

"Clever boy. That's it. The Eureka lead might be one of many. Of course, it was sheer luck that the diggers recognised the Eureka as a lead. Diggers might have found other leads already and ignored them, not knowing what they are. One of the early diggers used to say, 'There's gold all over the place at Ballarat. The trick is to find it.'"

"Have they found any more leads?"

"Yes. Late last year they found one at Red Hill."

"Is there more gold in them than on the surface?"

"Sometimes. Surface mining has been good, but apart from the new fields they find, it's nearly exhausted, so deep lead mining is what they are looking to do now."

"Why don't they just follow the leads under the ground, even though it's deep?"

"Two problems, Bill, but the main one is water."

"I thought you needed water."

"Well, when the mines go deep, they go below the level of water in the earth and they just fill with water. You can't dig gold out of a hole filled with water."

"I didn't know there was water in the earth."

Tom laughed.

"We'll make you an expert yet. Besides, you're supposed to be helping me in the shop. I've had enough of gold talk."

William thought he had shown too much interest and Tom might be afraid of losing him.

"I have to admit I'm intrigued by the gold. I didn't know that the earth has changed, that there are old rivers and water buried under the ground or that gold could be found in so many different ways. Scott said it's a good chance to learn and he's right. But, I'm grateful for the job and I'll stick to my end of the bargain."

Scott sat back, smiled at William and said, "Well said. Now, let's pour some more whisky. And Tom, tell me what else is happening. Are we selling everything?"

"Everything. I thought things might slow down as the surface gold played out, but it's not happening like that. There's plenty of other stores, mind you, but I think because we treat our customers well, they come back."

"Good. Is there still talk of trouble in the goldfields?"

"Yes, that's never stopped. Everyone hates the licence fee and everyone hates the way it's enforced."

"It irks me to pay it."

"What?" said William. "We pay it?"

"Anyone working in the goldfields pays it, not just the diggers. You don't have to worry. Tom gets a licence for you."

They sat in silence for a few moments.

"Enough of the doom and gloom, boys," said Scott. "One more whisky and I'm off to bed."

He filled their glasses and half the bottle was gone.

William was really enjoying the whisky and the company.

"How is it, Bill? You met some of the people here?"

"Apart from supper at Jack's tonight? I meet other people as they come to the store. Everyone seems friendly. It's a good place and I'm glad I came here."

"When it gets colder and the days shorter, store doesn't stay open so long and some of the diggers'll come here for some whisky and a game of cards. Do you play cards, Bill?"

"No, but I'd like to learn."

"Well, that's it for me," said Tom. "You two can stay up if you want, but I'm tired enough to sleep on a bed of thistles."

"No, no. I've had it too," said Scott. "'Night."

They rolled themselves in the blankets and William dreamed of gold.

# CHAPTER 10

# William and Tom

"He's working out well, Scott. I'm glad you found him. We'll lose him sooner or later though. You can see how he's interested in the gold."

William woke to the sound of Scott and Tom talking.

"Bill was interested before he came, so that's no surprise."

William yawned loudly before he got up, folded his blankets and joined Scott and Tom at the table.

"I suppose you heard us," said Scott.

William blushed.

"No harm done," said Scott. "Just hold up your end of the deal."

"I will," said William.

"Now, let's have breakfast and I'll be off. I can be home before nightfall if I get moving."

Scott left straight after breakfast and the first customers arrived soon after.

William could deal with small amounts of money and learned how to manage the scales for simple transactions. Tom managed all the larger amounts and no one seemed to mind waiting for him if he was busy. William decided he wasn't the only one that couldn't read, write or handle money, and that many customers came to Tom because they could trust him.

They settled into an easy working relationship.

Towards the end of the week, William decided that he'd go exploring on the Sunday. He asked Tom if that would be all right.

"Of course it will. I also thought that Saturday night we might finish Scott's whisky and I'll show you how to play cards."

William was surprised how much he looked forward to Saturday and Sunday.

Saturday night came, the last customer was gone and they'd finished supper. It rained heavily outside, wind lashed the tent, and between the wind and the rain they couldn't hear any noise from the goldfields.

Tom fetched the whisky, two glasses and a deck of cards. He spread a blanket over the table.

"What's the blanket for?" asked William.

"Stops the cards from getting dirty. You'll see. A deck of cards is worth its weight in gold out here."

When they were settled, Tom said, "I'll show you how to play poker. There's lots of games, but poker is the most popular. You play for money, too, so if you play well, you can make some good money at poker. On the other hand, if you play badly, you'll lose money."

"Money," said William, apprehension in his voice.

"Aye, money. But this is an even bigger night, because I'm going to teach you how to smoke, too."

"Drinking, smoking, cards. There's not much left."

"There's one thing, but I'll let that find you."

"Do we smoke while we play cards?"

"Some do, but not here. We'll get ash all over the blanket and cards and burn holes in them. No, we'll stop after a while and I'll let you borrow my spare pipe. If you like smoking, then one day we'll play cards for the pipe."

"So, if I win, I get the pipe. What do you win if I lose?"

"You'll have to put up something of agreed equal value."

"Can I choose when we play for the pipe?"

"That's the idea. Now, you fill the glasses and school's in."

"School?"

Tom looked at William and smiled.

"Don't look so frightened. It's not really school. And no, we're not playing for money tonight. That wouldn't be fair. Tonight we'll play for matchsticks. We won't get serious until you're ready to."

Tom was a good teacher, and William a quick learner. The pile of matches grew steadily on Tom's side of the table, but William did win a hand every now and again. William thought Tom might be letting him win to encourage him.

"You don't need to let me win," said William at one point.

"Now's a good time for a smoke," said Tom.

He went and got the pipes and tobacco and suggested William join him on the stools by the fire. He filled both pipes and handed one to William. He showed him how to light the pipe using a stick from the fire.

On the first intake, William coughed and spluttered.

"Christ. How do you do this?"

Tom laughed.

"Practice."

It reminded William of his first experience with whisky.

"Take it easy," said Tom. "It's like poker—you'll get better at it with time."

Tom leaned forward and puffed his pipe contentedly. William tried to do the same, but continued to cough and splutter.

"So you did let me win sometimes," he said, when he gathered his breath.

"Not at all," said Tom. "I never let anyone win. It's not what I do. Poker is about two things—luck and bluff. You don't know how to bluff yet, but sometimes you had a better hand than me and I couldn't bluff you, so you're off to a good start. I don't think you're enjoying that pipe, so let's get back to the game."

They returned to the table, refilled their glasses and went back to the poker.

William's head was addled by the smoking and the whisky. He struggled to remember the cards and the rules.

After a few hands, Tom said, "Enough's enough. I think we're done here. Next time, we'll have the smoke and the whisky after the game."

"I'm sorry, Tom. I can't think straight."

"Remember that, too, Bill. If you're playing poker for serious money, you can't afford to not think straight. I'm off to bed. Sleep well."

William went to the back, got his blankets and lay down. As soon as he did, the room started to spin.

He called to Tom in a panic. "Tom! Tom, the room is spinning! What's happening?"

Tom was beside him in seconds.

"Outside—quick!" said Tom.

He hustled William to the front of the tent, supporting him while he removed the locking bar, took him outside and held him while he was sick.

"Take it easy," said Tom. "Too much for one night. My fault. You'll be all right soon enough."

William was dry retching now and Tom sat him on the ground. The smell of the vomit mingled with the smell of animal dung and the smell from the town.

"You're not dying, Bill."

"I wish I was," said William.

Tom laughed.

"Stay here," he said.

"I'm not going anywhere," said William. "I couldn't if I wanted to."

Tom went inside and came back with a damp cloth and a cup of cold tea.

He wiped William's forehead with the cloth and pressed him to drink the tea. The tea tasted wonderful and took the taste of vomit away.

"You won't feel too good in the morning," said Tom, "So that walk in the hills might be a good thing. Anyway, you can decide in the morning."

The rain started again.

"Let's go inside," said Tom. "You can sleep inside the door tonight, so you can do a quick exit if you need to."

"The rain's nice."

"Aye, but only for a few moments. C'mon, let's go in."

He helped William up and helped him inside the tent. He stretched the blankets out again, and lay William on them.

William tried to sleep, but the room continued to spin.

When he woke in the morning, he had no idea how many times he'd been sick in the night. He hoped the rain would have washed away any mess from the front of the store. His head hurt like it had when he'd been injured on the ship, his mouth tasted dreadful, and he was unsure how he'd get through the day. He was sure of only one thing and that was that he'd never smoke or drink again.

He heard Tom walking towards him.

"Ah, Rip Van Winkle," said Tom.

"Who's Rip Van Winkle?" said William.

"Long story," said Tom. "How are you feeling?"

"Awful," said William. "Do you always feel like this after smoking and drinking?"

"No," said Tom.

"Why not?"

"Practice. Here, drink this."

He handed William a glass.

William sniffed it and said in surprise, "It's whisky!"

"Aye, that it is. Don't beat about now. Drink it all in one go."

"Tom, I don't think I can. I'll be sick again."

"You'll be all right. Just drink it. Lie there for a while. Sleep again if you can."

William inched his way closer to the door, looked at Tom, downed the glass, and lay back on the bed. While he was thinking about how sick he was, he went back to sleep.

When he woke, he felt remarkably better. He saw Tom working at the table.

"It wasn't whisky, was it?" he asked. "It was some sort of medicine, wasn't it?"

Tom laughed.

"No, it was whisky right enough. I don't know how it works, but it does. I'm sorry I didn't look after you last night. You can be angry if you wish. I forget you are new to this."

"I can't be angry, Tom. You didn't force me to do anything."

Tom nodded, but looked thoughtful.

"It's a nice day outside, Bill. Rain and wind have gone. Grab some tea and bread and then go for a walk. That will make you feel much better. I have plenty to do here. Just don't get lost. It's easy enough to do around here. Wherever you go, stay near to the roads. Once you know your way around, you can explore further. Don't drink any water from the creeks, no matter how good it looks. You won't believe it, but it'll make you a lot sicker than you were this morning."

"You're right. I don't believe it," said William, getting up and heading for the table at the back of the store. "I can't imagine I'll ever be that sick again."

He poured himself some tea and drank it nearly scalding. As hot as it was, it made his mouth feel better. He ate some bread and decided it was time to go.

"You'll be all right will you, Tom? I can stay if you want."

"No, you go. Just be careful and don't get lost."

"Where should I go?'

"Go out of the store and go up the hill. When you see a big, dark hill to your left, head towards that. It's called Black Hill. Climb to the top of it. You'll get a great view of the diggin's."

"Thanks, Tom. And thanks for looking after me last night. And for teaching me how to play cards."

"Don't forget, I also taught you how to smoke."

"I won't say thanks for that."

They both laughed, and William headed out the door and started walking up the hill.

There were people about and the sound of singing from the town. Most people acknowledged him with, "Mornin'". People were smartly dressed and every now and again he'd see a woman in a full length, colourful dress and bonnet. Sometimes, they'd have a hand laid affectionately on the forearm of their male companion. The men would mostly be in a full suit with a bowler hat. It all looked so out of place.

The air was cool after the rain, but was still tainted with the smell from the town. He tried not to focus on it as his stomach made unaccustomed flips.

He could see Black Hill easily, but waited until he came across a road that headed towards it. There were tent stores on both sides of the road, but only a few were open. There was no one outside those that were open, and from time to time he heard the sounds of laughter coming from inside.

Finally, he reached a road that headed toward the Black Hill. There was a wooden building on the corner and he marked its presence for the return journey. The road went downhill to his right and uphill to his left. As he set off on the road, he heard the sounds of laughter from the wooden building, too.

He started to sweat in spite of the day being cool. He was glad that he was out walking and felt better with every step. The hill was taking its toll though, and he wasn't sure how far he should go before turning back. There were fewer people about now as the hill levelled off. The road became a track through the trees. Birds called to each other, insects buzzed, and the diggings were lost behind him. Then, he came out of the trees and the diggings were in front of him.

*How did that happen?* He must have gone back somehow, but he knew he hadn't. The hill was still in front of him, so he'd simply come upon the same diggings from a different direction.

There was a sharp drop to a creek and there were tents on both sides. He decided to climb the Black Hill. It would help a lot to understand where he was. Threading his way past the tents, he reached the bank of the creek and it took several moments to find a way to cross. He fell more than climbed down the bank, sloshed through the muddy creek, and scrambled more than climbed up the far bank.

Once again, he threaded his way through the tents. There were a few people sitting on logs outside their tents, drinking and chatting. No one paid him any mind.

Reaching the hill, he started to climb. He hadn't gone far when he realised he should have planned it better. The hill was very steep and wooded. The trees helped him to climb and he used them as he fought his way to the top.

This couldn't be where Tom got wood. It was too far from the store.

Finally, he came out of the trees and turned to look back. He gasped.

The view before him was spectacular.

A creek wound its way past the bottom of the hill, to his right and then back to the centre in the middle distance. There were tents all down its length, mostly to the left of the creek, but there were some on the right, too. Smoke curled up from fires scattered among the tents. In the centre and in the distance he could see a range of hills and knew the rightmost one was the one above Jack's tent. People moved like ants in the distance. He couldn't make out Tom's store but knew where it must be, as he could see the town. Tom's store wasn't far from the town, although there were lots of tents along several streets to the left of the creek and going up onto the hill above Jack's, so the town might be bigger than he first thought.

*There might be gold under the tents, too. I wonder how they know there isn't? Or do they pitch their tents where they have already dug for gold?*

Once again, he was intrigued by the search for gold and was no longer sure he'd be able to stick to the bargain. He itched to try his hand at digging. Perhaps he could help Jack for a while next

Sunday, even though he knew they didn't dig on a Sunday. Jack might do it if William offered to help without being paid.

The wind was cold and blowing from the south. He shivered. It was colder now and he suddenly realised that night wasn't far off.

He hurried back down the hill, crossed the river, and found the road back as twilight fell on the valley. Music, singing and laughter accompanied him all the way back to the store. It was well after dark and he was relieved when he saw the lamps outside Tom's store.

"I was getting worried," said Tom as he went through the door. "I'd been working and didn't notice the time."

"I went to the top of the hill. Like you said, it's worth the trip."

"You get to see it all, don't you?"

"How do they know there's not gold under the tents?"

Tom laughed.

"I think you've got the fever, Bill. You just don't know it yet."

William blushed.

"Don't be embarrassed. It happens to everybody. Tell you what, how about we do some digging next Sunday? I've had my eye on a couple of places. Chances are, no one's been there yet."

"What about the store?"

"I'll get Joe to look after it. He'll do it for some tobacco. Would you like to do that?"

William nodded.

*I would love to.*

"All right. You get the supper—I'll finish here. I'm sure you're ready for bed. I don't think you got much sleep last night."

William blushed again.

# CHAPTER 11

# Meeting the Diggers

They were busy all week in the store and Tom was starting to fret that they'd need another delivery of goods soon.

"It's hard choosing what people want," he said to William. "Sure, there's the staples like sugar, salt, flour, and tobacco. People always want those. But the rest? It's always a gamble. Still, I've worked up a list and put it in a letter to send to Scott. I'll get you to take it to the post office tomorrow and it'll go Monday."

The next day, after a hurried lunch, Tom said, "I don't know why it's so busy. Here, take this letter to the post office. Go down the road from here to Jack's, but go to the right, then up the hill when you get to the creek. You'll be on the road to the post office. Well, maybe, not the final road, but you'll see the post office on the top of the hill."

As William left, several more people came into the store. Like Tom had said, things were unusually busy.

He headed down the hill and reached the creek, where he stopped and watched for a few moments. The noise from the cradles, paddlers, pans and dogs was constant. They were all up and down the creek, occupying every available space. There was a shout every now and again as someone exclaimed at a find, a disappointment, or an infringement of their space.

The road forked left and right, so he took the right path. It didn't go far until it crossed the creek and climbed the hill. There were plenty of tents about and his presence was enough to get all the dogs barking. All were tied to something, but it didn't stop them straining hard to reach him, barking loudly and frothing at the mouth.

The road wound its way through mounds and troughs of dirt where it had clearly been dug and piled. It struck William that the ground might have been dug several times. There was some scrub and small trees nearby, but all the substantial trees were at the top of the hill.

He'd learned to look for a flag outside any shop, but there were so many, it made it impossible to locate the post office.

At last, in frustration, he asked a man struggling down the hill with two large buckets of dirt.

The man stopped, put the buckets down and wiped his brow. He was wretchedly thin, covered in dirt, and looked exhausted. The buckets were big canvas bags slung on each end of a pole across his shoulders.

"Aye, it's a rest I've been wantin' anyways," he said. "You not from around here? Everybody here can find the post office."

"No," said William, wondering if it was the right answer.

"What're you doin' here, then?"

"I work in Tom Ballard's shop. Over the other side. He asked me to post a letter."

"Oh, Tom. Good man. You should've said so in the first place. You're nearly there. Keep goin' up the hill. I'll wait 'till you get back. You can carry one of my buckets."

William continued walking and found a tent with a queue out front.

"Is this the post office?" he asked the man at the back of the line.

"Aye, that it be," said the man. "I dunno what's happenin'. Not normally a queue. Mail might've been late and they're still sortin' it. Who knows? They got their own rules."

The queue moved slowly and William wondered how long it would be before he was served.

"You sound like one of us. Where're you from?" asked the man.

William studied the man. He was typical of almost everyone he had seen— dirty, ragged clothes, battered hat, and heavy boots. He looked to be as old as Scott or Tom. It seemed most people were about that age. He looked tired, already worn out, long before his time.

"Ireland," said William.

"Me too," said the man.

"Me too," said a voice behind William. He looked behind him and saw another man, looking just like the man in front.

"Is everyone from Ireland?" asked William.

"Seems so," said the man in front and laughed. It was a pleasant laugh, so much so that it surprised William. The man looked too worn out by life to laugh pleasantly.

"Next!" called a voice from the tent. William couldn't hear the exchange, but the man left empty-handed.

"See you," the man said as he passed William.

William went in and handed the man in the tent his letter.

"What do you want me to do with this," asked the man.

"Why, send it," said William, surprised. "What else would you do?"

"Hasn't got a stamp," said the man.

"What's a stamp?"

"Jesus. Another one. Where're they all comin' from? Not my fault the queue's so long, handlin' these all mornin'. A stamp's what you put on a letter to send it."

"Where do I get one?"

"From me. Costs two pence."

"I don't have any money."

"Then, sod off with your letter and don't come back until you've got a stamp or two pence. Next!"

William stood still, bewildered by what had happened. Tom had asked him to post the letter, but hadn't said anything about money.

*Is this fellow having fun with me?*

The next man stepped in, saw William's confusion and said, "What's up?"

"The man says it costs two pence to send a letter."

"He's right."

"I don't have two pence."

"If you're on the goldfields, you've got two pence."

"Why is that?"

"You'll wash two pence of gold in as many minutes from any of the wash-dirt."

"For Christ's sake!" shouted the postman. "Take your damned debate outside. If you don't want to be served, you can sod off too."

"Keep your shirt on. I'll pay his two pence. Here," he said, handing two pence to the postman who threw the money into a box, put a stamp on the letter and threw it in another box.

William protested, "But I have to repay you. Where will I find you?"

The man laughed.

"Wait for me outside. I won't be long."

William went outside and, true to his word, the man emerged in a few moments, some letters in his hand.

"Which way are yer goin'?" said the man.

"Why, down the hill."

"So am I. Mine's Murphy. Everyone calls me Murph," he said and proffered a hand.

"Bill," said William, shaking the hand firmly. "How can I pay you back?"

Murph laughed.

"Buy me a drink sometime."

They came upon the man that had showed William the way to the post office. William had seen him in the distance but couldn't believe that he'd still be waiting. He was sitting on the ground with his back to them, facing down the hill and sleeping soundly with his back against the bags. Murph laughed again.

"Hey, Patrick," he said, nudging the man with his foot. "Is this gettin' the job done, lyin' here and sleepin'?"

"Oh," said the man. "I didn't mean to fall asleep. There'll be trouble, for sure. I don't know how long I've been out of it. Can't be long. Doesn't take long to post a letter, does it?"

"Depends on where you're postin' it. Takes longer here I think."

"Will you still help me?" Patrick asked of William.

"Aye, and I'll be glad to," said William. He tried to pick up one of the bags and was astonished by its weight.

"It's not full of feathers, is it?" said Murph, once again laughing. It looked like he enjoyed laughing. "C'mon Patrick. I'll take one and Bill'll take the other. You carry my letters."

Patrick took the letters in one hand and his pole in the other. He watched the others load a bag each onto their shoulders.

*It's no wonder he's tired, carrying two of these down the hill.*

They'd taken only a few steps when Patrick said, "I'm not findin' much."

"Nobody's findin' much," said Murph. "Gotta start lookin' elsewhere."

"Where will you look?"

"Dunno. Anyway, if I tell you, you'll look there too."

Patrick looked hurt. Murph laughed again.

"You might be better off at Black Hill," said Murph. "You won't have to carry so far, either."

"I've heard that. This is me, just here," he said, pointing at a cradle by the side of the creek.

"Are you working on your own?" said William.

"Just here, doin' the washin'. My mate's up at the shaft. I'm runnin' late now, so he won't like it. Be wonderin' where I am. I can't leave the dirt, though. If I don't wash it, someone else will."

"We'll wash it for you," said Murph. "Take the bags back and get some more. We'll wait for you, but don't you fall asleep again, or we'll be gone before you get back. Off with you now. Be quick."

"I haven't done this before," said William, once Patrick had scurried away.

"Nothin' to it," said Murph.

"Why're you helping him?"

Murph shrugged.

"There were three of them, workin' different claims about the place, never findin' much. They worked their way all around the top of the hill. People laughed at them, but they always found enough to cover their expenses. Then, one day, not far from the old commissioner's tent, they found payable gold. It was said they'd found over a thousand pounds worth. Tried to stay quiet about it, but couldn't. People came by their tent after dark to congratulate and celebrate. Patrick went and bought some grog. They were passin' it around half the night. When Patrick and his mate woke in the mornin', all they had for their trouble was a headache. The other feller and all their gold had taken off in the night. It was terrible luck. You should be able to rely on your mates. I help him sometimes. Try to make up for it, I suppose."

"Did they find him?"

"Who?"

"The feller that took the gold."

"No. It's easy to lose yourself in Melbourne. Lots of diggers celebratin' there. People there don't care where you got the gold, as long as you spend it with them. C'mon, let's see if he's got anythin'."

Murph showed William how to rock the cradle as he poured the dirt and water into it. A few grains appeared once the dirt was washed away.

"Look, gold! That is gold, isn't it?" shouted William excitedly when he saw it appear.

"Yes, it's gold but not enough to be excited about. There might be enough for a postage stamp. Poor Patrick. He's got to start lookin' somewhere else I think. We'll leave it in the cradle. He won't be too long now and can get it when he comes."

"How long have you been in Ballarat?" asked William.

"About six months. I came after last winter. I'll go soon. It's too hard here in the winter."

"Where do you go?"

"Back to Melbourne. I've done all right here. I've got a wife and kids back there."

"Why don't you bring them here?"

"Here? This is no place for a woman."

"I've seen some here."

"Yes, they're here, all right, but that doesn't make it any place for a woman."

They waited a while longer and Patrick still hadn't returned. Murph walked over to some men who were cradling nearby.

"Can you look after Patrick's cradle? We have to go."

One of the men shrugged.

"That's what we do, anyway. Always chasin' someone away that wants to pinch it. Did you find anythin' for him?"

"Not much. There's a bit there. Some colour. He'll find it when he gets back."

Murph joined William.

"I've got to get back. I expect you do, too. Where's your claim?"

"I work with Tom Ballard."

"Ah. Lucky you. He's a good man."

"Where's your claim?"

"Over by White Flat. Come over some time. Bring Tom. Tell him he owes me two pence."

"Why does Tom owe you two pence? I thought I did."

"There's no way you were postin' that letter for yourself. See you."

Murph walked away, laughing. William laughed too, as he set off along the creek for the road back to the store. He enjoyed watching the men working the cradles as he walked along. Some were doing it on their own. It looked like hard work and on reflection, William was glad that he and Murph had done the task together. He wondered too, what happened to Patrick and why he hadn't returned? It was odd that Patrick's partner would steal his gold, but Murph casually asked the men nearby to watch Patrick's cradle, even though there was gold in it. There was a lot to learn about the diggings.

He found the road easily enough and set off up the hill back to the shop.

"There you are," said Tom as he entered. "I was about to send out a search party. I thought after you left that I hadn't given you any money. I hope you had some of your own."

"No, I didn't. A feller called Murph loaned us the money. Said to tell you that you owe him two pence."

"Murph? Which Murph? There's quite a few Murphs."

"He didn't say. Said he's got a claim over by White Flat. Said to come over sometime and to bring you."

"Ah. That Murph. Doesn't come here anymore. Used to come when he was digging near Specimen Hill."

"Where's that?"

"It's the hill behind the store. Anyway, we'll have to do as he says. It won't do for me to owe anyone. We'll practise poker again tonight, then if you want, we'll join Murph and some of the others for cards next Saturday."

"Do they play for money?"

"They sure do."

"I don't think I'm ready for that yet."

"I agree, but you can watch for a while, then join in when you're ready. You'll enjoy watching. You'll have to be careful though. If anyone's losing, they might blame you for their bad luck. Anyway, it's getting dark outside, so let's shut the shop, have some supper, and play some cards."

CHAPTER 12

# Prospecting

When he heard the sound of Tom alternately whistling and humming, William knew he was awake. He got out of bed and was startled by how cold it was. He joined Tom by the stove.

"You're happy this morning."

"No reason not to be. I'm looking forward to our day prospecting. Joe'll be here soon, so sit yourself down and have some breakfast."

*I'd like a change from chops, bread and tea. It's more than strange that Tom never tires of it.*

They were sipping their tea when Joe called from outside the tent. William let him in.

"We just finished breakfast. I left some for you," said Tom. "We'll be off now."

"Good," said Joe quietly, as though uninterested.

He busied himself at the stove, then sat at the table.

"Are you goin' fer the day?" he called as the others left.

"Yes," said Tom. "Might be dark when we get back."

"Not too late," said Joe. "I'll 'ave to see to the 'orses 'fore dark."

Tom nodded, picked up a musket that was leaning against the wall and they left. William followed Tom around the back of the tent where they collected a billy, shovels, picks and dishes. Tom stuffed a bundle of cloth he carried into the billy.

"Where's the cradle," said William.

"What do you know about cradles?"

"Murph showed me how to use one to get gold."

Tom laughed.

"We'll be panning. It's different. Here, help me carry this stuff."

They each carried a pan, a shovel and a pick.

Tom walked up the hill, the way William had gone on his recent walk.

"Where are we going?" asked William.

"Too hard to explain. Let's just walk and enjoy the sunshine. Winter's coming and warmth'll be gone soon."

They walked in comfortable silence. There were a few other well-dressed people about. William decided they'd be heading to church. He liked Sundays, doing something different, not working in the shop. This particular Sunday was beautiful—a crispness in the air, not a cloud in the sky and no wind to speak of. Their boots crunched on the road and the steady rhythm made it feel like they could walk forever.

It was no surprise to William that they followed his route towards Black Hill. He'd heard Murph tell Patrick that there was gold to be had there.

"You're becoming good at cards," said Tom after a while. "You won't have to wait long before you can join the others in a betting game."

"I'm nervous about it. I don't want to make a fool of myself. Nor do I want to lose money."

"You won't make a fool of yourself. As far as losing goes, just remember to never lose more than you can afford. Also, never chase your losses. You'll only lose more."

They crossed the creek at the bottom of the hill but, instead of climbing it, they followed the creek. It was easy walking along the side and it wasn't long before the tents were left behind them.

"Not far now," said Tom.

"Do you have a claim up here?"

"No. The idea of the claim is that no one else can take your gold. We're only panning, so we'll poke about and see what we find. Of course, if we find some payable gold, then we might stake a claim."

"Does the licence we have allow us to dig?"

"It does, but they won't look for us to have one up here. They're more interested in the diggers back there. I know you didn't bring yours."

"How do you know that?"

"Because I've got it. Just in case. But they won't look here."

"Is it dangerous where we're going?"

"Why?"

"The gun."

"Thought we might be able to shoot something for dinner. Been wanting to try this one out anyway—haven't had it long. Might even get enough for supper. I'm sure you're sick of chops and bread by now."

They walked until they came to another creek and then followed it along. They'd been walking for some time. William's load became heavier and he no longer noticed the crispness in the air. Tom walked without slowing and he had the added burden of the gun. William marvelled at his stamina.

*Must run in the family.*

"Be there soon," said Tom, as though he knew what William was thinking.

It was harder going now. The creek was narrow and heavily wooded, and they had to pick their way around fallen timber and large rocks by the creek. After a while, they came to another smaller creek and they started to climb alongside its course down a hillside. It wasn't flowing, but they did pass pools from time to time.

"Good," said Tom, as he stood for a rest. "There's some water to wash the dirt. I hoped there'd be some. Be a long way to carry the dirt to the other creek for washing."

They climbed for a few more minutes and Tom stopped.

"We'll try here. I'll fill the billy first. Water won't be much good after we're done washing."

He filled the billy and set it by a tree.

William bent down to drink, but Tom stopped him.

"We have no idea what's up stream. You should never drink from a stream that's not running, and be careful even if it is. Here, I'll make some tea. We can have a cuppa before we start. I brought enough tea and sugar."

In no time, he had a fire going and the billy boiled. It was very pleasant sitting by the pool sipping their tea. There was no wind and even though there was a crispness in the air, it was nice to sit after their walk. The sun flitted through the trees as the wind played with their branches. It was as though neither man had a care in the world.

"How do you know there's gold here?" asked William.

Tom laughed.

"I don't, but it's a likely place."

"What makes it a likely place?"

"The gold starts off in a quartz reef. Mostly, you can't see the reefs because they're buried, but over time, a very long time, creeks like this cut through them, the gold leaches out and stays in the creek. It gets caught on mud, or finds its way to the bottom of gravel beds."

"Did you see a reef?"

"No, but there're reefs all about here, so gold's as likely in this creek as anywhere."

"Why hasn't someone else looked here?"

"Too busy down on the flats. They'll get here soon enough. Thought we might beat them to it. C'mon, sitting here won't find gold. I'll show you what to do and you can look, too."

He filled both their pannikins with the remaining tea, threw the rest out and refilled the billy with water.

William was as excited as he'd ever been. Since he'd first learned about the gold, he'd wanted to look for it. His da sending him away, his time on the ship, the journey from Melbourne had all been about what he was about to do right now. He was about to look for gold. With a start, he realised Tom was talking.

"You find a spot like this," said Tom. "See here where the creek has cut into the bank and there's a shale ridge?"

Tom took his shovel and started digging into the dirt beside the creek, near to the edge and put the dirt to one side. He dug for a while and then exclaimed, "Ah, bottom!"

Now he shovelled the dirt from the hole into the dish. When the dish was about half full he went to the creek, dunked the dish in the water, and put in enough to cover the dirt. He washed mud and dirt off the rocks, checked them briefly, and threw them away.

"Just checking for gold. You sometimes get quartz pieces with gold in them."

Once he removed most of the big stones, he squatted by the creek, turned the dish such that the little groove was away from him and started to swirl the dirt in the dish, allowing some of it to wash out over the front edge.

"So now I'm throwing out the rubbish. The gold will fall to the bottom of the dish. Small pieces will get caught in the groove. If you see them there, you swirl them back into the dish."

Finally, he stood and swirled the remaining dirt away from the front of the dish.

"Let's have a look," he said.

William peered over his shoulder.

There at the front of the dish, like a shower of stars, was a swirl of gold.

William couldn't contain his joy.

"Gold!" he shouted. "We found gold!"

Birds nearby fled squawking from the trees.

Tom laughed and shook his head.

"There's not much. I thought we'd have found more. I'd like to give you a real reason to shout. Let's go a bit further up."

He took some cloth from his pocket and washed the gold into it, folded it and put it back in his pocket. He then refilled the hole, patted it down and made it look like no one had been there.

"No point in letting anyone else know we've been here."

They picked up their things and climbed a little higher up the creek. They hadn't gone far when Tom stopped.

"This is a better place, anyway," he said. "You see the line of shale across the creek? We'll dig on the high side of that."

"What's shale?"

"It's that grey-looking flaky rock."

They put their things down and William picked up his dish.

"Not yet," said Tom. "We know there's gold, but we're still looking for a good spot. Although, I'm willing to bet a week's wages we've found one here."

Once again he dug at the side of the creek and William stood by, struggling to contain his excitement and eager to contribute.

"Oh, Bill. I've won that bet. I can see gold."

William sensed Tom's excitement and his whole body started to tingle. He hopped from foot to foot.

"Can I dig too?" he nearly shouted.

'Wait. You'll lose it in the creek if you don't do it right. So, watch me again, then I'll help you to do it, then you're on your own. It's too hard to find to waste it."

Tom once again half-filled his dish and washed it in the creek.

"Oh, Bill. Look at this!" he exclaimed, standing up.

William looked over his shoulder. He shivered. There was about a half a pannikin of gold in the dish. More gold than gravel. More gold than William had ever seen. Riches in a creek. There for the taking. He and Tom were rich.

"How much is it worth?" he asked, once again struggling to contain his excitement.

"Two, maybe three pounds. C'mon, I'll show you. We'll do better with both of us working. You take the other side of the creek."

William grabbed his shovel and excitedly shovelled dirt into his pan.

"No, no," said Tom. "There's no gold at the surface. It's heavier and falls to the bottom, so you either have to find the bottom, or see the gold as you dig. So, dig carefully now."

William then went to the other extreme, scratching at the surface and peering intently at the dirt.

Tom laughed.

"Let me show you again."

He took his shovel and started digging near the edge of the creek, against the shale.

"Look," he said after a few minutes. "You can see the gold. Start washing what you get now. Wash everything you get from the hole until you get to the bottom. Don't put too much in your pan until you get the hang of it."

William put a shovelful into the pan.

"That'll do," said Tom. "Wash that."

William started washing the dirt vigorously.

"Whoa," said Tom. "Take it easy. You'll wash the gold out. You need to work the dish so the gold gets a chance to fall to the bottom. Then, you scrape the dirt away from the top. Repeat that process a few times, but keep looking in the dish for the gold and make sure you don't push it out."

William went more slowly and it wasn't long before he saw gold in his dish, like he'd seen in Tom's. He was so excited he couldn't stop laughing.

"What do we do with it?"

"When?"

"Now."

"Oh, I've put the cloth over there. I'll show you how to wash the gold into it."

Tom had placed the cloth in a depression on the ground. He put some water in William's dish and washed the gold into the cloth. The water went through and the gold stayed behind.

"C'mon, let's work the two sides for a while. Don't rush, there's plenty there and we don't want to waste it. Then, we'll stop and have a cuppa and something to eat and head home."

"But there'll still be gold here, won't there?"

"More than likely, but we need time to get home before dark."

"Shall we stake a claim?"

"No point. That'll only alert others to what we have found and anyway, you only get eight foot by eight foot and you and I are working on more than that now. No, we'll gamble that no one else finds it. We'll fix it up as best we can so no one else finds it and it'll be our secret."

"Can we come back tomorrow?"

Tom laughed.

"Bill, we've got the shop to look after."

"But, we'll make more money here."

"Here'll be gone in the blink of an eye, Bill. The shop'll be there as long as they are finding gold in these hills. We can come back a few times but sooner or later, others'll find it and we'll be squeezed out. We'll have some fun for a while and it'll be good pocket money. They won't be surprised when we sell it, because people will think it comes from the store."

"How do we know what's yours and mine? We've put it all in the same place."

Tom laughed again.

"We're partners, Bill. Half each is how it works. Do half the work each, take half the gold each.. You all right with that?"

"Of course I'm all right with that. I just didn't know."

"That's all right. You dig that side and I'll dig this and we'll stop in about an hour."

William set to work with a will and quickly learned how to get the gold to settle. He loved digging for the gold. It was like being back home, digging in the garden for money, not to plant vegetables. He laughed to himself when he thought what his ma and da would think now. Here he was digging for, and finding, gold. It was so easy to make money. He didn't want to work in the shop anymore. Now all he wanted to do was dig for gold.

The pile on the cloth grew and grew, each man contributing about the same amount.

At one stage, Tom looked over as William washed more gold into the pile.

"You're a quick learner, Bill."

Then he looked up at the sky.

"We need to finish up soon. We'll have a cuppa first, then head back."

He looked at their pile of gold.

"Might just fit in the billy. That's a good day's work. Make that one your last dish."

William was disappointed to stop. He wanted to dig and dig. He was sure there was more gold and he didn't want to leave it for someone else.

"You get the billy going," said Tom. "I'll clean up so it looks like we haven't been here. Bit of rain will help. Shouldn't be too long before there's some. It normally rains every few days this time of year."

"Won't the rain wash the gold away?"

"If there's not too much, it'll do the opposite. It'll concentrate more of it where we've been digging. Of course, if there's a lot of water, it'll scour the gold out."

William got the fire going, boiled the billy and made some tea. Tom had said there was some food, but William hadn't seen any.

"Did you bring any food?" he asked.

"Yes, some bread and some chops. I had them wrapped in the cloth we're using for the gold. I put them on that rock over there."

He pointed at an empty rock.

"Well, it was there. I guess the birds've pinched it while we were too busy digging. It'll be a hungry walk home."

"Can we shoot something?"

"Might be able to on the way home, but that won't help us now. We can have a cuppa though, then we'd better be going. I suppose I should've hidden it. It's not as though it hasn't happened before."

They finished their tea and Tom threw out what was left. He tied the corners of the cloth together and stuffed the bundle into the billy.

"That's a good day's work," he said. "It'll get heavy as we lug it home."

He stopped and looked about.

"Mark the spot in your memory," he said. "See that big tree? It's got an unusual fork. And that big rock? Looks like someone's head."

William looked where they'd been working. Tom had done a good job of concealing it.

They set off down the creek and William realised that, although there was some sun left, they'd be pushing it to get home before dark.

"We'd better move quickly," said Tom. "Maybe we shouldn't have stayed for that cuppa."

As they came out of the creek at the bottom of the hill, they saw a mob of kangaroos grazing.

"Look," whispered William. "Shall we shoot one?"

"We can," said Tom. "But then we'll have that to carry too."

"What about a little one?"

"All right," said Tom. "But you'll have to carry it. That all right with you?"

"That's all right with me."

"You should have told me you're sick of chops. These don't taste much different, but maybe we can make a pie. Even get some vegetables."

The kangaroos either continued eating or stood and watched, their ears flicking about. None of them were very big, so William's idea of shooting a small one still gave Tom a good choice. Tom primed and readied the gun. He knelt and took aim. The kangaroos still paid them scant attention, more occupied with eating than with the two intruders.

Tom pulled the trigger. There was a loud boom and large puff of smoke. All the kangaroos hopped away.

"Hmm," said Tom. "I suppose I should have practised first. It must be firing high. Just a minute."

Tom reprimed the gun, knelt, and took aim at a tree nearby. He pulled the trigger. Once again there was a boom and a puff of white smoke rose in the sky. There was a splat sound and pieces of bark flew from the tree.

"Like I thought—high. I'll have to adjust the sight. No time to do that now. He was a lucky kangaroo and that's for sure. C'mon Bill, we might even need to run. I don't want to be caught out here after dark."

"Is it dangerous?"

"We might fall down a mine shaft and there's plenty of those about."

They picked up their gear and headed off quickly. It was almost dark when they crossed the creek below the Black Hill.

"We'll be all right once we're on the road," said Tom. "Pity there's no moon tonight."

Finally, they arrived back at the store.

"Did you find anythin'?" Joe asked.

"Just some colour. Spent all day fossicking."

"Where did you go?"

"Left of Black Hill."

"Why so late?"

"Did a bit of shooting. Tried my new gun."

"I see you don't have anythin'. Not like you to miss."

"New gun's shooting high. I'll need to fix it."

"All right," said Joe. "I've done nothin' all day, but I'm ready to see to the 'orses and then for bed, so I'll be off. I've left you some supper."

"Thanks, Joe. Thanks for minding the store."

"That's all right," said Joe, stopping in the doorway. "Anyone asked me, I said you'd gone off to do some huntin' and show Bill around."

"Thanks, Joe. That was the right answer."

"Me, on the other hand, I reckon you got more than colour in one of those gullies to the right of Black Hill, maybe along Little Bendigo Creek somewhere. Doesn't matter to me, my diggin' days are long over. But if you do take a trick, don't forget your old mate Joe, back here at the store, makin' it possible. 'Night."

Joe pulled the door shut behind him and William looked at Tom in astonishment. They both burst out laughing.

"That deserves a whisky," said Tom.

# CHAPTER 13

# Card Night

The week went quickly and it was Saturday before they knew it. Tom hadn't talked about the cards again all week and William hoped he hadn't forgotten.

The cards were exciting but more than anything, he wanted to go back for more gold.

William reordered and repacked some goods while Tom worked on the accounts.

Tom looked up and said, "I haven't forgotten about the cards. Joe will be here soon. I want to get to Murph's before dark. I know he's on White Flat, but we'll need to find him and we can't do that in the dark."

Joe poked his head through the door.

"You fellers ready to go? I've seen to the 'orses. You can leave whenever you want."

"Good, good," said Tom. "I'll only be a few moments. You nearly ready, Bill?"

"Like you, only a few moments."

As they were about to leave, Tom said, "You'll need a coat. It'll be cold on the way back. You can borrow one of mine. We're about the same size. I'll get Scott to bring you one with the next shipment. We should sell them here, anyway. Don't know why we don't."

His spare clothes hung from nails on a corner post. He fetched a coat for William.

"Don't lose it. There's plenty out there that'll steal that from you given half a chance. Have you got your pipe?"

William flushed.

"I don't like it that much."

"You'll get used to it and you'll need it after the cards when they sit around and talk. Bring it. They'll think you odd if you don't have it."

Once again, as they were about to leave, Tom called to Joe.

"Sleep here, Joe. Not sure when we'll be back."

"That's all right by me," Joe replied.

They set off down the road. There was still plenty of daylight though fires were already going, anticipating a cool night. The ever-present smell wafted on the breeze, and there was the sound of music and laughter. A few people were out walking, going for a drink or to someone's tent, like Tom and William.

When the creek appeared they sloshed through it but took another road to the right, not the one that William had taken to go to the post office. The road skirted around the hill. There were tents all about, and men still puddling and cradling at the creek.

"They never stop," said Tom. "They'll work the shafts at night too, if they can."

"Can we go digging again tomorrow?"

"I know you enjoyed that," said Tom, laughing. "But we can't. Mike might be here with the shipment that I ordered. He usually comes on a Sunday, so we have time to unload it."

"I was hoping..."

"I know, I know. The gold's not going anywhere unless someone else finds it, and that's not likely. So, it'll still be there when we get another chance to go. Besides, you may not feel like going first thing."

"Why not?"

"You might enjoy yourself too much at Murph's."

They walked on, William struggling to control his disappointment.

Stopping to ask from time to time, they eventually found Murph's tent. It was bigger than those nearby, but of the same post and canvas construction. There were half a dozen diggers sitting on short upturned logs around the fire in front of tent.

Murph's face lit up in a huge smile when he saw them.

"Now, would you look at what the tide's washed in? I thought at first to reach for my gun. I figured you two for a couple of thieves."

He leapt to his feet and hurried forward to grip Tom's hand.

"Tom, it's been too long."

"That's your fault," said Tom. "I'm still in the store. Haven't gone anywhere and don't plan to."

"Aye. You're right enough. And Bill, it's good to see you, too."

He shook William's hand.

"Now, here's some fellers you need to meet. Tom, you might know everyone already."

"I do," said Tom and waved.

None of the men sitting on the logs moved. The two with their backs to the visitors made a half-hearted attempt to turn. It was as though the newcomers were intruders to the conversation.

"Now, now, boys," said Murph. "We can at least be hospitable. You all know Tom and he's a ring-in, but he's a right sort too. This is Bill and he works with Tom. Like us, he's a Tipperary lad."

"Why didn't you say so?" said one of the men, turning to face them.

*What's going on here? Why are they so hostile?*

The men all looked tired and worn. Some were smoking but all were dirty.

"C'mon, boys, make some room," said Murph. A couple of the men shuffled along and made space for Tom and William.

"We were talking about the licences," said Murph. "It's enough to make your blood boil."

The men all nodded and muttered under their breath.

"There'll be trouble, mark my words," said one.

"There's already been trouble at some of the other diggin's," said another. "Don't know what's wrong with the fellers here. It can't go on. The fee is bad enough, but ridin' through, chasin' people, hurtin' some folk is too much. And the traps? What a miserable lot they are. Chainin' people up and finin' 'em. I didn't come all this way just to pay to get my arse kicked every day. They do it for free back home."

"Calm down, Denis. Gettin' all angry won't do any good," said Murph. "What about the cards? That'll take your minds off it."

"I don't need my mind taken off it," said Denis. "I want other people's minds on it. Enough of us get together, they have to listen."

"Who's for cards?" said Murph.

"Dunno why else we came 'ere," said a voice.

"Too right," said another. "Why, with Tom 'ere, we don't have to dig for gold. We can take 'is."

A few laughed.

"You can try," said Murph. "The only way I can get money from Tom is to lend it to him."

"I haven't forgotten," said Tom. "I was hoping to play you for double or nothing."

"I'm game if you are," said Murph, laughing.

Murph laughed more than anyone William had met.

"And what about you, Bill? Are you in?" asked Murph.

William didn't know what to say. He was nervous about playing, but didn't want to look like a coward, either.

"I told him he can watch," said Tom.

"If he wants," said Murph.

"He's not watchin' anywhere near me," said Denis.

"Nor me," said another. "It's bad luck."

"He'll sit behind me," said Tom.

"C'mon then, everyone. Let's get set up inside. It'll be too cold out here soon anyway. Almost time to go back to Melbourne," said Murph, looking at the sky.

They set the logs up on the dirt floor around the table inside the tent. Murph slung a blanket across the table. Almost as soon as he did, bottles of whisky and grog appeared, along with a variety of drinking vessels—pannikins, glasses, cut-off bottles.

"This one's for Bill and me," said Tom, pulling a bottle from his pocket and putting it on the table. He pulled two glasses from his other pocket and winked at William.

Denis sat back on his stump, looked from Tom to William and back again.

"Bill can join us in the cards if he wants."

"Not yet," said Tom. "He'll tell us when he's ready."

"As you wish," said Denis, smiling.

Each man had a pile of matches in front of him. William was confused—he thought Tom had said they played for money.

Murph was on the opposite side of the table from Tom. He looked at William and smiled.

"I can see you confused by these brave men gambling for matchsticks," he said, laughing. "Each stick is an ounce of gold. Everyone starts off with ten sticks. If you lose all your sticks, that's it for you for the night. At the end of the night, we count our sticks. If you have less than ten, you put gold in the centre to cover it. If you have more than ten, you take gold out. Ante, bet and raise are always one stick. Makes it easy to work out what's going on. Better for these simple folk is the real reason."

"Nah. What it really means is that you can't lose too much, it doesn't get too serious and you can have whisky at the same time," said a balding, bearded man to Murph's left. "Anyway, what's the gold for if you can't enjoy it?"

"Can't take it with you, John," said Tom.

"You can't? Who told you that?" said John.

"My mother," said Tom.

"You've got a mother?" asked the man to Tom's right.

"He's got a mother, just doesn't have a father. Well, one that he knows, anyway," said the man between Denis and Tom.

"It's not going to work, Andrew," said Tom.

"What's not going to work?" asked William without thinking.

"They're trying to upset me, put me off my cards," said Tom.

"Enough of this," said Murph. "Let's get to the game. I'll deal."

Murph dealt the hand.

William could see Tom's cards, but not those of anyone else. It didn't matter. He studied Tom's, trying to work out what Tom would do. Then, he realised that the players opposite Tom were watching him to see if they could judge Tom's cards. William remembered what Tom had taught him.

"Some players can't keep emotion from their faces and the other players will try to read their face and get an idea of their cards."

At one point, he saw Murph smiling as though he had realised how hard William was trying not to show emotion and give Tom's hand away.

Once the game was underway, the players said nothing other than what was necessary to keep the game moving.

They played quickly. The dealing, the calls, the hands, the winning and the losing all took place at speed. Most of the players ignored their drinks. Glasses would be untouched for several hands. William thought he was improving. Most often, he would have made the same decision as Tom. Player's piles of sticks grew larger and smaller by turn.

Then Martin, to Tom's right, said, "I'm done. You fellers are too good. You want to take my place, Bill?"

William shook his head. He wanted to talk with Tom first about some of the things he'd done. He knew he still had a lot to learn. Also, he hadn't brought any gold with him either, so couldn't pay if he lost.

Tom said, "Go on, Bill. I brought enough gold for us both. You can't lose more than ten ounces."

"All right," he said, so nervous he could hardly speak.

He took Martin's seat at the table and Martin took his.

"That's not going to work, Martin," said Tom. "I don't want you learning my tricks."

"You're right," said Martin. "Wasn't thinking."

He took his whisky and stood by the fireplace, taking out his pipe and starting to fuss with it.

"Only a few hands left anyway," said Murph. "I'm almost done playing and would like to enjoy some whisky and a pipe. And I want to hear some of Andrew's stories. You'll like 'em, Bill. Tells a good story, Andrew does."

"It's just as well I can tell a story," said Andrew, pointing to his diminishing pile of matches. "Sure can't play cards."

Tom put ten matches in front of William, winked at him, and the game started again. William was so nervous his palms were sweating and his hands shook. His voice trembled as he responded in turn.

He lost three sticks on the first hand and won two on the second.

"Last hand," said Murph, pointing at his three sticks remaining. "I'm nearly done."

"Who put you in charge?" said Denis, pointing at his large pile of sticks.

"My tent, my rules. Besides, you've won enough."

"You can never win enough," said Andrew.

William had settled down, and wasn't feeling anywhere near so nervous. More than anything, he was glad he'd been pushed into the game.

Andrew, Murph and John folded early. It left Denis, Thomas, William and Tom, who had each put in a stick.

William had two kings, three hearts, and no chance of a straight.

Denis took three cards, Thomas two, William three and Tom none.

Tom taking none was a problem. He wished he'd known Tom would do that. Then he realised. Of course Tom would take none. He had nothing, but wanted to appear like he had everything.

William looked at his new cards. He'd got two more kings. He couldn't believe his luck.

Denis folded. Thomas put in a stick, then another one. William matched him with two, and Tom folded.

It was up to Thomas. He stared at William as though he wanted a nervous twitch, or a bead of perspiration to guide him.

William loved it. He stared back. Thomas drummed his fingers on the table. Then he ran a finger around his collar. Thomas was more nervous than William was. He must have thought William, as a new chum, would be easy to read.

"All right," said Thomas and advanced another stick.

"I'll call," said William and matched it.

They put their cards on the table.

William had four of a kind and Thomas, two pair.

"Well done, Bill," said Murph. "C'mon fellers, we're done. Let's settle up and get down to the serious business."

Thomas threw Murph a dark look as though to admonish him for putting his support elsewhere.

William had learnt how to play the game, and had won against a seasoned player—he was elated.

The men settled their bets according to their matches. William had nothing into which he could put his winnings so Martin, who had lost his stake, gave William his piece of cloth. Denis was the big winner of the night and couldn't keep the smile off his face.

Murph put some more wood on the fire and took the blanket off the table, and the men settled in with their whisky and pipes.

"All right, Andrew," said Murph. "Let's hear it. And it better be good after what I said to Bill here."

# CHAPTER 14

# Andrew's Story

Andrew filled his glass with whisky and stoked his pipe. He was tall and well-built with receding hair, twinkling eyes and a stern face. His beard was white, like some of the other men. Unusually, he had a collar and tie—though it was hard to see behind his beard. It appeared Andrew liked to dress for Saturday night.

William knew almost nothing about him, but wanted to know more. Andrew looked like an interesting man. He had a soft voice, which suggested he came from the south of Ireland.

"This story begins not that long ago in Melbourne. A n'er do well from England, a convict, arrived on these shores about ten years ago. In spite of the fact he was a convict, he was well educated, could read and write and was quite a hand at numbers. He'd been caught embezzling his employer and was sent to Australia for his trouble.

"He served his time in Van Diemen's Land, where he charmed all who met him. He was a handsome man with a happy disposition and was hard to dislike. Guards and soldiers who couldn't write would seek his help to write letters home and they were always sure of his discretion. No word of what was written was ever told to anyone else. It's more than passing strange that a man with a criminal background would be so thoughtful.

"When he was released, he signed on as crew and sailed to Melbourne. He wasn't much good as a sailor and they were pleased to see the last of him when the ship landed. Some people who knew him said he might have deliberately made a mess of being a sailor because it made it easier to leave the ship.

"He did some work around town, being very careful, as anything he did against the law would land him back in gaol. Finally, he found a job in a bank after the gold rush started. The bank failed to do their usual checks because it was so hard to find staff, with so many people in the goldfields, and him being so good with numbers. The bank couldn't believe their luck to find someone so gifted.

"They say that once a criminal, always a criminal and the man in our story proved the saying. At first he stole only small amounts, but temptation was too frequent and money too easy so, after a time, he'd stolen a substantial sum.

"How he stole the money required a good knowledge of the bank's procedures, but he was good with money and at first, if they didn't look too hard, there was no reason they would ever discover what he had done.

"Nonetheless, he'd made a mess of it because he took too much and it was only a matter of time before he was discovered.

"You can imagine it was difficult for him. Not because he'd fallen victim to his weakness, but because he feared he was now certain to go back to gaol.

"One night as he was heading home, he happened upon a chequebook in the street, lost by some person. The book belonged to another bank, so it was the perfect opportunity to settle his debts and leave town. Of course, it was consolidating a number of smaller debts into one large one, so the total amount stolen was still the same. The important thing was that the smaller debts would be cleared.

"A few of you are looking at me strangely. 'What's a chequebook?' I hear you ask."

William had no idea what a chequebook was and judging by the looks on the faces of those around him, most of the other men didn't either. He saw Andrew smile at him as though he understood what William was thinking. Andrew's face had a soft, kindly look and William guessed he was a good friend to many of the men in the diggings. Andrew leant forward slightly, as though to take his listeners into his confidence, and continued his story.

"For those of you who don't know and for those of you whose memories need to be refreshed, a cheque is used in place of money and a chequebook is a bundle of cheques. A man who has money in the bank can be given some cheques by the bank and can write a cheque up to the value of that amount. The person receiving the cheque will be given the amount for which the cheque is written upon its presentation to the issuing bank. The cheque is validated by the owner's signature. The bank will not honour a cheque without the correct signature.

"Most holders of chequebooks will write inside the book the total amount of their holding and reduce that amount for each cheque they write, so our man even knew how much he could steal.

"He knew that any signature he put on the cheque would not pass muster when the cheque was presented to the owning bank. However, any messy, illegible signature would do on a cheque which he could use in his own bank to cover his thefts. His knowledge of the procedures of his own bank told him it would be unlikely the bank would ever discover who had found the book and forged the cheque.

"He was so excited about finding a way out of his troubles, he decided to go to the pub and have a few whiskies to celebrate. As luck would have it, there were a few friends there and he decided he would be churlish to not invite them to join him.

"They, of course, were delighted to have some drinks on someone else's account and they all celebrated far into the night.

"When it came time to pay, he was well short of the money needed. Still, he had the chequebook and, without thinking, wrote out a cheque for the amount, signing a false name. The publican took the cheque without question.

"He awoke in a state of panic the next morning. He'd not intended to use the cheques other than to clear his own debts, and in so doing he'd be able to hide how the cheque was used, at least for long enough for him to get away.

"Now, under the influence of drink, he'd made a mistake. The bank would dishonour the cheque, the publican would be out of pocket and would come looking for him to make good the debt. He was running out of time before the bad cheque was presented. Of course, it would take a few days for the cheque to be presented to the issuing bank, so if he cleared his debts that very day and hid what he'd done in the bank's procedures, then it was only one forged cheque for which he was accountable.

"Of course, now he'd have to resign from the bank. The publican knew where he worked, and would tell the police. They'd come looking for him and it would come to light that he was a convict. Still, it would be easy to resign. He would tell them he was going to the goldfields. They'd believe him. Everyone was going to the goldfields. It wasn't that large a sum of money for the publican. He doubted the police would follow him to the gold-fields, even if he did go there.

"Still, he had made a mess of it. He could have cleared his debts, stayed at the bank and not been found out. He decided to never drink alcohol again.

"He went to the bank as usual, used another forged cheque to clear his previous thefts, and hid as best he could what he'd done. He resigned and left the bank that day.

"You can imagine his excitement. He was confident he'd got away not only with the bank's money, but also with the forged cheque. He decided that one last drink could do no harm. Why, his friends might be at the pub and he could have a farewell drink with them. He reminded himself to be careful and not to say too much. It wouldn't do to tell anyone he was about to leave.

"He'd hardly stepped into the pub when there was a shout, 'That's him!' He was startled to be accosted by two large policemen and confronted by an angry publican.

"It turned out the publican had been the victim of fraud previously where a patron had paid for his drink with a bad cheque. Being familiar with the process, the publican hurried the cheque to the bank the very next morning and it was refused on the basis of a false signature.

"The police, when informed by the publican of the crime, had asserted that the man would not be so foolish as to return to the pub the next night but eventually agreed to watch for him after the publican offered them free whisky while they waited. If our man had not gone to the pub, or had indeed gone later when the police would have been the worse for the free whisky, he may indeed have escaped capture. The police hurried him to the lock-up, left him there in a cell and returned to the pub to continue their enjoyment of the publican's hospitality. As it turned out, their job done, the whisky was no longer free.

"Our man was left to do some quick thinking. They didn't know who he was, nor about his record. He could give them a false name, spend some time at His Majesty's pleasure, then go to the goldfields as planned. The matter would be dealt with in the morning, so there was little chance he would be found out.

"The next morning, two still-drunk policemen ushered him into the police court.

"'Who's this man? What's this matter?' asked the magistrate. 'I have no brief for this matter.'

"'No, Your Honour,' said the prosecutor. 'The matter has been brought to our attention this morning by Mr Weeds, the publican. He wanted the matter dealt with as soon as possible, hoping for restitution of his money.'

"'What money?'

"'It seems the prisoner uttered a forged cheque in payment for an evening with friends at Mr Weed's establishment.'

"'Indeed. And, what's the prisoner's name?'

"'We don't know, Your Honour.'

"'You don't know? A person is brought into my court to face charges and you don't know his name? This court is not a joke and I'll not have you treat it as such. Mr Weeds, what's the name of this person whom you believe to have wronged you?'

"'I don't know, Your Honour.'

"Our man remains silent but with every passing moment, things do appear to be better for him.

"'All right,' said the magistrate. 'You, what's your name?'

"The court turned to look at our man.

"'Michael Pennyweather, Your Honour.'

"'Mr Weeds here said you gave him a false cheque. What do you have to say for yourself?'

"Our man leaned forward in the dock. He put on his most serious and self-righteous face, smoothed his hair back and looked the magistrate in the eye.

"'Your Honour, I would firstly like to apologise for my appearance. I was not permitted to prepare myself as one would deem appropriate. This is a serious charge, but one of which I am not guilty. If Your Honour has the time, I would like to appraise him of the incidents that frame this misunderstanding.'

"'Of course, of course, Mr Pennyweather. Get on with it.'

"'Well, Your Honour, I am a man of some means and in possession of several chequebooks, one of which I found by chance on the street on the evening that I went to Mr Weed's establishment. It was my intention to return the book to the issuing bank on the following morning, to be restored to its rightful owner. However, as matters transpired, I incorrectly used that book to pay Mr Weeds for his services. Had I used the correct book, I would not be here today. I would also have preferred if Mr Weeds had drawn the matter to my attention. I could have settled the matter quickly and easily without wasting the court's time.'

"'Well, Weeds. What do you say to that?'

"The publican stood, his mouth opening and closing but no sound forthcoming.

'Mr Pennyweather,' said the magistrate. 'I think Mr Weeds agrees with you. Mr Weeds, what is the amount of the debt?'

"Weeds recovered his voice. 'Fifteen pounds, three shilling and sixpence, Your Honour.'

"'Well, Mr Pennyweather. Can you settle that amount with Mr Weeds?'

"'I certainly can, Your Honour. But it is rather a large sum. Would the court agree to the matter being settled by cheque?' The last statement was accompanied by a wide and winning smile."

Andrew smiled and reached for his pipe to show that his story was finished.

The group all laughed heartily, stoked their pipes and replenished their whiskies.

Many of the words were lost on William. He understood the story, of course. For the first time in his life, he really wished he had spent more time at school. His mother had helped a lot with his speech, but the sound of Andrew talking was from another world. He wondered if all the men at the table understood. He looked around and realised that many were like him—they didn't know all the words either. How could he learn them and sound like Andrew?

He and Tom stayed on for a few more hours enjoying some more storytelling, and even some songs. Some of the men told poems and some sang. A lot more whiskies were drunk, and many more pipes smoked. William loved the evening—the company of the men, the cards, the stories, the singing, the drink, and the smoking.

It wasn't until late in the evening that the talk returned to the goldfields. The men were angry about the conditions and alternately counselled each other to be calm, or to take action. All agreed there would be trouble.

Nevertheless, as far as William was concerned, whatever would happen, whatever had happened, whatever the price to get there—Australia was better than Ireland.

CHAPTER 15

# The Morning After

His head the next morning told him that he'd had way too good a time the night before. Tom was right—he didn't feel like digging. In fact, he didn't feel like doing anything. He didn't remember leaving Murph's, much less the journey back to the store.

Tom was silent as they prepared breakfast. They both stumbled about, getting their own. William worried that he'd done something and upset Tom. He didn't know how to ask without telling Tom he had no memory of the trip home.

Finally, he had to know.

"Thank you for the evening at Murph's. I don't remember much about the trip home."

Tom gave him a slight smile.

"Don't thank me. Thank God we got home safely. I don't remember a thing about it. Joe says he came and got us. Said he was worried when we didn't come back. He heard some shots fired late in the evening and thought it might be to do with us. Hitched up a wagon and came looking."

"What about the store?"

"Left it. I told him someone might have known we were out and fired the shots to get him to leave. Said he hadn't thought of that. I told him not to worry. I was glad he came."

"Where is he?"

"Gone. Left early. Told me all about it before he left. You were sleeping, so we didn't wake you. Joe said he didn't want to go without saying goodbye to you. Said you slept with your head on his shoulder all the way back. He thought he might be able to make more of it."

William flushed with embarrassment.

Tom tried to laugh.

"Oh, that hurts," he said. "Don't worry. He probably made it up. They'll do that when you're too drunk to remember."

"Did he really come and get us?"

"Dunno. He might have made that up too."

William went out of the store, around the back, and threw up behind a tree. He didn't know you could feel so sick and still be alive. He washed up behind the store and felt a little better. Once again, it was a beautiful morning. The ground was hard and cold underfoot, so there had probably been a frost the previous evening. The air was crisp with just a gentle breeze and a hint of the constant smell from the town. William decided he was just growing accustomed to it. He marvelled that even with winter coming, there was no change to the appearance of the trees. They didn't lose their leaves like they did back in Ireland. He sat on a stump to enjoy the moment, and to give his thumping head a rest.

There was a shout from the front of the store.

"Is there anyone here?"

William walked around the front. There was Mike with a loaded dray.

"Morning," said William. Mike was startled. He hadn't expected someone to come from behind the tent.

"Where's Tom?"

"Inside. At least, he was a few moments ago."

A stranger appeared from the tent. It was William's turn to be startled.

"This is Jake," said Mike. "Jake, this is Bill."

"Is it catchin'?" said Jake, looking at William.

"Is what catching?" asked William.

"What you and Tom have got. You both look horrible."

Jake looked genuinely concerned. So much so that William couldn't help laughing.

Jake looked affronted.

"Just askin'," he said.

"Well," said William. "As far as I know, you can only catch it from a bottle or a pipe. But whatever it is, it's no good and I'll be glad when it's gone."

Tom appeared in the doorway.

"I see what you mean, Jake," said Mike. "Just what the hell have you two been up to?"

"It's a long story, Mike. I'll tell you over a whisky tonight."

At the mention of whisky, William thought he might be sick again.

They spent the rest of the day unloading the goods and rearranging the store. William was glad of the work. It took his mind off being sick and by the time the job was done, he actually thought he'd enjoy another whisky.

Mike took the horses and the dray to Joe's.

"How's Joe?" asked Tom when he returned.

"Why?" said Mike.

"Did he say anything about last night?"

"Why would he? What did you fellers get up to last night? And why would Joe talk about it?"

"No matter," said Tom. "Let's have some supper. We can talk about it after that."

Once they finished supper, Tom proposed a whisky and cards.

Mike and William were keen, Jake not so much. He didn't like cards much, he said—didn't like losing money and liked even less making a fool of himself.

Tom told him not to worry. They'd play for matches and Jake could fold as often as he wanted. Mike turned out to be a good player. They had an enjoyable time with none of the excesses of the previous evening. Nevertheless, William was pleased when the day ended and he could get some much-needed sleep.

Mike and Jake left early the next day.

The store opened and they were busy selling the newly arrived goods. It was always like that—the customers always knew when there was a delivery.

Tom and William settled into an easy life—cards on Saturday, sometimes as excessive as that first night. Then on Sundays, it was back to their gully to dig for gold. It was a good life, lived against the background of the frustration of the diggers with the authorities

There were often tales of physical confrontation between the diggers and the police, of diggers being harassed and locked up overnight for no reason, or to settle petty scores. For all its wealth and opportunity, for most diggers, the goldfields were generally neither happy nor lucrative.

But William loved it—the cards, the whisky, the companionship, and the gold.

# CHAPTER 16

# Scott Comes Back

One day Tom announced that Scott would be there soon and would swap with Tom, who would go back to their Melbourne property over winter. Scott would take his place for a few months. Many of the miners had gone back to Melbourne, believing the days too short and too cold to make for effective digging. It was only those who had nowhere else to go, or were zealous about working claims in spite of the miserable conditions, who stayed.

William didn't know how Scott's being there would affect him or his job, nor did he know how to ask Tom. He decided he'd just have to wait and see.

Scott didn't come until a few weeks later. It was an awkward goodbye with Tom. They'd been together for several months and there was no doubt that Tom would be back, so it wasn't really goodbye forever, like William had done before. Still, William was more worried about saying welcome to Scott than he was saying goodbye to Tom.

He needn't have worried. Scott was clearly looking forward to his time in the goldfields and threw himself into the shop, the cards and the prospecting. Some of the card players had already gone back to Melbourne, so there were fewer players, but no less fun. The days were shorter and much colder, but it didn't stop Scott taking time off to prospect. They'd often borrow horses from Joe to speed things up. Joe obviously liked Scott and would often come around for supper or a whisky. He never argued about minding the store, or lending Scott the horses. After a few weeks, William decided that Scott was as good a companion as Tom, if not better. He wasn't as good at finding the gold but riding the horses made the task much easier, and William loved the animals.

William was stiff and sore at first but, under Scott's direction, he quickly improved as a horseman.

It surprised William that the store continued to thrive despite the fact that so many of the diggers had gone to Melbourne for the winter.

"Always be grateful for the hardy souls," Scott had said once. "We'd be lost without them."

They were sitting in front of the fire one night after a long, hard day in the store, enjoying a whisky and companionable silence. Scott had fashioned some comfortable chairs from wood and canvas and they would sit in them most evenings. The wind howled outside and the canvas tent flapped and groaned, making conversation difficult. The pipe was a regular companion now and it would usually come out after supper. Scott had one too, and smoking was normally at his suggestion. He would fetch one of the good brands of tobacco from the shelves. He was more prone than Tom to using the store's merchandise.

"Storm's bad," said Scott, speaking louder than usual to be heard over the storm.

"I think there might be some rain in the wind."

"Might be snow later, too. Feels about right for it."

Scott leant back in his chair, then turned it sideways so he looked directly at William.

"So, what do you think, Bill? Do you like it here?"

William was surprised at the question and unsure how to answer.

Scott laughed.

"All right. I should have given you some warning, I suppose. It's nearly time for me to go back to Melbourne. I'll only be here another month or so. I thought I'd ask how it's going. You've been here about six months. Probably more. We agreed you'd stay for a month or two and we're long past that. Have you made any plans?"

William was still silent. It wasn't the question. He just hadn't thought about it.

*No harm in telling Scott.*

"I haven't thought about it. I like it here. I think I work well with Tom. I hope I work well with you."

"You were keen to dig for gold once. There'll be men returning from Melbourne soon who'll want a fresh start, some local knowledge and a good, strong pair of hands to help. I thought you might be keen to talk to them. I know they'll be keen to talk to you."

"You're talking like you have someone in mind."

"I do. Several of the fellers have asked me about it."

"Why'd they ask you?"

"They know you work with us. Wanted to be sure I was all right with it. They know good people are hard to find."

"What did you say?"

"I said Bill's his own man—whatever he does it all right with me."

William was embarrassed. No one had ever said such a thing to him. Scott topped up his whisky. How his life had changed. Here he was talking about his future with a man that he didn't know until just a few months ago, in a country he knew nothing about a year ago.

"Think on it, Bill. Tom and I would like you to stay on. You work well with both of us. The store is easier to manage with two and your company makes it easier to pass the time. We all have to make our way in this world. You have to do what you think best and like I said, whatever you choose is right with me and with Tom."

William just nodded his agreement. He didn't trust himself to speak, feeling overwhelmed by Scott's kind words and friendship.

The wind continued to howl outside, bashing the canvas, straining the ropes and poles.

William shivered.

"Ask Joe to get you an opossum coat," said Scott. "The blacks make and sell them. Joe'll get one for you. He deals with the blacks all the time and knows how to negotiate the price. Ask him next time you see him. I'm sure you've seen the coats on some of the others. I've got one, but I left it in Melbourne. You'll be as snug as a bug in a rug with one of those, and wonder how you survived before you got it."

"Where do the blacks come from? I saw some in England. Did they come from there?"

"No. They were here already. Every country has its own people. You're Irish. They're Australian."

"Do they talk like we do? I've not heard them speak."

"No. I don't think they spoke English before we got here. Ask Joe—he deals with them all the time and knows how to talk with them. He likes them. He says they make fun of us. They ask him why we bring food here when there's so much here already."

"Why didn't they take all the gold before we got here?"

"I don't think they value it like we do. They look for it now though, because they know we want it. They're very good at finding gold that we missed in the tailings."

"Are they dangerous?"

"I don't think they are now. They used to be. The men are pretty strong, resilient fellows. Used to be fights with the early settlers. Settlers didn't always win, even though they had guns and the blacks had spears. Some work with the police. I'd rather deal with them than some of the Vandemonians. They're a rum lot, if you ask me. Cause trouble every day."

"What's a Vandemonian?"

"Ex-convict from Van Diemen's Land. It's an island not too far south of us where they sent some of the convicts."

"Andrew told a story about one of them. He didn't sound so bad."

"You're right. Not everybody from somewhere is bad. It just seems that the worst of the convicts went to Van Diemen's Land and the worst of the worst came from there to here. Did your man come here?"

"Andrew didn't say. Is that all the blacks do? Dig for gold?"

"No. They work with the farmers. They're good guides too. They can find food and water where we'd starve or go thirsty. They're really good hunters, too. They've got a thing they call a boomerang that they throw. Joe reckons they can hit a sixpence at a hundred yards. It's even better than that. If it doesn't hit anything, it comes back and it's ready to use again—like having a gun where the bullets come back."

"I don't see many of them."

"Most of them have moved away. Gone further into the bush to get away from us."

"So we pushed them off their land?"

"I suppose we did, but they don't build houses like we do. They like to move around, so I think they'd just as soon be there, as here. Like I said, ask Joe. He'll tell you all about them."

They were silent for a while, each man lost in his own thoughts.

"Well, I'm off to bed. See you in the morning," said Scott.

"How come you don't sleep across the doorway, like Tom does?"

"Not too many thieves this time of year. I don't think they like the cold. Besides, it's warmer at the back. 'Night."

William lay in his bed, listening to the storm outside. There was something comforting about being rolled up and warm, listening to the weather do its worst yet not be able to reach him.

He thought about the store. It was easy to stay, but he didn't own the store so he wouldn't get rich. Panning for gold was easy and fun but, like the store, that also wouldn't make him rich. He wondered who it was that had approached Scott. Some names came to mind, but after a few moments he realised it was useless to think who it might be. It had to be one of the card players, yet none of them were rich either.

Then he wondered about the blacks. He knew the Irish didn't like the English much because they had taken their land, or so popular opinion said. Yet here he was, Irish, and taking someone else's land. In spite of what Scott said, he was sure the blacks would prefer it if they'd been left alone. Perhaps that was just how things worked, like the cards—winners and losers. But at least you could choose to play cards. You couldn't choose to play in the game of life. Everybody played, and not everybody won. There must be rules. He just didn't know what they were yet.

There was no doubt he'd have to move on from the store and he'd have to be ready when the chance arose. Still, for the moment it was safe. He earned money, learnt a lot, had some fun, had a roof over his head and a shirt on his back and food to eat. No, this wasn't all bad.

CHAPTER 17

# A Visit from Sir Charles

Winter and Scott left, summer and Tom returned. Life on the goldfields returned to normal. William found the summer months left more time to look for gold but daily life was made more miserable by the flies and mosquitoes, by muddy roads, by short tempers, by the heat, and by the smell from the town.

Days rolled into weeks and weeks rolled into months.

Cards and Saturday nights continued, but William's luck didn't hold. He wasn't sure if he was too adventurous, or not adventurous enough. Tom elected not to help him as they now competed fiercely to be winners on the night. William asked for Tom's advice sometimes on the way home, but Tom always replied that William was past being taught, by Tom anyhow, and he needed to work things out for himself. Not that William lost a lot of money—he knew when to stop. The gold he found on a Sunday was often lost the following Saturday night.

Tom and William prospected mostly behind Black Hill, but sometimes went into the hills above the Buninyong Road. If they did, the find was mostly small and they'd return to the store tired, hungry, and dispirited. They'd find little to talk about on those nights and both men would retire early, exhausted from the day's endeavours.

Noone ever approached William about working with them to find gold. He sometimes wondered if Scott had made the whole thing up, just to test his attitude.

William hadn't seen Scott since he returned to Melbourne. Mike and Jake brought any deliveries. It was always great to see them and a very pleasant evening would be passed drinking whisky and playing cards. Mike always reported Scott to be well, but busy.

The talk sometimes turned to politics and the state of the diggings. Tom and Mike always agreed that the diggers were angry about the squatters paying so little for land and the diggers so much in the way of a digging licence, and La Trobe's enforcing the licence fee. He too said there'd be trouble before long. They always said there'd be trouble, but William had not ever seen or heard of anything other than the daily hassles around the goldfields as the police ensured that diggers carried a valid and current licence.

Then winter came and Scott was back. William was delighted to see him. He hoped they could pick up where they left off and add riding to prospecting again.

Mike and Tom had gone. The goodbye was easier this time.

Scott and William sat in their favourite chairs. They weren't used in the summer, so they dragged them out from behind the shop where they'd been left last winter.

"So, how's it going now?" asked Scott.

"Still the same," said William, with a smile.

"No one talk to you?"

"No. No one."

"Well, maybe I can fix that, if you want."

"Why didn't anyone talk to me?"

"Maybe everyone's struggling with the cost of the licence fee. Most of the diggers can afford the fee and that's about all. Do you want to try your hand at digging?"

William put down his pipe and whisky.

"I think so, Scott. I don't know if I can make a go of it, but I'd like to try. Don't get me wrong—I like it here. I like working with you and Tom, but I'm ready to try my hand."

"Would you do it alone?"

William shook his head.

"No. I watched some of the fellers doing it on their own. It's too hard. It's like trying to run the store on your own. You can do it, but it's too hard and not worth it. They've found some more leads that are producing payable gold. I've a mind to join the hunt for them. Some are near to the surface, but most are deep, really deep, so the work is hard and dangerous. Murph's talked about it, but that's all he's ever done—talked. I don't blame him. It can be a lot of hard work if there's no result. And you still only get eight foot square, so if you dig a shaft a hundred or a hundred and fifty feet deep and find nothing, it's a lot of wasted effort."

"You don't sound too convinced."

"Like I said, they sometimes find them near to the surface. That's what I'd hope to do."

"I know about the leads. They're good for the store. Alluvial gold is harder to find, so the leads will keep the diggers coming. Bill, things're always quieter over the winter. Why don't you stick around for the winter and find something in the spring? Besides, La Trobe'll be gone soon and a feller called Hotham is taking over. He might change things, and looking for gold may not be so expensive anymore. They said in Melbourne he'll visit here soon, so that'll be interesting and we can get a first-hand look at the man. In the meantime, we can keep prospecting and if we find something good, you can work that full-time come spring."

"What'll you or Tom do here in the store if I do that?"

"Don't worry. We'll find somebody."

William had a feeling Scott had someone in mind already. Once again, his life would change by a decision about him that had already been made. He would need to think harder about what he'd do next.

A few days passed and both men were busy in the store, and the customers were all excited about Hotham's visit.

"They said his wife will be with him," said one.

"They say he's dour, but she's a real treat," said another.

The next day was blustery, wet and cold. Not many customers came in the first hour or so that the store was open. Those that did, complained about the weather.

"Today's the day," said Scott early in the day, after he'd been in quiet discussion with the last customer.

"For what?" asked William.

"It's Sir Charles and Lady Hotham day. Anyway, that's what I was just told. One of us should go to see them," said Scott. "I'll look after the store. You go and check them out."

The wind caused the tent to flap and shake.

"Where will I find them? They're unlikely to be out in this."

"Head for the commissioner's tent. If they're not there, at least someone there will know what's happening."

William took an oilskin jacket that they kept if they needed to work outdoors in bad weather. He pulled it on over his other clothes and stepped outside the tent.

There were a few hardy souls walking on the road, all heading down the hill.

William followed them and crossed the bridge over the river, heading into the town and to the commissioner's tent. He was soaked and cold in minutes.

*It would be good if they made an oilskin coat that actually worked.*

A few people gathered outside the commissioner's tent, looking soaked and miserable.

William asked one of them if he'd seen Sir Charles.

"No. Story goes that he's arriving sometime today from Bacchus Marsh. Man'd be a fool to travel in this, so I'm betting he'll come tomorrow. Missus wants to see Lady Hotham so sent me to find out when she'll be here. Papers say she's a looker, so I didn't mind coming. I'm not going to hang about though."

The men stood and looked at the sky and the rain, being buffeted by the wind and shivering from the cold.

"Name's Angus," said the man and thrust out his hand. "You on your own?"

"Bill. Aye, I am."

"Why don't we go to Bath's for a whisky? That'll get us out of the weather and give the Hotham party a chance to arrive."

"Well, I've got a mate holding the store. Don't want to leave him too long on his own."

"Bet no one's coming in this weather. Lord knows, we're fools to be out in it. C'mon, just a couple. Then we can come back, check on developments, and hopefully go home."

"All right," said William. "Just a couple."

It wasn't far to Bath's Hotel. William had not been there, but he had heard of it. He stopped outside. It was pretty flash. He wondered if it allowed the likes of himself and Angus to go inside. Angus didn't hesitate and went straight in.

The bar was busy and all manner of people were enjoying themselves. Angus pushed up to the bar, ordered two whiskies and brought them back. William had found a table inside the door, out of anyone's way, where they'd be sure not to attract attention.

"Bottoms up," said Angus, and the first two drinks were gone in no time. William was glad he had taken to carrying some money with him. A lot of the diggers didn't mind if someone couldn't return the shout. They were glad of the chance to have a drink and enjoy some company, but it didn't sit well with William. He'd been caught a few times and now carried some money just in case, as he was always more comfortable paying his own way.

William got two more drinks and returned to the table. The conversation always started with dissatisfaction with the licence fee and the enforcement of it.

"Hotham'll fix it," said Angus. "I've heard he's a good man. Things'll be better soon, mark my words. Anyway, if they're not, there'll be trouble. Diggers're sick of it."

Soon those drinks were gone too.

"We just can't leave it at that," said Angus. "You can't leave me either, Bill. Man can't drink in a place like this on his own."

"All right. Two more, but that's it."

"That's the spirit. This is turning out to be a good day, after all."

They had two more drinks and left the hotel. It was coming on dark when they arrived back at the commissioner's tent.

Angus asked a policeman standing out front if the Hotham's had arrived yet.

"They're here," said the policeman. "Arrived about an hour ago. Come back tomorrow—they won't come out again in this."

"All right," said Angus to William. "I'm off. Nice to meet you."

He shook William's hand and left.

William stood for a few moments longer, more to orient himself than anything. He was dizzy from the whiskies.

"Is your friend foreign?" asked the policeman. "I only heard Hotham. Couldn't understand the rest."

William stared at him quizzically.

"Sorry, mate," said the policeman. "I guess you don't speak English either."

William set off, slogging through the mud, rain and wind. The river was nearly up to the bridge when he reached it. He was sober enough to realise he wouldn't be able to cross in an hour or so, and pushed on up the road to the store. There were still some people about and lamps adorned some of the stores and tents, so the road home was clear enough to follow.

By the time he arrived back at the store he was soaked, muddy and miserable, and had to call to Scott to open the door.

"There you are," said Scott. "Are you all right? Not robbed or anything?"

"I'm all right," mumbled William.

"Ah, I see," said Scott. "What of Sir Charles and Lady Hotham?"

"Arrived late. Might be able to see them tomorrow."

"Supper and bed for you, I think. I'll catch up on some accounts. I don't think anyone will be up for cards tonight anyway. Might be nice to sit by the fire with whisky and a pipe. I haven't done that since last night."

William just nodded, feeling very unsteady on his feet.

Scott looked at William for a few moments then led him over to his bed, stretched him out, pulled off his boots, threw his opossum rug over him, and left him.

"Thanks," muttered William.

"You'd do the same for me," Scott replied.

\*    \*    \*    \*

In the morning, William woke and spent the usual few moments wondering where he was. He remembered meeting Angus and going to Bath's, but not much after that. Then he remembered it was Sunday and was glad of it. Unless they were prospecting or taking a delivery, Sundays were a nice slow day and that was what he needed after meeting Angus.

He could smell bacon, eggs and coffee. Was he really in the tent? Who was cooking those things? What a change from chops!

Rolling out of bed, he pulled on his boots and peered at the fireplace through the canvas curtain. There was Scott cooking up a storm and Jack sitting at the table.

"Ah! Here he is, Jack. Fresh as a daisy," said Scott. "Jack's brought us some eggs and bacon."

"Why?" said William.

"Well, seein' as I hadn't seen you for a while, I thought it might be an idea. I've come by a few times to see you, but you've been away or tied up. I came yesterday. Scott said come back today, so here I am. He said you've been celebratin'."

"I just need to clean up. I'll be back in a few moments."

William stepped outside and gasped at the difference in the day. It was fresh and cool, no clouds in the sky, and blue as he had ever seen it. The smell from the town wasn't as bad as usual—maybe the wind was from the southwest. He took a piss and washed his face and hands.

"That's better," he said to himself, and headed back inside.

Scott had poured him a pannikin of coffee. It smelt so good. He took it in both hands and warmed them—they were still cold from being washed.

Jack put three plates of damper, bacon and eggs on the table. William hadn't realised how hungry he was until he started eating.

It was wonderful after missing supper the night before, and after the incessant diet of chops. He looked up from an empty plate.

"You can come anytime, Jack," he said, sipping his coffee.

"Bridie keeps some chooks now," said Jack. "Dunno how she does it with the dingoes and the diggers. There's not a minute's peace since we got 'em, but the eggs're welcome."

"I don't think there any dingoes here. Might be wild dogs," said Scott.

"Well, somethin' sure fancies 'em. Bill, are the Hotham's 'ere?"

"I think so," said William. "I went to the commissioner's tent, but Sir Charles and Lady Hotham hadn't arrived yet. Met a feller on the same errand and we decided to have a whisky while we waited. It was warmer in the pub, so we stayed for too many. When we went back, I think the policeman said the Hotham's would be out and about today."

"That's what I hear too," said Jack. "The ladies are all keen to see Lady Hotham. The papers say she's a looker."

"I hear that too," said Scott. "Listen, I need to go out back. I'll leave you two for a while. Might even walk down town and see if the Hothams are about."

"Wait and we'll go with you," said William.

"Oh. I'll do the things I need to do then meet you at the commissioner's tent. How does that sound? Will you fellers clean up here? Joe'll be down soon to look after things. I went and saw him last night and asked him to come down. I thought we could both have a look at the Hothams. Joe said he's not interested."

He didn't wait for an answer—just put on his coat and went.

"Now, that's Scott for you," said Jack.

"How's that?"

"I want to talk to you, Bill. Like I said, I've been by a few times, but I've got you now and I'd like to talk if that's all right with you."

"That's all right with me."

"I'd like you to come in with me. Be my partner."

"Are you still digging on Clayton's Hill?"

"Near to there and yes. I'm not getting much, so I look elsewhere when I need some money. But I'm convinced there's gold there. Bridie and the girls can't help. Oh, they can with the cradling, but not with the digging. I'm having to go deeper than I thought, so I need some help. Will you come in with me? The girls'll help however they can but whatever we find, we go half each. What do you think?"

"Where will I live? I can't live in your tent."

"You can if you want. But, if you don't want to, we can pitch a tent near to us. You can eat with us then go back to your tent to sleep. There's plenty of space there now. Many of the diggers have gone back to Melbourne for the winter."

"I haven't got a tent."

"That's easy—I've got a spare tent. Some people just up and left it. You'd think they'd try to find a buyer, but they didn't. We can fit you out with a fireplace and all, so you'll be warm. What do you think?"

"I'll have to ask Scott."

"Of course."

"When do you want me to start?"

"Maybe in a month or two. Let the rain slow down a little. Can't dig when the rain fills the hole all the time. It's too dangerous. The Hothams are here now too. Everyone's bettin' he'll be easier on the licences. So you have a talk to Scott, have a think about it, and come by soon for supper and we'll talk some more."

"When should I come for supper?"

"Whenever suits you. You're welcome anytime."

They busied themselves with cleaning up after breakfast. They washed the dishes in a bowl with hot water from the fire. Bill then took the bowl and pushed his way through the door at the front of the store to throw the water on the road. Scott was sitting on a log out the front, smoking his pipe.

"You fellers done yet?" he asked.

"That Scott?" called Jack.

"Aye, it's Scott," said William, laughing.

"Tell 'im to wait. We'll come with 'im."

"He's waiting," said William, loud enough that Scott could hear too.

The three of them walked down the road in the sunshine.

"It's good to be alive," said Scott. "Especially on a day like this."

"It's always good to be alive," said Jack. "There's not a day goes by that I don't thank the Lord for my Bridie, for the girls, and for bein' alive."

When they reached the creek, Jack took his leave.

"I'll be off. Got some chores to do. Let me know what you think about the Hothams. Take your time with the thinkin', Bill. No rush."

William and Scott waved and continued on their way.

"Looks more like a town now, doesn't it?" said Scott. "Some houses, a theatre, a proper building for the hotel. I'll be sad when it's all gone."

"Is it going? Why will it go?"

"When the gold is finished, everyone will leave. Well, not everyone. The farmers will stay, but there's not enough of them to make a town."

"It's hard to imagine what it would be like without the people."

There were quite a few people about, chattering and laughing. It was such a beautiful day and, being a Sunday, many people were off to church or returning from it. Most people were dressed in their best clothes. Looking back, William saw Jack stopped in a group of people down by the creek. They were all much better dressed than Jack and he looked quite out of place.

"I wonder who Jack is talking to?" he asked.

Scott stopped and looked back too.

"Dunno," he said. "Jack's a pretty friendly feller. Let's speed it up a bit. I don't want to miss the Hothams."

They arrived at the tent, only to be told that the Hothams had already left for a stroll around town. They'd gone with an orderly but he'd been dismissed early in the walk and had arrived back, so no one knew where they were now or when they'd be back.

"It doesn't matter," said Scott. "Let's not waste the day. Have you been to the lake?"

"No, I don't think so. What lake?"

"Some people call it Yuille's Swamp, others Lake Wendouree. I prefer Lake Wendouree. It's where we get our fresh water."

"I wondered where it came from and never thought to ask. I'd like to see it. Why do you prefer Wendouree?"

"Well, Yuille was the first feller here so it was originally named after him. They say someone asked the blacks what it was called and they received the answer Wendouree, so they called it Lake Wendouree. The story I heard is that later they found out Wendouree means 'I don't understand' in the black's language. Who really knows, but if that's right, I reckon it's pretty funny. You should ask Joe. He'd probably know the truth. Anyway, it's not far and it's such a nice day."

"That's all right by me."

They walked along the rutted dirt track, standing to one side from time to time to allow carts to pass. The business of fetching water didn't stop for the Lord's day. It was cooler where the trees overshadowed the track, but Scott kept up a brisk pace that kept the winter chill at bay.

"What did Jack want?" asked Scott, and William laughed.

"All right. What are you going to do?"

"I'd like to join him. I'm nervous and excited at the same time. What will you do? Have you got someone else to work in the store?"

"No, I don't. But, I'll tell you what. Why don't you live at the store, work with Jack each day and help me when I need it? That way, we both win. If it doesn't work out with Jack, you can come back to the store. What do you think?"

"I think that's more than fair."

"By the way, I've got money for you too. I know you've lost most of your gold at cards, but I've still got most of your wages stashed away and you can take that whenever you need it. There's nearly forty pounds there."

"Can you keep it for me? It's safer with you."

"Of course."

They arrived at the lake and watched several people filling barrels. The lake wasn't as big as William had expected, but it was very pretty. It was nice to be away from the smell of the town. They sat on a log in the sun, which sparkled off the lake. Some birds dipped and swooped nearby, calling to each other, no doubt annoyed at human intrusion on their domain. There were some blacks nearby sitting around a fire outside a bark hut. William watched as the little black children laughed and squealed, chasing each other around some trees.

*They're just like us.*

"We'd best be getting back," said Scott. "Might be good in the sun at the moment, but it'll get cold come night and we don't want to get lost out here."

It was nearly dark when they passed the commissioner's tent and crossed the creek on their way back to the store.

William went to Jack's for supper the following Sunday to discuss their partnership. Jack was delighted that William would join him and suggested they celebrate with a few whiskies. They agreed that William would start in October when the weather was warmer.

Over supper, Bridie told William that she and Jack had met the Hothams the previous Sunday. "They seemed all right," she said. "He was very interested in the names of places and buildings, and she in the process of digging. She laughed when we told her we used a cradle to separate the gold from the dirt."

"Met 'em just after I left you two," said Jack. "Big Larry thought he'd died and gone to heaven. He followed Lady Hotham around like a puppy for most of the day and helped her cross the creeks and mud. One time, he picked her up. She didn't mind at all. Just laughed and thanked him. I think he'll dream about her for the rest of his life."

"Did Hotham talk about the licences?"

"Only to ask questions. We're still bettin' there'll be change for the better."

"I hope so," said Bridie. "Everyone's so upset. It's all just wrong."

"Do you want me to set up a tent?" asked Jack.

"No need. I'll stay at the store and come down each day. Scott said it would work better for him."

# CHAPTER 18

# William and Jack are Partners

William joined Jack and his family for supper from time to time. "It'll make it easier for you to know when to start," Jack had said.

They always talked about where Jack was searching for gold.

"Maybe we should look higher on the hill," said Jack. "It'll be easier with two of us. I suppose I've been hopin' to find it a bit lower, since I won't have to cart the dirt so far."

"Is anyone else looking there too?"

"Nah. They still think I'm mad."

"You're not mad, Daddy," chorused Missy and Polly.

"I don't think I am either, but Bill might think I'm mad if we don't find somethin'."

"You won't think Daddy's mad, will you, Bill?" asked Missy.

"No, Missy, I won't ever think that. But I'm glad other people do, since we'll have that spot all to ourselves."

One Sunday Jack asked, "Can you start tomorrow?"

"Yes. Scott's been wondering if you'd changed your mind."

Jack laughed.

"That's not likely," he said. "The days're better, longer and drier, so it's time to get on with it. Come here first thing in the mornin' and we'll walk up the hill together. I've worked out a claim for us and I've got a licence for you. The first month's on me."

William told Scott when he got back to the store.

"Good," said Scott. "I've been expecting it. I agree with him—best to get started. Tom'll be here soon. I wrote and told him you'd start with Jack soon. He wrote back that he's glad you're going to stay at the store. Said he'd miss your company and promises not to make too many demands on your time."

William woke early, had a quick breakfast, and walked down the hill to Jack's. It was quiet at the diggings.

"Bit early for everyone," said Jack.

They gathered up their picks and shovels and walked up the hill together, taking the same route they had originally. Jack had a billy full of water hanging off his pick.

"Be quiet if we find anythin'," Jack said as they walked along. "We don't want the others sniffin' around, nor do we want anyone jumpin' our claim. It's a bit out of the way up here and they think we're mad already, so we shouldn't be bothered by anyone. They'll see us as we cradle, so if we get anythin' we'll need to be careful there too."

They reached the spot where Jack had marked out their claim.

"Are we too high on the hill?" asked William.

"No, I've been tryin' further down and not gettin' anythin'."

"How deep do you think we'll have to go?"

"I don't know. Fifteen or twenty feet."

"I thought you said you had to go a lot deeper."

"That was what I said all right, but that's down there on the flats where they're findin' the deep leads. That's where we'll go if we don't get anythin' up here. If we find somethin' up here, we can take out a claim each and work them both. Anyway, let's get to it. Bridie made us some biscuits, so we can stop for a cuppa when you're tired. Don't want to go too hard on your first day."

They set to and William was surprised how hard it was to dig. The ground was hard, dry, and full of flat stones. He, Scott and Tom had been chasing gold in the creeks, so there hadn't been so much digging involved. Here, they had to sink a shaft. It was easy enough at first to dig then shovel but as the hole became deeper, they had to bucket the dirt out.

"When do we start cradling?" asked William.

"Gotta get some likely dirt first. I've been watchin' for it. I'll tell you if I see it, then you can look out for it too. These are old deposits, done when the valley looked a lot different to what it does now. The gold got stuck in hard purple-coloured clay so when we find that, we can expect gold. That's the theory, anyway. Seems they always find the gold above it, but never below."

"Won't the others know we're onto something when we start cradling dirt that looks like that?"

"No. They'll expect us to cradle at some point, but they won't come over to see what we're doin'. No, the main thing is not to shout and holler."

William laughed.

"That's what I did when Tom and I found some once."

"We all do it. It's very excitin'. But the longer you can keep it secret, the better off you are."

They stopped for a cuppa at one point and Bridie and the girls arrived with a meal a few hours after. William ached all over, and his hands were covered in blisters. The panning that he and Tom had done was child's play compared to this.

By the end of the day, they hadn't gone much deeper than four feet.

"A few more days and we might get some idea," said Jack. "Not sure what to do if we find nothin'."

They walked down the hill in the dusk, carrying their tools with them.

"Can't leave 'em 'ere," said Jack. "Someone'll souvenir them."

"I thought you said no one came up here."

"There's people wantin' to pinch things who'll go anywhere."

They parted at the bottom of the hill.

"Sleep well," said Jack.

"I've no doubt of that."

The next day they got down to about ten feet, and the hole became harder to manage. The dirt had to be hauled out in a bucket and dumped, but not so close that it would fall back in, or that it would it be a nuisance if they found gold and made another claim nearby.

Jack did all the direction and William provided the labour.

The third morning they were heading up the hill when they heard, "Joe! Joe!"

"What the devil?" exclaimed Jack.

They could see the police troopers moving among the diggers already working.

"I thought things would get easier under Hotham," said William.

"Me too," said Jack. "I don't like the look of this at all. I'll go down and find out what's happenin'. You stay with the tools. I won't be long."

There was a lot of shouting along the creek and on the flats where some deep holes had been dug. William thought that it looked like there were more troopers than usual.

Jack got back about an hour later.

"Hotham's ordered there to be more licence searches! I don't understand it. See what you can find out from Scott tonight. I'll check with the other diggers when we're done here."

Bridie and the girls brought them some lunch later. William loved the food she brought. It was always different. That was reason enough to be glad he'd joined Jack.

"The diggers are all angry," said Bridie. "There's talk of trouble, again. Oh, Bill. This is the worst thing, with you just starting. I hope you don't change your mind."

"It's early days, Bridie," said William. "If I change my mind, it won't be because of this. There's always been this trouble. I think we were all hoping it would be resolved."

William checked with Scott that night.

"I heard about it," said Scott. "There's a rumour going around that Hotham's misunderstood the mood of the diggers. He was so pleased with his reception here that he thinks the diggers'll not mind if the government increases the searches, so he's passed a law that says the commissioners will search for unlicensed diggers twice a week. It's hard to believe."

William left the store the next morning and noticed many more people on the road than usual. He tried to stop a few to find out what was happening, but all shook him off and hurried on their way.

He arrived at Jack's tent to find a number of diggers gathered, all enveloped by an angry mood.

"What's happening?" he asked Jack.

"James Scobie's been killed."

"What! How did that happen?"

"Seems there was a fight last night outside the Eureka Hotel. They said Bentley's mixed up in it somehow.

"Who's Bentley?"

"He owns the Eureka Hotel. I'm surprised you've not been there."

"I've walked past it."

"Many don't, most go in. There's a roarin' trade goes on there."

They stood around for a few minutes as the crowd vented its anger.

Then Jack said, "Bill, there's nothin' we can do, and these fellers are only standin' around gettin' angry. How about you and I head off and be about our business?"

"I'm all right with that. I only knew of Scobie anyway. Some of the fellers had played cards with him."

They started to walk away and someone called, "Where are you two goin'?"

"We've got work to do," said Jack.

"What about Scobie? He's been murdered."

"Aye. It's a terrible thing, but there's nothin' we can do at the moment. But if there is, let us know and we'll be there."

A couple of the men came forward, muttering about people not doing the right thing.

"Leave it!" someone called to them. "There's been enough trouble for now. If we're gonna get angry, for Christ's sake let's get angry at the right people."

Jack and William kept walking.

"We've not heard the last of this," said Jack.

They dug all day and got down to twelve feet.

Scott told William that night that there had already been an inquest into Scobie's death, and that the inquest found Scobie had died from a blow to the head by an unknown person. He said anyone that came into the store that day was angry about the murder and all saw Bentley as the culprit. Scott thought the government needed to do more, and he hoped that some of the diggers or storeowners with influence could push the government to reopen the case.

The next day, Jack and William got down to sixteen feet. William started to worry that the hole was a duffer, but Jack said it was normal.

The following day would be Sunday, so they agreed that they'd take the day off and catch up on their chores. William would help Scott if he needed it and start again the next day.

There was no more news on Scobie that night, though Scott thought a group of miners had visited the commissioner's tent to complain that more needed to be done.

The following Monday morning, William thought Jack looked worried, despite his assurances when they last met. They cradled some of the dirt, but it produced nothing.

"I think we need to go further up the hill," Jack said as they walked home that evening.

"How do you know?"

"I don't. I'm only guessin'."

"Should we go down to the flats? Others seem to be doing better there. Or maybe even Eureka."

Jack stopped and looked at William, and William noticed Jack looked tired and dirty.

*This is not easy for him—he's carrying my disappointment too.*

"Bill, there's more failure than success lookin' for gold. If there wasn't, we'd all be rich men. You can count on the fingers of one hand the number of men who went lookin' for gold and found it straight away."

"It's all right, Jack. I understand. Anyway, I'm not much good at counting. Perhaps it's harder because it's so hot and dry. I thought we'd get better days than this."

"I agree. You can pull out if you want."

"And miss out on Bridie's cooking? Not on your life."

"That's her secret plan."

"I thought it might have been."

That night, Scott told William that Bentley and two others had been arrested again.

"We're finally getting somewhere," said Scott.

The next morning, William and Jack decided to go further up the hill.

"I think the further, the better," said Jack. "No one else goes there, so it's been untouched. It's too far to carry the dirt."

William laughed.

"What's so funny?" asked Jack, looking hurt.

"I suppose that being too far to carry the dirt is as good a reason as any for a place to look for gold."

Jack laughed too, clapping William on the shoulder.

"You're all right, Bill. No wonder Bridie likes you."

They started to dig, but it wasn't long before they stopped. Winds from the north, dust, and oppressive heat made it more than difficult. Perspiration was pouring off them. They'd brought only the billy for some tea, and some of Bridie's cakes. They found a spot near the trees out of the sun and the wind and not too far from their claim, started a fire and got the billy boiling.

"Be nice not to do this," said Jack. "I get sick of hot tea on hot days. What I wouldn't give to put my feet in a cool mountain stream and sip beer. I've been diggin' too long, Bill. I hope we find somethin'. I'd love to move to Melbourne, get a small farm, and put the girls in a proper school."

The flies had apparently decided it was summer already and there was no protection out in the open. The diggers wore nets over their hats when they dug but couldn't wear a net when they ate and drank, giving the flies free rein.

"The little buggers know when your hands are full," said Jack. "I dug with a fellow once who used to crush them with his eyelids. He was always wipin' away the dead flies. No end to 'em, though. Must be a pretty good fly factory, somewhere."

"I think it's the rubbish in the town."

"Might be right for the blowies, but the little black ones come out of nowhere and doesn't matter where you are in the bush."

"I wonder what good they do. My ma said everything has a purpose."

"There's no good purpose for any of them, as far as I'm concerned. Let me know if you find one."

"I think we'll find some gold."

"What makes you think that?"

"I'm a new chum and you're due for some luck."

Jack laughed.

"Let's get back to it. Bridie'll be here soon and it won't do for her to find us sittin' in the shade and chattin'."

Bridie arrived with lunch and inspected the hole.

"Well, that's not going to get you to China," she said.

"What's China got to do with it?" said Jack, still flushed in the face from the digging.

"Don't you know? If you dig through the earth, you get to China."

William laughed. It reminded him of Hannah telling him that from Liverpool you could get to anywhere. He wondered if she knew you could get to China from Ballarat.

"Who wants to get to China?" said Jack. "I only want to find gold."

"Bill might want to get to China," said Bridie. "But that hole's not deep enough for you to find gold, or for Bill to get to China."

"It's hot up here. There's a lot of sun and no water. We're takin' our time."

"What's wrong with the flats?"

"That's what Bill says."

"Bill might be right."

"Bridie, there's gold here. I know it."

"You've dug a lot of duffers."

"Bridie, if it's a fight you're lookin' for, you've come to the right place. There's two fellers here that have blisters on their hands, almost run out of places to dig, moved tons of earth to no purpose and have despair gnawin' at their hearts. So, if you've got somethin' to say, say it. We're all ears."

Bridie's eyes welled with tears.

"Oh, Jack, I'm sorry. It's the weather—the heat, the dust, the wind, and the flies. Maybe it's the place too. Maybe we've been here long enough."

She looked around at the scrubby terrain, the sparse eucalypts, and the whirls of dust. Then, she held up her hand as though to signal them to listen.

All William could hear was the screeching of birds, the clattering of the cicadas, the occasional shouts of men, and the sounds of digging, cradling, and animals from the flats below.

"Why'd they put gold here, anyway? Who in their right mind would pick somewhere like this to put gold? And, who in their right mind would have come here to find it in the first place?" said Bridie.

She walked over to Jack, and held him close.

"I'm sorry, my love. You do what you think is best. Come on, girls. Help me with the lunch, we'll eat and we'll leave the men to it."

They ate and as the girls left, Bridie said, "Bill, come by the tent tonight for a whisky. You've both earned it. Maybe we've all earned it."

William and Jack went back to work. It was clear after an hour or so that Jack's heart wasn't in it. He stopped digging and sat on the side of the hole.

"What do you think, Bill? Is she right?"

"I have no idea, Jack. I'm the new chum. You weren't right when you said I reckon we should go to the flats too. I'll go where you want to go. I've got the time if you've got the patience and I reckon your hunch is as good as anyone else's. Let's at least finish this hole, now that we've started it."

It was too hot to dig by mid-afternoon, so they called a halt. They picked up their tools and headed down the hill, shoulders slumped and feet dragging, spirits at a low ebb.

When they arrived at the tent, there were six or eight men there already. All were angry, shouting and cursing. Bridie and the girls were nowhere to be seen.

"I wonder what's happened now?" muttered Jack to William.

"You won't believe what's happened now!" yelled one of the men when they came close. "We've been waitin' fer you. Town's in an uproar."

"So, out with it," said Jack.

This must be really bad, thought William. These men are more upset than they were at Scobie's murder.

"Gregorius went to visit a sick feller in the Gravel Pits. A trap stopped him and demanded to see his licence. Gregorius tried to explain that he didn't need a licence and the damned trap took offence, got off his horse, and assaulted him! As luck would have it, Johnston, the assistant commissioner arrived on the scene and everyone expected the trap to be in trouble. Didn't happen that way. Johnston supported the trap and said Gregorius would have to appear in court tomorrow."

When the man finished, the men started to talk all at once in angry overtones.

"Who's Gregorius?" William asked Jack while the others were occupied.

"He's an Armenian, works with the Catholic priest. Doesn't speak much English, and walks with a bad limp. He doesn't need a licence because he's with the Church. The trap would have known that. I wonder which trap it was?"

"Well?" said the man who had spoken.

"Well, what?" said Jack.

"Well, what are we goin' to do about it?"

"What do you think we should do?"

"How about givin' the trap what he's askin' for?"

"If we do, we'll all finish up in gaol. Why don't we calm down and let the police magistrate deal with it?"

"Who's idea was it to wait for Jack?" someone called. "He didn't want to do anythin' when Scobie was murdered, and he doesn't want to do anythin' now. Soft, if you ask me."

"No one asked you!" shouted another. "Jack's got more brains than your whole family put together, and that includes those three dogs you've got."

"Who said that?" shouted the first man. "He'd better be prepared to back it up with his fists."

"Settle down," said the man beside him. "You're only makin' 'im right."

"C'mon everyone," said Jack. "Think about it. I know we take a lot of matters into our own hands and that's as it should be. The traps don't help us much because they're here for only one purpose, and that's to hunt illegal diggers. But we can't rough up a trap. We'll all go to gaol. I, for one, don't want to do that."

"What should we do then?" said a man in the group.

"Like I said, let it go to court tomorrow. See what the police magistrate does. He'll sort it for the best. It's his job to uphold the law."

"All right, Jack, but you'd better be there too. No runnin' away from it this time."

"Aye, I'll be there. Now go home, have a whisky, and come tomorrow if you can. No need for you all to be there. It only needs one or two of us."

"I'll be there too," called a few voices at the same time and the men drifted away.

Bridie appeared in the doorway.

"C'mon, Jack, Bill. Come inside. I know it's too hot, but if you're inside, people are less likely to stop for a chat. Anyway, I've got the whisky ready and I'm of no mind to share it with anyone else."

Jack and William washed up and went inside. It was hot—too hot—but they quickly got used to it.

"Don't be angry with them, darlin'. They're just sick of the government ridin' roughshod over everythin' and everyone," said Jack.

"I'm sick of it too, but doesn't mean I'm ready to pick a fight with every policeman in town."

The two girls sat in silence, as though detached from everything.

"Jack, what do you think will happen tomorrow?" said William.

"We won't get any diggin' done is all I'm sure of. They say the police magistrate is crooked, so who knows what he'll do. If he does the wrong thing by the diggers, this'll only get worse. You can see them spoilin' for a fight now. The government must see it. They're blind if they don't."

"Why're you getting involved, Jack? Some of the men want a fight and they'll use good men like you to start it," said Bridie.

"I'm a digger, Bridie. We'll do better if we stick together. Some might want a fight, but they're all good lads. I know they'll do the right thing in the long run."

Insects committed suicide by the hundreds on the lamp by the door.

"Don't be like them, Jack," said Bridie, pointing at the lamp. "Don't join a fight you're sure to lose."

"Oh, Bridie, my love. You take everythin' so seriously. After you left today, Bill and I finished the hole, got to China, and got some of the Chinese fellers to come through and help us. They're up there now, workin' on some more holes."

"That's a good idea, Daddy," said the girls in unison.

William looked at the girls, smiling.

*How do they do that? It's like they read each other's mind.*

"You're right, girls. Your daddy is the smartest digger in Ballarat," said William.

"I think in the whole world," said Bridie.

They all laughed, but the tension didn't leave the adults' faces.

"Not too many problems a whisky won't solve," said Jack after the girls had gone to bed in the oppressive heat of the tent.

"Let's sit outside," said Bridie. "There might be some cool in the night air. I think the diggers are gone and I don't think the mozzies are about yet."

They chatted for a while before it was time for William to go.

"Shall I come to the court with you tomorrow, or go back and dig?" he asked Jack

"Come to the court. It might be useful for you to know what you're dealin' with. You'll see the legal system in action."

"Where will we meet?"

"Come here first thing. Court will be at the police camp. Let's have breakfast, then we'll walk up together."

"Please be careful," said Bridie. "I have a bad feeling about this."

Scott was already in bed when he got back, but he had to be woken to let William in.

"Sorry," said William. "We need a better system."

"This one's fine with me. I wanted to talk to you, anyway. Did you hear the news? I figured that might be why you're late."

"Aye. Jack and I are going to the court in the morning."

"Are you in trouble too?"

"No. Jack told some of the fellers he'd go to see what happened. He thought it might be a good idea for me to come."

"Be careful, Bill. I don't like the feel of any of this. I think it's going to get worse. Much worse."

"Everyone sounds angry."

"Mostly with good reason. By the way, Tom'll be back in a few weeks."

"Can I still stay here?"

"Of course—no reason not to. I'll stay on for a bit, so there'll be three of us."

"Jack says he's got a spare tent."

"No, you're welcome here. I'm staying on for a few weeks to introduce Tom to the new customers—lots of new diggers in Eureka and Gravel Pits, so we decided to take our time with the hand over. Too much competition now, so we can't afford to lose anyone. It seems everyone with a spare shilling and a tent has opened a store."

"If you need help, all you have to do is ask."

"I know that. How are you and Jack doing?"

"Nothing yet."

"Might be time to go chasing those deep leads."

"That's what Bridie says."

*    *    *    *

William and Jack arrived at the court early the next morning but were told to wait. Quite a number of people were already gathered there, but none of them were the men who had been at Jack's the previous evening. The only advantage of being early was that they could be assured of a place in the court. There were many disadvantages, not the least of which was a long wait, as the hearing didn't get underway until late in the morning. It turned out that many of those waiting were charged with being unlicensed at the diggings.

Finally, they were ushered in. The court was a tent just like many others in Ballarat, but at least it had a wooden floor. There were chairs for the public. Officials and the jury were at tables. The room was very hot and the police magistrate wouldn't allow anyone in that wasn't seated.

"Too bloody hot in here," he said.

Anyone that had a piece of paper was using it as a fan. There was a constant swish, swish sound from the paper, adding to the buzz of insects and the hum of flies.

There'd already been a number of cases heard, all for being unlicensed, when Jack nudged William and whispered, "Here he is. That's Father Smyth with him. He's the local Catholic priest."

The priest assisted his servant into the court and stood with him. It was obvious that his servant had difficulty in both walking and standing. The police magistrate gave the priest permission to stand and help him.

William was impressed by the formality of the court, how people addressed each other respectfully, and how much control the magistrate exercised over the room. There was a man seated near to the magistrate who read out the details of each case before the magistrate interrogated the person, anyone assisting him, or the police officer who had brought the charge.

Gregorius looked bewildered and was constantly looking at the priest, who was answering any questions that Gregorius had been asked.

The charge of being unlicensed was dismissed but then the charge of resisting an officer was raised, and ultimately found by the magistrate to be fully proven, and Gregorius was fined five pounds.

"He's already paid the five pounds," said the priest.

"That was for bail," said the man the magistrate referred to as Mr Johnston.

The priest just shrugged and helped his servant to leave the court.

William wanted to stay longer when the case was finished, but Jack said he'd had enough and wanted to go.

"He should have dismissed both cases," said Jack on the way home. "I know the boys won't like it. I'm glad I went, to hear it with my own ears."

"I wonder why the boys weren't there."

"You don't find much gold sitting in a court room, but they'll come by tonight sure enough, and they won't like it."

Jack was right and diggers began drifting in later in the day. No one apologised for not being at the court, and everyone expressed anger and surprise at the decision.

"Timothy Hayes was there. I don't think the Catholics'll accept the decision, so it won't stop there," said Jack at one point.

"What can they do?" asked one of the diggers who had arrived late and was already drunk. "The whole thing is rigged. There's no way out of this mess for any of us. Bloody Hotham came here full of promises and we have nothin' to show for it. They'll do nothin' if we just talk."

"He's right," said another.

"Well, there's to be another inquiry about Scobie's death tomorrow," said Jack.

"Bentley and the law are as thick as thieves, so it'll be the same result as before," said the drunk man. "You goin' tomorrow, Jack? Be good if you did."

"I suppose it's open to the public. I don't know, but there's no advantage to me being there. We'll all find out what happens soon enough," said Jack with a sigh.

They all decided to go for a drink, but Jack said he was tired and hungry. William said he was too. The constant complaining annoyed him, so he preferred to stay with Jack and Bridie.

When they'd all gone, Bridie spoke.

"I'm glad you're not going tomorrow, Jack. You don't owe them anything. Most of them are full of talk, too, just like the government."

"Ah, darlin'. It's not just them. There's lots of people spoilin' for a fight, but all they do is talk about it. Besides, talkin' can't do any harm."

"What'll we do tomorrow, Jack?" asked William.

"Let's go and help our Chinese friends dig for gold."

"Chinese friends?"

"Yes, the ones we found when we dug through to China."

"Ah, yes. I should have remembered them."

*   *   *   *

William and Jack spent the next three days finishing holes, and then digging some more. They were both dispirited by their search and poor results but agreed to stay in the same area.

On Friday night, Scott said that William hadn't played cards for a few weeks and suggested that they go together the next night.

"The fellers are missing your money," said Scott with a laugh.

Jack didn't mind at all. He said he'd be glad that William would catch up with his friends.

When Scott and William arrived at the cards, all the talk was that the further inquiry by Commissioner Rede and the others had produced the same result—Bentley was innocent. They were told that Magistrate D'Ewes had pestered witnesses hostile to Bentley and, once again, the wrong decision had been reached, the government was corrupt and there was no chance of the diggers getting a fair go.

The evening lacked its usual fun and banter. There was talk of another monster meeting to be held on the following Tuesday where Scobie was killed.

"More talk," said Denis. "All they do is talk. If I had a nugget for every wasted word, I'd be a rich man."

Scott and William walked back early.

"Is Denis right?" asked William.

"About the talking?"

"Yes."

"Talking is important. Helps people make the best decision."

"But, all that's happening is the government is deciding it's right and the diggers are deciding it's not."

Scott laughed.

"C'mon, Bill. While they're talking, they're not fighting. Will you go to the meeting on Tuesday?"

"I expect Jack will want to go. If he goes, then we'll both go. Will you go?"

"No, I'd better mind the store. These're good days for the thieves to be out and about."

*    *    *    *

William and Jack agreed to meet at the store on Tuesday and walk to the meeting together. It wasn't far from the store and despite the early hour, there were many people out and about. It seemed to William that all the diggers were going to the meeting. The crowd surged about, intruding on the area around other's tents, knocking things over and receiving abuse. The mood was sober though, meriting an occasion of remembrance for a lost friend. It wasn't long before the speeches became more aggressive. The sly grog sellers were doing a roaring trade, the talk was all against Bentley, and the mood of the crowd became more threatening.

The day wore on, the sun beat down, and the dust and the wind made people irritable and uncomfortable.

Some police had arrived early to provide protection for Bentley's hotel. It looked more under threat as the hours went by.

Jack and William went back to the store to get something to eat.

"There are thousands there," Jack told Scott.

"No one's come here," said Scott. "It's a slow day. If it wasn't for the thieves, I'd come with you."

"Can Joe look after the store?" asked William.

"Not today. He's closer than we are, so more likely to lose out to someone who would prefer to ride than walk."

Later in the day, Jack and William headed back to the meeting. There was a distinct change in the atmosphere.

"Let's go back to the store," Jack said. "This won't achieve anything. There's only anger and if I was Bentley, I'd get out."

A man Jack said was Commissioner Rede stood at the front of the hotel and exhorted to the crowd to be calm. It just made the crowd angrier. He might as well have tried to tell them to stop digging for gold.

People tore at the hotel structure—pulling at floorboards, fence palings, windows and curtains. Anything that could be held was torn away.

All of a sudden, a shout rang out and a lamp at the front of the hotel was hit by a rock and flames began to spread around the eaves of the hotel.

"Burn it!" screamed someone.

"Burn it! Burn it!" The cry was taken up.

The crowd surged forward.

William would never be able to recall what happened next, as everything happened so fast. He'd notice one thing, and then there'd be another that would take his attention. The crowd pushed and shoved around him—some trying to get closer, others trying to get away.

As the fire took hold, people ran in and came back out with goods. It appeared someone had found some liquor and some of the diggers were helping themselves.

Some were calling for calm and respect for the property, others were screaming for damage.

William had never seen a mob before. He saw it losing reason, causing wanton acts of destruction that led to more. The fever and excitement fed on itself, and men he had previously thought to be calm and measured were screaming for destruction.

His arm was being pulled strongly. He looked and saw Jack.

"C'mon, Bill. Let's get out of here. This isn't a meeting—it's a riot."

They pushed back through the crowd.

At one point, William looked back and saw the hotel burning fiercely.

*What a shame. There'd been a lot of hard work gone into that. And what of his wife and child? Does no one care about them?*

They got back to the store and told Scott what had happened.

"I could hear the noise," Scott said. "I'm glad you're both all right. You'd better get back to your family, Jack. They'll be worried about you. The noise, if not the smell of the smoke and the sight of the flames, would carry all the way to them, I'm sure."

"What'll we do tomorrow, Jack?" said William.

"Dig as usual," said Jack. "Might be a quiet day. There'll be plenty nursing sore heads."

Once Jack had left, Scott and William prepared some supper. They were well skilled now at working together on their daily tasks.

"What will happen now?" asked William. "About the fire?"

"I'm sure there were police there."

"Yes, there were, but they didn't do much."

"It's a brave man that stands up to a mob. The police'll identify some of the diggers there and they'll be arrested and tried. They'll identify men with previous convictions and bad reputations where the charges will be believable. With so many diggers there, it won't be hard to find a few to charge."

"What'll the diggers do?"

"Continue to agitate. Government is only fiddling with the edges. It hasn't done anything serious about the diggers' concerns. Besides, diggers won't care that Bentley has lost everything tonight. They'll still want him locked up for Scobie."

"Did he murder Scobie?"

"Doesn't matter—the crowd thinks he did and that's all it needs to support its case."

"I was frightened up there today."

"I'm not surprised. It was a big crowd that went there for one reason and found another."

Scott was silent a few moments before speaking again.

"There's a couple of events moving toward each other now. One is that the government is sure to be afraid it's losing control. It's not just in Ballarat that the diggers are agitating. So, they'll want to take action to regain control. The other is that the diggers are more confident they're gaining control and that the government will have to listen to their demands."

"What will happen?"

"Ever been involved in a fight, Bill?"

"Yes."

"And how did it finish?"

"Someone lost."

"That's what'll happen."

*     *     *     *

William headed off to Jack's the next morning. It had rained heavily overnight and the roads were soaked and muddy. The creek was flowing fast when he got there, and the roar of its water could be heard some distance away. There was traffic on the roads, but few diggers working at the creek.

*Jack must be right—a few sore heads this morning.*

"Any trouble at the store?" asked Jack as they walked up the hill together.

"No. All quiet. Any trouble down here?"

"No. There was a lot of noise as some of the diggers came back. They were shouting and yelling like men who'd succeeded in doing a difficult job."

"Did you hear anything of Bentley's family?"

"Why're you worried about them?"

"Doesn't seem fair. The diggers're mad at Bentley, but his family pays the price, too."

The next two weeks was like a game of cards where no one playing knew the rules, how many cards anyone held, when the game would start, or even when it would finish.

Bentley and his wife Catherine, and two others, were arrested for the murder of Scobie. An employee originally charged with the murder spoke out against them to receive the reward that would lead to the conviction of the murderer. In addition, the employee received amnesty for assisting the police. The trial was scheduled to begin in the Melbourne Supreme Court.

Three diggers were charged for participating in the riot that resulted in the destruction of Bentley's Hotel. Another monster meeting was held at Bakery Hill to raise money to aid in their defence. The trial was scheduled first to be held in Geelong, then in Ballarat, and finally in Melbourne.

The Catholics called a meeting to discuss the insult to the Catholics due to the charges being upheld against Gregorius. Father Smyth counselled forbearance, but the Catholics wouldn't hear of it—they wanted an apology.

By the end of October, there were two more companies of soldiers in the police camp, bringing the total number of soldiers to around two hundred and sixty. There was ongoing friction between the military and the police, who struggled to fit together into the small area allocated to the police camp. Scott reported idle chat from the store about frequent confrontations between them.

Hotham established a committee to meet at Bath's Hotel in the first two weeks of November to review the first dismissal of Bentley to see if there was any collusion by the law, and to see if the local police behaviour was such as to inspire respect in the local population.

Even while the committee was meeting, Magistrate D'Ewes was dismissed.

Five thousand diggers and storekeepers met on the Gravel Pits and decided to form the Ballarat Reform League with diggers from other goldfields. Armed sentries were posted to prevent any government spies.

Tom arrived from Melbourne, providing a welcome relief from the daily rumour and goldfield focus. He and Mike brought a fully-laden dray, and it took the four of them all day to unload it.

"Sorry about your Sunday," Scott said to William at one point.

"Don't be sorry," said William. "It's better than digging and finding nothing."

Tom looked at him in surprise and raised the matter again over a whisky that evening.

The four of them sat around the table. The heat of the day was still upon them and they agreed it was too hot to play cards.

"How's the digging going?" Tom asked William.

"Like I said before, it's all work and no joy."

"Where're you digging?"

"Near to Clayton's Hill."

"They say the deep leads are paying well."

"Aye, but you've got to go deep, slab the hole, and you need a group. There's just Jack and me. Jack doesn't want to bring anyone else in, nor look anywhere but where we're looking."

"You can't keep looking forever in the one spot. You might need to leave Jack and join another group."

"Jack's good to work with and I like his family."

"That might be true, but you're not in it to waste your time."

"I know. Can we talk about something else?"

Tom laughed.

"Sorry, Bill—none of my business. I hear the Bank of Victoria was robbed a few weeks back. It was all the talk in Melbourne. The diggers are glad someone else was robbed for a change."

"That's all right, Tom. They said it was four diggers because they were dressed like diggers, but who knows? They got away with a lot of cash and gold. I suppose if they were diggers, then it beats digging any day."

"It wasn't you, was it?" asked Tom.

"No. I wouldn't have thought of it. I suppose they'll be found."

"There's another public meeting next Saturday," said Scott. "I expect there'll be thousands there."

"What's the purpose of this one?" asked Mike who had shown little interest in what had gone before.

"It's been called by the Reform League. They want to elect some officers and discuss political changes."

"More of the same, isn't it?" said Mike. "These fellers are good at goin' in circles. Anyway, I'll be gone by then, so I don't know that I care."

"I joined," said Scott. "I'll do the caring for all of us."

Mike went back to Melbourne, William went back to working with Jack, and Scott and Tom worked the store. William came back each night and discussion was dominated by Tom wondering how Scott had managed on his own, with the increased business and the unrest in the goldfields. The three of them managed to play cards on two more Saturdays where the talk was all about public meetings, the trials of Bentley and his associates, and the trial of those held for the riot at Bentley's Hotel.

William became more concerned each day that he and Jack found nothing, and the talk at cards was of how much was being found on the deep leads. He was surprised that the mood at cards was still ugly even though Bentley had been convicted and sentenced to three years with hard labour for the murder of Scobie, and the rioters received light sentences. He talked to Jack about it one morning when he got to Jack's tent. There was a pot of coffee on the fire and William was glad to be asked to share some before going to their claim.

"It's been goin' on too long," said Jack. "Government's only pretendin' to be listenin'. Sure, they seem to be doin' somethin'. But it's as though they have to be pushed before they do anythin'. Besides, the build-up of soldiers at the camp's got everyone nervous. It's like they're spoilin' for a fight. Both sides are, if you ask me."

"Did you hear about the ambush last night at Eureka? It seems some military supplies were attacked in the dark by a group of diggers. Scott and Tom were talking about it this morning."

"I heard the noise. Didn't know what it was."

"Will there be more trouble?"

"Bound to be. There's another big meetin' of the diggers today at Bakery Hill. Becoming quite the place, isn't it?"

"Are you going?"

"Yes. I talked about it with Bridie. She's keen to get out of here. Doesn't like how things are developin'. Says she wants to go to Melbourne. Wants me to go with her. I said I'd go to the meetin' and find out if the diggers have any plans."

"What about us? What will I do if you go to Melbourne?"

"You're right to ask, of course. I'm just tellin' you what's happenin'. I don't want to go until we find the gold that I know is there."

"But Bridie might insist."

"Might she now?" said Bridie coming out of the tent.

William flushed with embarrassment.

"It's all right, Bill," laughed Bridie. "I know what you mean. Jack's his own man and I can't make him do anything. But, I am sick of this and I hate the tension between the government and the diggers. I think it's going to get worse and I don't want Jack mixed up in it. You know him—he can't help himself. The others'll ask his opinion and he'll want to advise what's best."

"You know I'm not lookin' for trouble, Bridie," said Jack.

"I know you're not, but it's going to find you—all of you. I've lost one husband to these goldfields and I don't want to lose another."

She walked over and put a hand on Jack's shoulder.

"You're all we have, Jack—the girls and I—you're all we have. I know you're not stupid but if a fight happens, it won't only be the stupid people involved. The military have guns, so they don't plan to settle the matter with fists."

"We have guns too," said Jack.

"See what I mean, Bill?" Bridie said, exasperated. "Guns? Do you think that'll make them scared? The military will run because the diggers have guns? Don't you bet on it, Jack. It will only make them more determined to fight. They're trained to fight and they want to prove themselves. It's their job, for God's sake!"

"All right, all right. Don't get your feathers up. We'll go to the meetin' and see what comes of it."

"Bill—you've got more sense. Don't let him do anything stupid. Please? For me and the girls?"

"C'mon, Bridie. It's not Bill's problem. Leave him out of it," said Jack.

"Of course it's Bill's problem. He's your partner, isn't he? You and him have hours and hours of digging invested in your claims and nothing to show for it. If something happens to you, he'll always have nothing to show for it."

"C'mon, Bill. Let's go to the meetin'," said Jack.

"It's too early," said Bridie. "You'll stand around in the heat, waiting. Stay here and let's talk some more."

"I've done enough talkin'. Besides, I want to see Scott and Tom. We'll see them on the way."

"That's a fine excuse, if ever I've heard one. All right, you go. But you be careful. And you too, Bill. I meant what I said—if Jack's right about the gold, you need him to find it, so don't let anything happen to him."

Bridie turned her back on them and slumped down by the fire, poured herself some coffee, and sipped it without another word.

"Do you really want to see Scott and Tom?" William asked once they were out of Bridie's hearing.

"No, not really," said Jack, shaking his head. "I'd had enough of the talkin'. Besides, I want to have a talk to you."

"Me? What do you want to talk to me about?"

"About all the diggin' and nothin' to show for it. Like Bridie says, we've done a lot of work and where we dig is all my idea. Maybe we should move to the deep leads. Find another couple of people. Might find someone at the meetin' today. What do you think? Are you ready to look somewhere else?"

"What's happened? Why have you changed your mind?"

"I'm ready to give it away, Bill. I don't want to lose Bridie and the girls. They're my world. Nothin' else matters and I think Bridie is ready to go. Has been for a while. She's just usin' the trouble

as an excuse. If we try the deep leads where the others are successful and find payable gold, we'll call it quits. I don't want to leave
you in the lurch, Bill. I'd rather leave you a rich man."

"Jack, I joined you, so you tell me what to do."

"I'll bet Scott and Tom have been tellin' you to look elsewhere."

"I suppose they have, but it's my life and my choice."

They arrived at the store and peered through the open flap.

"You're back early," Scott said to William.

"We're going to the meeting. Do you want to come?"

"One of us might as well. There'll be no customers."

"You go, Scott. I'm still working on the books, so I have plenty
to do," Tom said.

"Suits me. Coffee first? I think we'll be early otherwise."

The three of them set off in the sultry heat an hour or so later.
There were plenty of people about, most on foot, all heading for
Bakery Hill. It was obvious to the three of them that the mood
of this meeting was different to any that had gone before. The
meeting wasn't about one thing—it was about everything. The
diggers were sick of waiting. It was time the government acted on
all their demands.

Troopers rode around the edge of the crowd, incurring shouts
and threats from anyone nearby. The mood was heightened by the
sly grog sellers and their roaring trade.

"I'm glad Tom is back at the store," said Scott. "It looks like
everyone from Ballarat is here. The thieves'll be having a great
time robbing the stores. Police'd be better off to look after some
of them instead of riding up and down and annoying everyone."

Rumours were passed around that the Reform League had
been to see Hotham on behalf of those sentenced for the hotel riot,
but that any suggestion they should be freed had been rebuffed.
There was a big, old stump on which people stood to address the

crowd. There were a number of speakers, but one in particular got the crowd's attention.

"Who's he?" asked William.

"Feller called Peter Lalor, one of the leaders in the Reform League. He's Irish. Knows how to work a crowd."

There was also a huge flag, with a pattern of five stars on a blue background that diggers referred to as the Australia Flag, atop a very tall pole.

"I haven't seen that before. The flag, I mean. The stars look like the Southern Cross. I wonder what it's for," said Jack.

Lalor stood on the stump holding a rifle in one hand, its butt resting on his boot. The image screamed defiance and belligerence.

They couldn't hear what he was saying above the noise of the crowd, but his words seemed to affect those who could. From time to time there were shouts, clenched fists and raised arms.

"I'm going to get closer," said Jack. "I can't hear anythin' from back here. You two comin'?"

"We'll try," said Scott, "But it doesn't look easy. If we get separated, we'll see you back at the store."

Jack pushed ahead and was soon lost in the crowd. People knew him and wanted him to get closer. Maybe they valued his opinion and wanted him to have one. Scott and William tried to move closer too, but only found trouble. They weren't the only ones who wanted to be able to hear, so there was a lot of pushing and shoving with little result.

"They're pledgin' their allegiance," someone said.

"Who are?" asked another in the crowd.

"Why, the diggers. Lalor's got 'em all committin' to somethin'. I wish I was closer. I want to be part of it too."

"Part of what?"

"Whatever they're agreein' to."

"Let's get back to the store," said Scott. "I'm worried about Tom back there on his own. I can't hear a damned thing here and it's hot enough to fray tempers. I don't want to be around if there's any more trouble. You coming too?"

William stood undecided. He couldn't help Jack since he couldn't find him, and knew he never would in the crowd. And Scott was right—if he couldn't see or hear anything, it was a waste of time. Besides, Jack would find them back at the store.

"Yes, I'll come."

They arrived back at the store, pushing their way through the throng. Most people were on the move, either going to or away from the meeting.

"Any trouble?" Scott asked Tom.

"Couple of fellers came sniffing around. I showed them this and they left."

He pointed to a gun on the table.

"What happened at the meeting?"

"Too many people there. There's a different mood. Lalor spoke and urged people to do something. Those that were close enough to hear agreed and committed."

"What to?"

"Dunno. Jack went forward to find out and we lost him. I told him to meet us back here if we got separated, but I don't know if he heard me. They were flying a flag. I've not seen it before."

"Was there any violence?"

"Not that I saw. The mood was angry, but not about anyone or anything that was there. There were troopers about, but no one seemed to want to do anything about them. No, it was a quiet, reserved anger. Lalor was holding a gun."

"A gun? Why a gun? Who brings a gun to a meeting?"

"Well, Lalor did. But he never looked like using it while we were there. It was like he was telling the military that we have guns too."

"Bridie said that'll just get the military angry," said William.

"She might be right," said Tom. "Who's for a whisky while we wait?"

"While we wait? What for? For the military to get angry?" asked William.

"No. For Jack to get here," said Tom.

"That's if he's coming," said Scott.

"I think we can all have a whisky either way," said Tom. "Somehow, waiting and whisky go well together."

They had some whisky, some supper, and some more whisky. Jack didn't show, but William was past caring. They tried to play cards, but agreed after a while to stop playing as it wasn't much fun playing each other.

William woke late the next day, feeling guilty that he hadn't taken better care of Jack. Scott and Tom were already up, had eaten breakfast, and were busying themselves in the store.

"We left some breakfast for you," said Scott.

"You should have woken me," said William.

"It's not that late. I'm sure Jack'll be talking to other diggers for a while, so you don't need to be in a hurry to get there."

"Why? What's happened?"

"Couple of customers have come by this morning. Seems Lalor got members of the Reform League to burn their licences. Then commit to each other and to the flag they flew and remain steadfast until death, if need be."

"So, what's Jack got to do with that?"

"I heard he's a member of the League, so he's probably committed."

"So, why'll he be talking to diggers this morning?"

"They'll be wanting to know what happens next. There'll be lots like us who weren't close enough to hear what was going on."

"I'd best get down there. Bridie said to keep an eye on him. I've hardly done that."

"Have some breakfast first. You'll be better to face an angry Bridie on a full stomach."

William had some breakfast and gulped down some tea. He couldn't shake a feeling of foreboding.

He hurried down the hill and saw Jack in the distance standing at his tent, surrounded by a group of diggers. Bridie was nowhere to be seen.

"Ah, here he is," said Jack when William approached. "He was there. He can tell you."

"Tell them what?"

"About the meeting."

"I might have been there, but I didn't hear anything. I tried to push to the front too but got nowhere, so Scott and I left."

"Jesus," said someone. "You makin' stuff up, Jack? Makin' it sound like Lalor's gettin' us somewhere?"

"Jack doesn't make stuff up," said another. "If Jack says it, it's true."

There was a flurry of gunshots, dogs barking and people shouting.

"Where's that comin' from? Is it Bakery Hill again?" said someone.

"Over by the Gravel Pits."

"Christ. That's where my claim is. What's goin' on now? Another meetin'?"

"I'm not waitin' for an invitation. I'm goin' back."

"We'll come with you," said Jack. "C'mon, Bill—stay close this time."

They all hurried down the road and across the creek.

The area was in an uproar. A licence hunt was on in earnest. Cries of 'Joe! Joe! Joe!' were coming from everywhere.

Those cries were mixed with cries of alarm from those who had been caught, the barking of the dogs, the shouts from the traps for people to halt, and screams of 'Take it easy, mate!' from aggrieved diggers whose tents had been felled.

The diggers with Jack and William scattered, rushing to protect their families.

"The police're spoiling for a fight," said Jack. "They don't normally behave this badly. I'll bet they've heard we burned our licences and there'll be lots of unlicensed diggers."

William couldn't help but be alarmed by what he saw. There were diggers everywhere running for tents or holes or the bush, most being hotly pursued by police. Then, some diggers started to fight back. They threw mud, bottles and stones—anything they could—at the police. None, that William saw, even tried to use a gun. Some police were being dragged from their horses and others continued to fire their guns at the diggers, women and children—anyone that showed any resistance.

Commissioner Rede galloped into the fray, held up some papers and and tried to read the Riot Act. The words were lost in the noise, but his intent was clear. There'd be hell to pay for anyone defying the police.

To William, it was like the two sides had finally had enough of each other. The police were sick of not being obeyed and the diggers were sick of being told what to do. The enemy had every shape, as far as the police were concerned. If you weren't police and you were on the goldfields, you were the enemy. William thought the riot every bit as bad as what had happened at Bentley's Hotel, but this time the police were the aggressors.

"I can't see that anyone's been shot," said Jack.

"Someone must have been hit. All those guns, all those bullets."

"Let's get to Lalor. He'll know what to do."

"Where is he?"

"Dunno, but let's look at Bakery Hill first. If he's not there, there'll be someone there that'll help."

They headed up the road together. Others hurried along too, but it wasn't obvious if they were also looking for Lalor or simply trying to escape the fray.

"Have you joined the League?" asked William as they hurried along.

"Aye. Why do you ask?"

"Isn't that dangerous?"

"No, I don't think so. The League is our way to protect each other."

"Scott said you'd agreed to fight to the death, to protect each other's rights."

"Scott's right, but it won't ever come to that. The agreement is about solidarity. It means Lalor and the others can discuss things with the government and know the diggers are behind them."

"I hope you're right."

"That's what Bridie said," laughed Jack.

"I didn't see Bridie this morning."

"No, but she was in the tent. She's mad at me. Wants me to stay out of everythin'. Just wants you and me to look for gold, find some, make a fortune, and go to Melbourne."

"Most of that sounds good to me."

"Me too. But a man has to protect his rights, and those of his mates. A man can't hide when he's needed. You saw what the police were doin'. You can't pretend that didn't happen, but the government will want you to. No, Bill. Lots of diggers burned their licences in protest, so we have to support them now."

"But only if they're members of the League, Scott said."

"That's true, but most of 'em joined the League, so we'll be needin' to provide some protection in the comin' days."

As they neared Bakery Hill, they could see the new flag flying. There were hundreds of people gathered under it and William was growing concerned.

*This must be the rallying point. People like Jack will gather here. They belong now, to the League, to each other. They're united against the government. It's no wonder Bridie is worried.*

The crowd swelled in numbers all the time. Diggers, women, children—all afraid of what had just happened and all afraid of what might happen next.

Jack pushed through the crowd and William stayed as close as he could. The press of bodies was awful. Dirty, smelly people and chaos were all around— screaming children, frightened women and angry men.

Lalor was again on the stump. William was close enough this time to get the idea of what was happening. They were going to pull down the flag and make for Eureka. They could make a barrier there. It was a suitable area, on a bit of a rise, facing the camp the police and soldiers would come from. They would barricade the diggers who'd destroyed their licences and their families would come, too. They'd all be safe there. They'd organise men with weapons to put up armed resistance if it was needed. No more being chased like criminals all about the goldfields. No, if the police came again, like they did on the flats, they'd find a very different group of diggers to deal with. The shoe would be on the other foot this time.

"What about diggers that aren't in the League?" called a voice from the crowd.

"Yes, what about us?" called another.

"Why, join the League!" shouted several voices as the flag was pulled down and everyone started for Eureka. William stayed close to Jack. He wouldn't get away this time.

There was a purpose to the crowd now. They moved off, trampling the ground and falling into shallow holes that had been dug and not filled, but no one complained. Children still whimpered and women cried, the memory of the morning's licence hunt and its violence still fresh, but people took more comfort from each other. People stopped to help those who fell and offered to carry children. It wasn't far—just the other side of the creek. They all sloshed through the filthy water and slipped on the mud, crying out when they barked their shins, but safety was now in reach. And, they had each other.

"I don't know how we're going to build a barricade big enough," said Jack. "There's over a thousand people."

"And they've got to be fed and watered," said someone nearby.

Still the group moved on, with the flag and Lalor in the lead.

When they arrived at Eureka, plans were already in place. Jack left William sitting on a rock and went to get instructions.

William looked around. People were gathered in a triangular area bounded by three roads. It wasn't all that big, and it was filled with people. Someone nearby said that he thought there were fifteen hundred there. William had no idea what fifteen hundred was but if the man was right, it was a lot. Many tents were already pitched, not far from the Black Hill and Eureka Leads. Some diggers were already living there, so their homes were already in the safe area. Some of the diggers were taking their water and giving it to the children.

"What are we supposed to do?" cried the owner of a barrel.

"It's for the children," said a woman who had found a pannikin nearby. "We're all in this together."

"Yes, but not all of us want to be," said the owner. "Some of us are just in the wrong place at the wrong time."

Jack came back and said they were getting ready in case the police and military attacked.

"Some of the members are being organised into defence groups. Men with rifles, guns and pistols. Then, they're going to have a group of pike men. They're going to make a barricade with barrels, carts and slabs. People that aren't in the defence groups are asked to help build the barricade, or find food and water and bring it back."

"What're you doing, Jack?" asked William.

"I've never used a gun, so I'll be a pike man."

"What's a pike man?"

"They're putting a piece of steel on the end of a pole, so we can defend everyone if the police or military break through the barricade."

"Do you think they'll attack?"

"Some think so, but I don't. The fact that we're here and organised will make them negotiate. We'll negotiate what we want, give a bit, take a bit, and it'll all be over in a day or so. Once word gets to Hotham about what happened this mornin', he'll take action and get it fixed."

"Will you stay here until that happens?"

"Yes. I'm afraid our diggin' has to wait for a few days."

"What do you want me to do?"

"For the moment, help with the barricade and help with the food and water. The League will give a receipt for anythin' you bring in and will pay for it."

"Where will they get the money?"

"From the members. You pay to join, so they'll use that money."

"They've used all his water and I didn't see them give him a receipt," said William, jerking his thumb at the owner of the now-empty barrel of water.

"He's inside, so he gets protection. He's lucky if you ask me. He'll be safe whatever happens."

"I'll see Tom and Scott. Maybe they'll send some of their stores. I'll borrow a cart from Joe. Where do you want me to take them?"

"Good idea. See that tent yonder? It's the Diamond's. Take anythin' there. They'll arrange a receipt."

"Do you want me to see Bridie?"

"Good idea. Tell her I'll only be a day or so."

"She'll be mad."

"Better you see her, then," said Jack, laughing. "It'll be all right, Bill. You'll see. Both sides are angry at the moment, but they'll settle down. Tell Bridie not to worry. Worst thing that'll happen to me is that I drink too much whisky."

The day was still hot and dusty as William headed back to the store, but the dark clouds gathering in the sky signified a storm was about to come.

He didn't know whether to see Bridie or go to the store first.

*If it's going to rain, I'm better to get the stores first. Won't hurt to see Bridie in the rain.*

# CHAPTER 19

# The Stockade

"Stores might as well go to the diggers as get stolen," said Tom.

"What do you mean?" asked William.

"There're gangs of fellers going from store to store, in the name of the League, demanding food. They're handing out receipts, but no one knows if they're fair dinkum. So if you take it to the barricade, you can at least get a real receipt."

"Why do we want to send stuff anyway?" said Scott. "If Jack's right and it's over in a day or so, we'll only have to go and get it back again. Waste of our time, if you ask me."

"It's too late today anyway," said William. "I told Jack I'd go and see Bridie. I'll do that now and we can talk some more when I get back."

"Do they want people that can fight?" asked Tom.

William stopped and looked at him.

"I expect they do, but there's already hundreds there."

"There's hundreds of soldiers too."

"Jack says it won't come to a fight."

"Best way to stop a fight is to look ready for one. I'm good with a gun. I'll go if they need me."

"You go, Bill," Scott said. "Tom and I can talk about this. We'll sort out the stores when you get back."

William hurried off into the twilight and imminent storm, then quickly stopped and returned to the store.

"Can I borrow a lamp?"

"Take one of the ones out front."

"Thanks," said William before he hurried away again. He wished he'd brought his oilskins, too.

*Bound to need them before this night is done.*

He picked his way carefully down the road and across the creek.

*Should know this like the back of my hand.*

But he was continually astonished that there was always a new rock or rut to fall over, or new puddle to step in.

He was dreading talking to Bridie, but knew it had to be done. Jack's confidence wasn't catching and he wasn't sure he could lie to Bridie.

*Might be better to talk to Bridie without the girls.* He wished he had come later when they would be asleep.

He stopped in front of the tent and took a deep breath. He called, "Bridie?"

"Yes? Who is it?"

"It's Bill."

"Oh, Bill—thank God! Where's Jack? We haven't seen him since this morning and there's been all the talk about the ruckus on the flat. Come in, please come in."

Big drops of rain started to plop and there was a loud rumble of thunder. William was glad to step inside.

The girls sat at the table, their eyes round with worry.

"Have you seen our Daddy?"

"Yes, girls. He's all right—he's helping the diggers."

"What's he doing?"

"Well, the police raided Gravel Flats this morning, looking for diggers without licences. Daddy and some other men want to be sure that all the diggers are safe, so they're over at Eureka making sure."

"What do you mean, Bill?" said Bridie.

"Well, they've built a barricade over there, and any digger who burnt his licence is gathered behind it. Jack and the others are standing guard."

"Standing guard? Standing guard? What does that mean?" Bridie's voice was shrill. William's courage evaporated and he took a deep breath.

"Well, it means they won't let the police in to arrest any digger who doesn't have a licence."

"And how do they propose to stop them?"

William looked quickly at the girls and then at Bridie.

"They have a right to hear," said Bridie. "They have to learn about men and their madness, sooner or later."

"It's not madness, Bridie. Sure—they're armed, but Jack says the police won't attack. They'll negotiate and that'll be the end of it. Peter Lalor and the others have thought it all out. Jack says it's a good plan."

"He does, does he?"

"Oh, Bridie. I don't want to fight with you. I told Jack I'd come to see you so you'd know what's happening, but Jack says it'll be all right and I believe him."

Bridie's lips began to quiver and tears started to flow.

"Oh, Bill. I'm sorry. I'm not mad at you. Thank you for coming. I'm sure it's not easy. I might have my fears, and maybe Jack's right. But I hear the police didn't hesitate to use guns this morning. No, Bill, my experience is that a man who carries a gun is aching to use it. And they've got the military here, so if there's a battle, it'll be one-sided."

William couldn't stand the anguish in the family. He had to get out. He was frightened Bridie was right.

"I have to go."

"I know. Thank you for coming. Can I go to see Jack? Will they let me in?"

"Many of the diggers have their families with them. I'm sure they'll let you in."

"Maybe. I wonder if we can stay with him?"

"No, I don't think so. There's a few tents there, and a lot of people. There's not much room."

"We'll go anyway. All of us. Will you come in the morning and take us?"

"There's talk of me doing a delivery to the barricade, but I can come and take you first. Yes, Bridie. I'll do that."

He turned to leave the tent and realised the storm had arrived. There were lightning flashes, thunderclaps and torrential rain.

"You can borrow Jack's oilskins, if you want. Bring them back in the morning," said Bridie.

"I am most grateful," said William and bowed low to Bridie and the girls. The girls squealed with delight. William and Bridie laughed out loud.

"I'll do that every time I'm here, if you'll always laugh like that," said William, looking at the girls.

"We will! We will!"

William turned into the storm. His lamp was extinguished in seconds. The lightning helped him to see the path, but he slipped and fell many times on the uneven ground. He was a bedraggled, mud-stained, soaking mess by the time he arrived back at the store.

"My God!" exclaimed Scott. "Look at poor Bill!"

"Leave that mess at the door," said Tom. "You can't bring that in here."

William realised the oilskins looked like he'd hung an animal skin across his shoulders.

"Can't leave them outside," he said. "Borrowed them from Jack and can't afford to lose them."

"I thought he was at Eureka?"

"Well, Bridie loaned them to me, so Jack doesn't know about it."

"By the look of them, Jack might not want them back. C'mon inside, get dry and join us in a whisky. We're planning the revolt."

William hung the oilskins by the door, dried himself as best he could, and joined the others at the table.

"Tell me about your plans."

"Well, Tom here is going to go with you in the morning. We'll borrow a small cart from Joe, load it up with some goods, and you and Tom can take it to Eureka."

"Why does it take two of us?"

"The diggers stopped the soldiers' supplies, so the soldiers might be out to stop the diggers' supplies. Tom will help, if there's trouble."

"There won't be any trouble."

"I'll bet that's what they told the twelfth regiment that was attacked bringing the supplies and ammunition up from Melbourne."

"You're making it sound way too serious. You sound like Bridie."

"Bridie's a smart woman."

"She's a beautiful woman," said William, regretting it immediately and showing the regret with an embarrassed flush.

"No harm in being smart and beautiful."

William wanted to leave the topic as it was.

"That'll be all right, but I promised Bridie I'd take her and the girls to visit with Jack first thing in the morning."

"You can do that. We've had a head start with the whisky and we're not planning to open the store tomorrow—too many crooks about. So, you go first thing then come back and help us load the cart. I make it sound like there'll be a lot, but there won't be. Either way, this'll be over soon. We'll probably never get our money, so we don't plan on sending too much. A cart will make it look more than it is."

"So, what's the revolt?"

Scott put his head back and laughed loudly.

"It's our revolt against their revolt. Burning licences, building a barricade—who on earth thought it up? It's madness!"

"What's your revolt?"

"Why, taking a cart looking like there's lots of supplies, but there isn't much."

William bristled.

"This is important to the diggers there. I think they're hoping for all the support they can get. They're doing it for each other. I don't think they'd like it if they thought we were making fun of them," William said.

Scott was immediately serious.

"Bill, I'm not making fun of them. This is madness and either way, it'll be over soon. If we take a cart, the police will think there's plenty of supplies and the barricade can hold out. But it doesn't mean I agree with the League—I think it's madness! If I could stop it, I would."

"Sorry," said William.

"We're keeping the serious revolt for the government. If the troopers try to stop you taking the supplies, then Tom'll revolt against them."

They sat in silence for some time, sipping their whisky.

"C'mon," said Tom. "Let's all go to bed. I think you're more worried than you look, Bill. And I think you're worried for Bridie and the girls. By the way, they're lucky to have you to help tomorrow."

First thing the next morning , William was up and gone. He didn't bother with breakfast, as he knew Bridie would insist on him joining them.

The storm had raised the creek and the water rushed by, thundering over the rocks and carving away at its banks. It wasn't easy to cross and he wondered at the common sense in trying it with the girls.

*Probably best to let Bridie work that one out.*

Bridie and the girls were ready and there was no mention of breakfast.

No matter—he wasn't feeling hungry anyway. He was dreading a confrontation with Jack because he brought his family to the barricade, or a fight between Bridie and Jack because Jack wouldn't leave. Either way, the morning had little attraction.

They crossed the creek with William piggy-backing the girls one by one. He then held Bridie's hand to help her though the fast-flowing water. It was the first time he'd held the hand of a woman, other than his own mother, and the experience was both embarrassing and exhilarating. He couldn't look at Bridie's face and he hoped she wasn't watching him.

There were people out and about as they walked up the hill and past the store on the way to the barricade. Very few stores were open and, as most people were walking in the same direction, he guessed that they were all off to the barricade too. He felt better about that. Jack couldn't be mad at him for doing what others were doing.

Work had continued on the barricade since he last saw it and now it was starting to take shape. It still didn't look capable of stopping much, but he supposed that anyone attacking it would think twice if someone behind it had a firearm. More slabs and barrels were added as they came closer.

Men were gathered in groups learning how to hold weapons, marching up and down, and learning orders. There were many fires with people cooking, but very few tents about.

"How did they survive the storm?" he said to Bridie. "There was rain enough to drown an army!"

He wished he hadn't said anything. The sight of the men preparing for a fight and the mention of an army would do nothing to lighten Bridie's mood.

Glancing at Bridie, he saw her tighten her lips, but she remained silent.

There was a sentry at an entrance who challenged them. They weren't the only ones trying to get in. There were groups of women and children, and some men, pushing and shoving and shouting to be heard. The shouts from people within the barricade who recognised those at the entrance and the orders being yelled to those learning military skills wasn't helping.

"Who? Who do you want to see?"

"My husband," said Bridie.

"Who's this then?" said the sentry, pointing his shotgun at William.

"I'm his partner."

"Bridie!" came a shout. Jack disengaged from a group marching nearby and hurried to them.

"It's all right," said Jack to the sentry. "They're my family."

"You can see them outside then—not enough room in here anyway. Make sure you see me on the way back in."

"All right, all right," said Jack. "But it won't be hard to get back. There's more holes in the barricade than there are in Ballarat Flat."

They moved away from the entrance.

"Probably a good thing he didn't hear me," said Jack.

"But I did," said Bridie. "What are you doing, Jack? Have you taken leave of all your senses? That fence wouldn't stop a randy rooster."

"It's not meant to," said Jack. "We're just doin' all this for show. Let 'em know we mean business."

"And what will you do if *they* mean business?"

William didn't want to watch Jack and Bridie. Then he realised the girls didn't want to watch either. They stood behind him, each one using a leg for shelter from the spectacle in front. Bridie and Jack stood toe to toe—Bridie angry, Jack looking like he might get that way too. Bridie and Jack were silent for a few moments, but shouting continued to come from behind the barricade.

"Weapons ready!"

"Not like that! Like this!"

"Push it into his guts, if you can! That's right. Throw your weight behind it!"

"It's not a party, it's a fight! Put some heart into it!"

The girls started to cry.

"Mummy, please take us home. We don't like it here. Daddy, please come with us. We don't want you to get hurt. Mummy said you might get hurt. Mr Bill, please make him come."

William stared helplessly from Jack to Bridie and said, "I'm sorry, girls. It's up to your Daddy. He has to do what he thinks is right."

"Is that what you think, Jack? Is Bill right?"

"Yes, Bridie, he's right. But it's only for show, believe me. We have to show them we're willing to fight, even if we don't want to."

"Oh, Jack. I don't want you dead. Please come home."

"It'll blow over in a day or so. Besides, we're sleepin' under the stars. We're all too old to do that for too long. Please take the girls home. I'll be home before you know it."

William noticed the same scene being acted out all around him. There were many small groups with women pleading and crying for their men to come home.

"All right, Jack," said Bridie. "You do what you think best, but please be careful. C'mon, girls. Let's go home. Bill, thank you for bringing us. We'll be able to get back. You go off and get those supplies. Most of those fellers look like they need something to eat."

"What about the creek?"

"I wish the creek was my only worry."

She grasped Jack tightly, put her head on his shoulder and whispered, "The world has enough heroes. Just come home safely."

She turned and took the girls' hands and sloshed away through the mud, her long dress all wet and muddy where it met the ground. She didn't once look back.

William and Jack watched them go in silence while the noise continued unabated around them—shouts from the men drilling, small battles at the entrance as people tried to get in, and pleas from anguished wives and mothers.

"Anythin' good comes at a price," said Jack. "Off you go and get those supplies. They'll be welcome."

"You don't have to go back, Jack. There's plenty there to put up a show."

"Not you, too," laughed Jack. "Off you go. It'll be fine. You'll see."

William went and borrowed a horse and sulky from Joe. It was the best he could do—all the carts were gone.

"It's not much," said Joe. "But it'll do the job."

He went back to the store, loaded up the items that had already been stacked at the door, and then he and Tom set off for the barricade. They didn't have far to go, so William decided that Tom sitting up beside him with a rifle was all for show.

"Christ," said Tom when they came in sight of it. "What a mess."

There were more slabs, barrels and carts piled up on the barricade, more people inside and more noise. Drilling and marching continued, but it all seemed completely disorganised.

Tom looked up at the flag.

"That's one good thing, anyway. It looks good. I like the design."

They dropped the goods off at the entrance, got a receipt that Tom declared to be worthless, and took the horse and sulky back to Joe.

"All in a day's work," said Tom as they went back into the store. "What'll we do now?"

"Not much to do here except stand guard," said Scott. "Did you get a receipt?"

"For what it's worth," said Tom.

"We can use it anyway. Groups are coming by looking for stores and guns. If we show them the receipt, we can argue that we've already contributed."

"Better to show them this," said Tom, holding up his rifle. "Is it too early for a whisky?"

"I was about to get lunch. How about we have that, then have a whisky?"

"Good idea. You should see the barricade. It's a shambles, Scott. It won't stop a drunk on a lame horse."

"I don't think they expect to use it. I think it's just something to stand behind when the police come looking for the unlicensed diggers."

"That's what Jack says," said William.

They had their lunch and cleared up afterwards before enjoying a whisky. In between dealing with the occasional gang looking for stores and guns, they played a few hands of cards and talked about what to do the next day.

"I think we should stay closed," said Tom. "There'll be no one about and we don't want to encourage the fellers looking for stores and guns."

"I agree," said Scott.

"I might go and see Jack," said William. "Maybe there's something I can do to help."

"We could go and do some digging at your claim?" said Tom.

"I don't think Jack would like that," said William.

"Maybe, but we can't sit around all day. C'mon Scott, you're the ideas man."

"One of us has to stay here and I'm happy to do that. Why don't you both go to see Jack? You might be able to give them a few tips on how to fix the barricade."

They got up late the next morning, had breakfast and did some chores around the store. It was already late morning when Tom and William set out for the barricade.

It was much cooler that day, and more comfortable to be out and about. There were people streaming up and down the road and many of the men were carrying guns.

"You'd think there was a war on," said Tom. "Glad I didn't bring mine."

They could hear the barricade long before they reached it. There were more people inside it than the previous day.

"What are they all doing here?" asked William.

"Like us, I suppose—all wanting to help. I don't think it'll be easy to find Jack."

"We only found him by accident yesterday. He was near the entrance when we arrived."

The sentry on the entrance wouldn't let them in.

"Too many already," he said. "Everyone wants to help. That's good, but they'd be better to bring us food and water."

"We brought some yesterday."

"Then you've done your bit. Why don't you go home? There's no more room inside and it's a mess. They're usin' some of the old holes, but there's still piss and shit everywhere. There's even talk of some of 'em goin' home. There's never been a licence hunt on a Saturday and tomorrow's Sunday, so some'll be wantin' to go to church."

"Maybe, Jack's gone already?" said Tom.

"I don't think so," said William. "He'll be the last to leave. Let's stand over there for a while. We might see him like we did yesterday."

They stood at the barricade for a while. The sentry was right—there was an awful smell coming from inside.

"They'll need to clean it up a bit, or people will get sick," said Tom.

"Over there," said William. "See those people? With the poles? Jack said they're pikemen and he's with them. Can you see him? That's where he'll be."

The pikemen were practising forming up and thrusting their weapons. They didn't seem too enthusiastic, appearing to practise only because they were told to.

"How are they going to get close enough to use them?" asked Tom. "They'll be cut to pieces by the rifle fire before they get a chance."

"I hope not," said William, thinking of Bridie.

"This is a waste of time. Let's go."

"I'll walk down and see Bridie. Maybe Jack's down there."

"I'll come with you. Nothing better to do and I don't mind leaving this behind."

"Didn't find him?" said the sentry as they walked by. "He might have gone home already. Some have gone. Said they'll be back Monday."

"Thanks," said Tom. "Good luck."

The sentry laughed.

"It's the police and the soldiers that'll need the luck. The boys inside have been practising since yesterday and they're pretty good."

"Some of the soldier boys have been practising for twenty years," said Tom. "Don't underestimate them."

They headed back past the store on their way to Jack's.

When they reached the creek, William said, "Maybe it's not a good idea to see Bridie. If Jack's there, that's good. If he's not, she'll think we're bringing bad news and we might upset her."

"No, I think she'd like to see you either way. But, while you think about it, why don't we walk up to the government camp and see what's happening there? We won't be able to get too close, but let's have a look anyway."

"Good idea."

They crossed the bridge and went into the town.

The wind was strong and cold, but the walk and the sun kept them warm.

When they saw the camp in the distance, there seemed to be less activity than at the barricade—not so many people and many more tents. There was no drilling or marching, but the camp was barricaded too and there were sentries all along the sides. It seemed that they were also expecting an attack. The sentries saw them coming and raised their rifles.

"C'mon, Bill—let's get out of here. It looks like they are expecting trouble. The boys at the barricade might be right. Maybe show and threats are all that's needed. Maybe, these fellers don't want a fight after all."

As they headed back through the town, they saw Bath's Hotel was very busy.

"Let's stop here," said Tom. "Let's get some of the gossip about town."

They went in and got two whiskies with some difficulty.

"Might open a hotel the next time," said Tom when they managed to find somewhere to stand. "These boys are doing well in the crisis. Not like us—no one buying and anybody that comes is looking for a donation or to rob us."

Some of the patrons nearby had come from the barricade. They brought William and Tom into the group.

"You fellers from Eureka?" asked Tom.

"Yes," was the reply from them all at once.

"You going back tonight?" asked William.

"No point in goin' back 'till Monday," said one.

"If then," said another.

"What do you think the soldiers will do?" asked Tom.

"The talk is that they'll do nothin'. Lalor sent Father Smyth and some others yesterday to see Commissioner Rede about releasin' the unlicensed diggers they arrested on Thursday at Gravel Pits. Story goes that he wouldn't, but didn't set any deadlines for the diggers to leave the barricade either, so we think he'll just wait for the diggers to get tired of the game."

"And will they?" asked William.

"Who knows? There's nothin' happenin' on the diggin's and that's for sure. No dig, no find they say. So we can't afford to do this forever."

"Well, let me buy you all a whisky anyway. If you've got the time, of course."

"That's all we've got," said the man who had spoken before.

William and Tom stayed for a few more drinks, and William decided that it was too late and he'd had too many whiskies to visit Bridie and the girls.

"Funny place, this Ballarat," he said to Tom as they stumbled back to the store. "Hot as hell yesterday, cold as ice today."

"If it wasn't for the gold, no one'd be here," said Tom.

Scott was pleased to see them when they got back. He told them that nothing further had happened. He wished he'd got Joe to look after the store and gone with them.

"Did you find Jack?" he asked.

"No, there was an idea that he might have gone home already. Lots have left according to some fellers we met."

"I hope there's enough left if there's trouble."

"There won't be trouble. We went to the government camp and they looked more nervous than the diggers. Let's have some supper and another whisky and head for bed. Nothing more will happen for a few days."

*   *   *   *

William woke to the sound of pop! pop! pop!—it sounded like someone had left a lidded pot bubbling over the fire.

*That's odd. We didn't have stew for supper last night.* Maybe Tom or Scott had put some on after he'd gone to bed and forgotten it.

He got up to check, but there was nothing over the fire. Then he saw Tom standing in the doorway.

"What's happening?" he asked.

Scott was already up too, and he and William joined Tom near the doorway.

"I think it's coming from the barricade," said Tom. "I wonder what the diggers are shooting at?"

"Jesus, Tom," said Scott. "Do you think the soldiers are attacking the barricade?"

"If they are, the diggers're in trouble. It's the right time to attack—it's dawn and most of the diggers left last night. C'mon, let's get over there. They might need our help."

"What can we do to help?"

"We won't know from here. C'mon, let's get dressed and get over there."

They all struggled into their clothes and hurried out the door, Tom picking up his rifle on the way.

"Jesus, Tom. What are you going to do with that? Shoot someone?"

"Maybe," said Tom.

"Will we need a lamp?" asked William.

"Better off without one, even if we can't see. If the soldiers are there, no point in telling them we're coming."

They hurried down the road, their boots slushing where the ground was muddy and thumping where it was dry.

"How do you think they got there?"

"Who?"

"The soldiers."

"Dunno if it is the soldiers, but there sure is a lot of shooting."

There were a few other shadowy figures on the road and William was glad the police and the soldiers wore uniforms, so at least they'd know them if they ran into them.

The road was a gradual rise and they could hear the shooting more clearly as they came closer. There were now more bursts of shooting, rather than the sporadic shots they heard a few minutes ago.

"It's the soldiers, all right," said Tom.

"Can you see them?" asked William.

"No, but that's how the soldiers shoot. They'll be firing by section. God help the diggers."

The dawn's light was increasing and as they came around the side of the hill, they could see the barricade clearly.

The police troopers had ridden in from the south from Warrenheip Gully—some with sabres, some with revolvers, and others with rifles. It looked like they had nearly reached the barricade before they were seen.

The soldiers were massed at the north, marching at the barricade, kneeling and firing by rows. The air was filled with the white smoke from their rifles. The wind was still from the south, so the smoke was carried across the soldiers. It may have been harder to see the diggers due to the poor light and the smoke from their fires and rifles, but there was no doubt the soldiers still had a clear view of them.

The smoke cleared for a moment and William could see the chaos behind the barricade. Bodies were strewn about and puffs of smoke came from guns, pistols and rifles within the barricade—it was a fight to the death and the diggers were losing. There weren't enough diggers to hold off an assault from two sides.

William was astonished to hear Scott praying.

"Oh, dear God. Those poor men... help them, please... please don't let Jack be there."

He saw the pikemen. They were gathered behind a rude structure they had built within the barricade, facing the soldiers with nothing but a piece of iron fixed to the end of a wooden pole.

Both the soldiers and the troopers were close to the barricade now. A few of the soldiers fell, but the diggers could do nothing. The encirclement, the encroachment, the end, was inevitable.

The troopers broke in first and pursued any armed man, dispatching them with rifle and bayonet. Some of the men already lying on the ground were bayoneted again. The pikemen didn't know what to do. Their weapons were no match for the rifles, guns, pistols and bayonets. Some tried to fight, others tried to flee, but the soldiers and police showed them no mercy.

Tents were set alight and women and children ran screaming. Any man who tried to defend his tent was cut down.

"Bastards!" yelled Tom and readied his rifle.

"No, Tom. Don't be a fool," whispered Scott. "It'll be over soon."

Incredibly, William saw some diggers fleeing the barricade.

How had they survived?

"Look!" he whispered. "Some of them are getting away!"

The soldiers tried to shoot them, and a few of the troopers took off after them on horse. Some of the diggers ran across the creek, heading to Bakery Hill. Others took off through the scrub in the direction of Black Hill and Brown Hill. A few headed around the side of the hill towards Scott, Tom and William.

"Now's my chance," said Tom, readying his rifle as some soldiers started in pursuit. But the soldiers were ordered back and the diggers, realising they had got away, headed towards the creek and cut through it towards the town.

The nearby drama concluded and William looked back at the barricade.

Groups were huddled together and guarded by soldiers or police. It looked like the officers were taking control, and any diggers or their families still alive were placed under guard. Anything that would burn was alight. Every now and again, a shot rang out when a digger was found hiding, or attempted to escape. The flag had been torn down and was no longer visible.

In a few places, women and children wailed over bodies lying on the ground. Some of the soldiers were piling the bodies in a heap and pushing people roughly away if they tried to intervene.

It was impossible to see if Jack was there. In the manner of the diggers, many of the bodies were dressed alike, just as Jack was.

Some shouts of triumph came to them from the barricade. The military and the police exalted in their victory.

"Proud of themselves," said Tom. "I'll bet their mothers wouldn't be."

"I have to get down there and see if I can help Jack."

"He may not be there."

"But what if he is?"

"They'll shoot you, Bill—you're dressed like a digger. You're the enemy."

"I have to help if I can. I think the shooting has stopped. They've won, anyway. Why would they shoot anyone that's unarmed?"

"You just saw them shooting unarmed people," said Scott.

"Maybe he's right, Scott," said Tom. "There's holes all about in the barricade now. He might be able to get close enough to see if Jack's in the pile of bodies."

"If they see him, they'll shoot him," said Scott. "Don't be a fool, Bill."

"What if he's only injured? What if he needs help?"

"There's no one there that's injured. You saw them, Bill. Every soldier running by stuck his bayonet into every body, even if it was lifeless."

"All right. What if he's in one of those groups under guard?"

"Then he doesn't need your help. Someone else who's in the group will have to help him."

"It's not done yet," said Tom quietly. "Look."

William saw the soldiers setting fire to tents outside the barricade too.

"It's as though they like it now," said Tom. "How many will they set alight?"

The screams of women and the protests of men came to them across the dawn air. They could see people trying to extinguish the flames, others trying to run away and infrequent shots as the soldiers tried to stop them.

"They must have been hiding some diggers," said Scott.

Officers were moving amongst the men, distinguishable by their uniforms, and forcing them to stop. Smoke and flames rose on the air.

Small groups started to gather outside the remains of the barricade. Inside, the soldiers laid out the bodies in neat rows and stood guard over them. Two women came in and knelt beside one of the men, prostrate with grief.

"You might be able to go down now, Bill. It looks like they're letting people claim the diggers' bodies."

"Will you come with me?"

"Three men and one with a rifle? I think it'd get us killed. No, Bill. But I think if you want to check for Jack, you can do it. It's risky, but find a woman and go in with her."

"Shall I get Bridie?"

"Hell, no. There's women there, but it'll be a heartbreaking job. No, Bill. See if he's there—that's all. We'll wait here."

"All right," said William and he headed around the side of the hill, picking his way through holes and scrub. He watched the soldiers all the way as he went down the hill, but no one took any notice of him.

Two women were waiting outside the barricade and William went up to them. One was young, not much older than him, with dark hair and a pleasant face. The other lady was much older. Maybe they were mother and daughter.

"Are you waiting for someone?" he asked.

"I think my husband's in there," said the older woman. "But we're afraid of the soldiers."

"I'll come with you," said William.

"Oh, please," said the one who had spoken, and then she started to cry.

"I'm Emma, she's Alice," said the young one. "We're sisters. She's looking for her husband and I'm here to help. She might be afraid of the soldiers, but I'm not."

William helped them both through the barricade and towards the bodies. He'd never seen bodies like this—the blood, the cuts, and the wounds. It didn't seem possible that any of them were alive. Yet as they came close, some of the men groaned.

"Some of them need help," he said to a soldier without thinking what might happen next. The soldier just shrugged.

William was still with the women when Alice dropped to her knees beside a body and screamed, a heart-rending wail of loss.

"Oh, my poor man. What have they done to you?" she sobbed. She lay across the body, mindless of the blood.

Emma stopped too and grasped Alice by the shoulders.

"God, no," she said and knelt beside her for a few moments, then spoke again. "Think of the living, Alice. There'll be time for mourning later. Find one that's alive," she whispered. "Pretend he's yours, too."

"I can't," said Alice. "What have they done? What will I do? Oh, what will I do?"

"Can you get a cart, or something?" Emma asked William.

"Of course, but let me check the bodies first."

"Pick at least two, if they're alive," whispered Emma. "We have to help as many as we can. They're setting up a hospital at the London Hotel."

William had checked most of the bodies before he found Jack. He stopped, stunned at the sight. Jack must have put up the fight of his life—he had deep cuts to his arms and face, and bullet wounds to his chest, arms and legs.

Kneeling beside him, William whispered, "Jack? Are you alive?"

But Jack didn't move or answer.

Emma stood beside him.

"I think he's dead," she said. "Is he your father?"

"No," said William, incapable of saying anything further.

*Jack dead? How did this happen? Why would they kill Jack? What was the point?*

"Did you find any others alive?"

"No," said William, still trying to come to grips with Jack lying dead in front of him.

*What'll I tell Bridie? Oh, God. Bridie and the girls.*

"He didn't look hard enough," came a whisper. "I'm still alive. Will you help me?"

"Oh, my darling brother!" cried Emma as she knelt beside the man who had spoken.

"Can you get us something to take them away?" she whispered to William again.

"Of course," said William, glad now to have something else to think about.

He hurried off through the barricade and up the road, past the burnt out remains of Bentley's Hotel, then turned towards Joe's. Tom was coming up the street with a cart.

"How did you know?" asked William.

"We saw groups of people going in, some claiming and removing the bodies. We thought you or someone else would need help."

"They're trying to help as many as they can. Some of them are still alive, but the soldiers are doing nothing. A lady helped me, now I'm helping her, and we want to take them to hospital."

"Hop on. Let's go before the soldiers change their mind. Did you find Jack?"

"Yes, I did," whispered William, so quietly that Tom looked at him in alarm.

"I see," said Tom. "Damn."

They got back to the barricade and there were more people now, arranging to take the bodies. The women he had left were still there—Alice still lying across the body of her dead husband, Emma beside the digger that was still alive.

Taking the injured digger, they put him gently in the cart. Then they retrieved Alice's husband, struggling with her as she continued to lie across his body. Finally, they collected Jack. Emma went back to check for more that were living, but the soldier chased her away.

"They can't all be yours," he said laughing. "Unless you run a brothel, in which case most of these are no good to you."

Emma stopped, turned and walked up to the soldier. They were about the same age and the soldier took a step back.

"I'll check for any that are alive and you'll have to use that if you want to stop me," she said, pointing at the soldier's rifle.

"Don't tempt me, miss. I've not ever shot a woman, but I'll do it if I have to."

"All right, I'll go. But you'll be hurt and dying one day and no one will help you. Besides, when you die, there'll be a surprise for you," she said.

"And why is that?"

"God'll be waiting for you and He's got special things in mind for people like you. Good luck, soldier. Something tells me you'll need it."

The soldier stood open mouthed, staring after her.

She joined the others on the cart and they hurried away towards the London Hotel. The two women and Tom sat on the seat—William was in the back with the bodies. He tried to make the wounded man as comfortable as possible but it didn't matter—the man was unconscious. William hoped he wasn't dead.

"Why so far?" asked Tom.

"Don't know," said Emma. "I hear that's where they're being taken."

They dropped the wounded digger at the hotel, where a doctor said he would do his best to save him.

"Where would you and your friend like to go?" asked Tom.

"We have nowhere to go," said the woman. "They burned our tent. Where are you taking the other body?"

"His wife and children have a tent near Canadian Flats. We'll take him there."

"We won't go with you then. His wife will find it hard to grieve with strangers about."

"I wasn't thinking that you would. I have a store. I'll take you there and we'll work out what to do next."

William still sat in the back, unable to take his eyes off the dead bodies.

What would happen now? To him? To Bridie? To the girls? He'd become very close to Jack. *Oh, Jack—Bridie'd been right all along. You should have listened. Now you're dead. And for what? How have you changed anything?*

He remembered old Patrick, who saw all of the world he wanted through his one eye. Patrick was right. William had just seen way too much through two.

*What a stupid, pointless, waste.*

The tears started to flow and he couldn't stop them. Tom looked back.

"We'll be there soon," he said to Emma, loud enough for William to hear.

*I'd better stop crying. It's not what men do.*

They pulled up outside the store. Scott heard them and hurried out. He peered into the back of the cart.

"Oh, no," he said. "Bill, I'm so sorry. Who's the other one?"

"He's her husband," said Emma, climbing down from the cart, and nodding her head at Alice.

"We helped these two ladies," said Tom. "They have nowhere to go."

"I'm Emma and she's Alice," said the young lady. "C'mon Alice, I'll help you."

She stepped forward and helped Alice down from the seat. Alice couldn't walk and leaned against her sister.

"I'm Scott, this is Tom and that's Bill sitting in back. Bill, hop out. Tom, pull the cart around the side in the shade. They'll be all right there, for the moment."

Tom did as he was asked and when he came back, they all went inside. Alice staggered more than walked.

"I have to tell Bridie," said William, as soon as they got inside.

"Yes, but it'll wait a few more moments. We have to work out what to do with Alice's husband. Do you ladies have any friends where you can go?" said Scott.

"Not in Ballarat," said Emma.

"Where, then?"

"Melbourne."

"Alice, I know this is hard but we need some help. What do you want to do with your husband?"

"What can I do?" Alice wailed, breaking into tears again.

"While you work it all out, I'll walk down the hill and tell Bridie," said William.

"Don't you want to take Jack?"

"Not like he is. I'd rather tell Bridie first so she can get ready to see him."

"Can't it wait?" asked Tom. "I'll come with you once we work out what to do."

"No—Bridie'll be frantic. She'll have heard about how badly it went for the diggers and she'll want news of Jack. No, I'll go now and take Jack to wherever she'll want him to go, later."

Tom put his hand on William's shoulder.

"You're right, of course. I'll come if you want."

"No—best I go on my own I think."

He left, walking out into the morning sun. It seemed impossible that such a catastrophe had occurred on such a beautiful day.

There were occasional shots as he walked along. No doubt some nervous soldiers were trying to find the diggers who had escaped. He decided he'd better be careful, as the soldiers wouldn't know an escaped digger from one that hadn't even been there.

Arriving at the creek across from Jack's tent, he could see Bridie standing outside, looking in his direction. He wondered if she knew it was him. He still hadn't worked out what to say. How do you tell a wife that her husband has been killed in a battle? Or fight? What was it?

As he came close, Bridie recognised him.

"Bill?" was all she said. Then she raised her hand to her mouth and fainted. Her head made a nasty thud as it hit the ground.

"Mummy! Mummy!" screamed the girls, running from the tent.

"Oh, Bridie," said William. He bent and scooped her up. She was much lighter than he expected and he carried her into the tent.

"Is she dead too?" asked Missy.

"What do you mean, 'too'?"

"Our Daddy is dead, isn't he? Mummy said he might be. She said if you came on your own, he'd be dead."

William stretched Bridie out on her bunk. She looked so helpless, lying there. William would give anything to not be the one to bring the news.

*It's too late now. Now she knows, and I'll always be the one that told her.*

"No, Mummy's not dead," he said.

"Is our Daddy dead?" asked Polly, looking at William as thought he might know everything.

"Yes, Polly. Your Daddy is dead. I'm sorry."

Bridie stirred. She looked at William.

"Where is he?"

"At the store. Do you want me to bring him down here?"

"No, please don't. Would you bury him for me? I'll give you some money."

"I've got money. He was my partner. I'll bury him. Do you want to come to the cemetery?"

"No, we're going to Melbourne."

"When?"

"As soon as I can work out how."

"Would you like some tea, Mummy? We can get it."

"Yes, please. Some for Mr Bill too, please. Would you like some tea, Bill?"

"Yes, please."

The girls busied themselves at the fire. A little wood on the fire, a little water in the billy, then wait for it to boil, add some tea and the job was done.

"Would you pour it for us, Mr Bill? We haven't worked out how to do that part yet. We're scared of the hot water."

"Of course I will."

Two pannikins, some sugar, some tea and that job was done, too. William was glad to busy himself with a job, no matter how small. It avoided dwelling on the sadness.

"Bridie, I can take you to Melbourne—I'm going myself. I can't stay here anymore."

"Why not? What about the gold?"

"Everything here will always remind me of what I saw this morning. It was terrible, Bridie. Those poor men. They were outnumbered, the soldiers were trained and knew what they were doing. The diggers didn't, but they were so brave. Even when the soldiers broke through the barricade, they stood there and fought. Oh, Bridie. Poor Jack."

"Did you see him?"

"No. We heard the noise from the store and went around the side of Specimen Hill behind the store. We saw the fight, but I didn't see Jack."

"And, what about the gold? You could keep looking for it. You could join one of the deep lead teams. They'd be glad to have you."

"No, Bridie. I'd like to go away."

"Why don't you think about it? Talk to Scott and Tom. They might want you back at the store."

They sat in silence for a while, sipping their tea.

Then, William noticed Bridie had gone to sleep.

He looked at Missy, who put her finger across her lips to indicate William should be silent.

Missy leaned across to him and whispered, "Mummy's been awake since the noise started. We knew she wanted to run and help Daddy, but had to stay with us. She said, 'Mr Bill will help him.' Did you help him, Mr Bill?"

"Oh, Missy. I wanted to. There were so many soldiers, and they had so many guns. I don't think anybody could have helped your Daddy. He was a very, very brave man."

He started to cry again and was glad only the girls could see him.

Missy patted him on the shoulder.

"Don't worry, Mr Bill. Daddy's all right. Mummy said he's gone to heaven."

"Where is heaven, Mr Bill?" asked Polly.

"Anywhere but Ballarat," said William. "You girls look after Mummy. I'll look after your Daddy now. I'll come back later today."

"Bye, Mr Bill," the girls whispered at the same time.

William crossed the creek and headed up the hill to the store. There were patrols of soldiers still about, and the odd rifle or gunshot. He almost wanted a patrol to question him. The need to lash out at someone or something was overwhelming.

He arrived back at the store and everything was as he had left it. The cart was still parked at the side of the tent with the two dead men in it, but they had both been covered with blankets.

Flies had already gathered and William realised there was no time to waste in burying the men. The horse looked distressed, so William gave him some water.

"There, there, boy. We'll get you back to Joe soon."

Scott saw him come through the door and called, "Good, you're back. I won't ask how it went. Does Bridie want us to take Jack to her?"

"No—she asked if I'd arrange to bury him. I have no idea how to do that. Will you help me?"

"Of course, of course. Sit down, Bill—you look exhausted. Have some coffee. I opened a tin of biscuits as well. One or two of those will do you no harm."

William slumped into his favourite chair, surprised it hadn't been taken. Emma put a pannikin of coffee in front of him.

*She's one of those people who always knows when and how to help.*

"While you were gone, we decided to bury Alice's husband this morning," said Scott. "Now that we know what Bridie wants, we'll bury Jack too. I'll stay here. You and Tom can take the bodies to the cemetery. Alice and Emma will go with you."

"Aren't we rushing it, Scott?" said William. "I don't know much about this, but at sea the captain or a friend says some comforting words, so maybe somebody should do that. There's also the holes to be dug."

"Some lads have gone ahead to dig the hole for Alice's husband."

"Has he got a name? We keep calling him Alice's husband. Has he got a name, Alice? I'd like to know his name," said William.

"Steady, Bill. This has been hard on all of us. Yes. His name's George," said Scott.

"Do you have any children, Alice? Shouldn't they be here?" said William.

"No, Bill. We don't have any children."

"Bill, like I said. We've already been through all this. We talked about it while you were seeing Bridie. Sit there, drink your coffee until we're ready to go," said Scott.

"Sorry, Scott. I know I'm not thinking properly. It's just... It's just... So pointless," said William. "Jack was so brave. Foolishly brave! It's such a waste. And the silliest part? The best ones were behind that barricade. And now they're gone."

He sipped his coffee. There was no taste or comfort in the scalding liquid.

"Bill, we've all lost this morning. Some more than others," said Alice. "Yes, my George was a good man and I probably won't find another. We kept moving from place to place, always chasing gold and never finding it. It was a lonely life for me. We couldn't have children. I don't know why. The doctors said it was George's fault. I didn't care. I only wanted my George. But he took it personally. Always trying to prove he was a man, and always taking the most dangerous jobs. He loved the deep leads, digging one hundred and fifty feet down, every day he could show himself to be braver than all the others."

She was quiet for a while. William wondered if she was finished.

"It seems you and your Bridie have lost a good man too," she continued. "We'll bury these and other men today and we'll keep going, doing some things we hate and other things we love, but life will go on. In time, these men will only be memories, but they may have won more than we realise today. The government will look like fools because they allowed this to happen. This isn't the time of Jesus when a life wasn't worth a Roman sandal. This wasn't an armed uprising. It was a bunch of brave and foolish men trying to stick up for each other."

The room was quiet.

*The Alice speaking just then wasn't the Alice lying prostrate across her man, wondering what had happened and what to do next.*

"I'll always be proud of my George. You should be proud of your friend, too. I'm sure they achieved more today than we think right now, and only time will tell."

"Jesus said, 'No greater love does any man have than he lays down his life for a friend'," said Emma quietly.

"Then, let's bury those that did. Sitting around and talking about it won't get the burying done," said Alice.

She walked over to William.

"Now, you, young man. You can take my arm and give me some comfort. I think I'll be needing it before this day is done."

William rose to his feet and took Alice's arm before walking her out the door and helping her up onto the cart. The day was still nice and warm with little wind blowing. There were some darker clouds gathering in the south, showing the promise of more rain.

Alice looked down at William.

"I hope it holds off," she said. "There's not much that's nice about a cemetery and rain sure doesn't make it nicer."

Tom, Alice and Emma sat at the front. William got in the back with the bodies. He was glad of the blankets, but surprised by the amount of blood. It was impossible to avoid sitting in it.

They went down the hill, across the bridge and through the town to get to the cemetery on Creswick Street. There were some carts gathered, groups of people about, and quite a few men digging graves. William was pleased when Tom parked the cart such that the horse could get at some grass.

Tom went to find the men that had agreed to dig the grave for George to find out where it was and to ask them to dig another. He came back shortly after to say that he had found them and they had finished, and two of them would help with George before they started on Jack's grave.

William asked if it would be all right if he didn't help carry George.

"Take it easy, Bill," said Tom. "I expect you'll want to help with Jack though."

"Of course."

Alice thanked the men for digging the grave for George.

"That's all right, missus," said one of them. "Diggin's what we're good at."

Tom helped the men carry George to his grave.

William wasn't sure that he'd want to spend eternity there. The town and the mines didn't help. It must have been beautiful once.

"Please hold me, Bill. I think I need you now."

William took Alice's arm.

The diggers carried George while Tom and Emma walked behind, and William and Alice behind them.

Alice was praying quietly. William didn't know any prayers, and he didn't know George either, so he decided to hold his grief until they buried Jack.

The men accidently dropped, more than lowered, George into the hole.

"Sorry, missus," said the man who had spoken before.

"Pay it no mind," said Alice. "He's past caring."

She looked down at George. The blanket mostly covered him and there was only a flash of grey where it had slipped off his head.

"Please, God. Look after our George. You know he's earned it. C'mon, Bill, take me back to the cart. I fear my legs and heart won't be up to the task if I stay much longer."

"We'll cover him for you, missus," said the gravedigger.

"Thank you," said Alice. "I know your kindness will be repaid."

"We won't be long with the next grave, Tom. There's another we can use. They haven't brought the body for that one yet, so Jack can use it."

William, Emma and Alice walked back to the cart while Tom went to help the men.

They sat on the cart in silence, darker clouds rolled in and the breeze freshened.

"You can always trust nature," said Alice, and a drizzly rain began to fall.

William could see a sulky coming from the direction of town. He wondered who the new arrivals were. *It's going to be a busy day out here.*

Then he realised it was Joe with Bridie and the girls, who were dressed in black. The sulky pulled up beside them.

"Bill," said Joe.

"Bridie. Why?" asked William.

"I had to say goodbye," said Bridie. "The girls and I. A good man is leaving us today. We won't get another chance. We walked to the store, hoping to catch you in time. Joe was good enough to bring us. Have we arrived in time?"

"Yes, you have. They're still digging the... Uh... Bridie, this is Alice and Emma. Alice lost her husband today too."

"I'm sorry," said Bridie. "It's a sad day for Ballarat. This is Missy and Polly."

"Hello, girls," Emma and Alice said at the same time.

*Is this something that all women do?* William wondered.

"Joe, will you wait with us?"

"That I will, missus. I knew Jack too."

"Where is he?" asked Bridie.

"In the back," said William, nodding his head behind him.

Bridie climbed down and walked over to the cart.

"Please don't look, Bridie. Remember him as you knew him. We've not cleaned him up or anything—it's not pretty," said William.

"Stay seated, girls. Bill, I want to see what they've done."

"Bridie, please don't," said William.

Before he could say more, she reached the side of the cart and lifted the blanket.

Bridie screamed, but not in fright or surprise—she screamed at the sight of what had happened to her man.

"Oh, Jack. What have they done? What did you ever do to deserve this?"

William helped her back to the sulky.

"What have they done, Mummy? What did the bad men do?"

Bridie clasped her girls to herself fiercely.

"Bill was right, girls. I shouldn't have looked. I wish I hadn't. I hardly recognise your Daddy."

Tom came over.

"They're ready now. Hello, Bridie. We didn't think you were coming."

"I came to say goodbye, Tom. That's all."

Tom nodded.

"Would you put him in the grave and cover him with the blanket before we join you?"

"Of course, Bridie, of course. Bill, will you help us?"

William stepped down from the cart and helped Tom and the others to carry Jack to his grave. Once again, he was dropped into the hole, but there was no one to apologise to this time.

"I'll fetch Bridie and the girls," said William.

He came back with them a few minutes later. Alice, Emma and Joe stayed behind.

The diggers moved away. William, Tom, Bridie and the girls stood around the grave. All that was now Jack lay at the bottom of the hole, covered with the blanket. There were patches of blood all over it. The rain fell more heavily now, making little puddles in the folds and mixing with the blood.

"He's yours again," whispered Bridie. "We didn't have him for long, but we're grateful for his time, and proud to call him husband and father. He was a good man and that can't be said about everyone. Goodbye, Jack."

Bridie hugged the girls and all three walked away crying, sloshing through the mud and the rain.

*Like Alice says—nature doesn't fail to disappoint.*

"Let's get it filled and go home. I'm soaked," said Tom.

It took no time to fill the hole. William looked around and saw the other groups were finishing up too. The sounds of crying and grief could clearly be heard above the patter of the rain.

Bridie, Joe and the girls were waiting when they got back.

"Will you take Bridie home, please Joe?" asked Tom.

"No," said Bridie. "We're all going back to the store. I've brought a bottle of Jack's whisky. Jack would expect no less of us than to toast him farewell. And if you men won't do it, then all of us girls will."

"If that's what we're doing, then let's do it," said Tom. "This is no longer any place to be."

"If it ever was," said William.

They headed back to the store and Tom and the women went inside while William and Joe returned the cart.

"I'll leave yer the sulky," said Joe. "The missus will need it to get back later. You can bring it back when you're done."

The horse had other ideas and tried to follow.

"I think he wants to get out of the rain," said William.

"Don't blame him," said Joe. "Don't much like it myself. Looks like I'll need to tether him, but if you bring a nose bag back he might be happier to stay."

It wasn't far to Joe's. They removed all the harnesses and put the horses in the paddock and the cart in the shed.

"Leave the cart in the open," said Joe. "The rain'll clean it up a bit."

William nodded. He'd forgotten about the blood in the back.

"I won't come back with you" said Joe.

"I understand," said William, even though he didn't. "Thanks for the cart and the sulky."

"Glad to help."

When William arrived back at the store, he attached the nosebag to the horse. It no longer seemed to care about the rain or being left behind.

Then he went inside, and Bridie wanted to know what had happened to Joe.

"Said he wasn't coming," said William.

"We'll see about that," said Bridie, heading for the door.

"You can't go out in the rain," said William. "It's too wet out there."

"Well, Bill. The way I see it is that one of us has to go to get Joe. If you don't want me to go, then it has to be you. If you think Joe won't come with you, then it has to be me."

She was standing with her back to the room and her hands on her hips, her black clothes soaked with rain and making little puddles on the floor where she stood. Her cheeks were flushed and her eyes were blazing, and locks of her dark hair fell across her face.

*Perhaps she just wants something else to be angry about too*, William thought as he remembered how he had argued with Scott earlier. *The day has been hard on everybody. And she is beautiful.*

He realised he was very attracted to Bridie, even though she was old enough to be his mother. Despite trying not to, he flushed red with embarrassment.

"I'm sorry, Bill. I didn't mean to embarrass you."

"There's another option, Bridie," said Tom. "I'm still wet, so I can go and be back soon."

"Good idea, Tom. C'mon, Bill," said Bridie, taking his arm. "Come over by the fire and dry out."

Alice and Emma were busy drying out the girls and looked both absorbed and delighted by the task.

"How are you girls going?" asked William. "Getting enough attention?"

"Yes," they both said, giggling.

"I put some tea on," said Emma.

"Whisky first," said Bridie. "When Tom and Joe get back and get dry, we're going to drink a toast to our men."

"But then we'll have some tea," said Alice. "I'm ready for a good cuppa. I wouldn't mind some cake, too. Doesn't anyone here have a wife?"

"Only me," said Scott. "And mine's in Melbourne."

"Doesn't she like Ballarat?" said Alice.

"I've got a place down there. I come up from time to time to help Tom. He runs the store, I run the property."

"Tom doesn't have a wife?" asked Alice, looking squarely at Emma. "Is he engaged then?"

"What about Tom?" asked Tom, coming through the door, followed closely by Joe.

"Ah, Joe. Glad you can make it. I want to thank you for the ride to the cemetery and for looking after us. I know Jack would like you to join us in the toast," said Bridie.

"Thank you, missus. You're very welcome," said Joe, looking embarrassed. "At first I thought some thieves might be about, but they don't like the rain, so I'm pleased to be here. There's some others bringin' some horses and carts back later, too. It's been a busy day."

"And what about Tom?" asked Tom, again.

"You don't want to know," said Scott. "C'mon, you two get dry. I'm keen to try one of Bridie's whiskies."

Scott and William gathered the strangest collection of glasses and pannikins. They usually had to cater for only four, but now they had five more.

"Do you have some water for the girls?" asked Bridie.

"I have something better than that," said Scott. "I've got some ginger beer. Rowlands are making it locally and I got some in to try it."

"Beer? Beer? Did you say beer?" said Missy.

"You bet I did," said Scott and poured some for each of them from a tall bottle.

"Mummy? Can we?"

"I suppose so," said Bridie, looking doubtful.

"Don't forget the grownups," said Tom.

"We won't," said Scott. "But since Bridie brought the whisky, she should have the honour of pouring it."

Bridie picked a bottle up from the floor where she had left it earlier and poured a generous portion into the remaining glasses and pannikins.

They all drank a toast, first to Jack, then to George, then to all the men that had fought that day.

"Let's drink to the women, too," said William. "I've seen a lot of courage today, not only from the men. Why, Emma rescued an injured digger from the barricade. A soldier even threatened to shoot her!"

"Did he?" said Missy, trying to look grown up with a glass of ginger beer in front of her.

"Where are you staying, Alice?" said Bridie. "And I mean you too, Emma."

"Why, Tom said we could stay here for a while," said Emma.

"Why here? Don't you have a home to go to?"

"The soldiers burnt our tent. It was just outside the barricade," said Alice, bitterly.

"Do you have any clothes?"

"Only what we have on."

"Then, I must give you some things. This might be a store, but it doesn't cater for women."

"Oh, we'd be so grateful. It's been such a sad day and you have all been so kind—you with the clothes, Bill with the cart, Tom with somewhere to stay," said Emma.

"Yes, Tom is wonderful," said Alice, once again looking at Emma.

"How will you all fit in?" asked Bridie.

"We'll manage," said Scott. "It's big enough. Just for a day or so. Alice and Emma are going to Melbourne."

"So are we," said Bridie. "That is, the girls and me."

"I've been wondering what you'd do," said Scott. "What will you do, Bill? Will you stay and work the claim?"

William shook his head.

"No, I'm going to Melbourne too."

"Why?" said Tom. "You don't have to work your claim. You can join the others on the deep leads. There's gold there, Bill, and I know you like digging for it."

"It's not that, Tom."

William knew everyone was looking at him. He was the centre of all their attention. He flushed and hated himself for it.

"There, there, Bill," said Alice. "It's none of our business—you're your own man. You can do what you want and you don't need to explain yourself to anyone."

"It's all right, Alice," said William. "I work with Scott and Tom. They need to know what I'm thinking. We watched from the hill this morning. The diggers never had a chance. Ballarat will always remind me of that and what we lost today."

"We might have gained something, too," said Scott. "We don't know yet."

"Whatever we gained, Scott, the cost wasn't worth it."

"I'll tell you what," said Scott. "Joe, will you hire us some horses and a cart? Bill can take Alice, Emma, Bridie and the girls to Melbourne."

"Yes, I can do that," said Joe.

"Bill, you can stay at my place until you decide whether to keep going or to come back. My family knows all about you and would love to meet you. They'll put you to work with the horses. You might even enjoy it."

The room was silent and Scott continued.

"If you decide to keep going, Mike can bring the cart back with a load at some point. What do you think?"

The room was still silent.

"C'mon everyone, it's not that bad an idea!" said Scott.

"How long would the cart be gone for?" asked Joe. "Summer's a busy time. Might be needin' it sooner rather than later."

"We'll sort that out, Joe. I'll make it worth your while."

"I think it's good for Alice and me, but I worry that it's not good for Bill," said Emma.

"Let the man speak for himself," said Alice.

"It's good for me," said William.

"Bridie?" said Scott.

"Yes, it's good for us," said Bridie thoughtfully. "Besides, Bill'll be the most popular boy in Melbourne."

"Why's that?" asked Tom.

"Tuning up in Melbourne with a cartful of women, why wouldn't he be popular?"

Everyone laughed. Even the girls giggled.

It was the first time all day that William wasn't lost in a fog of sadness and grief. Someone offered more whisky and he was grateful to take it.

"C'mon ladies, let's give these men a break and get them a proper supper," said Alice. "I'll bet they've been living on chops and damper. Makes you wonder how these poor men get by, doesn't it, Emma?"

Emma sighed and said nothing.

William watched the women working around the fire, arranging the meal. He'd been lucky to go to Bridie's a few times, but he really liked watching how a group of women took to the task of preparing a meal. There was a briskness about the process and a sense of them settling into the familiar. It had been a very difficult day filled with drama, fatigue and sadness, but the women put all that behind them and got on with the job of living.

*That job is always there*, thought William. *Even the little girls are fussing with spoons and bowls, as though the job couldn't be done without them.*

He missed his own family, remembering the hugs from his mother and the day he held his father's hand, and Jimmy's adoring looks. Oh, how he missed Jimmy. It all seemed so long ago. But most of all, right then, he missed Jack. Jack was a good man.

Then, so were Tom and Scott, so he was lucky to have good men around him.

William admired all the men because they said they would do something and did it, no matter the cost. Going somewhere else meant that he'd be going away from people like them, so he would miss them now, too.

"Missus," said Joe. "I left the sulky outside. I can take you home when you're ready to go."

"Joe, that's very thoughtful of you. We're ready to go now. C'mon, girls. We need to go. We don't want to keep Mr Joe waiting. I'll give Joe a bag of things for you and Emma, Alice. We're all about the same size, so I expect they'll fit. Will you drop them back tonight, Joe?"

"Of course, missus."

"But you haven't eaten!" said Alice. "It'll go to waste!"

"No, it won't," said Bridie. "You have men enough here to feed."

"But, Mummy, I haven't finished my drink," said Polly.

"Be quick, then."

"They can take the rest of the bottle, Bridie. It'll just go to waste here," said Scott.

"Then you can have the rest of the whisky," said Bridie, laughing.

*Oh, how I admire her,* thought William. *She buried her man today and still finds a way to laugh. I know Jack would approve.*

"Bridie, when do you want to leave for Melbourne?" asked William.

"Day after tomorrow—Tuesday. Bill, are you sure you want to take us? Do you want more time to think about it?"

"Yes, Bridie, I'm sure. And I don't need more time," said William.

There were hugs, kisses and a few tears, and Bridie and the girls left.

"There's plenty of whisky here, Joe," said Tom as they were leaving. "We'll have a drink when you drop the bag for Alice and Emma."

"Thanks, but I'll see. It's been a long day," said Joe. "And there are others to help."

With the little girls gone, the mood in the store became more sombre. When the meal was finished, Alice and Emma turned to worrying about the sleeping arrangements, and that they were wearing everything they owned.

Scott, Tom and William would take their blankets and belongings and sleep at the front, near to the door.

"Be a good idea anyway," said Tom. "There'll be people about trying to take advantage of the trouble."

Joe came through the door with a bag. He was dripping wet.

"I won't stay," he said. "Best to get home and get dry. Here's the bag with the things. The missus said she don't want 'em back."

"Thank you, Joe. You've been most kind," said Alice.

"Happy to help," said Joe, and he turned and left.

"Now, boys, let's get set up. We'll need the fire," said Emma. "We'll dry all our things in front of it. We'll need to wash, so we'll do that here, too."

Tom conscripted some gold pans as washing bowls, and brought some water from the barrel outside.

After the men helped set up a screen, Emma banished them and their chairs to the front of the store with their whisky and pipes.

"If you want something from back here, just ask for it and we'll pass it though the curtain. Otherwise, this is strictly women only. We are very, very grateful for your help but we're both very tired. So we'll retire now," said Emma.

"Goodnight," said Tom and Scott. William remained silent.

They all missed the comfort of a fire, but they smoked their pipes and sipped their whisky and made small talk, aware that the women could hear everything that was said.

"Shall we open tomorrow?" asked Scott.

"Might as well. People may need some things with all that has happened today," said Tom. "Shame Joe didn't stay for another whisky."

It wasn't long before the events of the day caught up with all of them and they stretched out their blankets and fell asleep.

CHAPTER 20

# The Aftermath

Morning came and with it, the sense that he'd had a very bad dream. But William quickly realised it wasn't a dream and that in just a few short hours, everything had changed.

All was quiet in the store. Scott and Tom slept soundly only a few feet away and he could hear nothing from beyond the blanket-curtain. He got up, unlatched the door, and stepped outside.

Ballarat still looked and smelled the same. Dawn had broken and the early sun brought promise of a hot day. The sky was cloudless. Cicadas, insects and birds squawked, screeched, hummed and whistled from the bush nearby. There were wisps of smoke from early fires and the smell of burning wood was carried on the morning breeze. The ground was damp underfoot from yesterday's rain. He had forgotten to put on his boots. His feet were no longer hard and the stones and sticks hurt his feet as he walked up into the bush. He neither noticed nor cared—his mind was still filled with grief.

The smell of the bush was different in Australia, especially after rain. The gum trees dropped so much rubbish that there was always a layer of leaves, twigs and bark decaying and producing a pungent smell. He tried to walk where there'd been digging, to avoid the twigs, but wasn't too successful. It wasn't long before he regretted forgetting his boots.

He took a piss against a tree, then found a rock and sat on it. There was no need to review his decision to leave Ballarat, but he wanted to be clear in his mind about Bridie and the girls.

Would they be all right? Should he suggest to Bridie that he stay and help them, if only for a while?

He knew the answer—of course they'd be all right. Bridie was one of those people that would always be all right. If she was all right, then the girls would be all right. He also knew what Bridie would say if he suggested it. She'd tell him to get on with his life. She'd probably tell him to stay in Ballarat too, but he didn't want to.

*I wish Bridie was younger.*

Then he laughed at himself. He wasn't Jack and never would be. Other people wouldn't measure up to Jack for him, and he wouldn't measure up to Jack for Bridie.

*What to do when I get to Melbourne?*

He remembered some of the diggers talking about looking for gold in New South Wales. They said it was like looking for gold in Victoria—some found it, some didn't. Maybe he could work out how to get to New South Wales. He could make a fresh start— new place, new people, new memories. Like Alice had said, he was his own man and could make his own decisions.

Smoke started from the chimney above the store.

*The others are up—they'll be wondering where I am. Time to get back.*

# CHAPTER 21

# Leaving Ballarat

The cart with two horses stood outside the store. The horses stamped their feet and shook their heads as though they knew a journey was about to start and they were anxious to get on with it.

Joe had already collected Bridie and the girls. There was only one bag for Alice and Emma, so it wasn't as though it would take them time to load.

They decided that Alice and Bridie would sit up front, while the girls and Emma would make themselves comfortable in the back.

Bridie had brought everything but a few sticks of furniture and the gold digging gear. She left most of the tent, although she did bring some pieces of canvas they could use for protection when they camped. Scott and Tom would later go to collect the tent and other gear and sell it. Bridie insisted they keep any money it raised to contribute to the cost of the horses and cart.

Scott had taken William aside the day before and told him that he was owed around forty pounds for the time he worked for the store.

"Don't take it with you, Bill. Though if you insist, I'll get it for you. You'll be better to send me a letter when you need it and I'll send it to you through a bank. Just tell me where you are and what bank you want it sent to."

"You forget I can't write."

"No, I hadn't, but you should fix that someday. No—find someone to write a letter for you."

Scott handed him twenty pounds.

"Take this now and write your letter for the rest."

"Thanks, Scott."

The girls and Emma had fashioned places to lie or sit in the back of the cart and had put up a piece of canvas as protection from the sun.

Now they all just stood around outside the store, no one wanting to take the first step. A customer turned up and that made it easy.

"We have to go," said Scott, and he shook hands with William. "I know you have reasons for going, but you know you are always welcome here or at my home in Melbourne. Travel well."

He dipped his hat to the women and the girls and went back into the store.

Tom pressed something into William's hands.

"We didn't play for this, but I think you would have won it anyway. Think of us when you use it."

William looked. It was the pipe.

"Thanks, Tom."

"Safe journey. I put a pistol behind the seat—I hope you don't need it. It's yours too. Don't get confused between the pistol and the pipe though. I hope you come back—Ballarat will need people like you."

He too dipped his hat to the women and went into the store.

The others climbed onto the cart, William flicked the reins and the horses started the journey to Melbourne.

It was early in the day, but it already promised to be hot. William was grateful for his hat. He didn't want to push the horses, so he let them find their own pace.

He worried about the pistol, because Tom had seen the need to give him one.

What did Tom know, that he didn't?

Scott had said that they should be able to do the trip to Melbourne in two days, since the cart wasn't fully laden like it had been on the journey from Melbourne. He suggested they try to make Bacchus Marsh for the overnight camp and push on to make Melbourne the next day.

"James will welcome you. I know he will. If you don't want to spend money on a room, then at least the women can tidy up at the hotel. I'm sure they'll appreciate it after our arrangements here," said Scott.

*Maybe there's more reasons than a tidy up to stay at Bacchus Marsh*, thought William, wondering again about the pistol.

Having remembered the possibility of trouble on the road, he hastened the horses a little to be sure to make Bacchus Marsh that night. There wasn't much other traffic on the road so it wasn't as though they could join another group for protection.

After a while, he decided that trouble didn't bear thinking about and concentrated on taking the best and fastest route. He remembered little of it from the trip up, though he noticed that the road had been made more distinct by an increase in traffic. He supposed that the military and the heavy equipment used for digging to reach gold in the deep leads had all come this way.

There was some traffic going the other way and that surprised him.

*What reason would people have for going to Ballarat now?*

Some of the people wanted to stop and talk, but William ignored them and kept the horses moving. He worried about those in his care and wanted them to be safe. Alice and Bridie looked at him each time as though expecting more courtesy, but said nothing.

He'd never had such responsibility before and struggled to remain calm about it. He was responsible for Emma, Alice, Bridie and the girls. The guilt he felt over what happened to Jack would be nothing compared to living with the guilt if something happened to his companions now, especially the little girls. Too much had happened to them already.

No one questioned that he only stopped once to boil a billy. Scott had packed enough food for two days, most of which didn't need to be cooked. William took advantage of it and kept moving. There was some mild disquiet and criticism when the others all struggled to drink their hot tea while the cart swayed and lurched. William remained silent in the face of it. His passengers then decided it would be easier to drink if they let it cool a bit.

He did stop briefly when they crossed the creeks to allow them to disappear behind the trees, or take a drink if they were thirsty, and to allow the horses to take a drink too.

Nonetheless, he was relieved when they crossed the last creek and came down the road at dusk with Bacchus Marsh in sight.

They pulled up at the hotel and William knew to take the horses and cart into the yard beside it. He offered to let the others out in front, but they elected to all go into the yard with him. There were several carts, some wagons, and quite a number of horses grazing there already.

When they pulled up, Bridie leaned sideways and kissed William on the cheek.

"Thank you," she whispered. "You can stop worrying now."

They all climbed down, stretching limbs and groaning from the soreness of the long ride.

William couldn't look at Bridie. He had such a flush of pleasure from her kiss and didn't want her to know.

"I'll see to the horses," he said. "You can all go in if you want."

"We'll wait for you," said Alice. "Scott says you know the owner, so we're better to go in with you."

"We don't have any money, Alice," said Bridie. "I'm not expecting Bill to pay for anything, so we'll all be sleeping out here, as far as I'm concerned. So let's busy ourselves setting up a camp. Perhaps we should go to the other side of the road, closer to the river and away from the people here who are staying at the hotel?"

"Oh, Bridie," said Alice. "You're right. I hadn't thought of that. Sorry, Bill. Please forgive me."

"Nothing to forgive, Alice," said William. "Let's go inside, and see what they have. Maybe we can all squeeze into one big room and you can all use the water closets, at least."

"Now, Bill," said Bridie.

"This is not your decision to make, Bridie," said William. "Scott gave me some money—said I was to treat you all to something to eat and a room if we can afford it. And Tom said he wanted to be sure you were all safe tonight."

*Well, Scott did give me some money. And Tom gave me a pistol.*

"They're wonderful men aren't they, Emma? Especially that Tom," said Alice.

"No wonder you play poker, Bill," said Bridie. "All right. Let's wait while you see to the horses and cart and then let's all go in."

"No," said William. "Let's all go in first. If they have nothing and we have to move, it'll be easier if the horses are still harnessed."

They left the yard, walked across to the steps and up into the hotel.

The first person they saw was James.

"Well, here he is!" shouted James with a big smile on his face. "Bill! How good to see you! With a family, too? Are these all yours? You sure didn't waste time. Scott said you were doing well in Ballarat, but he didn't say how well!"

"Hello, James," said William, sticking out his hand. James took it and pumped it furiously. "Alice and Bridie here lost their husbands on Sunday at Eureka. I'm taking them back to Melbourne."

"Alice and Bridie?" said James.

"I'm Alice and this is my sister, Emma."

"I'm Bridie and these are my girls, Missy and Polly."

"Oh, I'm so sorry to hear it. That was an awful business. We only know what we've heard from travellers," said James. "Please be my guests at the hotel. It won't cost you anything. I'm sure you've enough to worry about without worrying about somewhere to stay and something to eat."

"James, I—" started Bridie.

"Bridie, you can protest all you like and sleep outside if you've a mind to, but I think it's the least I can do. I'm proud to meet the wife of a man that stood at Eureka, and proud to meet his family. So, the hospitality is there. I won't be offended if you refuse it for whatever reason, but I'd feel a lot better if you'd take it."

"Thank you, James," said Bridie.

"Good, good. I'll find someone to look after you all."

"I need to see to the horses," said William.

"You do that, Bill. I'm sure the ladies will take some time to freshen up. Oh. What have I said?"

"It's all right, James," laughed Emma. "We know what you mean. We are so grateful for your kindness. It's been a very difficult time."

"Thank you, Emma," said James, looking relieved. "Bill, you see to the horses, and I'll see you in the bar."

As William went to see to the horses, he heard James tell the others, "I'll find someone to help you with rooms. When you are ready for supper, go to the room at the back and ask Edie to come find me."

William went to the horses. They were pleased to see him and to lose their harnesses. He poured some oats into nosebags for them, and attached one to each horse in turn. The horses bickered and pushed each other as they waited for the oats, but there was little William could do about that. The oats were finished soon enough. He removed the nosebags and set the horses loose in the paddock. He presumed that there were still men about to guard the animals and the carts, though he couldn't see anyone.

The bar wasn't noisy but was crowded when he entered. There was an assortment of travellers and local people. James was standing in the middle of a group talking, but not drinking. He saw William.

"Ah, Bill. Welcome. Let me get you a drink. What'll you have? Beer, isn't it?"

"Yes, I'd like a beer. Thank you."

James signalled to the barman for two beers.

The barman brought the beers over and James suggested that he and William stand where they would be alone.

"The others wondered if you'd come from Ballarat," he said. "I told them 'no', as I thought you may not want to explain to them what happened."

"Thank you. I don't want to talk about it. Do you still have men guarding the horses and carts?"

"Not so much. It's been some time since we've had trouble. Maybe it's because there are more men camped there, or it might be because the thieves concentrate on the road. There's been trouble off and on by four particular fellers. They pulled off a daring robbery between Ballarat and Creswick Creek a few months back. There's a place called Graham's Refreshment Tent and they robbed the owner and patrons alike. We hear about them from time to time, but the police are too busy elsewhere to do much about them."

"Do you think we'll be all right if we push on to Melbourne?"

"I think you will. We don't hear of much trouble between here and Melbourne. Having said that, there's still trouble for anyone travelling through the Black Forest near Mount Macedon, but that's on the Bendigo Road and a long way from where you'll be. There aren't many places for the bushrangers to hide around here."

"What's a bushranger?"

"Oh. Used to apply to escaped convicts who took to the bush, hiding there and robbing travellers. Now it applies to anyone that does it. They're mostly not bad men, though some are. They're usually only after money."

"I hope you're right."

"Normally I'd say to wait for the gold escort and go with them but with the disturbances in Ballarat, we don't know when that will be."

"Disturbances?"

"That's what the papers are calling it."

Edie appeared in the doorway and waved to them.

"C'mon," said James. "Supper's on."

They went out back to the dining room. Alice, Emma and the girls were at one table, and Bridie on her own at another.

"Let's pull these tables together," said James.

"No," said Bridie. "Edie wanted to, but I want to sit with you, James, and thank you for your thoughtfulness."

James and William sat with Bridie—James opposite her.

*She really is beautiful.* He wished he'd had a bath too and couldn't suppress a pang of jealously that Bridie wanted to sit with James.

Bridie's dress was colourful, with long sleeves and a frill around the bodice that was tight to her neck. The colours were in stark contrast to her dark hair and sparkling eyes. She'd pulled her hair tightly from her face and it showed off her perfect nose, lips and chin.

"Please think nothing of it, Bridie. I meant what I said—I'm proud to help and it's the least I can do."

"I know I shouldn't be surprised, but everyone has been so kind. Bill here has been wonderful. Did he tell you he was my husband's partner?"

"No, he didn't, but we haven't had much time to chat. How did you go, Bill? Are you rich and haven't got around to telling me?"

"No, nothing like that," said William. "We weren't having much luck. Jack was talking of moving to the deep leads if our luck didn't improve."

"They worked well together," said Bridie. "Jack said Bill was the best partner he'd ever had."

*Here I go again*, thought William as he felt the familiarity of his face blushing.

"Sorry, Bill," said Bridie. "All I ever seem to do is embarrass you."

"What will you do in Melbourne, Bridie?' said James.

Edie arrived with their meals and William was pleased to have attention diverted from him, pleased that he didn't have to order, and pleased to see a steak on his plate.

"I'd like to open a clothing store, but I'll need to work somewhere first and get the money together. I'll try to find a clothing store that wants help or a manager. Not much point in being too ambitious."

"I might be able to help with that. I'll write out some people for you to visit and give it to you before you go. I'm sure one of them will help."

"What sort of people?"

"My sister for a start. She owns a store—ladies' fashion. Is that your experience?"

"It certainly is. I made this dress," said Bridie, indicating the dress she was wearing.

"Talented as well as beautiful," said James.

"Now it's my turn to blush," laughed Bridie, wrapping James in a warm smile.

William struggled to control his jealousy. He knew he had no future with Bridie, but it didn't stop him being in love with her.

*Oh, to be a few years older. No—who's fooling himself? She still wouldn't be interested.*

William finished his meal quickly.

"Thanks for the supper, James, but I'd best see to the horses."

"I'll be done soon. Do you want a beer before you go?"

"No. I'd best be getting out. We rented the horses in Ballarat, so I want to be sure nothing happens to them."

"I'll find out your room number."

"No need, I'll sleep under the cart. That way, I can make sure the cart and the horses are all right."

"It's up to you, Bill. There's a room and a bed if you want it."

"Thanks, James, but I'm all right. Bridie, I'd like to be away early. Can we leave with the sun?'

"Of course. I'll make sure the others are ready."

"We'll see you at breakfast, then, Bill," said James.

"No, I'll see to the horses. Just come out when you can, Bridie. I'll come in then, James, thank you again. It was wonderful to catch up and I'm sorry to say farewell so soon."

"Of course, Bill. Whatever you want to do is all right with me," said James.

William turned and walked out.

"Goodnight, Mr Bill!" called the girls as he left.

"'Night, girls!" he called over his shoulder.

William's emotions were in turmoil. The emotion of jealousy was new to him and he didn't like it.

He got to the cart and fetched his blankets, rolled himself in them, and tried to sleep. It was denied to him. All he could picture was Bridie's beautiful smile for James. He remembered Bridie's quick kiss on his cheek and took momentary comfort from that. It didn't last long as he imagined James enjoying more than a peck on his cheek from Bridie.

After a while, he realised it was pointless trying to sleep so he went to talk to the horses. They were grazing quietly in the paddock, along with some others who were just dark shapes in the moonless light. He took comfort from the horses nuzzling against him, even though he knew they were only looking for more oats. It amazed him how the horses that knew him came to him and the others stayed away.

There weren't any other carts or sulkies about, so the horses must belong to riders staying in the hotel. *I'm the only idiot sleeping under the stars in Bacchus Marsh tonight.*

He went back to the cart and wrapped himself in the blankets once more, this time falling into a troubled sleep. He dreamed that Jack was begging for his help in the battle, but his hands and feet were stuck in something and he couldn't move. The sounds of guns, swords, horses and shouts were all about and he could see Bridie not too far in the distance. She was laughing at him, telling him that he was too young to help anyone. At one point he woke and tried to sit up, bashing his head underneath the cart.

The sun finally appeared and he was glad to get up. There was a mark and some blood on his forehead that he could feel, so he went down to the creek for a wash. It was warm enough to take off all his clothes and have a swim. He was glad he did and felt much better, although he still wasn't sure how he'd explain the mark on his forehead to the others.

When he got back to the cart, the others were already there, making him feel foolish that he'd asked to leave early but hadn't yet harnessed the horses.

"We'll help you, Bill," said Alice. "Better still, you pop in and see James and we'll do what we can while you're away."

William was pleased by the offer as he was regretting being so short with James the previous evening.

"Thanks, Alice."

William headed to the hotel and found James cleaning the bar.

"Time to go then? Last I saw Alice was shooing everyone along like an old mother hen. Bridie told her you wanted to be gone early, so the pressure was on. Is everything all right, Bill? You aren't worried about the trip to Melbourne, are you?"

"It's probably a lot of things, but thanks again for everything."

He put out his hand.

"You're always welcome here, Bill. By the way, the ladies definitely think the world of you. We pulled the tables together after you left and all they did was talk about you."

William flushed. *Damn!*

"There's more. Here's the list I promised Bridie—I forgot to give it to her. Tell her the first name is my sister, the second is my wife and the third is my wife's sister. I think she'll have the best luck with my sister though—I know she needs some help. She's about six months pregnant with her first, so she'll be looking for someone and last I heard, she hadn't found anyone."

William was overcome with shame.

*Why was he jealous of a good man like James, always helping and just making a compliment to Bridie? And married? Why didn't he even think of that?*

"Thank you, James. I'll tell her. Hope to see you again."

"I hope so too. You are welcome here anytime. Don't worry about the trip. You'll be fine. If you're going to run into trouble, it'll be in the first hour or so. So, if anything looks like trouble, come back."

William nodded, turned and left. When he got back, the harnessing was nearly done.

Finally, they all got on and headed for Melbourne. No one said anything, nor was there much noise from the horses—just the jangling of the harness and the soft patter of the hooves on the ground. Insects and cicadas welcomed the day with their ceaseless buzz, and the sun flashed from time to time through the canopy of trees that hung over the road.

The view ahead gave them a good look at the road and the bush beside it. If anyone proposed a robbery around here, they'd at least have plenty of warning. Then they crossed the bridge and headed towards a wooded creek.

"Is that a man seated on a horse in the shadows? It's hard to see, but it looks like it," said Alice.

"It is," said Bridie. "I don't like the look of it. Emma, girls, pull that canvas over yourselves and don't come out or make a sound."

"There's only one," said William. "And I've got a pistol."

"It's never only one," said Bridie. "Bill, give me the pistol."

"What? It's all right. I know how to use it."

"If it's a pistol, it's only got one shot and there'll be more than one of them. We need an advantage. They won't expect me to have the pistol, so we'll get one shot they won't expect. We don't have any time, Bill. Give it to me, quickly."

William reached behind and fetched the pistol to give to Bridie. She hid it in the folds of her dress.

"Hope it works," said William. "I didn't check it."

"Where did you get it?"

"Tom."

"Then it'll work."

As they came closer to the man they could see he was on a beautiful, big bay horse, at least seventeen hands tall. The man looked young—about Emma's age—with a clean-shaven face and dark eyebrows and hair. He wore a black pea jacket and a wideawake hat. Both he and the horse were watching the cart and its occupants with interest.

"So, what do we have here?" he said as they got close.

William stopped the cart just short of where they would go down into the creek. The road was so rutted and torn by traffic that the cart's wheels were in the ruts on one side and on top of them on the other, listing towards the stranger. He and his horse were just off to the side of the road, still in the shadows.

"We've come from Ballarat," said Alice.

"What do you have in the cart?"

"None of your business," said Bridie. "What's your intention? We have no time to pass the time of day. Drive on, Bill."

"Steady there, missus. No need to be unfriendly," said the man. "I've just watered my horse and saw you and thought to stop and help you if you need any."

"We've no need of your help," said Bridie. "Now, Bill, we'll be on our way."

"Not so fast," said another man, who had ridden out of the trees from behind them. He had reached the side of the cart without any of them knowing. "Like the man, said, what's in the cart?"

William turned to look at the man. This man had light hair and a fair complexion. Sitting atop another tall and beautiful horse, he was wearing a black pea jacket and a wide awake hat just like his companion. The man rode right up to the cart and was only a foot or two from William now.

"What do you men want and why do you want to know what's in the cart?" said Alice.

"Oh, we're down on our luck and thought that you might share whatever you have in the cart."

"You're thieves, you mean," said Alice, her voice trembling with anger. "We've had trouble enough and would appreciate it if you'd just move on."

"We've all had trouble enough, madam," said the first man.

"That horse is not yours, is it?" said Bridie and started to get down from the cart.

"It's none of your business whose horse it is and you'll stay on the cart. But I do like feisty women, so you may get more than you bargained for before this day is out."

"Talking about that," said the other man. "The old boiler will suit me fine."

"You've always been like that. Me—I like them young, and the younger the better."

"I know that brand," said Bridie, now standing beside the cart and looking at the rider's horse. "I know it doesn't belong to you."

"Stand your ground, missus," said the man, taking a gun from his belt and levelling it at Bridie. "Take a look in the cart, Sam. We've wasted enough time."

Sam had to lean down from his horse to pull the canvas to one side. The other man had his gun levelled at Bridie. William saw his chance, turned in the seat and threw himself on Sam's back. He gambled that the other man would take a moment or so to notice, and another moment or so to turn his gun on William.

Three guns fired almost at once.

William didn't realise that Sam had his gun out and held it in his other hand. It fired uselessly into the ground. As Sam fell, his head smacked against the wheel with a sharp thud and his weapon slipped from his hand.

The other man had turned his gun and fired at William, but he took the shot too quickly and without aim. The bullet whistled past William and made a thwacking sound as it hit the ground under Sam's horse, startling it and causing it to back away from the cart, leaving William in full view of the other rider.

Bridie saw her chance and fired at the other man. Her bullet thudded into his shoulder. He was unsteady for a moment, then raised his gun and pointed it at Bridie.

"You bitch," he said. "You'll pay for that."

He fired and Bridie fell to the ground. The man turned his weapon back to William who had picked up Sam's gun. William pointed it at the man and pulled the trigger but the bullet whistled harmlessly past him.

"Not as easy as it looks, is it?" said the man before firing again at William. He also missed.

William realised that all the women were screaming. The screaming from the cart had startled the stranger's horse. It was now prancing about and the stranger struggled to pull its head around so he could get a clear shot at William, who had rolled under the cart. As he dived under, he saw that Alice lay across the seat and William could only hope that she was unhurt. He didn't know about Bridie, who lay motionless like a bundle of rags. The screaming from the back of the cart continued.

"Sorry, horse," he whispered. He had a clear shot at the rider's horse's chest from under the cart and he took it. He fired and the horse fell, throwing the stranger heavily to the ground. Unfortunately for him, he landed on his wounded shoulder. He struggled to get up, work out where William was, and get a firm grip on his revolver.

The stranger saw William pointing his gun at him from under the cart. He looked like he was saying 'no' yet bringing his gun to bear on William, who fired. The bullet hit the stranger in the chest and he slid to the ground, his gun falling from his hand. His horse struggled to get to its feet. William got out from under the cart, walked over to the horse and put a bullet in its head.

Then, he walked over to Sam and put a bullet in his head too.

"Oh, Bill, he might have been alive," said Alice who was now sitting up.

"That's why I did it, Alice—we've had enough trouble for one day."

Later, he would be surprised that he was more upset about shooting the horse than he was the man.

Alice was down from the cart now and holding Bridie.

"Bridie," she whispered. "Oh, Bridie."

"Is she alive?" asked William, kneeling beside her.

"I don't know," said Alice. She put her cheek close to Bridie's mouth. "I think she is—she's breathing."

"Has she been hit? I don't see any blood."

"She must have been hit. She fell when he fired."

"Can I help?' asked Emma from the cart.

"No, please look after the girls. Tell them their Mummy is all right," said William.

"Oh, Bill. I hope that's true," whispered Alice.

"So do I. Please look for the wound. We won't know until we find it."

After a few anxious moments, Alice said, "I think it's here, on her head. She's not bleeding anywhere else, and there's blood on her head."

"She might have hit her head when she hit the ground."

"No, the bullet has grazed her head. Look, here—enough to knock her down. Bill, I think you're right. I don't think it's a bad wound at all. It's bleeding, but we'll be able to stop it. We'd better go back to Bacchus Marsh and get some help."

William thought for a moment.

"Alice, if we can, I'd rather keep going. If we go back, we have to do this again. If we keep going, then it's safer and there's more help in Melbourne. Will your friends help us?"

"Of course they will, but I'm no doctor. I only think the wound's not serious, but I don't know. At least if we go back to Bacchus Marsh we can ask a doctor."

"There may not be a doctor. Let's give her a chance to wake up and see what she wants to do."

"Is our Mummy all right? She doesn't look all right," said Missy, standing in the back of the cart.

"Yes, she's all right. We're just waiting for her to wake up. Emma, can you bring the girls down, please?"

There was a sound of rustling canvas and feet scraping on the side of the cart. Three anxious faces leaned over Bridie as she began to wake—small groans at first, then full words of curiosity.

"Where am I? What happened? Are the girls all right?"

William left Alice to answer the questions, unsure that he could control his emotions. He'd already done enough crying for a lifetime.

He walked over to Sam's horse. It nudged Sam on the ground, as though to tell him the day was wasting and it was time to move.

"There, there, boy," said William. "A change of plan for you today."

He took the saddle off and threw it in the back of the cart. Then he took the horse to the creek to give it some water, but it wasn't interested.

*They must have been waiting by the creek for a while. I'll bet if we look around we'll find where they camped last night.*

He took the horse back and tethered it to the back of the cart. There was nothing he could do about the other horse, but he wrestled its saddle off and dumped that in the back of the cart too.

The bullet wound to its head was obvious. Hopefully, passers-by would think it had been lame and needed to be destroyed. The bushrangers were a different matter—no point in arousing attention by leaving them about. He picked up the two bodies one at a time, walking them some distance into the bush and dumping them

"There you go boys," he muttered when he dumped the last one. *Keep each other company. You'll probably both go to the same place and you'll meet Emma's soldier at some point.*

When he got back, Bridie was sitting up with her back against one of the cart's wheels.

"How are you?" he asked gently, kneeling beside her. Emma wound a piece of material around her head. He had no idea where it came from and thought he'd better not ask.

"I've been better."

"Looks to me like you're all right, given you've just finished a gun fight."

"They tell me we won."

"They're right."

"Thank you, Bill. I don't know where we'd be without you."

"Probably safe and sound in Ballarat. And don't thank me. You're the one we need to thank."

"Perhaps they might have just taken our money and left."

"I doubt it. But who knows, Bridie? What's done is done and we need to work out what to do next."

"Alice thinks we should go back to Bacchus Marsh."

"We go back, or we go on—two choices. And the one we make depends on how you are. What do you want to do?"

"Go on to Melbourne. I'm tired of this, Bill, tired of the violence. Doesn't matter which way we turn, someone's out to rob us."

"Or worse," said Alice.

"If there's any chance you're hurt worse than we think, then we'll go back," said William.

"No, Bill. I'm lucky. The bullet took a few hairs and I've still got plenty of those. Please, let's go on."

"All right. Let's get you in the back of the cart then. Polly and Missy can be your nurses. Alice and Emma can sit up front with me. Emma, could you get a billy of water from the creek? Our patient might need some water."

"Of course," said Emma, taking a billy from the back of the cart and filling it at the creek.

They all helped Bridie on to the cart and made her as comfortable as possible. Then they all got onto the cart and continued the journey to Melbourne.

Sam's horse complained at first, pulling on its bridle, not wanting to go with them, then it settled down and plodded along at the same pace as the cart. No doubt it was more accustomed to being ridden than led.

The day was hot and flies buzzed about, and the girls did their best to keep Bridie comfortable. William continued to fret about whether they'd made the right decision by pressing on. He knew it was the sensible thing to do, but it would be a long day.

They stopped at a creek around the middle of the day to have some food and to water the horses. William stopped the cart short of the creek and everyone got down. Then he moved the cart to the creek so all the horses could have a drink. He got off, untied Sam's horse and led it to the creek, talking to it and trying to reassure it that everything would be all right. It was better behaved after that and Alice remarked that 'Bill has a way with horses'.

Night had already fallen when they finally reached Melbourne. William had no idea where he was now and Alice was directing him through a number of streets but it was taking too long. He was anxious to get help for Bridie.

"Please, it will be all right, Bill—you'll see when we get there," said Alice.

Finally, well after dark, they went up a long, looping road and Alice told him to stop at the front of a beautiful, big home. William couldn't hide his surprise.

The home had verandahs on the front and the sides, and a set of steps going up to an impressive entrance door. He could see spectacular gardens despite the darkness. It was a single storey home, but quite wide and rambling, and lights showed in many of the windows. They could hear the sound of a piano playing.

"This is your friend's house?"

"Yes. They are well to do."

"Who are they?"

"No matter," she said as a man appeared in the doorway of the house, carrying a lantern.

"Who is it?" he called.

"It's Alice—Alice, Emma and some friends. One of us needs a doctor—badly."

"Yes, missus. I'll be back soon." He disappeared inside and came back a few minutes later with a man and a woman, and they all hurried down the stairs to the cart.

"Alice? Alice?" said the woman. "Is it you or Emma that needs the doctor?"

"No, no, Lucy. It's not us, but a good friend. She saved our lives."

"Where is she?" asked the man.

"In the back, Robert," said Alice.

"Harold, help to bring her into the house, there's a good man," said Robert, taking the lantern from the man who had first seen them.

"Hello, Robert," said Alice, putting her hand on his arm.

"Alice. What's your friend's name?"

"Bridie."

"C'mon inside everyone. Lord, there's enough of you," said Lucy.

Harold carried Bridie while Alice walked with her hand on Robert's arm. Lucy, Emma and the girls hurried along and William followed behind. He saw a number of children gathered in the doorway.

"Shoo! Shoo!" said Robert. "Remember what curiosity did to the cat."

Harold knew where to go and carried Bridie into a small room at the side. Robert followed quickly, pulling the doors closed behind him as he went in.

William must have been looking bewildered, because Alice said, "It's all right, everyone. Robert's a doctor. See, William. I told you it would be worth it."

Nodding his agreement, William looked for somewhere to sit. He was very tired after the day's drama and journey.

"You poor man," said Emma, noticing. "Lucy, we've had such a day."

Harold came out of the room and closed the doors behind him.

"Is she all right?" asked Alice, fearfully.

"I believe so, missus," said Harold.

"Have you had supper?" asked Lucy.

"No, not really. Not much since breakfast."

"Where have you come from?"

"Bacchus Marsh."

"Oh, Lord—so far! Emma, Alice—you can have your usual room. We can put these two little ones in with mine. They'll show them where to go and you, young man," said Lucy, looking at William, "I could give you a paling fence, I think."

"I'm sure we can do better than that," said Robert, emerging from the room laughing.

"Is Mummy all right?" asked Missy.

"My word, she is. She might have a headache for a day or so, but she'll be just fine. She's sleeping now, so we'll leave her there for the moment. It looked to me like she had some excellent nurses. So, who is everybody?"

"Oh, sorry," said Alice. "How rude of me. These are my good friends, Robert and Lucy. This is Bill, Missy and Polly."

"We nursed our Mummy," said Polly.

"I know you did," said Robert, laughing again.

"Bill, Harold will show you to a room you can use," said Lucy. "Why don't you all freshen up and we'll meet in the kitchen for some supper."

"I need to see to the horses," said William.

"I'll do that, sir," said Harold. "I'll do that after I show you to your room. You're looking worried, sir. Let me assure you that it won't be me that attends to them. I'll tell the stable hands and they'll know what to do."

"I'm sorry," said William, "I meant no offence."

"And none taken, sir."

"Harold, would you fetch their bags from the cart before you see to the horses?" asked Robert.

"Very good, sir," said Harold and he left the room.

"Now, where's my lot?" said Lucy.

"Here we are, Mummy!" called a voice from the doorway where five children were gathered, peering around the corner.

"Good. Now you take these two girls and make them welcome. Don't split them up, unless they want to. Do you want to be split up?"

"No," said Missy and Polly.

"I thought not. Put them in your room, Edith. You can go to Lucy's room. I know you'll both like that. See? It's an ill wind that doesn't blow someone some good. Now, everybody, off you go and make yourselves beautiful. We'll see you all in the dining room when you are ready."

Harold came back with the bags. There was the bag that Bridie had given to Alice and Emma, a bag for Bridie and the girls, and a worn-looking canvas bag for William who blushed with embarrassment as he took it.

All the children went off, trying to talk at once. Lucy took Emma and Alice, and Harold took William.

"Harold, show Bill the smoking room on the way. Bill, come to the smoking room and we'll have a whisky before supper. Take your time though—I always like to get a head start."

Harold and William walked down a hallway.

"That's the door to the smoking room. You'll find Mr Robert in there later."

They walked further down the hall, then up a short flight of stairs. Harold stopped outside a door.

"This'll be your room, sir. I hope you'll find it comfortable. Now, come with me."

William followed Harold further down the hall again.

"This is a bathroom, sir. Please give me a few moments and I'll arrange for some hot water. Perhaps if you just sit here and wait. I won't be long. Then, Mr Robert was concerned you may not have a change of clothing, so he has asked me to put some in your room. You'll find them there when you finish in here. There's a gown on the rack there that you can wear when you finish washing. Wear it back to your room, if you please. Just leave your other clothes here and they'll be collected and washed."

"Harold. I don't know what to say."

"Then say nothing, sir. Mr Robert is very pleased to offer you his home and he's most grateful to you for what you have done for Mrs Alice and Miss Emma."

"How does he know?"

"Miss Bridie told us, sir. Now there's a good man. I won't be a jiffy."

William sat on the stool and was sound asleep when a maid came in with the water.

"Oh, dear, I'm sorry to wake you, sir. I'll just put the water in the bath and I'll be gone. There's soap and towels there, sir. You help yourself."

Once she had gone, William took off all his clothes, folded them and put them on the stool. They looked a sorry collection of rags.

Everything reminded him of his treatment in the surgery on the ship. He could easily become accustomed to living like this. Neither Alice nor Emma had given a hint that they ever lived like this, and William was intrigued to know more.

*What were they doing in the goldfields, when they had friends like this?*

He lay down in the bath and enjoyed the warm water's embrace. In a few moments, he felt himself nodding off again and decided that it wouldn't do. Using the soap, he lathered himself up and washed himself quickly. Once he got out of the tub and towelled himself dry, he put on the robe and returned to his room.

As Harold had promised, there were some clean and welcome clothes laid out on the bed. There was a nice flannel shirt, some corduroy pants, some socks and a nice pair of soft leather shoes. Once attired, he felt quite the gent. He left the room, found his way to the smoking room and tapped on the door.

"Oh, please come in," were the welcoming words from inside the room.

William opened the door and stepped into the room.

Robert sat in a large leather chair with a paper spread out on his lap, a lit pipe in his mouth and a whisky on a table beside him.

"Ah, Bill. Please come in. Sit there. Make yourself comfortable. Would you like a whisky before supper? I'm having one. I can assure you it's a good brand and you won't be disappointed."

He got up and poured a whisky for William. When he sat back down he raised his own glass and said, "Your health."

"Thank you, sir. And yours," said William, raising his glass too.

"Robert, please. Bridie said you've had a long and difficult day. She didn't say a lot though and if you don't mind, I'd like to hear about it."

"Now?"

"Yes. You won't be asked again over supper, I assure you. A topic like this has no place at the supper table, so I'd like to hear about it over a whisky."

William explained what had happened, leaving out the details of how the bushranger called Sam was killed.

"You've done well, Bill. Not only to survive the incident, but to relay your story in such a fashion. I agree that some of the details relayed by Bridie are best left out."

William flushed, as was his habit.

"No, Bill. Please don't be embarrassed. I mean what I say. And while we're discussing it, do you want to report the matter to the police? They won't need all the details, but it may help to avoid any investigation when the bodies are discovered. The dead horse may lead some curious person to the dead men."

"What do you think, Robert? What would you do?"

"Well, Harold said there are some saddles in the cart and a very fine extra horse that could lead an investigation back to us, then back to you. Do you think you might want to keep a saddle and the horse?"

"No, I don't think so."

"The saddles are worth some money."

"Then, you take it as our gratitude for your help."

"No, my boy. We don't want anything. But we can see the horse goes back to its rightful owner with no questions asked and the saddles to someone that can make good use of them. If you are happy with that, then we can leave the matter there."

"Yes, sir—more than happy. I'm very grateful."

"Then let's finish our whiskies and go to supper. I'm sure the ladies are ready now. Perhaps we can come back for another whisky later."

Bridie didn't join them at supper and it was probably just as well as there were more than enough people around the table. True to Robert's prediction, no one spoke about the morning's events at supper, nor did they speak about the disturbances at Ballarat. Conversation mostly covered the goings on in Melbourne, what the girls were learning in school, how much Missy and Polly would like to go to school, and how good William looked in his fine clothes.

Once supper was done, William and Robert went again to the smoking room.

"Ah, it's so nice to have another man in the house," said Robert as they settled in. "I have a spare pipe, if you would like one."

"No, thank you. I have one in the cart, but I don't feel the need for it at the moment. I'm content with the whisky, if that's all right with you."

"Of course, of course. Talking about the cart, is it yours?"

"No we rented it in Ballarat and it has to go back there. Our plan was to go to Scott Mallard's, but we came here when Bridie was hurt. Do you know Scott?"

"No, I'm afraid I don't. Where's his place?"

"He's near Williams Town. Our plan was to get directions at the *Sailor's Inn*. That's where I met him."

"I know the *Sailor's Inn*—you were better to come here. There would have been some difficulty finding his place in the dark, no doubt."

"Yes, it wasn't much of a plan, was it? Anyway, I'll have to take the cart and horses to Scott's sooner or later."

"No matter, my boy—plenty of time for that. You're here now. What do you plan to do next? You didn't tell me why you came to Melbourne. I know why Bridie, Alice and Emma are here, but why are you here? Surely, they haven't run out of gold in Ballarat?"

William sipped his whisky.

"I'm sorry, Bill. It's none of my business. Please forget I asked. I, like my children, sometimes forget what curiosity did to the cat. Anyway, would you like to work here for a while? Alice said you are very good with horses and I need a man that's good with horses. So, if you don't have any immediate plans, perhaps you could work here. What do you think?"

"What would you have me do?"

"Work with my horses. I'm expanding the work we do here, so I need more. I want to build up the herd. There are two men now, but I don't think that's enough. Anyhow, I'm not sure how good they are so I want to find out. You might even like it here."

"That's funny. That's what Scott said."

"Well, what do you think?"

"Do you mind if I think about it?"

"Of course not. Take all the time you need. But, I will need to know in the morning."

He laughed when he saw William's face.

"Don't worry, my boy. I'm just having fun."

"How do you know Alice and Emma?"

"Emma is governess to our children. One of our children is named after her. She is like part of the family. Alice came to visit her once and met George, who used to work in our garden. Everybody loved George—he was so full of life. It was love at first sight. They hadn't been married long when gold was discovered and we couldn't stop George. He and Alice were off to make their fortune. I'm sorry it turned out the way it did. We all lost a good man."

William finished his whisky.

"More? Another? Just one more?"

"No, thank you, Robert. If you don't mind, I'll go to bed."

"Mind? Of course not! You've had a long day. Please don't hurry out of bed in the morning. We'll have breakfast when you are ready. And don't worry about Bridie. I've given her something to help her sleep through the night. Not as good as whisky, mind you. Goodnight, my boy. You've earned a good rest. Thank you for what you did today."

He got up and shook William's hand.

William found his way to his room. He took off his clothes, put on the nightgown that was laid across the end of his bed, crawled under the covers and was immediately asleep.

CHAPTER 22

# Robert and Lucy

The sun was streaming through his window and William was suddenly hot under the covers, so he pushed them to one side and took a few moments to work out where he was. The events of the day before rushed back like a bad dream and it took a while before he realised they weren't a dream and, once again, he was a murderer. In his own way, he was no better than the soldiers at Ballarat. He hoped that Emma's God wasn't patiently preparing a place for him too.

Sounds of animals and workmen came through his open window, so he got out of bed for a look. The window looked out on rolling green hills, although none of them was high. There was a river or creek in the near distance, some outbuildings nearby, and a variety of animals grazing in the fields. There was no doubt they wouldn't waste the best views on a guest bedroom, so perhaps the views from the other side of the house would be even better, but there was no disappointment here either. He was in no hurry to go down for breakfast although, from the angle of the sun, it might have been way past breakfast time. Someone had been in his room and had laid out some more clothes for him. They looked lighter, more comfortable and more suitable to an inevitably hot day.

*What would it be like to work here? Robert seems like a good man, so it might just be easier to say 'yes' and see what happens. It might be good to be near Robert too, in case the police start asking questions about what happened on the road.*

Just as he had once been dependent on Eddie saying nothing, he was now dependent on Emma, Alice and Bridie saying nothing. He was pretty sure the police would find in his favour, but he'd also seen in Ballarat that the police didn't always act in accordance with the law.

He liked Lucy, Robert and the children, though he hadn't seen much of them. He wondered what Bridie and the girls would do. Bridie said she was looking for a clothing store and William had forgotten to give her the piece of paper with the names on it. He felt a sudden pang of guilt at his behaviour.

*And what about the piece of paper? What if it's been washed?* He would have to check when his clothes came back. If they did, of course. The clothes he was wearing now were much better than those in which he'd arrived, so they might have thrown the others away.

After dressing quickly, he left the room and went to the dining room. Only Lucy and Alice were there.

"Here he is," said Lucy. "Welcome. We thought you'd never get up."

"Sorry," said William. "Has everyone had breakfast?"

"Don't mind me," said Lucy, laughing. "Yes, and gone about their business. Alice and I were reminiscing on happier times. Emma is looking to all the children, and you should hear Polly and Missy! You'd think Christmas had come early. Why don't you sit down and have some breakfast?"

"I'd like to see Bridie first, if she's awake."

"I don't know if she's awake, but I know she'd like to see you. Do that now and have something when you get back. By the way, Lily asked me to give you this."

Lucy gave William a piece of paper. He recognised it as the one given to him by James.

"Thank you. I was worried I'd lost it."

William went to the surgery and tapped on the door.

"Please come in," said Bridie.

William stepped into the room. Bridie sat up in bed and smiled broadly when she saw him.

"Oh, Bill. So wonderful to see you! Are they looking after you? Oh, you do look so smart!"

William thought it impossible that someone could look so happy with such a large bandage on their head.

"How are you, Bridie? Did you sleep well?"

"Oh, I've nothing to complain about. I've been so looking forward to seeing you, but every time I asked about you they said you were sleeping. But I don't mind. Your rest is well deserved."

They looked at each other for a few moments. Then, Bridie looked serious.

"Bill, thank you for what you did yesterday. I knew from Ballarat that you worried about the responsibility. But when it came time to protect us, you didn't hesitate. My father used to say 'a man is not a man until he accepts the responsibility of one'. Please come and sit by me on the bed. I want to be sure you're all right."

William sat on the bed, a little nervous. He had never sat on a woman's bed before, and certainly not one of a woman that he loved.

"Alice told me what you did."

"What do you mean?"

"Why, that you shot the bushranger."

"I shot them both."

"That you shot the one called Sam as he lay on the ground."

"Oh, Bridie. Aren't we better not to speak of it?"

"That's what I told Alice. She promised not to speak of it again. I wanted you to know that no one will know of it. I know why you did it and I want you to know I would have done the same. So, there's only three of us that know."

"I think Robert knows too. I think Alice might have told him."

"She didn't tell me that."

William shrugged. They sat in silence, each one trying to work out if Robert knowing changed anything.

"I have a confession to make," said William.

"Let me hear it. I love confessions," said Bridie, laughing, obviously wanting to lighten the mood.

"James gave me a piece of paper with the names of contacts about your shop. I forgot to give it to you."

"I thought he'd forgotten. Oh, my. Please give it to me."

"I left it in my pocket and they'd taken my clothes to be washed, but Lucy just gave it to me."

"Wonderful. I thought he'd forgotten and I would have to start my search from nothing."

William smiled with relief and gave her the piece of paper.

"There are three names here, but nothing about who they are," said Bridie.

"James said the one at the top is his sister, the next one is his wife and the last is his wife's sister. I think that's what he said. I think he also said the first name was your best choice. I've been worrying that I'd lost the paper and that I wouldn't get his message right."

"You silly man," said Bridie. "Imagine worrying about that! Now, Alice tells me that Robert has offered you a job. How exciting. Will you take it?"

"I think I might, Bridie—just because it's easy. I'd like something easy after the last few days."

"I think you should. I'll see James' sister, too, as soon as Robert says I can leave. I don't know this address. Do you know where it is?" she asked and passed the paper to William.

He looked at it and said, "No, I don't," before passing it back. He wasn't about to tell Bridie he couldn't read or write.

"I'll ask Lucy, or Robert. Thank you for coming to see me. And don't worry about Alice. She won't tell anyone else."

William nodded, turned and left. He knew Bridie was wrong about Alice and there'd be a reckoning one day.

# CHAPTER 23

# A Troubled Visit with Scott

Robert took Bridie to meet James' sister. They were instant friends, and Bridie was welcomed into the clothing store. She and the girls moved to Melbourne to be closer to the store where, by report, the girls were going to school and loving it.

William moved out of the house and into the servants' quarters. He was given a modest but comfortable room. It was so much better than anything he'd ever lived in that to him it was luxury. There was even a shared bathroom and an outdoor privy. Hardly a day went by that William wasn't grateful that he'd taken the job with Robert. He loved working with the horses and delighted in learning about them. The older stable hand, who went by the name of Rocky, was smart, hardworking and knew what he was doing with the horses. But the young man was insolent and indifferent and it wasn't long before he was fired and William took his role.

After a number of enquires, Robert found Scott's address and offered Harold to go with William to return the cart and horses. It was thought that it would take a day to make the journey there and Robert offered Harold because it was necessary to go to

Melbourne first, then take the Ballarat Road, cross the Saltwater River at Solomon's Ford, and from there proceed to Scott's near Williams Town. Harold said he knew the roads.

Harold was excited as a child with a new toy and Robert was envious of them both.

"I'd love to go too," he said. "But I just don't have the time."

It was already hot when they set out. They'd brought two spare horses for the return journey.

William enjoyed the rolling landscape. Harold told him that the river to their left would often be visible all the way to Melbourne, and laughed when William suggested the river might be a better way to get around.

"Good idea," he said. "Some people used to use it to take produce to the markets, but the road is better now. You'll soon see that it's been sealed, so it's suitable for all weather."

They chatted amiably and Harold confided that he liked to get out of the house.

"Mr Robert is a good man," he said. "But I do get tired of being in the house all the time. He used to take me on trips to Melbourne, but not so much anymore. The road is better, faster and safer now."

The road became busier as they came closer to Melbourne, then they veered off onto the Ballarat Road. They crossed the river at Solomon's Ford and soon turned left onto the road to Williams Town. Once they did, William thought he recognised it as the road he, Mike and Scott had used to go to Ballarat. The day was well advanced and Harold fretted that they wouldn't get to Scott's before dark. William encouraged the horses to move faster.

Just when it looked like they would have to camp out over night, they saw a wooden house with wide verandahs, not unlike Robert's house. Smoke curled up from the chimney and the smell of burning eucalyptus came to them on the evening air. They pulled up out front and Harold got down to see if they had come to the right place.

A young voice came from the house.

"Daddy! Mummy! There's some men here!"

Scott appeared in the doorway.

"Bill! You son of a gun! We wondered where you got to! It's so good to see you. Hop down and come on in. Introduce me to your friend."

"Scott, this is Harold. We're working together."

"I was hoping you'd work here, but no matter. Come on in. Meet my family. You can tell me everything over supper and a few whiskies. Come on, Harold, you too. I don't know where you've come from, but you'll both be tired, I'll warrant."

"We've come from near Warringal," said Harold. "But we had to take the long way around."

They all went inside to a large room that was well furnished with leather chairs and sideboards. Some lamps flickered, but there was enough light to see that Scott and his family lived well.

"This is my wife, Kathy. Kathy, this is Bill and his friend, Harold."

"I'm very pleased to meet you, Bill. I've heard so much about you. You are both welcome. If you'd like to wash up, there's a room through there. Supper's nearly ready and there's plenty for us all."

Kathy was about Scott's age, lively, pretty and quite small. William realised with a shock that Scott had not ever spoken about her, so he couldn't reply that he'd heard so much about her too.

"And this little man is young Scott," said Scott, lifting a little boy up who looked at William and Harold as though he'd not ever seen another human being.

"Who are these people?" he asked.

"They're friends of Daddy's."

"Do you have any children? I can show them my pony," said young Scott.

"No, we don't have any children," William replied warmly.

"That's a shame," said young Scott. "I'd like some children to play with. Sometimes, I meet some when we go to church. Mummy said she and Daddy might find a brother or sister for me, but you've been saying that for a long time, haven't you, Mummy?"

"C'mon, young man. You need to wash up," said Scott hurriedly.

"Where's Mike?" asked William.

"He and Jake left for Ballarat yesterday with a delivery. Joe's been asking for his cart so he'll be pleased to get it back, but he'll have to wait for the next trip."

"I'm sorry," said William. "It would have been hard to bring it back sooner."

"No matter," said Scott. "Joe'll survive."

"Wash up, everyone. I'll put the supper out and you can tell us what you've been up to, Bill," said Kathy.

"C'mon, Bill. Let's see to your horses, then we'll wash up," said Scott.

After supper, Kathy put little Scott to bed and they all sat outside on the wide verandah on chairs made of canvas and wood. The men nursed whiskies and Scott smoked his pipe. He didn't remark that William wasn't smoking his.

"So, what're you up to, Bill?" asked Scott.

"I'm working with some friends of Alice and Emma," said William. "We took them there when we arrived back from Ballarat, stayed a few days, one thing led to another and now I'm working there."

"Good for you," said Scott. "We miss you, of course. Hardly a day goes by in the store that someone doesn't ask after you. And what of Bridie and the girls? Are they all right?"

"Yes—Bridie got a job at a store in Melbourne. I'm told she loves it and the girls are going to school nearby."

"And Alice and Emma?"

"Alice has gone to be with some friends in Melbourne and Emma works with us. Turns out, she's a governess."

"And a good one," said Harold, speaking for the first time.

"And what do you do, Harold?" asked Kathy.

"I'm a valet, sir," said Harold. William had never heard the term, but thought he'd remember it—it sounded so good. It was like a word that Andrew who told the story about the cheques would use. He loved words and loved learning new words. Robert was a great teacher and delighted in expanding William's knowledge.

"Another whisky, anyone?" said Scott. "I'm certainly going to have another to celebrate things turning out so well. See, darling, I said they would."

"Yes, you did," said Kathy, nodding her head.

Scott returned with the whiskies, sat down, and restarted his pipe.

"You were lucky that you had a safe trip back," he said.

"Why is that?" asked William.

"I suppose it happened after you went through," said Scott. "Some travellers found a dead horse beside the road this side of Bacchus Marsh. It'd been shot, but strangely there were two bullet wounds, so it didn't look like it had been deliberately destroyed. Anyway, the travellers scouted around and found two dead men in the bush nearby. They'd been shot too. The police were called in, but they were too busy in the aftermath of the disturbance at Eureka, so it took them some days to get there. I believe they decided the two men had been killed by bushrangers because they had no money on them, but no one could work out why they had only one horse. So, they decided the other horse had been stolen, so the police are on the lookout for it."

"How do they know what horse they're looking for?" asked Harold.

"I suppose they expect it has the same brand as the dead one."

"Of course," said Harold. "How silly of me."

"I'm surprised you haven't heard about it," said Scott. "We were worried it was something to do with you. James from the Woolpack Inn said you had left early in the morning, not many days before the horse was found, and he hadn't heard from you. He'll be pleased to know you're all right. I'll get a message to him when I send the next shipment to Ballarat. Tom'll be pleased too—we were all a little worried."

William and Harold saddled up early the next morning and left on the return journey. There were hugs and kisses from Kathy and young Scott and a very warm handshake from Scott. William agreed he would come back to visit as soon as he could. They rode back the way they came. Harold said he thought there might be a shorter way, but it was easier to stick to what they knew. They stopped at the Ford and brewed a cuppa.

"We should have kept the other horse," said Harold as they sat under a tree by the riverbank. Birds called and the occasional fish jumped. Water was bubbling over the rocks and the sunlight glinted through the trees from time to time.

"Why?" said William, though he'd had the same worry. It was the only link back to him.

"Well, I know Mr Robert returned the horse to its owner. If he's not discrete, then the police will find you."

"What's it matter if the police find me?"

"Mrs Alice told Mr Robert what happened and I overhead. I know there could be trouble if the police come looking like Mr Scott said they might. Some things might be hard to explain."

William just nodded and said quietly, "Yes, they might be."

"I'll speak no further of it, Bill. I'm sure Mrs Alice won't either."

"I'm sure you're right. Let's be on the road."

William knew now for certain that Alice would lead to his undoing.

Life became very comfortable for William on Robert's farm. There was plenty to do every day. He became a very good judge of horses and always went with Rocky when they bought or sold them. There was no further discussion of the incident on the road near Bacchus Marsh and it was now as though it never even happened.

Robert sometimes invited William to his smoking room for a whisky and a few times he joined the family for supper. Emma was always there and said that Alice was doing well in Melbourne and she'd heard that Bridie's shop was very popular.

"We must go sometime, Bill," said Emma one evening. "I know Alice would like to see you, and we could stay with Bridie. I'm sure she and the girls would be delighted. Let's write and see what she says."

"I'm sure Bill has no time for writing," said Robert. "Why don't you do that, Emma?"

Despite the best of intentions, and several letters back and forth, the visit didn't happen. Nevertheless, if there was such a thing as a perfect life, William had found it. He became great friends with Rocky, who taught him to play chess. They spent many wonderful hours together drinking whisky, smoking their pipes and trying to outdo each other on the chessboard.

Robert was wonderful, thoughtful and courteous—the best employer imaginable. He never let on that he knew William could neither read nor write, and never made an issue of it. Yet he would always help him with the pronunciation and meaning of new words. It became like a game to them.

Emma was always busy with the children, yet always making plans that didn't eventuate. William decided she was one of those people that liked to have a plan. The planning of an event was more important than the doing of it.

Lucy was always there, fussing and making sure the house ran smoothly. She had little to do with William and he had little to do with her.

The days, weeks and months rolled by until nearly eighteen months had passed since William and the others had left Ballarat.

William and Rocky were locked in a fierce game of chess. Rocky had won the last three but William thought he had a good chance to win at last. The game had been going for several days, continued each evening after supper. Harold appeared in the doorway.

"I'm sorry to interrupt. Mr Robert would like to see you, Bill. And, I believe it's urgent."

"Don't you move the pieces, Rocky. I'll be back soon."

"Who, me? I wouldn't dream of it."

"He's in the smoking room, Bill," said Harold as they walked to the house together.

"Is everything all right?" asked William.

"I'm sure it is, Bill. But you'll know soon enough, won't you?"

William laughed.

Robert was pacing up and down when William opened the door after knocking.

"Oh, Bill. Please close the door behind you. Sit down, my boy and let's enjoy a whisky. I do love our chats."

"Is there something wrong?" asked William, sensing all was not right.

Robert sat in a chair opposite.

"I'm sorry to tell you this, my boy. In hindsight, we should have destroyed, or at least kept, that damned horse. I arranged for it to go back to its owner, but he's put it all about that it's been returned. Says no one can get the better of him. I understand the police are now interested and planning to visit him. I suppose that it's taking so long led me to believe that the matter was behind us."

William, too, was surprised the matter was still current— nothing had been said for so long. He was sure it had been shelved, with other more important matters needing attention.

"I think it's for you to decide what you want to do," continued Robert. "We can go to the police and tell them what happened. They'll wonder why it's taken this long and why you've been hiding, but if you decide to see them, we can work something out. I've a friend who's a very good lawyer. I know he'll help."

"Robert, we've not ever talked about the matter. I know Alice told you what happened. What did she tell you?"

"That you shot the injured bushranger in the head as he lay wounded on the ground. Is that what happened?"

"Yes, sir. Well, he might have been dead, but she's right. I shot him as he lay on the ground."

"I'm sure you had your reasons. I'm sure any sensible jury would find you innocent of any criminal behaviour."

"And if they don't?"

"Let's not even think about that. It'd never happen. You were protecting the women and from what I hear, it was a job that needed to be done."

"Robert. We both have always known this would happen. The police would come looking for me, I mean. I'm not sure what I could have done differently. Buried the men, hidden the horse, or destroyed both horses. Who knows? Things can always be done differently. When I killed him, and he might have been dead already, it was because I couldn't guarantee anyone's safety while he was still alive."

"I know, my boy. You did what you had to do. He made himself a bushranger and he paid a price for it."

"I knew when I saw Alice's face she didn't agree with me. I don't think either of us knows what Alice will say when the police question her as the only witness to what happened."

"I can talk to Alice."

"We could both talk to Alice, but we still wouldn't know what she'd say."

"I suppose so."

"Thank you for telling me, sir. You've been a good friend. I'll think about it overnight and we'll talk again in the morning, if that's all right with you, sir."

"Please call me Robert. Of course that's all right."

"Goodnight, Robert. And thank you for offering to help, but it may be that this is one of those things a man has to do for himself."

"Goodnight, Bill. And don't worry. There's nothing to worry about. I have some powerful friends."

"No, Robert. You must always deny all knowledge of it."

"Despite what Alice says?"

"Particularly despite what Alice says."

William went out the door and returned to the servants' quarters. Rocky was sound asleep in his chair.

*I wonder if he moved the pieces?* William smiled inwardly. *God does. God moves the pieces all the time.*

CHAPTER 24

# On the Move Again

William rose early the next morning, sure in his own mind
of what to do. He'd go back to Ireland. The police weren't
looking for him by name yet, so he'd go before they were. The plan
was simple. Go to Melbourne or Williams Town, sign on as crew
to a steam ship or sailing vessel, and head back home. He'd sign
on under his own name, so the police would know he'd left and
wouldn't trouble Robert to find him. He doubted they'd charge
Robert with any crime, since he could deny any knowledge of
what happened on the day.

The sun was a glow on the distant hills as he set out. It had
taken no time to pack, nor had he made any goodbyes. The less his
friends knew, the better. Once again, the sound of gravel crunching
under his feet, the birds whistling at him from the nearby trees
and the incessant buzz of the cicadas provided background noise
to his journey. The morning was chilly, but he soon warmed up.
If he was lucky, someone might happen along and give him a
ride. He was sad to be leaving. Robert had been good to him,
and he'd broken his promise to talk to Robert again. He knew

Robert would forgive him, as the less Robert knew, the better. Nonetheless, there were others he would miss too. It was the worst part about leaving.

Sure enough, it wasn't long before he heard the clatter of horses' hooves and the rattle of wheels coming from behind him. He stood to one side and hoped he could convince the traveller to give him a lift. It was probably unusual to see a lone walker on the road and that would make the traveller wary.

Relief turned to concern when he saw that the traveller was Emma, driving a horse and sulky. She pulled up beside him and wrapped him in the warmth of a welcoming smile. William was, in spite of himself, very pleased to see her.

"Hello, stranger," said Emma. "Fancy seeing you on the road."

"Fancy seeing you," said William. "Where are you off to? And so early?"

"I'm off to Melbourne, so hop on and I'll give you a lift."

"What's in Melbourne?" asked William, climbing on to the sulky.

"Alice."

"Why today?"

"Last minute decision. Robert came into breakfast and said that you had left some time during the night. We were all surprised to hear it and asked why. He said you no doubt had your reasons, but he was not aware of them. He then suggested I take a horse and sulky and visit Alice in Melbourne and thought I should leave as soon as possible to avoid driving in the heat of the day."

Emma was then silent for a while. William wondered if that was the end of the story.

"As I was leaving, he pressed these two envelopes into my hands. He said that I should give them to you if I saw you, perhaps even give you a lift if you were going to Melbourne too."

She passed two envelopes to William who just stared at them.

"Well, aren't you going to open them?"

"I'll do it later," said William, stuffing the envelopes in his pocket.

They rode on for quite a few minutes in silence, and then Emma pointed out where the road came close to the river.

"Let's stop here for a few moments," she said. "It'll be pretty among the trees and I can let the horse have a drink. I'm not in a hurry. Are you?"

William shook his head and liked the idea of stopping, though he was nervous about Emma's reason for doing so. He was certain the horse wasn't ready for either a drink or a rest. There was an indistinct track going down to the river and Emma walked the horse down it. They both got down when she pulled up amongst the trees. It was cool out of the sun and the horse found some grass to its liking. They sat on a log in the shade, watching it eat.

"You can't read, can you, Bill?" Emma said after a few minutes of uncomfortable silence.

"No, I can't," he said quietly.

"That's a shame. You should have told me. I could have taught you."

"It doesn't matter—I get by. Not much reason to know how."

"There's reason enough in your pocket right now. Give me the letters. You'll need to know what to do with them."

William passed the letters without comment.

"The first one is to you. It has money and a note. The note says that Robert has more money for you and he'll send it to you when you want it. The second envelope is addressed to Robert. He says you can put any name you wish and the address of a bank on the piece of paper inside, post it to him and he'll send the rest of your money to the person at that bank. Do you understand?"

"Yes."

Emma gave William the money, tore the first letter into small pieces and threw them in the river. They watched the pieces float away.

"Take good care of that money," said Emma.

"I will. And thanks for your help."

"Do you know, Bill, if you hadn't been so besotted by Bridie, you might have noticed me."

"Noticed you? I thought Alice had picked Tom for you."

"I'll pick my own man when the time comes, thank you very much," said Emma. "Now, let's be on the road. We don't want to be late."

"Late? Late for what?"

"For whatever is going to happen next."

The horse was reluctant to leave the grass but did so quickly when encouraged by Emma with a sharp flick of the reins, who now behaved as though in a hurry. They clattered along at a fair clip. William stole a glance at Emma who sat tight-lipped, looking angry.

"Where are you going?" she asked finally.

"Aren't you better not to know?"

"And why is that?"

"Well, for when the police come asking after me."

"And, why will they do that?"

"Robert said they are asking questions about what happened on the road that day."

"They can ask. If they ask me, I'll tell them exactly what happened. We were attacked by two bushrangers, and you killed them defending us."

"Alice might tell a different story."

"And why would she do that?"

"She didn't like how I shot one of the bushrangers in the head when she thought he was only injured."

"That's not what she'll say. She'll say he shot himself in the head as he fell from his horse."

"And why would she do that?"

Emma looked at William briefly.

"Because that's what happened."

William liked this Emma. She had a fierce, determined look on her face. Her eyes flashed and she handled the horse like she'd been doing it all her life. It reminded him of the Emma who confronted the soldier. Her dark hair was cropped short. She wore a dark checked dress made fulsome by petticoats. It reminded him that he'd seen Mary for years, yet hadn't noticed her at all until the wake. And now, he noticed Emma as he was leaving.

*You can't change the truth though. You can pretend whatever you like, but you can't change the truth.*

"No, Emma, that's not what happened at all."

"But, Bill. Alice will say what I tell her to say. You can come back to Robert's. You look after the horses, I'll look after the children. Why, we'll have some of our own one day. That would be nice, wouldn't it? We'll be good for each other. Alice won't say anything against you, I promise."

"I'll spend the rest of my life looking over my shoulder. It'll be a bigger story too, since a rich and well-known man like Robert is involved and the papers will make more of it. No, Emma.—it's best that I go. There'll be no story without me. I thought I did the right thing at the time, but people have a habit of seeing things differently in hindsight."

"What do you know of the papers? You can't even read," snapped Emma.

"Not being able to read doesn't mean I don't know what's going on. Scott, Tom and Rocky all told me what the papers said and I knew it wasn't always the truth."

"I'm sorry, Bill. I didn't mean that. I'm just so upset. I wanted to talk to you every day and now I get the chance, you're leaving."

William looked at her and saw that she was crying. He found it very distressing. She hadn't cried at Eureka where he thought there was a lot more to cry about. Not knowing what to do, he sat in miserable silence.

Was this to be the pattern in his life? He only noticed girls when he was leaving?

They came closer to Melbourne and Emma slowed the horse.

"Come back with me, Bill. Change your name, grow a beard—the police'll never find you even if they come looking and who's to say they'll do that? I'll talk to Alice. You're running for nothing."

"My mind's made up, Emma. I decided last night. It's not just about me. My being here is a danger for everybody."

"Why are you being so pig-headed? A girl'll think you want to go. Come with me to Alice's. If we can't convince her to tell the right story, then you can go."

The old, fighting Emma was back. She'd stopped crying and her jaw was set firmly again. William was sure Emma was proposing they get married. He'd never heard of such a thing and suspected Emma was mostly thinking about herself and what she wanted, not what was good for William. Nevertheless, he'd come to respect and like her, and didn't want things to end badly between them. Still, he wasn't sure how to handle the accusation of being pig-headed. But he knew that however badly he handled the matter, nothing would be as bad as being married to the wrong person.

"Emma, I don't know why you waited until now to talk about this. It wasn't an easy decision to go, but having made up my mind, I'd rather get on with it."

"Don't I mean anything to you? Don't you even want to think about it? Let's go and talk to Alice, then you'll know better what to do."

"No, I don't want to waste time. You make it sound easy, as though the police aren't smart and they'll be easy to outwit. Robert said they are already looking into what happened on the road that day, so for all I know they're only a half-step behind me. It's time for me to go, Emma. This is not only the easiest way, it's the best way."

"What about us?"

"I haven't thought about us."

"Because all you've thought about Bridie. I could have told you that was a waste of time."

"But you didn't."

"Well, I'm telling you now."

"It's too late, Emma. It's time for me to go."

They rode on in silence for a few moments. There was more traffic about now and Emma had to give more of her attention to driving. William was glad of the respite.

William was startled to hear Emma laugh. He looked at her in surprise. She looked at him and smiled.

"I've not proposed to a man before, Bill. I know you're young. I don't know how young, but you do handle yourself well, so I thought we might make a good match. Who's to know what makes a good match? I suppose we'll not ever find out about each other, but I do like that you've made your mind up and won't be diverted. So, let me take you to the docks— I'll drop you there and you can work out what to do next. It's not far now, so let's talk of happier matters for the little time we have left."

Emma continued to chat gaily about the children and some of their mischief. William struggled with her change in attitude, but was glad of it. It was easier to chat about daily matters than it was to talk about the rest of their lives.

They soon arrived at the docks and Emma skilfully manoeuvred the sulky to the side, away from the busiest area.

Emma turned to William and said, "Now, you kiss me properly Bill Smith and be on your way. I want something to remember you by."

William had never kissed anyone but his mother and he had no idea how to respond. He looked at her helplessly, blushing crimson.

Emma stared at him, then put her head to one side and said, "You darling man. Oh, what have I missed?" She held him fiercely for a moment, then let him go.

"Be on your way and may God protect you all the days of your life. I believe I owe you my life, and if not my life, then certainly my virtue. I don't care what Alice thinks. You did the right thing and I'd pray that if you needed to, you'd do it again. Melbourne needs men like you, Bill and I can't tell you how sad I am that you are leaving."

William got down and stood with his bag. Emma drove off without another word.

The docks were bustling with activity. William was on his own again and with only his wits and good fortune to help him on his way. He looked around, wondering what to do next.

How long ago was it that he had landed on the shore at Williams Town? It seemed just the blink of an eye. He picked up his bag and went in search of a ship.

# About the Author

Peter Clarke is only one of many Australians who are intrigued by the stories of the immigrants who helped create a nation. Where did they come from? Why did they come? Why did they stay?

Born in Mudgee and raised in the Blue Mountains, Peter is familiar with the challenges of drought and fire, but these challenges are nothing compared to those faced by the early pioneers.

A working life in the computer industry has not in any way prepared Peter to write about the pioneers. However, a lively interest in early Australia and an adequate Irish heritage has contributed to a curiosity that has only been in part satisfied by several trips to Ireland. Thus motivated, Peter used the new technology to surf world history and events, to create a story of one man's journey which reflects the difficulties of the time.

www.ingramcontent.com/pod-product-compliance
Lightning Source LLC
Chambersburg PA
CBHW030353030726
47497CB00002B/321